Literature of the American West
William Kittredge, General Editor

The Last Paradise

Other Books by James D. Houston

FICTION

Between Battles (New York, 1968)
Gig (New York, 1969)
A Native Son of the Golden West (New York, 1971)
Continental Drift (New York, 1978)
Gasoline (Santa Barbara, 1980)
Love Life (New York, 1985)

NONFICTION

(with Jeanne Wakatsuki Houston) *Farewell to Manzanar* (San Francisco and Boston, 1973)
(with John R. Brodie) *Open Field* (San Francisco and Boston, 1974)
Three Songs for My Father (Santa Barbara, 1974)
Californians: Searching for the Golden State (New York, 1982)
The Men in My Life (Berkeley, 1987)
In the Ring of Fire: A Pacific Basin Journey (San Francisco, 1997)

The Last Paradise

A Novel

By James D. Houston

UNIVERSITY OF OKLAHOMA PRESS : NORMAN

This is a work of fiction. Names, characters, places, and incidents are either the product of the author's imagination or are used fictitiously, and any resemblance to actual events, locales, or persons, living or dead, is entirely coincidental.

The Last Paradise is Volume 2 in the Literature of the American West series.

Library of Congress Cataloging-in-Publication Data

Houston, James D.
 The last paradise : a novel / by James D. Houston.
  p. cm. — (Literature of the American West ; v. 2)
 ISBN 0-8061-3033-4 (alk. paper)
 I. Title. II. Series.
 PS3558.087L37 1998
 813'.54—dc21   97-31878
                     CIP

The paper in this book meets the guidelines for permanence and durability of the Committee on Production Guidelines for Book Longevity of the Council on Library Resources, Inc. ∞

To Jeanne

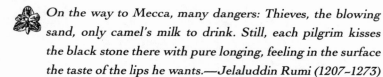 *On the way to Mecca, many dangers: Thieves, the blowing sand, only camel's milk to drink. Still, each pilgrim kisses the black stone there with pure longing, feeling in the surface the taste of the lips he wants.—Jelaluddin Rumi (1207–1273)*

The Last
Paradise

What Angel Heard

On the island of Hawai'i, usually called the Big Island, the rocky leeward shore is always dry. The windward shore is always wet, lush with ferns and macadamia groves and every variety of orchid. In that kind of moisture, cars quickly turn to rust. They gather in the yards and along the roadsides. Rusty cars and orchids and mosquitoes and the best singing in the islands—these are some of the things you would have found in Hilo, the main town along the windward shore, on a rain-soaked day in 1952, the year Evangeline was born, the year both of them were born, Evangeline Sakai and Travis Doyle, born in the same week, one in Hilo, one in San Jose.

"That's probably why we met," she will tell him, since in her view nothing happens by coincidence, not even births three thousand miles apart. She could be right. They say everything in the corporeal world affects everything else— earth, air, fire, water—from the engine spark to the ozone layer. What if the inner moments of all our lives could be linked in such a way, a great web to stitch together the ragged histories of the human heart?

The rain beat down on corrugated roofing. The unborn infant squirmed and kicked her tiny, restless kicks. The mother had been told to lie back on a narrow cot in a screened-in sleeping porch to receive the name. It was the grandmother's name, being called, groaned, as if squeezed *from the chanter's throat by force, while eight hands covered the swollen belly.*

To the young mother's ears the sound was familiar, but the words were strange. It was a very old chant, that much she knew, coming up from the soil, from the porous rocks that made the soil, out of the tunnels where the lava used to flow, rising through the loins and throat of the elder, a dark pulsing in the throat that filled the room and made the air throb and the body throb.

4

Next to the chanter the grandmother stood with two other Hawaiian women. The young woman on the cot looked up into the brown face of her grandmother, whose eyes were closed in concentration, and remembered how those eyes looked two days earlier when the grandmother stopped her outside the house and said, "Pele came to me in a vision and told me this baby will be a girl, told me she will be the first girl grandchild and so must be the one to receive my name, and told me no one else is to receive it."

This had been a troubling story, one the young woman was not ready for, standing in the driveway beneath the carport, with the clatter of rain on corrugated roofing and the Ford's engine ticking as it cooled. Driving home from the market she had been listening to "Slow Boat to China," singing along with the crooner. As she opened the car door, reaching across for groceries, there stood her grandmother, who perhaps had chosen the carport for its soundproofing clatter, no one else close enough to listen through it. She was tall and regal and still handsome, unless she had been drinking. Drink made her eyes ghostly and her face gaunt. At first the young woman thought she was hearing a drinker's vision. But the steady voice and steady eyes told her this was something that would only happen once and should be trusted.

That night they drove up to the crater, the two of them and the man who now was in the room there chanting and naming. In the dry cold air of the high country he led them, clearing the way with his guttural song, cutting a path through the darkness, out to the lip of the firepit they say is Pele's home, out to the edge of Halema'uma'u. While he chanted his long blessing and tribute to the lava goddess who destroys and creates, to her lineage, to her barren terrain, the women stood back, waiting.

They had been out there before like that, because the grandmother believed she was descended from Pele, said she was of Pele's line, and of all her offspring the young woman was the only one who would come along on such a pil-grimage. She did not know what it meant to be of Pele's line or understand how this was possible. But she knew how it felt to be there in the dark. The firepit was a crater within a crater. In daylight its walls were streaked with rust and yellow sulfur. Day or night the air was charged with some-thing you could not name. It hugged you like a cloak. It tasted like sulfur, but not in a way that bothered her. Sometimes she liked the smell and its nostril-burning after-math. She did not agree with the oldtime missionaries who considered this to be the devil's smell, a sure sign that Pele and Lucifer were allies. It worked on her like horseradish. With the steam it came seeping through the cracks and tiny blowholes from chambers underground. The sinuses turned to flame, and as that flame subsided, the mind seemed clearer.

At the firepit's edge the chanter fell silent, his voice swal-lowed back into the rock. The grandmother walked out to where he stood, with nothing visible beyond but darkness, nothing but sulfur scent to tell you the rocks were steaming, sending plumes toward the sky. Into the void he threw a sack *filled with the baked flesh of a pig, and a bottle of gin, in a paper bag an unopened quart of Beefeaters. Just to be safe, grandmother said. According to some people, Pele likes gin. She wasn't sure why, but might as well give her the best.*

Now this man with the night-cutting voice and the grandmother and the two Hawaiian women the young mother did not know, they were all listening and laying hands on the mound of her belly where the half-formed baby was listening too, and listening hard. Nothing else to do in there but listen, and wait. Listening to the name that throbbed in the room and to the benediction that came after the name. The infant heard and felt the vibration in the chanter's throat, which passed down his arms and through his hands, through all their hands to transmit the prenatal message that it is all one, all the same, the dark fleshy womb of the mother and the fiery womb from which the words come rising. Inside the chant the unborn child heard the low hum of the island's ancestral song.

Many years went by before she learned of her naming day. She was told about the origin of her name, but not about the ceremony. After the grandmother passed away, the mother kept it to herself, a secret she was afraid to share. It was a Hawaiian secret, and the Hawaiian in her moved cautiously, overwhelmed and outnumbered by the other races, the other voices in her body and in the islands.

The old grandma, Auntie Malama, had been the family renegade, one who refused to be ashamed of brown skin and island ways. She believed the flame of tradition should be kept alive. Like the candle in the room where the name was passed on, it was a covert flame, burning in the back rooms and chambers, in caves and groves of ironwood trees, and in the hearts of islanders who would not forget the sounds of the language or where the bones were buried.

The short version of the daughter's name was Evangeline Malama Kawailani Sakai. When she was seven they moved to Oahu, two hundred miles north and west. It was the year the first 707 touched down, cutting the time from San Francisco or L.A. to four and a half hours. The future would be in tourism, her father predicted. He was practical, a survivor. His father had come from Japan as a contract laborer. His childhood memories were filled with sugarcane. He did not want to farm or be a plantation hand. He went to work for Pan Am and bought a house at the edge of Honolulu, with a view of rain forest rising behind the neighborhood, while the view toward the road was screened by plumeria and flame trees that made scarlet umbrellas every summer.

His daughter called him Papa. He called her Angel. She was slender, a swimmer, a beach girl on weekends, a collector of shells and coral heads, a camera bug. She moved with a grace that captivated him because it seemed unlearned. Watching his daughter, he pondered the mysteries of creature grace. In her face he saw both his mother and his wife. He liked to take her places, to show her things he understood. He took her to the zoo, to the shave-ice stand. When she was sixteen he took her out to Pearl Harbor to see the remains of the warships. For him this notorious lagoon was a zone of power, with the same magnetism the crater had for Angel's mother and grandmother, a place where the dead linger on and speak to the living.

Part One

Traveling Music

November 1986

Sipping coffee from his wide-bottom road mug, Travis listens to Sky One, the overhead traffic reporter. A freight truck has jackknifed a hundred yards beyond the Bay Bridge off ramp, spilling chemicals over three westbound lanes. As the cars in front of him slow to a standstill he changes the channel, punches in KJAZ, loud and clear from Alameda right across the water. Mose Allison is playing the blues, voice and piano, block chords and rippling right hand. On the road Travis prefers jazz and blues, always listening for guidance.

I'm a deepsea diver, I know I can't go wrong.
Deepsea diver. Know I can't go wrong.
Dive underwater, and hold my breath so long.

Two minutes go by. He shuts off the engine, steps over to the railing and stands looking down at the water's sheen. Perhaps the time has come to abandon his car. How much longer will they really be useful, he thinks. Why can't he just leave it here and walk on into San Francisco? All he would miss is the sound system. Mose Allison comes toward him through the open window. Good traveling music. For walking away. Or for jumping. Distantly he considers a plunge, a low and gliding fall toward the dove-colored breast of the deep.

Behind him a horn honks, then two, then three.

He hops back into his 1978 Volvo Deluxe, wondering how he has ended up this way, morning after morning, doing exactly what he has tried for so long to avoid. Twenty thousand cars, he thinks, slowed down by a chemical spill. And why now, at 8:35, with all these jobs and urgent A.M. agendas on the line? He feels an old self-pity rising. He thinks of Marge, his soon-to-be-ex-wife, and their last excursion. From here he can see the islands. They took the bay cruise around Yerba Buena, Alcatraz, underneath the bridges. Two days later she walked out for the second and final time. What went wrong? What did he say? Or not say?

"You talk in your sleep," she said.

"Is that a crime?"

"You still thrash around. Last night you were yelling again."

"You said it was getting better."

"It is."

"Well, then . . ."

"It's more than that."

"Can't we talk this through?"

"We have. We are. That's all we do. It's just not working, Travis."

That was three months ago Where is she now? This morning? Remorse pours through him, a wave that loosens his neck. His head lolls sideways. He misses her. Maybe he still loves her. He isn't sure about love. He has lost his nerve about love. He doesn't trust his feelings now. He is stuck again and knows he's stuck.

As the traffic around him picks up speed, as his car surges forward, as Mose Allison swings into a final chorus, Travis is thinking about the music. It occurs to him that the blues and the traffic have something in common. Aren't they both versions of that which cannot be avoided? Aren't they both versions of destiny? He plays with this. He is free-associating now. Groping. Grasping. He isn't going to dwell on Marge. It's easier to think about the blues and destiny than to puzzle over the mysteries of Marge, and love.

He is not a musician by trade or training, but he is a half-decent back-porch guitar player. He has noodled around enough to know that in each blues chorus there are twelve bars, no more, no less, four beats to each bar, and a standard chord pattern laid out by pioneer piano players in nameless honky-tonks many years before he was born. If you want to play the twelve-bar blues, this is what you have been given to work with. As he listens to wizard Mose on the keyboard he also sees and hears the endless variations that have been offered up chorus after chorus, year after year, by all the guitar pickers and harmonicats and clarinettoes and songsters throughout the ages. And isn't that—Yes! By God! This comes to him both as sound and as a warm and illuminating rush—isn't that free will?

Twelve bars of four beats each, that's all you get. But you can play it loud, you can play it soft, you can play it sweet, you can play it dirty, you can play it fast or slow or stop-time. You can pile on thirty-second notes or leave empty spaces, cry, laugh, whisper, groan, belt it, squeeze it, fake it, jump and shout!

By the time he pulls into his basement parking space he believes he might be on the verge of something. The blues have raised his spirits, which have been going up and down a dozen times a day. At thirty-four he is poised again for change, for possibility, though who knows how long this mood will last. Thirteen years since he came back from the war, and Travis is still coming back. Still en route. Still circling, circling, looking for the place to land.

When the elevator door slides open, Carlo is standing there in his candy-stripe shirt, his red tie loose. He has assumed a linebacker's crouch, as if expecting sudden violence. Though he appears to be waiting for someone, Travis knows he is not. After three years he knows all Carlo's habits. He knows Carlo was returning from the men's room when the elevator ding took him by surprise. The worried eyes bulge, the fingers flex. Trying to cover his pointless show of alarm, Carlo demands to know where Travis has been.

14

"On the road, on the freeway. What a madhouse out there!"

Carlo grabs his arm, guiding him along the corridor, describing an assignment. They step through the door marked 20/20 CLAIMS, APPRAISALS, and the stern look turns boyish.

"You are going to have to take this one, Doyle. You are the only one who can get away. Jesus, when I think about it, you may be the only one I can ask."

He likes Carlo. He understands the man's anxiety. Carlo recently watched a wife walk out, and it hit him hard. They have two kids. He is forty-one now, hanging on by his fingernails. The harder Carlo works, the farther he falls behind, reminding Travis of a fellow he knew in Vietnam, a reserve captain who had returned to active duty hoping this would save his marriage. It was a crazy and demented hope. The captain worked day and night, always in a frenzy, as if the effort itself would somehow give him new stature in the eyes of the wife who was eight thousand miles away.

Carlo falls into the chair behind his paper-strewn desk, his eyes roaming, pleading. At 20/20 it sometimes seems to Travis that a grass fire of fear is racing across the land, a fear that all insurance policies will soon be canceled or priced so far out of reach no one can afford them. Sometimes he can almost taste the panic, the jittery greed. In the past three weeks two of Carlo's adjusters have quit. Everyone still on the payroll is off on one crisis assignment or another. Now, out of nowhere, has come a claim from the lava fields of Hawai'i.

"This doesn't make any sense," says Travis.

"You are right, it's goofy. Perhaps absurd. These people wait till the last minute to file, then it's rush rush rush to put the documents through."

Travis sits down on the rattan settee. In Carlo's office everything is rattan or wicker, the lamp shades, the picture frames, enhancing what he calls "the Pacific effect." A poster hangs on the wall behind his desk, an overhead of Borobudur, the great mandala-shaped temple in central Java. Carlo, who has never been there, has several times mentioned that he hopes to visit Borobudur and climb up onto the shoulders of one of the many Buddhas who guard the temple.

"Somebody in Honolulu should be checking this out," Travis says. "They could do it in half the time, for half the cost."

"Believe me, I have looked into that. I just talked to this guy we send business to. Their backs are against the wall. He has never seen so many claims piling up. It could be weeks before they get around to it. They had a hurricane, you know. All this shoreline property is wrecked. Pleasure boats ripped off their moorings. Owners are suing the Coast Guard. Meanwhile, a whole neighborhood is getting carried away by termites, one house after another. Not to mention hillsides caving in, taking houses with them, and saltwater intrusion doing things to the pipes. He says to me, long distance, on my calling card, 'Carlo, you ever get the impression the world as we once knew it is all coming apart at the same time?' Tell me about it, I said."

"I don't know much about volcanoes, or drilling for steam, or any of that."

"Steam is not the issue, Travis. It is an ordinary fire. An equipment shed, with property loss."

"It's not my area. You yourself told me expertise is a style of life."

"You know human character," Carlo says, with a mentor's smile. "That is really what we're appraising here. You know deceit, Travis. You know treachery when you see it. I trust you."

What can he say? Few people have ever complimented him like this. He is touched by these remarks. He wants them to be true, though he wishes they came from someone other than Carlo, whose judgment does not fill him with confidence—a man divided against himself.

To break the spell of Carlo's insistent gaze, Travis has to glance away. He looks out the window, just as the floor begins to vibrate. The frame around the window quivers.

"Jesus Christ," says Carlo softly, "you feel that?"

The office lurches. He reaches wide to grab the edges of his desk, as if to keep it from sliding. Again the room lurches, with a blood-quickening lift. They stare at each other, waiting for something worse. But that is it. The floor is still and firm again beneath their feet. Carlo's hands relax. He sits back.

"I never get used to it," Travis says.

"What do you figure? Four point five?"

"Less. Four."

"I have to get something closer to the ground," Carlo says." "You're fucking marooned up here. Where were we? What were we talking about?"

Out the window nearby buildings stand as they have always stood, seemingly unperturbed by this roller that has come and gone. They frame a view of the Bay Bridge, and beyond its metal scaffolding a broad slice of metal blue water. From Carlo's downtown office, at this hour, everything looks metallic and blue. Travis can see an arching segment of elevated roadbed where cars still inch along. The inbound lanes are stalled again. If he were tuned to Sky One, the overhead traffic reporter, he would know that this time a Winnebago has rear-ended an armored van from Brink's. The long bridge is clogged again, as well as all feeder routes onto the bridge, six miles of cars, motionless yet airborne, suspended above the waters of the bay.

In his mind's ear he can hear again the voice of Sky One, blurred by wind and rotor noise. In his mind's eye he rises toward the voice. He is up there in the chopper sitting next to Sky One, in the salty air above the bridge, looking down upon the waiting cavalcade. Together they observe the many-colored lanes that stripe the bridge, and beyond the bridge the many lanes of vehicles fanning outward from the van and the hapless mobile home.

When, in his mind's eye, Sky One rises away from the spectacle, banking and climbing, heading west toward Marin, Travis rises with him awhile, then leaves the chopper down below, rising higher still, released on his own recognizance. He rises until the whirling rotors disappear, until the bridges are strips of wire and the bay a squid-size inland sea and the sails off Tiburon are points of white.

If Travis continued soaring he would soon see the cities become a wash of gray and white against the tawny ridges of the long Coast Range, rippling north toward Ukiah, south toward the halfmoon curve of Monterey Bay, where his family's house stands somewhere in the shoreline forest, the house he grew up in with his brother and his father, his mother and his mother's mother too, until she died. Somewhere inside the foggy uplands between the ocean and the first brown peaks, a skylight makes a spark among the trees.

Underneath the skylight, in the loft where she keeps her tapestries and spools of yarn, her filing cabinets and her mailing lists, his mother sits wondering how she can spend so many days alone, after a lifetime in the company of men. From the loft she hears the mail truck stop on the road below the house and wonders how long it has been since she's heard from Travis, marvels that a son can be so near and still so far away.

But Travis doesn't see that spark among the coastal trees. He cannot yet soar high enough. With the shore far behind him he has leveled out. He is gliding westward like a seabird, his skin atingle at the thought of such a trip. It seems uncanny that Carlo would just offer it to him, like a book he has not asked for but has been itching to find and read. For months Hawai'i has been on his mind, an old and distant haven he would one day return to. But who knew when, or how? He sees a curve of green medallions across dolphin blue water. He sees green mountains as they appear from the shoreline, cut into a Technicolor sky. He is winging toward them now. He is already gone.

To Carlo he says, "Pacific Gas and Electric has some geothermal wells out near Geyserville. Maybe I should stop there first. A day to two is all I'm thinking. For the background."

"Steam is not the issue. It is fire, Travis, an ordinary fire. Go over there. Look around. You'll be doing me a huge and personal favor. Think of it as part of our executive training program. I want you to play a bigger role in what we're doing here."

Carlo would like to sound generous, as if this has just come to him. Travis knows he has saved it for last, a little enticement, a lure. The eyes are moist and fatherly.

"We learn by doing, Travis. We learn, we grow. I see this as a three- or four-day job at the outside. But take the week. Give yourself some R and R. When you get back we'll both be wiser. We will debrief then, and we will reassess."

The Veteran's Tale

Twenty-four hours later he is ticketed and packed in with a planeload of travelers bound for the islands. As the DC-10 lines up for take-off he sits back and closes his eyes. This time we are keeping it simple, he tells himself. Simple means no alcohol, no drugs, no women. This time, he thinks, I will do the gig and not get derailed. The gig itself will be his guide, another form of destiny.

The plane's low-frequency hum settles his nerves. Acceleration and the high-angle lift releases him, like a muscle relaxant. As soothing as Valium. Soon the coast is out of sight. For ten minutes he sits very still, with the pale blue sea chop far below working on him like a mantra. Then he opens the folder in his lap, labeled "Energy Source," and reexamines the claim, the cryptic drilling data, the detail maps, the columns of figures, the glossy eight-by-tens, the close-ups and the aerials, even the résumé.

The company is a subsidiary of Western Sun, a sprawling multinational out of Houston, Texas, with wells and oil fields and uncountable miles of pipe pushed deep into the earth and into the sea, all across the western United States and Canada, across the South Pacific, and now penetrating Asia. Their holdings encircle half the globe, from Alaska to Indonesia, from Bakersfield to the far side of Beijing.

He closes his eyes, trying to imagine the scale of it. Out of somewhere a voice breaks his concentration.

"Nice hat." A man's voice.

Travis has already rented earphones from a flight attendant. With a plastic loop hanging underneath his chin, and his brand-new panama slanted like Jack London might have worn it, he sits as if absorbed, as if listening to something oceanic, to Beethoven's Ninth Symphony. Keep it simple, he is thinking. No entanglements. Each moment contains enough space for one thing and one alone.

"Just don't lean back too far," the voice says. "Be a shame to crease that brim."

A shred of cloud passes beneath the plane. Watching it move against the distant water, Travis feels steady eyes upon his neck, upon his profile, his hatband of tiny peacock feathers.

"Looks like you might of been to the islands once or twice before." He isn't ready for an in-flight conversation, but something lonesome in the voice moves him to extract one earphone and say without turning, "What was that?"

"Your first trip?"

"My third."

"I was there in '41."

"An active time, from what they say."

"I was stationed at Pearl when the *Arizona* went down."

What he hears in this voice is a familiar melancholy, an old warrior with a tale to tell. When he turns to look at the face, the eyes, he sees no hidden agenda. The fellow just wants to talk and remember. His eyes are the same pale blue as the ocean from this altitude. In them Travis sees the same distance. The voice is near, the eyes are far away.

"Haven't been back since," the fellow says.

"Can't blame you for that."

"I had to watch it burn. I can still see it, plain as day."

The man speaks as if they have discussed the event a dozen times, and this detail has finally emerged, a piece of fresh and surprising information he did not intend to share.

"I have seen the hulk," Travis says. "Thought about what it must have been like."

"It was no party, I can tell you that."

"My dad took us out there for the tour, the motor launch. I was still in high school, mind you. I remember looking down into that incredibly clear water, and when it moved it looked like the ship was moving, swaying under there. It was ghostly. It's a ghost ship, isn't it, the USS *Arizona*."

"Couldn't say. I haven't seen it. Not since 1941. Never thought I'd have to. But there is this reunion next month. That's why I'm going back."

"You don't look that old. I mean, old enough to be going to a Pearl Harbor reunion."

This pleases the man. He flashes a grin. "I was eighteen. I'd only been in the service six months, didn't know my ass from a hole in the street, as they used to say. Sad fact is, the reason we're having a big reunion, a lot of these guys know five years from now, or ten, they won't be around to celebrate, or feel like traveling. I probably would, of course, but I was the youngest guy in our unit, just a kid out of Dayton, Ohio, and I'll tell you right now I have never seen anything like it before or since. Can you imagine being that age with the whole lagoon on fire and watching half the fleet go up in flames?"

A spasm passes through Travis, causing his head to shiver. Perhaps the old sailor thinks this means no. But it means yes. It means he can well imagine the scene. He can see it all. He too had enlisted at age eighteen, had seen other lagoons and other fires. Again he sees the thrown grenade arcing toward him, dark against the sky, a dark sun exploding white. He sees dry palm fronds sparking and spitting fire on the night the corporal who had never flown a plane decided to fly one anyway, fly it home to safety. He sees the end of the jungle airstrip ignite and make a fiery tower with the corporal somewhere inside it. In those days everything around him seemed to be going up in flames, though Travis is not in the mood now to dwell on that.

He turns toward the porthole. Feigning drowsiness he pushes padded phones over his ears and appears to be fooling with the dials marked Volume and Control. Dropping his seat back a notch, tipping the panama to shade his eyes, he watches all the rolling flames subside, dissolve. The famous ships slide underwater until only the topmost towers show. The oily, smoky surface of the tropical lagoon turns smooth and becomes blue-green again, serene again, and he sees himself at age sixteen on the day they motored out there.

It was a summer day, the sun still high, the water glinting, the kind of day young Travis had imagined when he thought about spending two months with his family in Honolulu, a day for beaches. But his father was another survivor of the Pacific war, from the same era as this veteran beside him on the plane. His father had fought in islands and atolls farther west, had fought well and earned a Purple Heart, and the time had come to visit the place where the war began, to show his two sons where the battleship had been resting on the bottom since December 7, 1941, the day it was sunk with all hands on board.

Travis remembers his father's silence as their tour launch skimmed across the harbor. As they neared the hulk, with its sunken towers poking through the surface, his father was blinking fiercely and Travis remembers not wanting to know why. He had never seen his father on the verge of tears. It confused him. He turned away and found himself standing next to a woman of about his age, an island girl whose eyes met his, as if she had been watching him and waiting for him to turn. She too was traveling with relatives, on an outing that was obviously someone else's idea . . .

With his hat tipped forward and his seat tipped back, an hour west of San Francisco and thirty-six thousand feet above the water, this is the scene that begins to replay, a scene from the dream time before he enlisted, Travis and his island girl side by side, eyeing each other, then peering down at the ghostly turrets of the USS *Arizona*.

She too was sixteen, and she too was seeing the ship for the first time. Later they would call it their first discovery, the first of many firsts in that long-ago summer of discovery. But before they spoke they stood shoulder to shoulder for quite a while, gazing at the shreds of algae that had gathered like the beards of elders around the rusted turrets. They studied the algae, both of them, trying not to notice their fathers' tears.

Later, with a shrug and a wistful grin, she would tell him, "I guess my Japanese side was feeling guilty out there, and it's crazy, when you think about it. I've never been near Japan."

Her name was Evangeline. Her father had also fought in World War II, a foot soldier in Italy, a sergeant in Germany, Bronze Star, oak-leaf clusters. On that day a great-uncle had just arrived in Honolulu, a man who had flown for the Japanese navy. A quarter of a century after the war he had come to make his peace with this branch of the family and make his peace with the dead.

Evangeline's father and her great-uncle were close enough in age to be brothers, both trim, severe-looking, golfers, dressed like golfers, carrying armloads of carnation leis. When the motors of the launch were cut and the tour guide's voice subsided, they began to toss the rings of bright red and white carnations toward the remnants of the battleships sunk by Japanese torpedo-bombers coming in low from the north at 8 A.M. Eleven hundred men had died that Sunday in 1941, their bodies interred with the ship, their spirits still hovering in the luminous air.

As the garlands fell and floated on the water, the great-uncle's stoic face was streaked with tears. Evangeline's father was weeping then, and so was Travis's father, weeping openly, all three of them, the man from Nagoya, the man from Honolulu, the man from California, each bringing to that translucent grave his wartime regrets, the memories of lost comrades and lost innocence, the pride and the grief for the folly of war, sharpened by the painful beauty of the tropical setting, the glassy water, and farther inland, beyond the city's skyline, the green-scoured ridges edged with perfect Polynesian clouds.

For the two sixteen-year-olds who could not yet know where these tears were coming from, the naked intimacy of the moment overwhelmed them and bonded them in a kin-ship that was electric and, before the launch had returned to shore, erotic, their young eyes already making promises.

They spent most of the next eight weeks together, giving themselves to sandy days and trade wind nights. They drank white wine from paper bags. They hung around outside clubs in Waikiki, where Hawaiian bands were playing, listening through the doors. They hiked and swam and talked about everything, it seemed. It was easy to talk, to joke around, to dream. They were going to travel. They would always be together. They made vows, and they made love, in the car, on the beach, in the back room of her family's house, with the clatter of rain on broad green banana leaves to muffle their squirms and groans.

In full detail the days come back, her eyes, her mouth, the glowing limbs. Steamy pictures. Rain made the air wet, and the air made the skin wet. You had to surrender to the slippery heat, and those wet days and nights were better than anything that has happened since. In his memory they were the best. Why? Because she was the first one, he used to tell himself. It was the first time for both of them, slender bodies discovering everything every day. But no, that wasn't it. Or only it. There is a place that sometimes opens for him, an interior place that will open like a flower or a sleeping eye. It is a light-filled chamber that he associates with her, or with the two of them together. A globe of honey-colored light. He has not words for this. It is not a memory. Not a scene. If he tries too hard to call it up, it will elude him, fade away and leave him emptied, or it will recede as if along a corridor until it's a pinpoint, a faraway glint at the end of a tunnel.

Connecting Flights

Beyond the ropes that guide him through the passenger lounge he sees a forest of white signs and notices. Small handheld signs show hand-lettered names. Is one of them meant for him? He isn't sure. There might be somebody waiting for you, Carlo said. On the other hand, maybe not. A typical Carlo arrangement. "They have a lawyer in Honolulu," he said, "but he could be in Tokyo this week, or Seoul."

He scans the cards and the eyes above the cards, the limo drivers, the VIP escorts. Higher up, large placards say ALOHA TOURS Assemble Here. PARADISE TOURS Welcomes You. TROPIC ADVENTURE Welcomes Phoenix Board of Realtors. These are tacked to tall sticks held high by brown-skinned men and women who wear flowered shirts, lava-lavas. Leis hang from their forearms and around their necks, filling the lounge with heady scents of tuberose and ginger.

The fragrance surprises him. It is a call from across a channel, a call he can't quite make out. If he stepped in closer he might hear it, and he would also be that much closer to one of these astonishing women. If he had signed up for the TROPIC ADVENTURE he would have the perfect excuse to be leaning for a flower necklace and a seductive glance from a dark-haired greeter.

Following the overhead signs toward BAGGAGE, CON-NECTING FLIGHTS, he watches faces coming toward him, searching for his name, looking for the eyes that will smile with recognition.

Honolulu International is made of concrete and shaped in long broad promenades for funneling crowds from asphalt runway to asphalt boulevard where the cabs and vans and ALOHA TOUR buses wait. But those promenades are open to the weather. All the doors are breezeways. This day the temperature is eighty degrees. The skies are clear. Tropic air and light surround him as he walks, the air balmy, the light amplified by the all-surrounding sea. The air is on him like a favorite shirt he forgot he owns, a shirt of weightless velvet. Then the light comes bouncing off the broad leaves of a tree rising next to the promenade. A concrete overhang blocks his view of sky and sun, so he only sees the fall of light, a radiant downpour, and the tree is not part of a forest or a garden or a park. It may not be joined to the earth. It has appeared in the midst of Honolulu International, with no tie to anything before or after, and so suddenly, with leaves so green and glossy and keenly edged, his eyes brim with water ready to spill.

In the flow of travelers moving toward the escalator he has to stop and wait and blink, thinking, Christ, what is *this* all about? Shake it. Shake it now. Be attentive. Shift the bag to the other shoulder. Take your time. There's the newsstand. Good. Let's stop. Stand still. Let the world scurry by, and buy a paper. The *Honolulu Advertiser* is what we need. News of the day. News of the islands.

From the alcove stacked with tabloids and magazines he checks the promenade one last time for anyone who might have a placard with his name. He folds the front page open and lets his eyes drift across the columns, reading but not reading, until he feels his strength return. The tearful rush has cleared his head. He has reached page four, scanning but not retaining, when a small headline stops his eyes. DRILLERS PLAGUED BY MISHAPS. He stares so long the rest of the page goes gray, while the headline acquires a slender, word-shaped aura. The brief story makes his eyelids sting.

> Unforeseen setbacks in recent weeks have slowed the progress of Energy Source, Western Sun's Big Island subsidiary. Plans to develop geothermal reservoirs a mile or so below sea level have been hampered by vandalism, equipment breakdown, and possibly arson, according to Puna District fire Marshal, Nelson Asato.
>
> Local opponents of geothermal development suggest that arson is too easy an explanation for the company's latest misfortune. Abner Kalaheo Bengsten, who chairs the Sacred Lands Foundation says "You cannot invade Madame Pele's domain and get off scot-free. Lots of people try to steal her lava rocks and take them back to the mainland, and they have paid the price. You think it's going to be different with her steam?"

He reads the story twice, then focuses on two phrases— *latest misfortune* and *possibly arson*. He rolls these around in his mouth and in his mind, to get the full taste. Latest means more than one, more than two. Possibly arson means a lot more than an ordinary fire. Has he missed something? Did Carlo mention this? The last thing they need is a protest group or an issue or a jinx. It could take up time. And time is money. Maybe Carlo doesn't know.

There is a hooded wall booth outside the newsstand. He dials and after three rings hears the click of a lifted receiver, then a voice that does not mention 20/20 Claims. A woman's voice. An island voice. Making a sound he has forgotten. The lilting rise of her slow "Hello?" is as soft and as smooth as a flower petal. The hairs on his forearms prickle. He recognizes the voice. His heart catches. He cannot breathe.

Again the slow and lissome rising word. "Hello?" Almost like singing. He knows now that he dialed the wrong number, the one he wasn't going to dial, and this is Evangeline Sakai's mother, five miles away on the outskirts of the city. He sees the house, the side street of slant-roof houses he has not seen since 1968. He sees the yard, red flowers glowing in the yard, flat banana leaves, the mother's brown and thoughtful face. For the first time he understands the layers of feeling in that face, the warmth and sadness and humor and compassion all at once. Her single word of greeting conveys that too. Her voice has opened a portal in his heart. He cannot speak. If he speaks, his own voice will break. He covers the mouthpiece with his hand and waits until she hangs up.

In his wallet he has the number on a faded strip of torn blue paper Evangeline gave him the day they met. He'd almost called from San Francisco before his flight departed, but decided it was too early, 6 A.M. in Honolulu, and better to be there where he can check the current listings, and then again thought, No. No, do not get sidetracked. She could be anywhere on earth by now. Just do the gig, he thought, get that taken care of before you start calling up old flames.

But here she comes again, floating into memory. Again he sees dark mountains as they rise from the shoreline, and in the foreground he sees Evangeline against the railing of the launch. The USS *Arizona* is out of the picture now. Completely submerged. Invisible. The fathers and the uncles are invisible, and his mother and his brother, too, though Grover was there that day and close enough to touch.

Evangeline stands alone, surrounded by light bouncing off the water of the still lagoon, her hair black against the water, the dream girl he has conjured so many times to ward off loneliness and his deepest fears. On the wall of his mind she has hung like a pinup in the barracks above the cot of the private waiting for orders. He remembers the day his family flew back to the mainland. She was at the airport carrying a lei made of vine leaves called *maile*, a fragrant and ceremonial vine that flourishes in the upland forests. She placed it around his neck, weeping helplessly, kissing, clinging, pressing her body next to his in an agony of last-minute desire. If he had said, Come with me, Angel, she would have done it, or tried to. He told her he'd be back. Three times she said, Promise me, and three times he promised.

He wore the lei on the plane and wore it to school for a few days, just starting his junior year, until the leaves began to curl. He hung it in his room, amid all his teenage artifacts, his Janis Joplin poster, his first guitar.

All that year and the next and the next, their letters traveled back and forth across the water. When he joined the army in 1971 the writing stopped. The maile leaves had turned brittle and paper dry, and yet, as of the day he left for the recruiting office, he could still lean in close and catch a dusty whiff of their perfume. And that is how you might describe his memory of her after he landed in Vietnam and learned how to die but not how to come back to life.

Evangeline was always surrounded with fragrance and summertime perfume. His Pacific dream girl. Eventually he would say it took him years to get over her, though maybe he never did. Maybe she spoiled him forever. As Marge walked out the door, her parting line had been, "You don't see me, Travis!"

"That's not true!"

"You never see anybody but yourself!"

Ten minutes later the rebuttal had come to him.

"If I could see myself," he said to the empty room, "maybe we wouldn't be shouting like this!"

Leona Doyle

Back across the water, in the house Travis seldom visits now, the big family house half concealed by shoreline forest, Leona sits next to an upstairs window reading from the Bible. She wears jeans, blue work shirt, her silver hair pulled back in a bun. The slanting light of late afternoon gives her face an ivory cast.

She quit going to church many years ago, but she will still dip into the stories from time to time, selecting out her favorites. She loves the look of Jesus transfigured on the mountaintop, his face and clothing ablaze with light so white all those who witnessed it had to turn away. And Saul of Tarsis blinded by a light from heaven as he traveled to Damascus, thrown to the ground, born again as God's true servant. And the rushing wind that filled the house in Jerusalem on the Day of Pentecost and set tongues of flame burning on the heads of the Apostles.

"Think of that," she will say to the dog or to anyone else within earshot. "Tongues of flame! In Jerusalem! In the year—what are we talking about here? 33? 34 A.D.? Wouldn't you love to witness a scene like that?"

Travis first heard such stories in Sunday school, where she would send them when they were young, Travis and his older brother, Grover. For three years of Sundays they sat below a long, floor-to-ceiling picture of Jesus in his *incandescent robe. Leona sent them mainly to please her mother, an ardent New Testament Christian. When Grandma passed away, the family's churchgoing habits went with her. Leona blamed it on the mileage. "It's the hateful part of where we live," she would explain to congregation members wondering where the Doyles had disappeared to, "up in the hills, and that long old country road. Driving anywhere will take you half the day."*

32

But along the way the New Testament had whetted her appetite. When Travis was growing up, Leona talked and talked about the mysteries large and small, the invisible currents, she called them, Christian and pagan, Druidic and Navajo, prayers that had been answered, healings she had heard about, the way a waxing moon can draw new-planted seedlings toward the surface, the way a car inherits energy from the previous owner, the way a future can be read in the ocean's ring of fire.

Travis was a scoffer earlier in life, because it was fashionable to scoff. With his father around, it was easy to scoff. Montrose Doyle was a very literal man. In his world there were no apparitions and few miracles. In Leona's world such things abound. Growing up between these two, Travis wanted her to know he wasn't listening to her stories. But of course he was. How can you silence your mother's voice? It all sank in. It all sank in, including her version of the story of his conception, which she tried in several ways to pass on to him. "Conception is the key, Travis—not where you were born, but the actual spot where a person was conceived."

There had been a love nest called "The Ditch," where she and Montrose used to meet when they were courting and where they would sometimes meet after they were married, to recapture the abandon of their courtship days. Years later they learned that this low spot in the hilly land beyond their house was a feature of the fault line that borders the ranch and runs through that part of California.

"My grandmother would have kept all such information hidden," she will tell Travis, "and my mother too, being from Oklahoma and a woman of an older time. But I am a woman of another time, and I want you to know as much as I can tell you."

This will be after he has been out among the islands for a while and has finally come back home. They will be walking together down through rows of apple trees bristling with new buds. Her work shirt will be knotted over her belt. They will leave by the porch door, down the back steps, across the yard, past the vehicle shed where he spent his high school years, where some of his posters still hang, and out into the remains of the orchard Monty's father planted in the 1920s, soon after he came west from Texas, when three hundred acres of sloping hillside was something a man could actually afford. They have forty acres left, thirty-five in the long gnarled rows of Red Delicious, and this is where she leads him, under the boughs and across the clumps of loamy soil, taking her time, his native guide through territory both recognizable and strange. He seems to be entering it for the first time, seeing it for the first time. Light filtering through the yellow-green leaves is magical light, and he is a child again, he is five again and thirty-five and a hundred and five.

The top of her head is level with his shoulder, but Leona has an erect way of standing and a forceful way of walking that seems to give her more height. They stroll all the way to the ditch, because she wants him to see "the touch point." In each life, she says, there is a touch point. She wants him to see with his own eyes where his seed was planted.

It is just a grassy hollow in the springtime earth, but it holds him transfixed as he tries to imagine the two of them entangled, youthful, in the grass, naked under apple boughs *the open sky. He doesn't know what to say. A hot current sears his skin. A wire running through him has touched a wire buried there. Leona is silent. She doesn't expect him to speak. She is giving him time to absorb the scene, until she thinks he is ready to hear her version of his life.*

For a long time, she says at last, she thought the conception spot accounted for his patchwork career, his years of restlessness and roaming, a natural-born son of earthquake country.

"As I think through the things you are telling me, Travis, maybe there is another way to read it. Maybe we have been looking in the wrong place. We have been looking back over our shoulders, the way we have come, seeing this ranch of ours as hanging off the farthest edge, like some piece of the continent that could break loose at any moment and float away. What happens if we look straight ahead and think about this ring, this rim we are on, whatever you want to call it? Aren't we on the edge of some great big wheel here?"

What does Leona mean? What is she seeing?

In her view the place where they are standing, where he was conceived, at the bottom of the ranch where he spent his early years, this acreage and the county spreading out around it, is about as far west as you can get without a boat. Yet it is not the West with a capital W. That is somewhere inland and behind them. This is the coastal strip of the western shore, a different place, a curving borderland with ridges, shaped by water, by the oceanic tides, by the dreams and fears of all the millions like herself and Montrose and Grover and his wife, who need to live within an hour of the water. The long borderland fits neatly into her picture of a rim encircling the Pacific, a jagged circle made of fault lines and hot springs and geysers and volcanoes. For her it comes as no surprise that he has been drawn toward the hub of the wheel they call the ring of fire, where lava churns and leaps

and oozes through the cracks, no surprise at all, Leona
being the good mother she is. A mother will always look for
some way to arrange her child's life, give it a shape that
appeals to her.

"I have peeked at the map a time or two," she will tell
him. "I have seen where that island is located, like a big old
eye out there."

This is the way her mind works. This is the way Leona
sees. It still appeals to her, that vision. It redeems him, her
younger and more prodigal son, once thought lost. It
redeems her too, gives her own life the kind of drama she
secretly enjoys. It locates her. In such a scenario the very
location of their house has meaning now, along with all the
random chances that led them there by way of Oklahoma,
Albuquerque, Needles, Bakersfield, Salinas.

Don't we all do this? Live our days one at a time, plunging
along, driven by who knows what? Years later, looking
back, some pattern may appear. The mind will seek it out,
the pattern that gives order to the day, the season, the bliz-
zard of events. Was a pattern really there? Who knows? But
the mind needs one. His mother needs one. Travis needs one,
though it may not be the one she would imagine for him.

Only now, as this trip gets underway, is he beginning to
be ready to look at where he comes from and where he is
headed. Travis Doyle. five eleven. 175 pounds. Brown hair.
Gray eyes. Blue Volvo. Purple Heart. Wells Fargo savings
and checking. Home phone unlisted. High school varsity
track and field. Accident-free discount with Mutual Life.
Reformed smoker. Frequent flyer. Born in San Jose. Conceived in the rift zone midway between Point Reyes and San
Simeon about four in the afternoon while the sun backlit the
apple leaves, making them translucent, according to his
mother, who was gazing upward at the time, with her eyes
wide open, not wanting to miss anything.

Hawaiian Time

On the interisland flight, heading farther south, he watches Diamond Head wheel past, its famous tiara peak flattened and green. Seen from above, the shallow brushy crater is a green bowl that makes its own round peninsula. Beyond it, Honolulu's quilt of districts spreads out and up toward ridges so wet and steep and forested, no one has ever thought of living there. As he drinks in the view, the rare and isolated beauty fills his chest with a longing for he knows not what, a double-edged longing, part gratitude, part premonition. It is wild up there in the ridges above the city, wild and trackless. They rise, as the whole island rises, from a sea of glittering light.

Across the channel his plane skirts the windward coast of Moloka'i, its empty canyon valleys, and dark walls of surf-edged cliffs streaked with ribbon waterfalls. They pass the red-dirt prairie, thick with cane, that joins Maui's western mountains to the dormant crater, Haleakala. Then the Big Island is looming very big in front of them, lush and misty, creased with gorges. As the plane banks, Mauna Kea comes into view, upper third of the great volcano that grew high enough to catch snow. He can see white patches gleaming at the very top of what was once a lava fountain. Then they plunge into the mist, into cloud cover, and land in a blinding rain.

Travis has never known such rain. Driving from the airport in his rented Toyota he cannot see street signs. He cannot see streets. His wipers are useless. It takes him fifteen minutes to drive two miles. At the registration desk there is one message. In his room there is a baby orchid on one pillow of the queen-size bed, with a card nearby welcoming him to the Orchid Isle Hotel. On a table next to the phone there is a magazine called *Round the Island* with a cover photo of a golf course. "Where to Go," it says, "What to Do. Free Maps. Dining. Shopping."

He stares at the cover, stupified with travel, the end of travel, and the sobering truth that two automobiles and two jet liners in and out of three airports have brought him to this solitary room at the bottom end of a world-class deluge.

A table and two chairs are positioned near a wide picture window that ordinarily offers a view across Hilo Bay. At the moment the bay seems pushed right next to the window. Falling into one of the chairs, he sits and gazes at the sheets of rain, cursing himself for letting Carlo talk him into this expedition, cursing Carlo too, who did not tell him about the rain.

How long does he sit there? Thirty seconds? Thirty minutes? He is in a paralysis of melancholy. When the phone rings, its jangle tears through him like a claw. On the table, two feet away, it seems alive. On the fourth ring he grabs the receiver.

"Travis Doyle here."

"Good afternoon, Mr. Doyle. This is Ian Prince. With Energy Source? Welcome to Hilo."

"Thanks. Nice to hear from you."

"You received my message?"

"I did, yes. I just checked in. Both my flights were held up. And then this storm, as we hit the coast."

"Rain like this tends to slow everything down."

"Is this a big one? A small one? I have no idea. It feels pretty serious to me."

"Let's just say it's not unusual, not unexpected at this time of year."

He hears a wistful note. This fellow sounds like a diplomat stationed at some embassy overseas, in a foreign country he does not quite approve of.

Travis says, "I suppose you and I should get together."

"That's why I've called, to see how your agenda looks."

"It's wide open, Mr. Prince. I am here to serve."

"You'll probably want the afternoon to rest up and gather your thoughts."

Something about the voice puts him on guard. What is it? Too formal? Too clipped?

"Actually I feel good. I slept on the plane."

"Hmmmmmm," he says, as if troubled.

"I wouldn't mind looking at the site this afternoon, if it's possible."

"Everything is possible, Mr. Doyle. Just bear in mind that we are on what they call Hawaiian time."

He knows this means letting things slide. He isn't prepared to let things slide, or to let Prince slide, if that's what he is trying to do.

"Hawaiian time?"

"In this kind of weather I doubt anyone is out there. The gate to the facility is probably locked, and the security man, who would be the closest person with a key, might be hard to raise this late in the day. By the time he met us it could be dark. Twilights are short on the windward side. When darkness falls, it falls all over you."

"Suppose you and I met somewhere for a drink . . ."

"I look forward to that, I honestly do. But I am about forty miles north of town, that is, an hour or so on a clear day. An errand that could not be postponed, and now, in this kind of weather it's just not advisable to be out on the road. Getting together today really isn't feasible, as much as I'd like to . . ."

"Tell me what *is* feasible. Is there someone else in Hilo who can start to fill me in?"

"I'm confident the weather will break tonight. Which will put me back in town tomorrow morning. I propose we meet, oh, eightish, for coffee, a bite to eat, at your hotel, and take it from there."

This sounds final. Prince is ready to hang up. Travis has been looking around the room, out into the gray downpour. On top of the TV set an illustrated card lists cable movies you can watch this week, with show times and ratings—PG, R, and X—with letter codings for Strong Language, Nudity, and Violence. The thought of sitting out the afternoon fills him with despair.

"I have to be honest with you. I am a restless person. I am a bundle of kinetic energy. I feel like I could run a marathon uphill. I would at least like to drive out toward the site and begin to get the lay of the land. If there is no one to go along, I can probably find my way."

Travis can hear him blinking, forty miles up the coast, if that's really where Prince is, blinking into this same eternal rain. five seconds go by.

"If I were in your position," he says at last, "I would relax a while. Enjoy the hotel. They have an excellent buffet, fresh mahimahi is a specialty, and some very fine performers in the lounge. I'm sure you're familiar with the hula."

"I love the hula. But I am not on vacation. The truth is, I am on a no-frills expense account. The sooner I get started, the happier we'll be."

Prince offers him directions now, his voice full of new sincerity, as if he genuinely wants to please. Whether they are the wrong directions, or Travis gets them wrong, or a blowing squall obscures the signs at a couple of crucial turns, he will never be able to say for sure. Two hours after landing on that island he finds himself lost and cursing with impotent rage, groping his way along a broken roadbed somewhere south of Hilo, cursing Ian Prince and cursing Carlo. He understands why three adjustors have walked away in the past six weeks. This is rain that can change a person's outlook and career plan. It is the last rain, the apocalyptic cloudburst.

The town, when it appears, seems otherworldly, as if he has indeed passed through some dark and dripping gateway. It comes toward him through falling water, its asphalt puddled and shiny, its rusty roofs shining as if polished. Along the short main street, stores have a frontier look. Wooden posts support overhangs of corrugated metal. Though the sky is heavy, light leaks under the cloudy darkness of late afternoon, coating the old wood with silver.

He needs something from this silvery town. He cannot say what. Reassurance. Relief. Revenge perhaps. A cup of hot coffee. He pulls up next to a public phone, half thinking he will call Western Union, though he knows he won't. The storm has siphoned away his anger. With the engine running and rain spattering the tinfoil lid of his Toyota, he riffles through folders spread across the seat. He studies printouts, a topo map.

Across the narrow street two elderly filipino men on a warped and soggy porch seem to be observing this. He would not be able to explain why the good opinion of these two strangers matters to him, men he will never see again. He does not want them to think he is lost and without direction. He turns off the engine, opens the door and leaps onto the nearest porch, where the phone hangs, and notices then a painted sign that says TRADEWINDS LAUNDERETTE. Around these words pastel socks and shorts and T-shirts tumble in cartoon suds. A young woman stands in the open doorway watching the rain and watching him.

He steps inside, scans the rows of white machines. A couple of them churn with gobs of clothing. Bleeps come from a distant corner, where a local kid concentrates on a standup video game.

"Can I help you with anything?" the young woman says.

She looks to be sixteen or so, filipina plus something else. Her skin is the color of honey, and glows with health. Her voice is gentle. Her eyes are large, reminding him of someone, holding him with an innocent, laundromat beauty.

"Yes. Yes, maybe you can. I'm looking for a road called Pumahi."

As he says this he sees the old photo in his wallet, stuffed in behind his driver's license and his Social Security card. This girl's eyes are like Evangeline's. She looks so much like Evangeline used to look, she could be a niece, or a close cousin. His wet skin feels suddenly dry. His blood is pounding. It occurs to him that if he stopped in this town for a reason, then he entered this room full of washing machines for a reason, and she is it. She is going to lead him somewhere.

"Pumahi," she says.

"I don't think it's very far from here."

In the silence her radiant smile turns tentative. Then she says the name again, and asks, "How far do you think?"

"I'm not sure. That's why I'm asking."

Yet again she says, "Pumahi," as if trying to memorize the word.

"That's right."

She gives him a vacant look. She could be watching afternoon TV. Her smile fades. Her lips close.

"Let me get the manager. Okay?"

"It's not too much trouble?"

"She's in back. She knows more than me. I just make change and sell detergent. Like that. You got anything to wash?"

"I'm just passing through."

She moves toward a doorway, and he is alone, disappointed yet relieved. Life is simpler without synchronicities and guides. Duller, but simpler.

He inhales the bleached and humid air, the sanitized heat of drying clothes, and watches the local kid pull levers. He wears a thin-strap body shirt that features his young muscles, round and brown and solid. His eyes never stray from the machine, which fills the Tradewinds Launderette with its electronic song: *bleep bleep blup blup bloop bloop oooooo-eeeeeeeee bleepedy bleep*.

A second fellow is in there, though Travis doesn't notice him until he stands up. He's been hunkering in front of one of the dryers. He is moving now, a Caucasian fellow wearing boots, faded jeans with a red knee patch, a pale brown mustache. His T-shirt says LOVE LAVA. His head is buzzed but not to the skin, the close crop you sometimes see on inmates and on Zen novices. A pillow case of laundry is slung over his shoulder like a duffel bag.

As he approaches, the girl returns and says to Travis, "Did she talk to you?"

"Not yet."

"Pretty busy back there, I guess."

He waits. That is the end of it. Her face shows both apology and pleasure, saying they have all tried their best.

He turns to the other fellow. "It's my first day on the island. I'm looking for Pumahi Road. I'm sort of off course."

The eyes go wide. The whites are very white, the pupils brown, nearly black. The smile, at first, is saintlike. The voice is low, with a back-throat scratch. It could be a doper's voice, but he doesn't have doper's eyes.

"I've heard of it," he says.

"I'm looking for a drilling site out that way, some outfit prospecting for steam."

The smile doesn't move, though its quality seems to shift. Thin lips pull in closer to the teeth. He creases his brow.

"A lot of people appear to be interested in steam these days."

"This outfit is called Energy Source."

He glances at the girl, who is no longer listening. He pulls at his mustache.

"South of town you'll come to a fork. Bear left. Seven, eight, nine miles down that way you'll come to a store. It's called Nakamura Store. Ask there. They'll know. That's about the best I can do when it comes to that end of the island."

Travis thanks the girl and thanks the man, receiving again his somewhat saintly smile. In the car he thinks of the way he said "that end of the island," as if it is two mountain ranges away. He wonders if this fellow too has recently arrived. Or has he been here so long the island has assumed the dimensions of a continent? He thinks of Prince's explanation for postponing any meeting until tomorrow. He is forty miles away. In the world Travis has been accustomed to, the world of the Bay Area and the L.A. basin, everything is forty miles away. You don't think about it much. Other terms are operating here, no question about that. Prince mentioned Hawaiian time. Maybe there is also Hawaiian space, a world where time expands and so do distances. "That end of the island" turns out to be ten miles of gradually sloping terrain with almost nothing else between the town's edge and Nakamura Store, nothing visible from the road at any rate, a few houses, arching corridors of ancient mango trees, backcountry thickets of scrub brush and 'ohi'a, lava outcroppings here and there, slick and black and furred with gray-green lichen.

A Silver Waterfall

Bearing east he finds Pumahi Road, then finds a wider track of new crushed lava rock cutting through a neglected papaya grove. Past the papayas, wet walls of sugarcane make a long, green corridor. Half a mile in he passes a small sign attached to a metal stake:

HAZARDOUS AREA
AUTHORIZED PERSONNEL ONLY

Underneath that, in smaller print, it says *Western Sun*.

The cane field ends, and he enters a forest of high, slender 'ohi'a and strawberry guava and sprawling ferns. After another half mile he reaches a chain-link fence and another sign:

NO TRESPASSING

But the gate, which Prince imagined would be locked, is wide open and unattended. Around the first curve he comes upon a plateau of slightly higher land where the remains of the gutted equipment shed stands skeletal and black, blacker than the flat spread of lava it was built upon.

Fifty yards beyond the shed, two pickup trucks are parked, with hoods raised. Between a house trailer and a half-built carport, four men watch him ease the Toyota to a stop. It is still raining, but not like Hilo. This is rain you can walk around in and see through, rain turning to mist, under foggy clouds that now touch the treetops.

The men wear ponchos, boots. Two wear beat-up ball caps with inscriptions he can't make out. Before he has the door open, one fellow is standing by the car, signaling to roll the window down. He could be a tag team wrestler. His face is big and thick and smooth, and he has blue eyes that cut through the rainy mist.

"Might as well switch that engine back on and turn it around and keep moving. We don't want any reporters out here"

"I'm not a reporter."

"Good. Because there is nothing to report."

"My name is Travis Doyle."

"Jesus Christ Almighty!"

"I just flew in from San Francisco."

"You're not supposed to be here until tomorrow! Where's Prince?"

"The last I heard he was somewhere up the coast."

"What do you mean, the last you heard! What the hell is he doing up there?"

"He called me at the hotel."

"The last you heard? You talk like you've been talking to him for months."

"I told you, I just got off the plane. I figured I'd drive out and see what's what."

"You sure picked a pisspoor time."

"Your company filed the claim, my friend. You want to change your mind? fine with me. It makes my report a whole lot shorter."

The blue eyes ignite. Travis expects him to yank the door open and start punching. Though the guy looks to have a fifty-pound advantage, Travis would take him on. He is ready to. They are both on a short fuse, glaring. Later, he will look back on this as one of his life's stranger moments, pulling into a fenced compound at the bottom of the island, in late afternoon with the drizzle settling on them like light-filled motes of dust, settling on the hoods of all the vehicles and on the silent leaves beyond the trailer, while he sits behind the wheel, eye to eye with a man he has never seen before, who could break his arms and legs and has three friends watching.

With his hands on his hips the man calls to the others, "Go on! I'll catch up with you!"

They stand looking at him, and Travis sees then that each man carries a bundle wrapped in burlap.

"Another thirty minutes," the man says, "it's going to be too dark to see what we're doing."

They move away, past the trailer, through a line of trees.

When he turns to Travis again, his eyes have changed. They say, Let's start over. His voice says carefully, "I'm Dan Clemson, the site engineer here. We happen to be in the middle of something. You'll have to stand by for a while, until we get it resolved. It's just a couple of our vehicles giving us some trouble."

"What's the problem?"

"They won't start. They're wet."

"They look pretty new."

"They're brand new. They are the replacements for two trucks we lost in the fire. We couldn't wait for the settlement. We need 'em, so we went ahead and bought 'em. The sonsa-bitches have been out here three days and now they won't even turn over. As soon as I deal with that, you and I can talk."

"Maybe I'll just take a preliminary look around."

"Tomorrow would be better. I mean, the light will be better. A lot of things we haven't touched, until you got here.

You want to be able to see what you're doing. If you can sit tight a while, I'll be with you as soon as I can."

It's a request, not an order, Clemson talking faster now, distracted. He walks back to the twin navy blue pickups. Something gives them a sinister look. The spotlights over each cab look like ears. The raised hoods make Travis think of two yawning Dobermans. He watches Clemson pause and gaze in at one of the engines, then slam both hoods shut and walk off toward the trees.

It strikes Travis as an odd way to deal with two wet engines.

It is too odd. A cold stream of panic drains through him. They have him surrounded, these four guys. They are spreading out in the twilight undergrowth, just waiting for him to step away from the car. He has heard stories about this island, about marijuana empires bigger than anything in northern California. If drilling for steam is their cover, if that is what he's stumbled into, he figures he is about to be badly injured. Sweat begins to drip underneath his shirt. In the still and sultry heat his skin is coated. Sweat runs on top of that, as he stands next to the Toyota, magnetized. There is no breeze, not a whiffle. The wet, thick air is charged with something he needs to identify. Is it the acrid scent of damp charcoal? Is it the specter of the drilling rig that now appears, in blurred outline, as the foggy mist thins and lifts? Metal legs, maybe a hundred yards farther in, come rising from the trees like a spider craft from another galaxy.

The mist dissolves, and the rig stands in sharp silhouette. He listens. Now voices are coming from that direction. They rise and fall. He can't make out words, but as he concentrates on the sound, it persuades him that all four men are somehow together, in the same place. His panic subsides. He reaches into the car for the little camera he always carries, a Nikon Touchmatic. The clearing has filled with a soft and milky light. He decides to take a few shots for the record, and while he has the chance—the rig, the trucks, the trailer, the shed from a distance and closer up. His Touchmatic is handy at times like this. No settings. No accessories to haul around. A built-in flash. Indoors and out, it gives him all the detail he needs.

He listens again, hears a single voice from beyond the trees, above that voice, above the silence, the flute notes of the forest birds. They call and wait. A trill. A trickling arpeggio.

The shed is older than the drilling project, thirty-five or forty years old is his guess, and mostly wood, roofed with the corrugated metal you see all along the windward shores of these islands, brown with weathering and rust. Two sloping panels are shiny and silver, perhaps tacked on for temporary cover. In this light they seem to glow. They make a sloping silver waterfall. Everything else looks burnt or smoked, the half-charred ends of dangling timber, the shell of a flatbed truck, the ruined claw scoop of what once had been a backhoe. Lengths of pipe look as if someone has worked them over with a blowtorch.

He goes through a couple of rolls, click click click. It is nearly dark when he walks back to the Toyota and hears the men returning. One at a time they emerge from the trees. The first two don't acknowledge him. They head for an old Pontiac sedan. Clemson approaches and says he wants Travis to meet his maintenance foreman, Tiny Kulima, a massive Hawaiian or part-Hawaiian who nods and extends a hand thick with calluses.

Tiny wears Levis and heavy-weather boots with the buckles flopping, so that they click loosely when he walks, like armor he is about to remove. His ball cap says HILO MARINE AND BOAT REPAIR. It sits atop a curly fringe of thick black hair streaked with gray. In the gloom his dark beard looks menacing, but his brief smile puts Travis at ease, a courteous and youthful smile, white teeth showing through the beard and through the dusk.

Tiny doesn't want to linger. To Clemson he says, "We check 'em out in the morning."

He slides behind the wheel of the Pontiac. As their engine recedes into the sudden night, Clemson slaps his forehead, nailing the first mosquito, and says, "Let's move inside."

The Driller's Tale

Travis has seen enough wreckage to verify the claim. His mind is already playing with numbers, the per-foot cost of pipe, the freight charges for replacement parts, the effect of such losses on a production schedule. For the sake of formality he may quibble with Energy Source here and there, but he does not plan to challenge the numbers in any serious way. If his luck holds he can have this job wrapped up in a couple of days. As he steps into the musty, mildew-scented trailer, that is his vision of the immediate future.

Clemson hangs his poncho on a hook under the little metal awning that makes his porch. He switches on a fan and a gooseneck lamp. "If this is the wrong time to talk," Travis says, "I can come back. I wasn't planning to barge in unannounced. Prince told me the gates would be closed."

From a mini-fridge Clemson brings out two sweating bottles of Dos Equis. "I can also offer you tequila. Or Irish whiskey."

Travis regards the long-necked amber bottles and distantly hears his vows of abstinence, but a louder voice is saying that if a man cannot have one cold beer at the end of such a day, during which he has more than earned his keep and paid his dues, the Earth itself would be a poorer place to live.

"The Dos Equis looks pretty good."

Prying the caps off, Clemson says, "Don't give it another thought. I had tomorrow set aside. But this is fine. This is better, as things turn out. Tomorrow could be lively."

"You mentioned reporters."

"We might see one or two."

"Anything in particular they'll be looking for?"

Clemson lifts his bottle in a little toast and with a cryptic smile says, "Welcome to the Big Island."

They are sitting next to a long flat desk, layered with reports, charts, and graphs. Beyond a narrow corridor Travis sees bedding, clothes on the floor. The gooseneck lamp shines down on the sprawl of paperwork. In this reflected light the thick tanned face is aglow with moisture. The eyes look startled, as if his mind is elsewhere, or following two tracks at once. Travis decides not to be troubled by this. Clemson has allowed him in and doesn't seem appalled to have an adjuster on the premises. Travis has been in situations where the hostility filled the air like smoke. He takes a long pull and concentrates on the soothing icy sting along his throat and waits.

"Everything that goes on here," Clemson says, "is everybody's business. It's taken me a while to adjust to that. Maybe I still haven't adjusted. My job is drilling holes in the ground. That's what I know how to do. I have never worked in a place like this, where so many people are watching, and every day something comes along that has to be handled, something you didn't expect at all."

"Like an insurance guy who shows up one day early."

Clemson tips his head back, guzzling half the bottle, the way you can do in the tropics when your whole body feels parched, drinking like a camel driver who has finally reached the oasis after nine days of nothing but sand. The long draft brings glitter to his eyes, and with these eyes he holds Travis, seeming again to weigh two or three options.

"No need to apologize, Mr. Doyle. I'm glad you're here. I've been looking forward to this. Since that claim was filed, certain things have come to light. Maybe you are the man to help us sort through it all."

Not me, thinks Travis. "The paperwork as it stands seems pretty complete."

"The claim may have to be refiled."

"I mean, from our point of view, it is certainly . . . satisfactory. No coverage problem, as far as I can see."

"Mr. Prince thinks he has located a culprit."

"Someone who set the shed on fire?"

"That's his theory, though you should know right now we do not always see eye to eye. He is the one handling the correspondence on this."

"How about you? What's your theory?"

Clemson stands up, blocking the light. Travis has become aware of his forearms, tanned and bristling with sun-bleached hair. For an instant, as the engineer hovers there, his profile suddenly huge, these arms put Travis on double alert. But Clemson is only moving toward the cupboard above the cluttered mini-sink.

"I have a craving for the taste of tequila next to this beer." He brings out an open quart of Jose Cuervo Especial. "There's ice in the fridge, though I seldom use it."

Travis too is ready for tequila. "I suppose I'll pass on the ice," he says.

Clemson pours the tumblers half full and pushes one across the desk and takes a slow sip, followed by a slow grin.

"I don't have a theory. That is Prince's department. I don't have time for a theory. All I want to do is get this well drilled. If somebody set a fire, of course, we damn sure better know who it is before they hit us again."

"And who is *they*?"

Clemson shoves some charts aside and comes up with a folder full of clippings. The one on top, from the *Hilo Tribune Herald*, says COURT WILL RULE ON PUNA PROTESTOR. It describes an episode a week earlier, when a fellow named John Brockman tried to stop construction at the site of a new luxury hotel/resort on the leeward side. An accomplice lashed him to some scaffolding where concrete was being poured.

There are other clippings, along with police reports, and a deposition from a cane field worker who remembers seeing a vehicle pull out of the access road not long before the shed caught fire. "A white or light-color late-sixties model," this witness said. "You could tell by the size, real wide, like a Dodge or something, maybe a Dart with the slant six, which I know pretty well because I drove one while my brother was on temporary transfer to the mainland."

Clemson gives him plenty of time to browse. He isn't in a hurry.

Travis says, "I gather this guy Brockman drives a white late-sixties Dart."

"He does, yes, which is part of the problem with Prince's theory. It is like saying he was last seen riding a bicycle in Hong Kong. I'll bet you could find four hundred white Dodge Darts on this island."

"But not all driven by people willing to tie themselves to scaffolding."

Clemson laughs a comradely and conspiratorial laugh. "Very good, Mr. Doyle. Very good indeed. Maybe I was right. Maybe you *are* the one who can help us get to the bottom of this."

He is reaching for the tequila bottle. Travis places a hand over his glass and reminds him that he is driving back to Hilo.

"Tequila is not like whiskey," Clemson says. "Tequila clears the head and sharpens the vision and gives focus to every task."

Travis, having swallowed just enough to be persuaded by this logic, removes his hand and watches the tumbler fill again to the midway mark. They have finished the beer. It is the tequila now. After they sip, Travis says, "This is what you were talking about—a typical Big Island situation."

"How do you mean?"

"Every day something takes you by surprise, you said. That's exactly how I feel. And I haven't even unpacked."

Clemson laughs again, loud and long, a sonic boom of a laugh. It pushes him past the sound barrier of his own caution and reserve.

"I might as well tell you what's been going on out here today. It'll be in the fucking papers sooner or later anyhow. Reporters are the same all over, as you probably know. They are like bird dogs. They are trained to sniff things out and carry back the carcasses. This is just the kind of thing they love. I only hope the sales rep from the dealership gets here first, before the shit hits the fan."

His eyes have the riveting steadiness of a man who is right where he thinks he wants to be, feeling bulletproof and fearless.

"You met my maintenance guy. Every time something has happened out there, Tiny has come to me and said, Dan, it's not good. And I have said, I know that. And he has said, The spirits of this place have been offended. And I have said, Tiny, we are dealing with machinery that either works or does not work, and when it doesn't work we fix it. You are not a believer in the supernatural, are you, Mr. Doyle? I mean, do you believe in miracles?"

"I don't know. It depends on the miracle."

"Or curses?"

"I suppose it would depend on who is getting cursed."

What Clemson said about tequila seems to be correct. In his own eyes Travis feels the same steadiness he sees across the desk. This seems to be a moment of high clarity, high recognition.

"How about coincidence?" Clemson says. "Where do you stand on coincidence?"

"Give me an example."

Clemson begins a long story about Tiny Kulima, who came to him today and said the guys have been talking. Two brand-new pickups going dead at the same time is not good, they said, it's another sign, and Dan has to do something. Drilling was scheduled to start ten days ago, he says, and they still don't have a bit in the ground. It has just been one thing after another. There have been shipping delays— to be expected, given the distance. And personnel problems (read drunk and disorderly)—also to be expected, given the delays. Then one afternoon a wind came up and blew open both doors to the trailer, sending a sheaf of crucial printouts flapping into the iron-red mud. Then came the fire. And now the rain, along with two temperamental pickup trucks.

He has a whole crew of Wyoming and West Texas roughnecks living in motels and getting into trouble waiting for the show to start. Today he had to let everyone go right after lunch because no one can fight the kind of weather they were getting. When Tiny said they had to do something, Clemson said, "My God, Tiny, we're doing all we can, under the circumstances. It could be those trucks are damp, or it could be something the sales rep can handle."

"The guys think you got to make peace with Pele," Tiny said, "or they're gonna walk off the job."

"We can't shut the project down, if that's what you're talking about. We've got too much into it now."

"Then maybe ask forgiveness, ask her to forgive you for what you're doing."

Dan reminded him that someone already did that. Two months back, before the crew arrived, a kahuna was brought in to walk the perimeter and speak to the land. Tiny told him it wouldn't hurt to try that again, it wouldn't hurt for Dan himself to tell Pele he respected her, to approach the earth in person and ask forgiveness for anything he had done to offend.

"Tiny," Dan said, "I am not a guy who goes around talking to volcano goddesses. I am a guy from Lubbock, Texas, who was raised a Baptist and who still has an uncle who preaches for the first Baptist Church in Fort Worth."

Tiny said, "I too am a Christian, Dan. But this is her island. If you want, the guys will pick some ti leaves and bring them to spread around the platform."

"Okay," Dan said, "suppose we do all that, then what?"

"We wait."

"How long?"

"Overnight."

"What if it doesn't work?"

Tiny shrugged. "You can't lose nothing. Try it. Otherwise, the trucks maybe keep sitting there and maybe you have to hire a whole new crew."

"So he had us between the proverbial rock and the hard place," says Dan, as he finishes the tale, "because the men who will actually work the rig are fellows I have worked with before. We have worked all over hell together, from Waco to Wyoming. The deal we have with the county is, a certain number of local people have to be on the payroll. Tiny and his crew do all the driving, the hauling, the moving, the clearing. You name it, they do it, and they're reliable, and we need 'em. Tiny, I said, I got a sales rep coming out from Hilo. If he can't get those pickups rolling, they're going right back to the dealership. And you know what he tells me? Do 'em both, get the sales rep and the ti leaves too. It would be good for the guys on the crew, he says, otherwise they might not come back. I said, When you say *they*, does that include you? Then he says—and I have to confess that this touched me, this got to me—he says, Dan, you are going to drill your holes here and go on to the next project, but me, I live here, my family lives here, all us guys are going to stay on this island after you are long gone.

"That is really why I went out there with the leaves and talked to her. It can't hurt, I was thinking. As long as my uncle in Fort Worth doesn't find out. We spread the leaves around. Tiny said some kind of blessing in Hawaiian. That's what we were getting ready to do when you pulled in, and that's why I blew up. I was already in a double bind. You made it a triple."

Travis feels obliged to look skeptical, although he is not. Not very. This story appeals to him. He wants it to be true. He likes the idea that something under or near the drilling site can shut down two glossy pickups. At the part about Tiny Kulima knowing he and his family would remain on the island, his arm hairs and neck hairs prickle in a rush that lasts until Dan stops talking. He has been waiting a long time to hear the driller's tale. Months. Maybe years. The timing is perfect. When you are ready for the story, they say, the teller will appear. Why did he tell Clemson he isn't sure about miracles? Before long he will see that a miracle is what he's out here searching for, and you say such things to protect yourself against not finding what you yearn for most.

In the long silence Clemson sits regarding him, then knocks back the rest of his tequila. Travis does the same, feels it burn his throat and melt into golden heat as it descends, while the heat spreads outward to make a second skin of golden moisture around his body.

"That's a pretty good story," he says at last.

"It's daily life down here in Puna."

"But you yourself, you're not the kind of person who thinks throwing leaves on the ground is the way to start a stalled truck."

Clemson grins broadly. "I haven't seen it mentioned in the owner's manual."

"You didn't want me coming down here until that was taken care of."

"Didn't seem like the best time to be entertaining a stranger, if you know what I mean. Nothing personal."

"I could have waited. It was Prince's voice made me nosey."

"Just between you and me, he can be a big pain in the ass."

"You think he would deliberately pass out wrong directions?"

"He usually overdoes it."

"Overdoes what?"

"He refers to himself as middle management. He's here about half the time. You want my opinion, he belongs in Las Vegas. His father used to own a chunk of Western Sun."

"Where does he stand on coincidence?"

"He keeps his distance. If you didn't tell him what I've just told you, I'd be grateful."

"You mean the blessing."

"He knows we had some kind of security situation. That's how I described it on the phone when I asked him to keep you in Hilo. He can live without the small details."

"So he didn't hear about the trucks."

"They stalled. Let's say the rest he doesn't want to hear."

Travis waits. He could press for more, but prefers not to. The more he knows, the more complicated his job is going to be. He does not want complications. Suddenly his eyes are sore, his shoulders ache. It feels very late. Clemson reaches for the tequila and asks if he'd like another drink. Travis pushes up out of his chair and says he should probably be starting back.

Night Sounds

It is 8 P.M. when they step through the door and into the tropic night. According to his body clock, still on Pacific Standard Time, it is ten. It could be the jet lag, or the drink, or the no-dinner, or all three that give the air outside the trailer such density. He thought the air inside was getting thick. The air outside is thick enough to lean against.

"You here by yourself?"

"Tonight I am. We're taking turns. We have had a hell of a time finding local people who will stay overnight. They just won't do it. They say they can't sleep. We tell them you don't have to sleep. It's better if you don't, we tell them. They say they feel things, they hear things."

"What do they hear?"

"They don't stick around long enough to find out."

"How about you?"

"I'm not worried. Once we start drilling, we'll go around the clock."

"I mean, how do you feel about whatever it is they say they hear?"

"Night sounds have never bothered me. Out here I can work as late as I want and be up with first light. I guess I like the solitude."

They stand there for five more minutes, for ten, without speaking. Listening. The air is charged with inaudible static, the kind of quiet that lets Travis hear his own internal circuitry. The crackling of nerve-ends becomes a tiny sizzle in his ear.

Eventually he moves through the darkness toward his car and starts the engine and turns the car around. Clemson is a bulky silhouette against the dim light from the trailer.

He is a couple of miles along the road north when he notices a far-off glow above the treeline to the west, a reddish halo that could be the aura from a large neon sign, if there were any theaters or casinos or malls out that way. Somewhere in the distance something is on fire. That's what he registers at the time. It is taking all his concentration to stay awake and not lose his way again. In the days to follow he will learn more about the origins of this light and how the lava burst forth in the hours after sundown. No one was near enough to hear the first roar and whistling explosion, or see the first gush of liquid flame and sparking gobbets of molten rock come leaping from the Earth. It is out there by itself, miles from anywhere. The first show of color against rain-heavy clouds was swallowed, in the early minutes, by the sun's final brilliant orange wash. But it did not take long for the news to spread.

By the time he drove away from Clemson's trailer, a USGS helicopter was already circling to see what could be seen, looping close above the pulsing scarlet fountain. Around its base a thickly bubbling swamp spills outward into blackness.

Travis will sleep through the night, while the lava is fountaining not many miles from his hotel. Later he will think about this and how it takes some getting used to. Every night the lava moves, whether seen or unseen, above-ground or below, the orange rivers sliding along through silent tunnels of older rock.

Montrose Doyle

Travis is up early for a hike around the curve of Hilo Bay. Sometime during the night the rain stopped. While the trees still gleam with water, the weight is off the air. From a rocky point he sees the first yellow beams of a rising sun caught in the windows of low buildings along the farther shore, and in the windows of houses scattered along the slopes above the town.

Higher up, the double peaks that build the island hump against a brilliant blue. Mauna Loa, "Long Mountain," makes a perfect sine wave, reddish brown. On Mauna Kea, "White Mountain," rippled crater rims of the same red-brown are edged with snow. A breeze comes off the water, the slightest of sunrise breezes, to touch the skin, gentle fingers waking him, waking him, as old histories move closer to the surface now. But how? And where are they coming from?

Perhaps the islands work on him the way they once worked on his father. Travis knows his father has gazed at these mid-Pacific mountains. But can he ever know what his father felt? Will he ever know that Montrose watched a receding profile of inland peaks dissolve against the horizon, thinking he might never see them again, or see anything else again?

It was 1944, and Private Montrose Doyle had never traveled anywhere. He was a kid from California heading for the combat zone. Underneath the wisecracks and the bravado and the bragging of their exploits along Hotel Street in moonlit Honolulu, his stomach drew tight. As he stood on the troopship deck, the old craters seemed to have a razor edge, a cutting edge, perhaps his final panorama.

He never talked much about what happened next, the atolls they assaulted, or the blood-filled lagoons, nor did he ever talk much about the Hawaiian Islands, though his heart had swelled with homesickness when he saw their ridges for the second time—not home, but still a refuge, first safety zone in the long, homeward-bound Pacific crossing. Hawaii was not then one of the United States, but it already held that place in the mind. America's farthest outpost.

Monty had a photo taken, which still hangs near the kitchen door in the house where Travis spent his childhood. He is wearing army tans, grinning with the overseas cap tipped back, cutting up, performing a little for some comrade holding the camera. His face says he is eager to consume every moment that remains. The war is over, and Montrose Doyle is a hungry victor, the water behind him bright with glare, as if backlit by a pro for the cover of a magazine.

Prince

In the Orchid Isle coffee shop Ian Prince is reading. Travis wants to feel generous toward this man who gave him useless, perhaps malicious directions. The early hike has refreshed him and cleared his head. He is ready to give Prince a second chance.

It is an open-air place and still cool, nicely ventilated, with greenery outside, yet Prince looks overheated, his face pink, his blondish hair faintly damp across the scalp as if he has just jogged a couple of miles.

"Mr. Doyle," he says, half standing.

"Yes. Good morning. Am I late? Are you early?"

"I may be a shade early. Giving a moment to the paper."

He wears a monogrammed polo shirt that somehow adds thickness to his heavy arms. He is a large man, in his early forties, who may have lifted weights for several years and let it go, now large and corpulent. Underneath the spreading fleshy surfaces there is still some meat and muscle. A corpulent man wearing white deck shoes and wrinkled slacks and several rings. A light blue canvas shoulder bag is on the table next to him.

As his copy of the *Tribune Herald* falls open on the table, Travis sees the story of last night's eruption occupying most of page 1. The headline reads, PELE SHOWS HER STUFF. In what he thinks will be an amusing and offhand and perhaps worldly remark, he says, "Not many places nowadays where a fire goddess makes the front page."

The lips form a semi-smile of cautious restraint, as if Prince wishes he knew Travis well enough to speak his mind.

"You've been taking the air."

"It's nice out there, once the rain let up."

"A man of your word."

"I try."

"Restless was how you described yourself."

"Time change. I couldn't sleep."

"Dan Clemson tells me you paid a call, began to get acquainted with our operation here."

"I'll know more after I get back down there and see it all in the bright light of day."

"Yes . . ."

Prince ponders this as if it holds the key to something. "The bright light of day," he says. He looks past Travis, into the dense branches of a nearby bougainvillea vine.

"My apologies if I sounded evasive on the phone. It was just a bit of confusion about the vehicles."

"What about them? Any news?"

"I beg your pardon?"

"Did the rep show? Did they start this morning?"

The blond eyebrows squeeze together, above another restrained smile. "Dan didn't mention it."

"I wonder if anyone happened to check the plugs or the carburetors."

"I would hope so. I've been telling him to keep those trucks out of the weather. As usual, he is only half listening. That is the key, don't you think? Listening to one another? If we don't listen, how can we communicate?"

Prince's voice is rising. He catches himself, places his hands on the table, palm down, as if for steadiness, and regards them.

"I am a liaison person, Mr. Doyle. The right hand *must* know what the left is doing."

His fingers are delicate, oddly narrow. Whatever filled out his neck and arms has not yet reached his extremities. The nails are white rimmed, perhaps manicured. Travis notes these fingers, then the eyes, gazing down. A sadness crosses the florid face. Has Prince's attention wandered?

He wears five rings, three so elegant and finely tooled your eyes can be drawn to the rings and almost miss the scarring along the insides of the fingers and the edge of one palm, small white scars that curl underneath the right hand. From a distance you wouldn't notice them. You would only notice the rings—on the right hand, three, of turquoise and silver; on the left, a birthstone and a military ring, the kind Travis once bought, after bootcamp, in the PX, silver plate with a simulated stone.

Prince looks up at last. "We are very eager to get this matter settled, Mr. Doyle."

"Please. Call me Travis."

"I'm sure Dan explained that more than fire is at stake."

"He showed me some clippings."

"We are in the midst of a battle here."

He reaches for his shoulder bag, just as the waitress arrives with a coffeepot. She looks part Hawaiian, brown skinned, thick hair pulled back in a bun. Her uniform is too snug, as if she recently put on a few pounds. Graceful pounds. On rubber soles she moves across the shop with a dancer's grace. The name plate below her collar says LINDA.

"You folks ready?"

"I haven't looked at the menu," Travis says.

Prince says, "I can recommend the Portuguese sausage."

"Home made," says Linda. "Lotta spice."

Her eyes light up. Talking about it seems to whet her appetite. Travis imagines that she will fry herself a couple of slices while his order is on the stove.

"I'll have that, with scrambled eggs and whole wheat toast and half a papaya."

"Rice or fries?"

"Rice sounds good."

"How many scoops?"

"How big are they?"

"You know. Regular size. Lunchtime we use it for the ice cream." She says this with a broad grin. Linda is a kidder.

"Two sounds about right."

Prince orders French toast, double shot of maple syrup, hold the rice. His mind is not on food. He has been flipping through folders. He hands Travis a white page, saying solemnly, "Here. Americans tend to think all the terrorists are in the Middle East."

It's a letter on a plain sheet of typing paper, the kind you buy in a package of two hundred at Pay-n-Save, and typed on a manual machine. It already has the look of an aging document. It was sent to the editor of the *Hilo Tribune* a couple of days after the fire. The writer does not take credit for the fire but celebrates its effect, saluting anyone who had the nerve or vision to start it, condemning the geothermal project, and reminding Energy Source that their troubles have just begun.

"As you can see, this wasn't signed, so it was never printed. But we now know it was written by John Brockman."

"How do you know that?"

"We know. And it has changed the complexion of our claim."

"What's the story on this guy? Is he Hawaiian?"

Prince shakes his head. "He isn't even local."

"Who is he? What's he doing here?"

"From all I can gather, he is another tree-hugging expatriate with an acre of pot planted somewhere to pay the bills and finance his extended vacation."

"You sure about that?"

"It's a safe guess."

"So you know him, you've talked to him."

"We are just starting to pull this thing together. We are working with the district attorney's people. Brockman is an elusive figure. I have tried to get through to him, and it's impossible."

"You can't find him?"

"He is arrogant. He is self-rightous. Maybe you will have better luck."

"I doubt that I will have to be spending any time with John Brockman."

"We're counting on your assistance, Mr. Doyle."

"I'm not a police detective."

"But you are here to investigate the fire."

"You want my candid opinion, I don't see much of a connection. An unsigned letter. A guy down the road maybe saw a white car."

"This man is an obstructionist. He has already been indicted. We're going to throw the book at him."

"Then what? You have a two-hundred-thousand-dollar claim here. You think he is a guy you can collect that much from? Is he insured? Does he work? Does he own anything?"

Prince picks up the letter and reads aloud. "If an assailant is loose in your neighborhood and the police just look the other way, what then does the concerned citizen do? The laws of rape apply to all rapists, including those who violate the Earth."

His breath comes in small gasps, as if he just climbed three flights of stairs in the hot sun. In his hand the page quivers. He sets it down and leans toward Travis.

"I am a lifetime member of the Audubon Society, as was my father. There is no one who loves the earth more than I do. But I have to tell you, I have run out of patience with people who are still living in the nineteenth century and if you don't agree with them they think they have a God-given right to destroy your property in the name of environmental preservation. Why aren't they over in Honolulu blowing up the oil storage tanks? That's the real polluter in these islands! Oil is the alien product here. Steam is the available resource. What's immoral about pushing a pipe down into a reservoir of steam that has never been tapped? Frankly, I am stunned. I am mystified! We're over here with a lot of money at risk, a million dollars a hole. That's the level of our commitment, in the hope that we can develop a local source of energy so you can light towns and run machinery. And yet there are people who think we're here to wreck the island forever!"

This is starting to sound like a speech Prince has delivered somewhere, to the Rotary perhaps. It sounds scripted, and Travis doesn't think Prince himself believes it, though he seems to want to, or has been told it would be in his best interests to believe it. Again his voice has risen. Two tables away a cab driver looks up from the sports page.

Linda chooses this moment to return with the orders. "Here's something to keep your teeth busy."

She is being playful. She hasn't heard what he said, she only heard the sound. Prince seems to take it another way, as a scolding. More color rises to his face.

She turns to Travis. "You want hot sauce?"

"Yes. Thanks."

From the next table she grabs a slender bottle of Louisiana Red and sets it by his plate. As she walks away Prince gulps the last of his coffee and stands up.

"I have to be at the County Building at nine. You're welcome to come along."

"What about breakfast? Aren't we having breakfast?"

"I've already eaten."

"Why did you order the French toast?"

"It was a mistake. I shouldn't have ordered anything."

He opens his shoulder bag, slides the letter into a folder, purses his lips, changes his mind. He places it on the table again, with another page beside it, another letter, dated two weeks later and signed by John Brockman.

It is addressed to a construction company on the leeward side, mailed the day he lashed himself to the scaffolding where the new resort is going in:

Cover me with concrete, and let the world know what we here on the Big Island already know. These are the new temples, and we are the new victims.

Both letters are obviously typed on the same machine, using the same kind of Pay-n-Save paper. The delicate fingers line them up precisely, side by side on the Formica tabletop.

"He has gone too far, you see. In a way, he has exposed himself, making these allusions to ancient practices many islanders would just as soon see relegated to the history books."

"Practices?"

"Victims. Temples. Human sacrifice. Equating first-class modern hotels with the barbarism of the past. He's making enemies right and left."

Travis studies these pages, thinking again of Carlo, of calling him. It is ten to nine, which means in San Francisco it is ten to eleven. Mornings are better for Carlo than afternoons. If he can catch him before lunch, maybe he can break the news that Carlo has sent the wrong man to Hilo, the wrong man for the wrong job at the wrong time.

"Mr. Prince," he says, giving it one more try, "our paperwork says a fuel tank exploded and a shed caught fire. So far I don't see any reason to alter that."

Prince grimaces and bites his lip. "I wish you and I were on the same wavelength."

"Correct me if I'm wrong, but what we both want is to get this claim settled and some kind of payment on its way."

"The picture has changed. Dramatically. We are finally starting to clarify the picture."

He runs a hand through the hair on his heated scalp. He shoves the letters into his blue shoulder bag and zippers it, looking with reproach now at the plate of food, and poised fork and knife, as if it is a failure of courage to choose food over his crusade.

This has spoiled Travis's mood. It has not spoiled his appetite. As Prince stands watching, waiting for who knows what, Travis shakes some Louisiana Red over the sausage and scrambled eggs and consumes a forkful, thinking about this man who seems far too impressed with his own detective work. Travis does not want to like him. Prince is petulant. He appears to have a vindictive streak. He strikes Travis as a man who was once handsome, who has come quite a way on his looks and his connections and knows these cards are about played out. And yet, just a moment ago, as he rose so abruptly from the table, he was reminding Travis of someone. Who? Carlo? Yes. Carlo standing in the hallway, startled by the elevator bell—caught, and ready to be angry, and also needing something, reaching out. Travis finds himself on the verge of reaching too. But toward what? Toward whom? What grief does he see in these eyes? Could Prince be another man whose wife has walked away? Travis feels a strange, inexplicable kinship. He almost reaches across to touch the fleshy arm, to offer reassurance. Relax, he wants to say, we'll work this out.

Maybe he should look up Brockman after all. If nothing else, Travis tells himself, it will be a way to keep things simple. Eliminate Brockman as a culprit and proceed with Plan A. An ordinary fire. Between his first and second mouthfuls Travis says, "Where does this guy live?"

The eyebrows raise a quarter of an inch. The lips curve in a small, boyish grin, as if it pleases Prince that they have at last begun to understand each other.

"I knew we could count on you."

The eyes are suddenly eager. Too eager. Travis has to glance away.

"Don't count on anything, Mr. Prince."

"We can make your stay here very comfortable."

"I'm already comfortable as can be. What I need now are the reliable facts."

"You have my word."

Linda

"Something wrong with the French toast?" Linda says. "It looks good to me."

"He didn't even touch it."

"He has a lot on his mind."

"Going to get an ulcer, that guy, drink coffee, talk loud, don't eat."

"You know him?"

"He comes in. He did that twice already. Order food, then leave. Bucky in the kitchen he don't like to see food come back."

"Just leave it here."

"Hurts his feelings."

"I'll eat it. Bucky will never know."

"You from the mainland?"

"San Francisco."

"I been up there. My brother used to work for Pan Am."

"I would have flown Pan Am, if they still came into Honolulu."

"How long you staying?"

"Three days, maybe four."

"My name is Linda."

"I'm Travis."

"You with those folks getting set to drill, down Puna way?"

"Not me. But the more I hear, the more I want to know."

"I guess you heard about the pickup trucks."

"The ones that didn't start?"

"This morning my sister told me they started right back up again. She lives over that way now."

"She say when?"

"Real early, she said. Last night dead. Today alive again."

"Must be the rain."

"Maybe so."

"You think it could be something else?"

"Got some lava last night too. You hear about that?"

"I saw the paper. Does that mean something?"

Linda shrugs, her eyes playful. "Could be. Lava don't come every day."

Part Two

The Navel of the World

Early that morning, about a mile past the airport, on the other side of town, while Dan Clemson stretched and stepped out of his trailer into the postdawn quiet, and while Travis plugged in the warmer for a courtesy cup of in-room coffee, Evangeline Sakai woke from a dream she wished she didn't have to remember. She had seen herself inside a ranch house they used to own, though in this dream the house had too many rooms. Each room had a window looking out upon a windy desert that seemed to spread forever, while overhead the roof had fallen, so that every room was open to the sky, gaping, ragged, as if a tornado had recently come and gone. In the dream she felt isolated, but not alone. She felt imprisoned.

Awake she is grateful to have a bed to herself, with green plants showing everywhere she looks, and hoping Walter will keep his promises now, keep his distance, keep the payments coming for just a while longer. She hopes for this, but not too much.

She can't trust him now, wonders if she ever trusted him, and wishes the answer wasn't yes. In those days, when they were first married, good-looking and good were still synonymous, and Walter was elegant to look at, this fellow she had dated a couple of times in high school, a handsome island mixture, mostly Portuguese, with dark wavy hair and a black mustache and a smile other women fell for. Or seemed to. Back then. When nobody she knew knew anything.

Why hadn't she been able to see that he would turn out to be a husband of the old school, who would use his money like a weapon? Maybe she did see it. Maybe she wanted it that way.

She was waiting tables down in Waikiki, with no clear sense of what would happen next, while he had a plan for himself. He was going to make it big in the hotel business, and her father approved of this. "Walter has initiative," her father would say, "he's on his way up."

The two men played a lot of golf together, until the West Coast transfer came through, his first big break. The fear she felt then seemed to be a fear of travel. She had seen the world on TV. She had heard the sounds of a dozen languages. But she had never left the islands, sometimes described as the most isolated on the planet, farthest removed from any other major chunk of land. Was it fear of the great unknown across the water? Or was it a premonition of what her life with Walter would become? She still wonders how else things might have gone if she let herself really listen to that warning.

After two years in a tract house south of San Francisco, they moved to Reno, Nevada. By that time Marilyn had been born. From the ranch house where she nursed the babe, Evangeline could see the eastern rise of the Sierra Nevada range. The high desert, she told herself, was like the ocean. The mountains were islands rising from a pale and windy sea. Those promontories spoke to her, and soon Walter was threatened by the promontories.

When Marilyn started second grade, Evangeline signed up at the community college. Life drawing. Photography. She wanted to photograph the desert, its subtle forms.

Walter sabotaged her study program. He invented parties that had to happen the night a project was due. He started hiding the keys to the car. One day he sold the car. They couldn't afford two, he said. He took her name off the checking account. When he began to accuse her of seeing other men, she tried that a couple of times. But there was no satisfaction in it. Reno was not her place. Maybe it was Walter's place. It wasn't hers. Something had made him frantic. If she'd loved him she might have tried to figure out what. She didn't love him. Maybe she had never loved him. All he cared about was making a killing in the hotel business. She believed in making a living. But not a killing. There was a difference. It had to do with balance. Their life was out of balance. Somehow altitude was a factor in all this. She was not born to live at six thousand feet. She grew up at sea level. At sea level her whole attitude improved.

She flew back to Honolulu—Marilyn had just turned nine—and spent a couple of years at her folks' place, working in a camera shop, trying to finish up a university degree. She almost married one of her instructors, but changed her mind at the last moment. It wasn't right. The city wasn't right, too crowded now, growing too fast, with high-rises everywhere you looked, and something was pulling at her, something she could never have put into words. The Big Island was pulling at her, her first island, her first anchorage.

Angel's mother felt it too. In her daughter's eyes she was seeing glimpses of a look that reminded her of Auntie Malama, dead for twenty years. Where did it come from, Mama wondered. How does such a thing get passed on, a look in the eye, a turn of the head, even after you have spent all this time in a place as strange and faraway as Reno?

One afternoon when they were alone in the house— Marilyn at hula class, Papa at the driving range—Mama found herself telling Angel about the naming ceremony. There was a sudden shower, the rain blowing down off the mountainside. Maybe that was it, the sound reminding her of the day Malama stopped her under the carport. When the shower passed she made iced tea and sat out on the porch with Angel, sipping, listening to water drip through the ginger next to the house.

In Hawai'i when someone tells a story that makes your arms prickle and your neck hairs rise, they call it "chicken skin." She barely began the tale when Angel shivered and rubbed her arms and pressed both hands against her belly and said, "Ooooohh, mama."

"It's true, Evangeline, everything I'm telling you."

The first story released a second, one she had thought she'd never be able to tell. Before Auntie Malama passed away she asked Mama to do something. She asked her favorite granddaughter to throw her bones into the firepit at Halema'uma'u.

"I said, Why do you want me to do this? And she said because she was of Pele's line, and the fire was her 'aumakua, her guardian spirit. She wanted to be reunited with the flame. And I said, But Grandma, there is no more fire in Halema'uma'u, it went out a long time ago. She said, It is still the same, it is Pele's home, it is still steaming, there is fire underneath. Then she told me that *her* grandmother's bones were thrown down in there back in the old days and she was a powerful woman, a *kahuna lapa'au*, a healing kahuna, so this was what Malama wanted too."

It put a great burden on Mama. Bones did not mean the whole body. Bones meant bones. In the old days flesh would first be steamed away. But how could she do this, even though it was her grandmother's final wish? Where could she do it? People would find out. Papa would find out, and he didn't like those old Hawaiian things. Mumbo jumbo, he called it. In this day and age, throwing Grandma's bones into the crater was impossible.

"The only thing I could think of was to get the body cremated, then wait."

"Wait for what?"

There was a long silence while Mama summoned the will to describe what she'd done. Her voice dropped so low Angel had to move over next to her, slide across the step and watch her mouth.

She had arranged for the cremation, and on the day of the burial she had exchanged urns. She bought an identical urn and filled it with sand, so that it had similar weight. A month later she flew to the Big Island and rented a car. She looked up Tutu David, the man who had presided over Angel's naming. He was an uncle, or half-uncle, Malama's son by her second husband. At first he refused to come along, telling her that bones should not be burned. It was an insult to the departed. This was Malama's final wish, she told him. Then she waited a long time, while he stood thinking. At last he nodded, and they drove up there. David chanted, and she scattered the ashes into the darkness, into the firepit, into the sulfur-tasting night.

By the end of this story Mama's face was haggard, as if she had confessed to a killing. Angel touched her hand.

"Malama was guiding you. And she thanks you. I know she does. She is where she wants to be."

Mama broke into tears. "It's terrible."

"Don't say that."

"It's terrible to do something all by yourself and keep it locked up so long."

She let Angel take her in her arms. They were both weeping tears of relief, Mama relieved to have the story told, Angel relieved to know why the home she had come back to was not feeling like home, relieved to know the mainland had not hardened her heart. Once again she felt the dread and the excitement of approaching unknown territory.

They had family on the Big Island, two uncles, the old half-uncle, numerous cousins and calabash cousins. She had a little money saved. She found a small frame house, some studio space. With two cameras and a fat portfolio she set up shop. Her father said she was crazy. Yes, you are probably right, she said. He told her, "I'm going to get stomachaches thinking about this."

Her second month in Hilo she drove alone to the crater, a place she had visited only while floating in her mother's womb. In the forty-minute climb she moved from shoreline to four thousand feet. She moved past rain forest and into the treeless moonscape that begins at Kilauea Caldera, fanning southward. The morning sky was blue that day, the cobalt blue that comes with altitude. Around the caldera she followed the perimeter road, to get her bearings, gazing across the rippled plain where steam plumes rose against the flat dark lava. Inside this caldera the firepit, Pele's home, is like a dry lake within a dry lake. Nowadays it is quiet most of the time. For centuries it was a boiling pot of lava, with bright fountains spewing and spurting. To the Hawaiians it seemed to be the wellspring, the island's source. They called it the navel of the world, the point through which the earth itself is born and reborn.

On that morning it was surrounded with wisps and veils of silent steam that rose dissolving in the wind. Angel had brought along some red anthuriums, not quite sure what she would do with them. As she reached the guard rail, she saw other offerings laid along the jagged edge. Leis, some new, some fading. Cut flowers. Bowls of fruit. A bottle of gin wrapped in flat green leaves. The gin was for the goddess, that much she knew. The flowers and the fruit might be for Pele, or for ancestors like her own, whose remains had been left there. Offerings for the goddess of destruction and creation, and for those reunited with the power of her flames.

As she stepped around the guard rail, Angel was trembling. As she hunkered and placed her anthuriums on a slab of black, burnt rock, she thought of the days when she had carried Marilyn, the way her belly bulged. She saw her mother's belly when the hands had gathered to bless it, and she saw herself underneath those hands, inside the belly. In the cool wind of early morning she thought she heard their voices, her great-grandmother's voice, speaking names. She had an urge to follow the voices, down into this jagged bowl. She felt a sob rising and didn't know where it came from, as if someone was sobbing through her. She listened. Yes. There were voices all around her. Voices in the blood, in the rocks, in the wind.

The Expatriate's Tale

Brockman isn't hard to find. He lives near the southern shore, a few miles beyond the drilling site. To reach his place Travis follows the coast road, which is a strange road, the most southerly road in the islands and in the United States, three full degrees inside the Tropic of Cancer, and unlike any other road he has traveled. It leads through a two-minded landscape, alternately lush and barren, green and black, ancient and new. For a mile or two jungle foliage rises around him, banana palm, bougainvillea, hala, and hibiscus. Then, as if sliced with a huge machete, the foliage ends, and he is crossing a strip of dark volcanic rock where a river of lava once cut through coastal greenery on its way to the sea.

A few yards past one such rocky field he finds what he is looking for. Two matching coco palms form a gateway through a low wall of stones much older than those in the nearby field. It is an overgrown parcel of what Hawaiians call a *kipuka*, an oasis of soil and growth surrounded on three sides by lava flows.

He turns onto a dirt track that seems to end in a thicket. But he eases through the overhanging fronds and finally enters a clearing where a low house stands under palms, old palms with thick gray trunks like elephant hide. He turns off the engine and gets out of the car. A breeze is coming from the ocean, maybe a hundred yards away. He can hear radio music, guitars, ukulele.

A large vegetable garden has been planted next to the house. A few papaya trees stand between the rows like pale green umbrellas, high stalks with each branch curving up to a five-fingered leaf, the green and yellow and orange globes clustered where branches meet the stalk. Though he has never cared about owning or maintaining even the smallest plot of land, Travis feels a stab of envy for whoever has access to these papayas, can walk out before breakfast and pick one and carry it to the kitchen counter and slice it open and scoop out a spoonful of its just-picked succulence.

The house is wooden, maybe forty years old, with a vaguely Polynesian line—raised off the ground on posts, for ventilation underneath, and a long peaked roof with eaves sloping on all four sides, to shed rain and shade the windows and doors. Next to the house two vehicles are parked, a GMC pickup with off road tires, and a mud-spattered white Dodge Dart.

He hears the voice first, a soft and graveled voice, disembodied, hanging in the sun-thick air.

"Good morning."

"Good morning. I'm looking for John Brockman."

"You've got him."

He appears in the doorway then.

"My name is Travis Doyle. . ."

"I know. We've been expecting you."

As Travis approaches the deeply shaded porch, he sees that it is the fellow from the laundromat—jeans, mustache, close-cropped hair—the fellow who did not know exactly how to find the drilling site but knew someone who knew. He wears the same T-shirt with the fiery lettering across the chest. LOVE LAVA.

"Haven't we met already?" Travis says.

"Briefly, yes."

It is not a friendly remark. Neither is it hostile. They are like dogs sniffing at each other in the street. From the indoor radio a male voice is singing in Hawaiian, a plaintive song that causes the singer's voice to break, a whole lifetime squeezing through the notes.

"I'll get right to the point."

"We can skip the preliminaries, Doyle. Yesterday I didn't know who you were. Two thousand people a day land on this island. A lot of them don't even stay overnight. You're a claims adjuster, right? You've been talking to the people at Energy Source. And they are telling you I torched their shed."

"Something like that."

"It figures."

"They are not a hundred percent sure what they think you did."

"I'm not surprised, since I have not done one fucking thing to them or their project."

"Except write a letter to the Hilo paper."

"Along with fifty other people. Is that a crime? Tell me honestly. Do you think I set that fire? In your heart of hearts? Do I look like a guy who could do something like that?"

If looks are the measure, Travis would have to say, yes, you do look like that kind of guy. Brockman has a wildness in him. It occurs to Travis that his Zen monk haircut, shaved a quarter inch from the scalp, could be a Zen punk haircut, some kind of sociopathic statement.

"I'm not a judge. I'd just like to ask you a couple of questions."

"Ask, man. My life is an open book."

"You are the guy who tried to stop some construction over on the leeward side."

"You would have done the same thing."

"You called the hotels temples."

"That's right."

"And used the word 'sacrifice.'"

"I don't believe I used that word. That sounds like an Ian Prince translation. But next time I probably will. Have you seen the ocean front they are trashing over there? Old fishing lanes. Perfect little beaches. That is the crime on this island."

"What do you mean, next time?"

"You have a minute, Doyle? I want to be straight with you, which is my policy with everybody. Be straight. Be open. I got nothing to hide. I was not anywhere near their shed that night. It was a bad night out. They probably didn't tell you that. But you ask anybody. We had thunderheads building. I was right here at home. We were having a meeting about how to raise money for my attorney's fees. I have eight witnesses. That is what's so silly about this whole fiasco. It turned into an electric storm. The power went out. There was *nobody* on the road that night—"

"An electric storm?"

The low and scratchy voice goes lower.

"The word I have is that's what started the fire."

"How do you know?"

He grins, pleased by this show of surprise. "It's called survival. It is in my best interest to know anything I can about what went on, although it hasn't been easy finding out."

"Why? How would anyone hide an electric storm?"

He tilts his head back for a long, an excessively long laugh.

"Why would they want to?" Travis asks.

"Everything depends on who you ask."

"I don't get it."

"Call it another local mystery. This is the island of mystery, Doyle. Underneath these balmy skies it is Spookeytown, USA. There is always a huge gap between what you know and what gets reported. Imagine the scene. A weather system comes rolling in. The sky is dark with thunderheads. The power goes. Inexplicably the shed starts to burn. Just about the time the fire department shows up and unrolls the hoses, the storm breaks wide open. This flood comes down like an extinguisher from heaven to douse the flames. The crew goes home to dry off, and it is days before Energy Source will let anyone inside their compound. The nosy and inquisitive are told that a fuel tank exploded, and until last week this was the official story. You don't believe me, do you?"

He doesn't know what to believe. The voice has become soft and smooth, hypnotic in its flow. But the eyes are larger, round and fierce.

"I'm listening."

Brockman touches his elbow to turn him around. "I want to show you something."

Travis follows him down the steps, past the corner of his house, and toward the garden.

"There are people who will tell you exactly what I just told you, so you can believe me or not believe me, I don't really give a damn. I am just down here trying to live my life. My crime is not torching somebody's equipment shed, although I confess I did not weep salty tears when I heard the news. My crime is doing a couple of things that have made me a thorn in the side of the local economy. Did they tell you I grow dope out here?"

"It was implied."

They are standing next to one of his papaya trees, the fingered leaves shading their eyes. He has squash growing, tomatoes up on stakes. He spreads his arms wide to embrace his plot and also display the rocky logo on his slender chest.

"I grow papayas and vegetables, and we do pig traps and T-shirts and bumper stickers . . ."

"Pig traps?"

"Wild pigs, man. They're tearing this island to pieces. I figured out an original kind of trap. But a lot of people, they don't want to know about that. They think everybody who comes over here to live is growing dope. You are looking at a guy who has grown *past* dope. I don't need it. I don't want it. All I want—and I am telling you this because you look like a guy who can relate to what I am about to say—all I want is time and space. Is that too much to ask for!"

This is not a question. It is an outcry. His eyes are expanding. Spittle has appeared at the corners of his mouth.

A girl steps through the wall of foliage that frames the clearing. She looks to be eight or nine, wearing shorts and thong slippers, some kind of Eurasian mixture, with dark hair tinted red-brown by the sun. She stops when she sees Travis. She carries a plastic bucket filled with yellow guavas.

"How many did you get?" Brockman asks her, suddenly calmer.

"This many," she says, with a crafty little smile.

"Let me see."

She runs to him and holds the bucket up for inspection, checks out Travis with a quick glance, then skips off toward the house. Something on the ground catches her eye and she hunkers to study it. Her brown back and shoulders seem polished by the sun.

"This afternoon we're making jelly," Brockman tells him. "You ever made jelly?"

"My brother does that kind of stuff," Travis says, with another pang of envy for all the crop-tenders and daddies of the world whose girls and boys come running to them. The arrival of this beautiful kid takes the edge right off his interrogation. What is he doing here? What right does he have to pry into this fellow's life?

Where the garden meets the border of wild foliage a bench has been installed, a rough-cut two-by-twelve set on a couple of lava chunks. Brockman walks over there and sits in the shade with his elbows on his knees. With insistent eyes he urges Travis to sit beside him. Music drifts toward them from the house, a female voice now, contralto, mingling joy and sorrow.

After a while Brockman says, "You know L.A.?"

"I wish I didn't. But sure. Who doesn't?"

"I grew up in L.A. I watched the world's most beautiful lemon groves transformed into asphalt. I finally said, I don't want this. I can't stand to watch it. I left. I went up to Sonoma County, outside Santa Rosa. You know Sonoma?"

"I've been through there."

"I got there just in time to watch the sky turn from bright blue to fuzzy, which was the Bay Area creeping north like the morning fog, except that once it creeps in, it never creeps out again. Pretty soon the water is trashed, the soil is filling up with toxic wastes, sewage is on overload, and it is all starting over!"

His voice has the purring insistence of a man ready to burst forth with sudden laughter or sudden fury. The spittle is showing again. Travis is about to stand up, but a hand falls upon his knee.

"I had already seen that movie, right? So I came over here, and I got into this piece of land, only to find the same thing going on that's going on everywhere else I've been. The same people who paved over Orange County want to fill this island with destination resorts and rocket launching pads. They want to send two miles of pipe down under the volcano to fuel their high-tech fantasies, and one day it hit me! Jack Brockman, I said, you cannot go back, and you cannot go any farther out this trail or that trail. There is nowhere else to move to. This is where you are going to have to take your stand!"

Travis has heard enough. He has to get away from here and think things through. He stands up.

"Hey. You want a cup of coffee? A beer?"

"I can't. But thanks for giving me a few minutes. I do appreciate it."

Brockman walks along beside him, a hand squeezing his elbow.

"You know what the D.A. said at the arraignment? 'This is not your island. You want to take a stand, go home and take a stand.' I can see his point. But what I told him was, Okay, I wasn't born here, but Hawai'i happens to be located on my home planet, and that is what's at stake. I am not talking about ownership. I am not talking about state or nation. I am not talking ethnic or indigenous, who is native, who is not! I am talking about human beings on the planet Earth! The question is, How do we survive!"

Travis pulls his elbow free and opens the car door and slides in behind the wheel. Brockman leans on the window-sill, his eyes unblinking. His voice dips to a gravelly whisper.

"You don't believe me, do you."

"Stop asking me that."

"You think I'm nuts."

He is smiling his saintly smile again, a John-the-Baptist smile. Travis starts the engine, lets off the emergency brake.

"I'm still talking to people. I'm looking around."

"Then do me a favor. Or don't. Makes no difference to me. You want to see what's happening, get over to the drilling site. I'd be there myself, but my attorney tells me discretion is the better part of valor. It's better for me to lay low right now, keep a low profile."

"Why? What's going on?"

"A gathering you should know about before you start writing your report. Too many people come over here with their notebooks flapping, hang around a couple of days, go home, write up their reports, and they miss ninety-five percent of it. You don't strike me as that kind of person, which is why I'm telling you this. Take my advice. Check it out. And give Mr. Clemson my salute."

A Nagging Question

In the predawn light while she puttered around her tiny lab, checking negatives clipped to the drying line, Evangeline had heard again the voice of her great-uncle and thought she must look in on him today. She would take a gift, a little something, and sit awhile and talk. She would do it first thing, while the air was cool. She had a bottle of pretty good white wine in the fridge, a chenin blanc that would be just right. Tutu David enjoys white wine, but not too dry. A little sweetness on the tongue.

She set out some breakfast cereal for Marilyn, who is a late sleeper, never eats enough in the morning, left her a note, then drove ten minutes to his cottage, where she now finds him sitting on the front porch in a straight-back kitchen chair, wearing a fresh white shirt, his good trousers, drinking coffee from a big white mug and watching the road.

"Uncle, you're all dressed up."

"Figger you might be coming by."

"Well, you were right. Here. I brought you this."

"Nice and cold, " he says, reaching down into the bag.

"For later, of course."

"Sure," says David with a raspy giggle. "Not so good in the coffee. Red wine maybe. But not the white."

Evangeline pours herself a cup and brings out another chair and pulls it close.

"Your voice sounds better."

"I think so."

"The swelling went down."

"You tell me, sister. Touch right here."

She touches the bony cup above his sternum. "Yes. it's smaller. Did you tell the doctor?"

"I don't like the doctor."

"He'll be glad to hear about this."

"I don't want to talk to the doctor."

David sips his coffee and turns toward the road. She looks at his face, the rimless glasses, the silver-white hair combed back, the soft brown and unwrinkled skin, still smooth against protruding bones. David is eighty, at least. Probably older. Sometimes she does not have a reason to visit him. She will sit, as so many others have come to sit, and listen to whatever flows from Tutu's mouth, and she will learn the lesson later. Though he never mentions it, the memory of Angel's naming day, when he placed his hands upon her mother's belly, is always in his eyes when they talk. Everything he says to her rolls outward from that day, as a form of confirmation, or a form of prophesy.

This morning she has a reason. In her mind there is a nagging question about money and whether or not to take a certain job if it comes along. Her cousin Tiny drives truck for the new drilling company, and he has heard someone talking about acreage that needs to be photographed. He has mentioned her name and told her someone may be calling. If the phone rings, she isn't sure what to say. She needs any kind of work she can get. She isn't sure about the drilling, which some say will be good for the island, and some say will be a catastrophe.

The steam does not belong to the company, that much is certain. Yet the drillers bring in jobs. Tiny can stay home with his wife and kids now, instead of moving to the other side where all the hotels are going in. Tiny has told her privately, with his quiet, rascal laugh, that he hopes the project fails. He has heard talk that this well may just be the start. University people have been over here doing studies. Department of Energy people too. One day there could be ten more holes, or twenty, and steam converters as big as gymnasiums, and there will be a power cable thicker than his leg running from the volcano and across the island, down into the deep channel between here and Maui, then across Maui and into the water again, past Moloka'i, all the way north and west to Honolulu. Federal money is coming in. State money too. When Tiny describes this cable his hands are dancer's hands. They dip and swoop, making serpent curves.

"These haoles," Tiny said, "they start dreaming things, pretty soon they don't know where to stop. Two hundred and fifty miles, they say. Four billion dollars worth of cable and towers and power poles."

He hopes they will drill until he has a down payment for the car he wants, then fail, miss the mark by half a mile, lose heart, go away, and leave Pele's steam where it has always been.

She pretty much agrees. She is wondering if the company will pay attention to this eruption she heard about on the early news. She mentions it to David, who says that two days ago a young woman in a long red dress stopped by his gate. She had straight black hair, and her face was shaded by the angle of the sun. She stood looking across the yard and called, "Eh! Tutu!" "Komo mai," David said, "Come, sit with me. Eat." He beckoned and the woman in the red dress raised her hand, then turned and moved away.

Evangeline shivers. "Ooooohh, Uncle. She waved to you?"

"She always come like that, before the lava starts."

The humid stillness is edged with just a hint of cooling breeze. They sit side by side, feeling it, listening, until the old man's voice cuts through the stillness.

"Sister. You remember the big eruption down Kapoho way?"

"I've heard about it."

"We should drive down there sometime."

"Not much left, from what they say."

"That's right. Not much. When I was young, that was a village with a store and a post office, a school and all that. Used to stop there with the horses whenever we went down that end, which is not so far from where the drilling will go. Maybe you still see a sign or something, I don't know. Haven't been down there since the lava came. When was that, sister? 1960? Around in there? They couldn't stop it, not with airplanes, not with trenches or bulldozers. Pele wanted it back, you see—the roads, the store, the cane fields, everything. So she came and she took it. I had a good friend, a Hawaiian man with family down there from a long time back. His house got filled up with lava, caught fire. He cried. He missed his house, like anybody would miss a house you live in for a long time. But this friend of mine, he was never angry. He prayed. He chanted. He saw Pele's face in the smoke over the cinder cone. He saw long hair that looked like flames, and he knew she had returned. It was her land in the first place, my friend told me. She just wanted it back."

His voice has become thin, as if someone has grabbed him by the neck.

"You want some water, uncle?"

He shakes his head and sips his coffee, looking at the road, then turns, with a cough and a little smile of apology that says he won't be talking for a while. This is all right with her. The unasked question has been answered. There will be no harm in accepting a little of the company's money, if the phone rings, since Pele will have the final say in the matter of steam and the island's fate.

Ancestors

A mile from Brockman's place Travis pulls off the road and double-checks his film. The sky is clear, cloudless and immense. Where it meets the sea, a thread line divides two shades of vivid blue—an excellent day to survey the damage, take some inventory notes, a few more photos while the sun is out.

Heading inland he still has this in the back of his mind. But when he sees the vehicles along both sides of Pumahi Road, he knows it's going to be another kind of day. Vans and pickups and dusty sedans are parked at odd angles, windows open, or doors ajar, as if someone out this way suddenly announced a luau. With no houses around they have an eery, abandoned look. The only driveway is the new access road, where grassy shoulders have been recently trod upon.

Once again he follows the track of crushed rock through papaya groves and cane field. Half a mile into the forest the road makes a rising bend, from which he first sees the crowd, just then reaching the fence line, sees the back side of a banner lifted high on poles.

He eases in closer and parks, figuring it's no time to drive through, even though he has reason to, and the right. He has been in this position once before, and drove right past a crowd gathered to protest the clear-cutting of some first-growth redwoods. Thousands of trees were at risk, some of them ancient, as trees go. Opponents of the logging had ripped a few planks from a temporary one-lane bridge built across a creek that ran through the acreage in question. A loaded timber truck had fallen halfway through the bridge, tearing out more planking. The driver had whacked his head on the dash, maybe injured his back. Travis's job was to go in there and look at the bridge and look at the truck and talk to the driver and not think about the trees, which he somehow managed to do, although later it ate at him and he's regretted it ever since, regretted not calling Carlo from a booth, regretted not telling him to put someone else on the case.

With his engine off he can hear the steady beat of a skin drum, *pa-tump pa-tump pa-tump pa-tump*. It rises over the chatter and challenges from the crowd, who number about a hundred. All their eyes are on the gate and five security guards with their heads close together.

The marchers are indecisive, agitated, shouting, but not militant. Not yet. On this island public protest runs against the grain. These people have never gathered in this particular way. No one is in charge. No bullhorns. No clipboards to be seen. No agenda. One moment they were milling around, nailing a hand-drawn banner to a couple of poles, while the cars pulled in and the marchers piled out. The next moment they were moving along the new road, a loose-limbed parade, all races, dark and light, all ages, moms and dads, grandads too, and kids pulled out of school, and part-time teachers and transplanted Mendocino hippies, Eurasian college girls, a couple of geologists, a couple of fishermen. They wear T-shirts, shorts, backpacks and fannypacks and ballcaps saying HILO GARDEN SUPPLY and BIG ISLAND DIARY. With a a blue sky blazing down upon them after two days of heavy rain, they have had a good time making it up as they go along, sorting out what draws them here. Now they have reached the fence line and finally have a clear view of the symbol of their common concern.

The banner that has led their way says

EARTH HOME ISLAND HOME

It rises above the front rank. Above the banner, beyond the fence, presiding over this scene, the top of the drilling rig shows through a break in the tallest trees, a crisscross tower, huge and solitary. Travis has seen them before, around Bakersfield, when his family used to drive over there from the coast to visit relatives. It has the same alien look of the metal spires you see rising from the center of a cotton field where some speculator has sent pipe down toward a new and untapped pool of crude. But this rig is larger than Travis or anyone else here remembers seeing, and more alien here, because the drill it houses is ready to enter earth that has never been entered in such a way. The islands have been bombed and strafed and gouged at with bulldozers and pounded with pile drivers. Roads have been tunneled and harbors dredged, but a drill bit heading for the deep interior with twenty thousand feet of pipe behind it, this is new, this is ominous, this has stirred people who are slow to be stirred.

From where he stands at the edge of the throng, Travis sees that everyone is watching a tall Hawaiian man who carries in his arms a large parcel wrapped in cloth and ti leaves. It seems to have weight, a stone, a piece of statuary. He wears Levis and a flowing white shirt with long sleeves and maile leis hanging thick, bunched with leaves bright green against the white. He hiked the long mile barefoot, as a form of penance and as a show of strength. He stands under the "Earth Home" sign, talking with one of the guards, also Hawaiian—navy blue shirt and blue trousers with a side stripe, hip pistol, silver badge. These two obviously know each other.

"Hey, Sonny," the tall man says, "what about that notice back there says 'Authorized'?"

Sonny doesn't like the role he has to play. His dark brow gathers in deep, troubled lines. "Road's closed. You folks know that."

"I used to hike up this way with my grandfather, Sonny. You came with us one time. You telling me I'm not authorized?"

Sonny shrugs with a painful smile. He turns to look at his four colleagues. They are outnumbered twenty to one. They all wear pistols, but this is not going to be a pistol situation. More likely a restraint and handcuffs situation. The crowd is not so cheerful now, after a mile in the sun, and after observing the rig at such close range. The drum still pumps out its leathery one-note signal, *pa-tump pa-tump*.

Dan Clemson chooses this interval to come barreling down the road in one of his new blue pickups. The tires spit gravel as he swerves to a stop. His jaws are squeezing. Travis can see the flat muscles twitch. Clemson leaps out and heads toward a man and a woman standing apart from the crowd, next to the fence. He walks with his butt pushed back, and rocking a little, as if his jockey shorts are filled with gravel. The half-sleeve khaki shirt gives him a colonial look. His face is flushed, and he is talking through his teeth, through the fence, while the man scribbles in a notebook, evidently one of the journalists Clemson predicted would come sniffing around today. The woman carries a couple of cameras and a leather case slung from one shoulder. The way her dark hair falls, Travis can see half a profile. She has a slender build and a languid stance that is so familiar it stops his heart. He realizes that for the past two days every woman he has seen has stopped his heart. He tries to put the resemblance out of his mind. He wills himself not to stare. He watches Clemson break it off with a muttered curse. The final words look like "Fuck you!"

Then he is striding toward the tall fellow. They are about the same size—the Hawaiian large and dark and gentle-eyed, Clemson florid, his blue eyes piercing the air as he says, "The site is closed."

"This is Hawaiian forest land," the tall man says. "You folks come in and desecrate the place, and now you tell me I cannot walk where my ancestors walked."

"We're not desecrating anything," says Clemson hotly.

"These are ancient lands."

"We're aware of that."

From near the front a gray-haired woman calls out, "You've already trashed O'ahu!" Her voice is brittle with sudden anger. After twenty-five years with the Oregon Department of Motor Vehicles she now lives in a tract about three miles away, and she fears the hydrogen sulfide fumes they say can surround a plant with the stink of rotten eggs. "More power?" she cries. "More roads? Is that it? More cars? More consumers?"

"You people have missed the whole point!" says Clemson.

"The point?" says a bearded fellow who owns an ice cream store in Hilo and who believes in solar energy, tapping into the sunshine that pours down all around them. "What exactly *is* the point?"

"We shouldn't even have to be here," the woman from Oregon shouts. "But who listens? We write! We sign petitions! We follow the rules! Look what happens!"

She raises an accusing finger toward the rig, which looms beyond Clemson, the embattled engineer.

"You people want to burn oil for the rest of your lives?" he says. "You want to keep spending eight hundred thousand a day on oil that has been shipped three thousand miles?"

The man in the BIG ISLAND DAIRY ball cap calls out, "Start with cars! Almost all of that is burned by cars!"

"Why can't you leave this island alone?" the Oregon woman shouts.

"Because we are next," says a Chinese Hawaiian man in a faded aloha shirt who would like to speak out for the welfare of herbs and healing plants. "Everybody knows we are next!"

Clemson's eyes seem to penetrate the crowd, as if committing each face to memory. Behind the mask of his rugged features he is overwhelmed. He has never had to deal with anything like this. He has never been the bad guy, nor has he been the diplomat watching a wave of agitation roll through a crowd. Later Travis will talk with him again and will ask what it's like to have charge of such a tower and the pipe to push down through rock and past sea level, past the level of the sea floor, if need be. "Have you ever looked at new soil samples?" Clemson will say. "Rock samples? Chunks of stuff that has just come up from a mile down, or two miles? It's amazing what this stuff can tell a person." Travis will watch a radiance come into Clemson's face as he says, "It's what my granddad used to call the substance of things hoped for, the evidence of things not seen. Maybe something else is going on around here, but I have to tell you there's already more than enough mystery for an old country boy like me."

Clemson's passion is to find out what's down there. He has never seen so many people near a drilling site. He has never heard the sound of grief so close to all the metal and machinery. As the woman from Oregon asks again, "Why can't you leave this island alone?" a deep and resonant grief breaks her voice, and they all push in closer to the gate, with the kind of rippling push you see in flights of seabirds who make a collective and instantaneous decision to veer.

The tall Hawaiian steps forward.

"I have the right to worship in this forest, to speak to my *'aumakua*, and to speak to the spirit of the place that has been defiled."

Clemson inhales deeply. He does not want a shouting match, yet he can barely restrain his urge to shout and denounce. "You people think this is a cathedral out here? We're trying to get into production. We have already blessed it twice. What the hell else do you want?"

"I have a right to go down this road. As a native of these islands I have rights you cannot take away "

"I don't know about native rights. That is not my area. Later today we'll have an attorney here from Honolulu. But I have to tell you, this is not a good time to be asking for a tour. We're on a schedule. Men are working at the site. We just cannot have this many people roaming around without permits."

The tall man stands taller. "I am not *people roaming around.*"

"If you come past the gate, we'll have to arrest you! You don't want that! I don't want that!"

"My family been on this island a thousand years."

The tall man looks back and seems surprised to see so many in his wake. Yesterday he heard a rumor that today the broad bit would make its first splintering cut into the rock layer from which these trees have sprung. Early this morning he heard about the fire fountains and a new lake of lava in the high country. Walking in here was his idea. But he did not organize the walk. Though he is leading now, he is not the leader. Since dawn he has been hearing the voices of those who guided him along the road, his grandfather, his great-grandfather.

Each one here is doing this, a hundred people meeting for a hundred different reasons, Travis among them now, pushed by all the ancestors who have brought them to this little intersection, though for the tall Hawaiian man the old voices are louder than anything else in the air because he is standing on his own ancestral land. It gives him great dignity, and authority. With his armload of ti leaves he steps forward, while around him others move. Bodies lean in his direction. Travis feels a pushing surge, and he too is yearning toward the fence.

The tall man steps past the gate, and past Clemson, who looks at Sonny the cop, who does not know what to do. Sonny's dark face is made of stone. He doesn't move. He can't move, until another man and woman step past the gate together, a Caucasian couple in their early fifties. They stop beyond the fence, like Quakers waiting peacefully to be arrested. Now Sonny reaches for his handcuffs, but others are suddenly rushing through, six or eight at once. Clemson holds his arms high like an umpire.

"Goddamn it! This is a hazardous area! Don't you people get that?"

Someone shouts, "Who made it hazardous?"

And someone else, "It wasn't hazardous a year ago!"

"That's right," the woman from Oregon shouts. "Where did the hazard come from?"

Then everyone is shouting, surging. Before the guards can close the gate, two dozen marchers crowd past. Some gallop away down the road with cries of jubilant escape, ignoring orders from Clemson and the guards, who manage to catch the slowest and snap cuffs around their wrists. When the gates close, a few marchers head for the trees, as if to skirt the fence and outflank the guards. Travis would be joining them, but the surge has pinned him next to the fence, and this is when Clemson spots him.

"Doyle? Is that you?"

The dark-haired photographer has stepped toward the action. At the sound of his name she turns, then looks away.

"Jesus Christ, Doyle!" Clemson shouts. "What the hell are you up to *this* time?"

Before he can reply, Clemson is sprinting for the pickup. The engine roars to life and he speeds away, in search of loose marauders.

Slowly, reluctantly, the woman turns again. She is standing very near. He sees her brows gather as if to fend off pain, or sun glare. A kind of wonder comes into her face, both guarded and exposed, a look he knows, releasing a pang he has not felt in eighteen years. It is not a pang of pleasure. It is closer to dread. A bucket of ice water drops through the sultry air and spills all over him.

Old Flames

He takes off his silvered driving glasses, pushes his hat brim back.

She says, "I can't believe this."

"Angel."

"Nobody calls me that anymore."

"Evangeline, then."

"Is it really Travis Doyle?"

He moves toward her, stops. The reporter has looked up from his page of scribbling with the frown of a man whose work is being interrupted.

"The one and only."

Her mouth opens but nothing comes, her eyes so full she can not speak. She is trying to cover. She can't. Neither can Travis. He feels naked. He is sixteen again, emotionally sixteen, unsure and aching.

"You two seem to know each other," the reporter says.

"We've met," Travis says, with a sardonic shrug that makes her laugh, a rippling nervous laugh of recovery, as they both recover from the first shock.

"Roland, this is Travis, a figure from the distant past. Travis, meet Roland Fernandez."

They shake hands. Roland is suspicious, though trying to appear cordial. He has smoky eyes, a mustache, thick black hair, and wide shoulders underneath an industrial-style blue shirt. In the midst of the turmoil on both sides of the fence, in the middle of the Puna forest, they make a silent tableau— Angel eyeing Travis, Travis eyeing Angel, and Roland eyeing both of them, his glance darting in a way that says he is closely attuned to her. He does not like this. He knows something is going on, or has gone on, though he doesn't really want to have to think about it. He has a story to cover.

The tall man is chanting now, a slow rumble like river stones rolling across the skin of a drum, a kind of chanting Travis will be hearing many times. There is history and mercy in it, pride and loss, and the old yearning to honor the earth, to be one with the earth. Around their sudden reunion it fills the air. It seems to be a voice much older than the body of the man, as if his grandfather or great-grandfather is singing through him. It is a sound Travis feels in his own silent, yearning throat, and all the other voices soften. The air goes still. The leaves wait, as if the trees too are listening.

It is a long prayer, one you listen to with your head up and your eyes open, and he cannot take his eyes off Angel, who has not changed. She is thirty-four and looks thirty-four, no younger, no older, yet her looks are the same. The hair pulled back from her forehead, falling past her shoulders, is set against a white shirt with buttoned shoulder flaps, a bush-jacket shirt tucked into her jeans. There is an Asian lift at the corners of her eyes, and in the lips a hint of Polynesian fullness, barely a shadow of that. In profile it edges and rounds her upper lip. Her skin is the color of cocoa butter, and in this light it seems radiant, though not in the angelic way. It is nearly noon. The sun pours down upon them through the branches overhead, surrounding her with a very terrestrial light.

She is looking him over too, taking him in, playing how he looks now against some inner snapshot of Travis in his teens. He is unhinged, melted by her gaze, which seems to have two layers. Her body, her face, her eyes all keep a proper distance from this stranger/former-lover appearing out of another lifetime. But from behind her eyes someone else is observing him, perhaps herself at age sixteen, or a gaze coming from the other side of age. For him it is a glimpse into some place he is still approaching, within reach but still unreachable, right behind all the surfaces of what this island appears to be.

Roland's voice cuts between them. "You local? You involved with some of these people?"

Hands up. Innocent. "I'm just passing through."

Her eyebrows rise. He doesn't know how to tell her what he's really doing, afraid she'll be disappointed.

"How do you know Dan Clemson?" Roland says.

"I don't. I mean, I just met him. I'm a writer," he says, which is at least partly true, since this is how his labors usually end up.

"A reporter?"

"I write reports from time to time. But I'm not strictly speaking a reporter."

Roland waits, half suspicious, half interested.

"Freelance stuff," Travis says.

Though Roland's look is formidable, his voice is soft. His face looks capable of amusement. In other circumstances they would probably enjoy each other's company. But there is a charge in the air. Roland feels it. Anyone would feel it. Her skin is the same, and her smile is the same, a time-capsule smile, older and more worldly now, yet still the same, and the feeling in the air between them, there is no mistaking that. After all this time the same flame has blazed forth, a singular flame Travis associates with her and her alone, a flame that only she can kindle, or that they two can kindle.

Roland glances at his watch. He has a deadline to meet. The first arrestees are already being released on their recognizance, told to report for arraignment in a couple of days. The guards don't know what else to do. When they first got wind of today's demonstration, four of them drove out from town. They have one car and five sets of handcuffs, and there are still the wild roamers to be rounded up. While Angel finishes out the roll in her camera, Roland moves to talk with the tall Hawaiian, who is shaking his head in disgust.

"You got two laws out here. Haole law says I'm the trespasser now. Misdemeanor trespassing is what they gonna hit us with. Then you got law from the old time. You don't have cops to enforce it. But you know in your heart if you follow it or you don't. You listen to the land, and the land helps you remember what is the right thing to do."

He shakes his head again. "Cutting up roads like this, ripping out the trees, putting holes a mile down through Pele's lava, or two miles or whatever . . . Maybe no cop is gonna call them for trespassing. But these folks breaking laws just the same."

This is what Roland has been waiting to hear. He has enough now to file a story. He hopes Angel has the pictures. He is heading toward the jeep. But she is not. With high color in her face she is looking again at Travis. Whether she is moved by what the tall man said, or still giddy from the strangeness of this meeting, as Travis is, or both, he can't be sure. Her hands are flapping. Her head seems to shiver with astonishment.

"I still don't get this. What are you doing here? Did you say some kind of assignment?"

Roland is behind the wheel, switching his engine on.

"I'll explain when we have more time," Travis says.

"How long are you staying?"

"A few days. Maybe a week."

"That's not long."

"It's a rough estimate."

"And you're still on the mainland?"

"The Bay Area. How about you? Over here from Honolulu?"

"I live here now. I was born on this island. Remember?"

He does remember. She used to talk about her kid days in the rivers and in the north coast valleys.

"Your folks were born here too," he blurts, groping for anything to say, to delay Roland, who is swinging the Jeep around for take-off.

"That's right." Her eyes are wide with acknowledgment, as if on the verge of larger matters.

He is in turmoil, panicking, unable to think. What to do? What to suggest?

"Listen. We ought to get together, for a cup of coffee, a drink or something."

She looks worried. She glances at Roland. Maybe she can call, if she knows where he is staying. Maybe tomorrow. She wishes he had more time. He tells her the hotel, and she hands him a card that resembles a small patch of tapa cloth. Black letters on brown spell out her name, *Evangeline Malama Waimalani Sakai.* Underneath that, a phone number and the simple word PHOTOGRAPHY. The card not only resembles tapa, it has a dark cloth texture, an expensive and finger-pleasing card, a card she has thought about.

He holds it between thumb and forefinger and watches dust puff up beside the deep-tread tires of the jeep, watches until it takes the bend and disappears.

Behind him the coolers are springing open. In the shade of roadside trees there is going to be a lunchtime picnic/vigil/sit-in. Two ukuleles have emerged from someone's pack. A few people are singing. The woman from Oregon offers him a sandwich, which he accepts. He is famished. He is exhausted. He sits down, frail and drained. Yet jumpy. Too edgy to sit. She and her husband are ready to hike back out the Pumahi Road, where they left their van. He gives them a lift.

A Recurring Dream

At the Orchid Isle Hotel two messages await him, one from Ian Prince saying, "Please call, urgent," the other from Angel saying, "I can meet you at 7:30 at the Blue Dolphin Lounge," noting the street and telling him to ask at the desk for directions.

A woman named Connie tells him Prince left unexpectedly for Maui.

"For how long?"

"He wasn' t sure. It came up all of a sudden."

"Before or after the demonstration?"

"May I ask who's calling?"

"I'm returning a call. The name is Doyle."

Her voice lifts. "Oh yes, Mr. Doyle. There's an envelope here for you. To be picked up as soon as possible, Ian said. If I have to go out I'll leave it in the box by the door. Some supporting documents he wants you to have."

"And how about the claim?"

"We're rewriting it. Taking recent developments into account, of course."

"Of course."

"Ian's very keen on this, as I believe you know. There is also something from the Manu Kona. "

"Which is . . . ?"

"The new place over on the leeward side. They say it's fabulous."

"Sounds like a hotel."

"In a way. Though it's more than that. They say once you get there you never want to leave. You're very lucky."

"Why?"

"It's a gift coupon. Ian says it would be a shame for you to visit the Big Island and not see the Manu Kona. Here's his note. 'Tell Mr. Doyle this is a small token of my regard.'"

"His regard?"

"I'm quoting."

"Any rough idea how long he'll be gone?"

"It's hard to say. His therapist lives outside Kahului."

"Is he all right?"

"Why do you ask?"

"You said his therapist."

"Well, yes, of course, he's fine. It's just always a little hard to say."

He thanks her and hangs up and laughs a laugh of self-disgust. Travis thinks he knows where this regard has come from. Go along with Prince's scenario, call it arson, an act of sabotage, help him tighten the noose around Jack Brockman, and get two free nights at a luxury resort, with snorkeling lessons, the floor show, a courtesy maitai at sundown.

Am I that superficial? he asks himself, laughing at whatever may have led Ian Prince to believe he can be purchased this way. And for so little.

"Carlo," he calls aloud, to the walls and the ferns and the phone and the *Round the Island* magazine and the TV listings marked PG, R, and X. "Why did you do this to me!"

He sits down on the bed, confused, suddenly so groggy he can't keep his eyes open. He wants sleep and only sleep.

By midafternoon the heat and humidity and time change have caught up with him. He falls back across the queen-size thinking he is not cut out for this kind of work, murmuring his vows of abstinence like a rosary. They drop through his mind not as words, but as tiny signals, beads of sound:

No drugs.
No alcohol.
No women.
No entanglements of any kind.
Each moment is its own doorway.
And you pass through it.
Into the next moment.
And so on.
And so forth.
With no regrets.
No.
No regrets at all.

He lies there like a corpse until dusk, when he dreams a dream he has never remembered, though it has rolled through his mind dozens of times. He is underwater, looking up at a blurred face he cannot quite recognize. In this dream he stands on something solid, which may or may not be the sea floor. He can't tell. The water moves around him in slow currents, blue-green water shot through with wavering bars of light. The face above him is distorted by the surface. Maybe the mouth is moving, calling to him in the blue-green silence. Maybe the only movement is in the water's undulating flow. He can't be sure. His feeling in this dream is anguish, the gnawing ache of some unnameable loss.

When his eyes spring open he is hungry and thirsty, cotton-mouthed, craving a drink, and the dream he has dreamed so many times goes unremembered once again. The face fades, the water dissolves. But the feeling stays, an anguish he cannot identify, a dark flow gripping him in the first moments of wakefulness, dripping through his limbs and belly. He knows it well, but where does it come from, he wonders, and why now? Why now?

116

The Blue Dolphin

In the shower he stands under a cold spray and thinks about Angel's message, telling himself it would be folly to get his hopes up. Men surely fall in love with her every other day. Roland, for example. Roland is crazy about her. Her message is a courtesy call, for old times sake, nothing more, and if they meet he will have to be guided by Vow Number Three—No Women—which means he will once again be taking a small liberty with Vow Number Two, to fortify himself. At the hotel bar as he orders a glass of white wine, he is thinking that vows, at best, are ideals. Guides. Your noblest intentions. Only a monk with iron will could live up to all the vows he has made in recent years.

At the main desk, when he asks for directions, the pretty clerk wrinkles her brow.

"The Blue Dolphin? Just you?"

"Unless you'd like to join me."

She shakes her head as if he has offered her a sky-diving lesson. "I think that used to be some kind of Korean place."

Halfway across town he pulls into a block-size mall of shops and offices, new buildings in the plantation style, with porches, low-slung roofs, extended eaves, old trees rising here and there. The twilight sky is the color of dark red roses. Overhead lamps have just come on. The door marked ENERGY SOURCE is locked. Venetian blinds screen the wide picture window. On a round cardboard clock, cardboard arms point to 11:15, and happy lettering says, "Returning Soon." In a slot by the door a nine-by-twelve manila envelope has his name on it. A sheaf of paperwork is clipped to a folded card showing the Manu Kona logo—a stylized sun, a cresting wave, the profile of a feathered helmet.

What the hell is Prince really up to here? Ensnaring Brockman? The more Travis thinks about that, the less it holds together. Something else is in the air. But what? He throws the packet into his trunk, deciding to keep this to himself. He will tell Prince he has updated the San Francisco office and in that way buy some time, a day or two or three, in the hope that he can figure out who, if anyone, is telling the truth.

His sympathies at the moment are with the tall Hawaiian, whose voice is in his head. Other voices have faded, while the tall man's chant comes back to work on him. He would not be able to say quite why. It has something to do with trust. Can you trust a sound? He does not know the man's name or the name of the chant or what the words meant, the words he chanted on the road to the drilling rig, but Travis recognized the sound coming through the chest and throat. It had some quality akin to what he has heard in gospel music, a striving with the voice, a crying out, calling toward an older time. It speaks to him and stays with him, and he does not want to do anything that might betray the feeling he heard.

Nor does he want to do anything that will discourage Carlo from paying him quickly. He still hopes for a simple outcome, an ordinary fire that can be summed up in twenty-five words or less, in a short concise report, followed by some serious pocket money, enough to do whatever comes to mind. As he drives across town he can imagine spending every nickel he possesses on Angel, if it comes to that. He dares not hope it will. But if it does, he is ready. What is money, after all? A tool. A symbol. Nothing, really, until you have transformed it into something else. Food. Time. Power. Peace of mind. Or a certain glance from the girl of your dreams.

"What's your definition of money?" he says to the bar-tender at the Blue Dolphin Lounge, as the icy glass of draft appears.

It is the wrong thing to say. He is a tall swarthy fellow wearing a blue aloha shirt filled with leaping dolphins. He stands in front of his long row of bottles and glasses, his smile slow, automatic.

"You here on business?"

The bartender glances at a man six stools away, hunched over a long-neck Budweiser, a bearded man in sunglasses, his cheeks dark, his arms as thick as coconut trunks. He too wears a blue aloha shirt. Larger than extra large. No dolphins. He rotates from the waist and looks at Travis, as if to say, "Who let this smartass haole in?"

Travis turns toward the doorway, calculating his exit route, hoping, as he hoped when he pulled up outside and saw the look of this place, that he will be able to have a drink and escape without bodily harm. The appetizers spaced along the bar tell him it isn't a place where visitors from the mainland are expected—pickled cabbage, shredded seaweed, spicy chunks of raw fish called *poki*. The lights are heavy on the reds and purples, and across one wall there is a stage long enough for four or five topless dancers to writhe and kick. Tonight it is set up with speakers and mikes waiting in the semi-dark, but no band visible yet, and not much of an audience, just a few early drinkers like this Goliath at the bar who Travis figures would gladly dislocate his shoulders.

He is into his second glass when Angel shows. He sees her pause inside the neon-painted entry, wearing stylish trousers, a white blouse, her hair black against the wide white collar. His vows of abstinence dissolve forever, along with any lingering doubts about why his lifetime of zigzag travels have brought him to this barstool on this particular night. If he had never seen her until this moment he would drop everything, swallow his fears, cancel his agenda and all flight plans, and follow her through the lounge or back out into the semi-mud of the parking lot on his hands and knees. The fact that he already knows this woman fills him with wonder, not only knows her but once knew her in the biblical way, slept with her, touched every inch of the body inside the clothes now reflecting blue neon. The knowledge and memory of that rises within him, making him suddenly powerful. He feels huge with luck.

She carries a lei in a polyethylene bag, and he's glad he stopped at the stand outside the hotel. You can never go wrong in the islands if you show up bearing a lei. By the time she reaches the bar she has lifted out the garland of tuberose and orchid and raises it with both hands, saying gently, "Here, Travis, this is for you," giving him then the welcome he dreamed of at the airport, though there is no flirtation nor any covert flicker in the eyes.

As she places the flowers, lightly touching her cheek to his, in a quick and intimate greeting, he is melting again. He has always been partial to the potent scent of tuberose, and she remembered that. Her body scent mixes with the fragrance rising from his shoulders. With a smile unexpectedly tender she steps away and says, "Welcome back."

He brought along a lei made of small orange flowers pressed tightly in a ring. The flower is called *ilima*. From a distance the lei resembles a ring of coral, a special-occasion lei, highly regarded, often used in ceremonies. This is not lost on Angel. As he places it around her neck her eyes are moist. The bartender's eyes are also moist. He too is moved by their flower choices. He and his huge companion are witnessing this reunion, and they feel what has passed between Angel and Travis. Welcomed by her he is less of a stranger. They are willing to meet him now, to hear his name. The bartender is a longtime ally. The big man is Tiny Kulima, though Travis didn't recognize him in the murky lounge, without hat and poncho, and with the eyes screened off. Tiny is a distant relative, a third cousin to Angel's mother, by marriage, and he recently formed a band that happens to be playing in the club tonight.

"Tiny," she says, "meet an old friend from California."

"He don't look so old."

"Didn't we meet yesterday?" says Travis. "At the drilling site?"

"Hey," says Tiny, as the face opens with a slow and curiously bashful grin, "that's where I seen you."

He slides off the stool. An enormous hand comes toward Travis for the brotherhood grip, the thumblock and sturdy clasp followed by a linking of the four bent fingers. The eyes are black ovals rimmed with silver, and the white teeth seen through his beard are dazzling. The smile seems both generous and sinister, which might be an effect of the light in here. Travis can't be sure. It makes dark colors darker and whites extremely white. Small white blossoms on Tiny's shirt shine like distant moons.

Island Music

For old time's sake he orders a bottle of white wine and they move toward a table back away from the bandstand, against the dusky wall. They sit down and he fills the glasses. For thirty seconds they look at each other.

"I had to think about calling you," she says.

"For how long?"

"About two minutes."

Her smile is shy, playful. It makes him laugh. They both laugh.

"I had to talk it over with Roland. I didn't want him to get the wrong idea."

"Roland is?"

"A friend."

"A close friend?"

"We see each other. He'll be here later, along with some folks I want you to meet. I've told them about you."

"What did you tell them?"

"Not much. I'm still waiting to hear the details."

She asks again what he's doing on the island. Before he answers she asks how long he stayed overseas. She knows he enlisted right out of high school. She wants to know where else he has been. She wants to know everything. At first he tries to keep it light, hoping to see her laugh again. He tells her he is like one of those people you read about on the dust jacket, where it lists what the writer did before his first book was published.

"After service in the military, Doyle worked as a health club janitor, a short order cook, a speed reading instructor, a body guard, a piano mover, a fortune cookie editor, a tuba player with the Salvation Army . . ."

It works. She laughs. One thing about Angel that has not changed—she enjoys laughing. As he watches her face open wide, her mouth, the light from her eyes, it dawns on him that his ex-wife Marge has never been an easy laugher. She has to be coaxed and teased along, and her smile, when it comes, is like a reward you have finally earned. He had forgotten how generous Angel can be.

"And now you're happily installed somewhere with dogs and cats, a whole house full of kids."

"No ma'am. Not Travis. No live animals. No kids. No wife to speak of. I was married for a while. I guess technically I still am."

"You guess?"

"I mean it's finished."

"What went wrong?"

Her mouth waits with a small expectant smile that tells him she wants a real answer, not a clever one. In this moment the past and the present come together with a click. It was this way in the old days, though he could never have described it then. She calls forth true answers. Kidding amuses her, but the effort to be honest brings into her eyes a richer light. He starts telling a story he hasn't told anyone, or thought of telling, not really a story, more the recollection of a scene, a meeting, a look that crossed another woman's face one night in a bar on Geary Street, during the last weeks with Marge, when he happened to be drinking alone.

This was a woman he had seen there a couple of times, though they had never talked. As he was getting up to leave she touched his elbow and said she'd like to know him better. He was lonesome, looking for any reason not to go back to the apartment until Marge fell asleep, and this woman was being more than friendly. She was available. She was offering herself. She wore a low-cut top that featured a lot of skin, a lot of cleavage. She was dressed for seduction, and he was aroused, there was no denying it, aroused by her flesh and by the fact that she had, for whatever reason, chosen him. He sat down again and ordered some drinks, and in scraps and fragments they began to talk about their lives.

She smiled continuously, a large, open, toothy smile, her eyes on his, eyes clouded the color of zinfandel. They were almost lovely, almost glowing, almost empty. He wondered if his eyes looked that way to her, wondered if she had recognized in him some kindred spirit and this had emboldened her to cross the room. The woman's eyes, just then, were like Marge's had become. He could not remember if Marge had always looked that way, but he saw that staying together as husband and wife was hopeless. There was no longer any use trying.

Angel says, "Did you go to bed with her?"

"I couldn't. She reminded me too much of my wife. While we were sitting there I had this little revelation. After five years I saw that we had married for all the wrong reasons."

"Why does it take so long?"

"So long?"

"To see these things."

He doesn't have to ask her which things. She wants to tell him, as if they have never stopped being companions and confessors. She leans toward him, her face eager, compassionate. Her words come quickly, but without a sense of speed, the tongue moving, the voice melodious and smooth, like her mother's, that flower petal softness, talk/singing her recent past, her marriage, Walter, the Reno years.

Her story takes him by surprise. In his imagination she has never moved. He is the roamer and the traveler, while she has stayed put, like the photo in his wallet, his Pacific pinup, backlit by tropic water. It is hard to let go of this. He despises Walter, and yet he sees that they have been co-conspirators. Travis too has kept her boxed in all these years, kept her in his pocket. Even as she sits across from him he looks for signs that she is still who she was, signs that they still can be the way they used to be. Everything has changed, of course, yet aren't they already talking as they talked so long ago? Suddenly, and nakedly, about whatever comes to mind?

At their table back from the bandstand, with the white wine working, and the tuberose scent, he is in a quiet ecstasy. He feels himself awakening, as if for all these years Rip Van Winkle Doyle has been asleep. He understands why he was compelled to tell the story about the woman in the bar. Angel's face called it forth. While she talks it occurs to him that everything that has gone bad with other women has been the result of lying, in one form or another, to himself, or to someone else. He makes a silent vow not to lie to Angel about anything large or small. There would be no point to it. Whatever has happened in these past eighteen years has given her eyes that seem to know the whole history of the world.

His life with women begins anew, right there in The Blue Dolphin Lounge—that is how it feels to him—as he clears the decks by confessing he is not a writer.

When he hands her his card she studies it, as he studied hers, reading the type, reading between the lines.

"Nice," she says. "Professional."

"Not as nice as yours. Next card I get will have more class."

She seems relieved.

"I probably shouldn't tell you what Roland said."

"No, you shouldn't."

She makes it a Roland imitation, gruff and watchful. "Any off-island guy who knew about that rally and was standing there in dark glasses calling himself a writer has got to be one of two things—a narc, or he works for Western Sun."

She lets this sink in.

"Is he right?"

"Twenty Twenty has a hundred clients. Every job is different. I don't work for anybody, Angel. Five days ago I'd never heard of Western Sun."

One of Tiny's guitar players has just stepped onto the stage, lifting his wide-body Gibson from its stand. He wears running shoes and jeans and a big loose T-shirt. He flicks his amp switch, adding a low hum to the murmuring babble, like the lowest note from a Tibetan Buddhist's longest horn.

Travis sips some wine and launches into the story of his trip, his mission. The details themselves validate something, making him more trustable, since Angel knows the story in advance, can play his version against her own. She knows the names before he speaks them. From Tiny she knows about Dan Clemson. From the paper she knows about John Brockman and doesn't much like what she has read. An opportunist, she calls him. And just this afternoon she had a call from Ian Prince, looking for a local photographer who knows the terrain and won't cost an arm and a leg, to fly over some land the company might buy or lease.

When Travis tells her how they spread leaves around the rig, she nods yes. She knows about the pickups. Driving down there this morning, Roland wasn't expecting to see a crowd. He'd heard talk of two stalled trucks, the kind of story the Honolulu paper might run, where readers enjoy ghostly news from the outer islands. They stopped at the dealership, she says, to talk with a sales rep who was still mystified and apologetic. The rep had seen trucks like those make it through flash floods with water up to the headlights. They were built for trouble, he said, the damp-weather champs. And yet such things are not uncommon, according to Angel. There are many stories she could tell him about cars and trucks and buses that have stalled for no mechanical reason, at midday and late at night, near burial sites and along back roads and in plowed fields where workmen will be trying to move a large and stubborn stone that does not want to be moved.

The way she says these things, the certainty in her voice, makes the small hairs rise along his arms and legs. He asks a question that seems to ask itself. It simply springs forth.

"What about lightning?"

"Lightning?"

"I heard there was an electric storm the night the equipment shed caught fire."

"I guess everybody knows we had a storm that night. I have heard folks say it was lightning, folks who live down that way."

"What do they say?"

"Oh, you know, they never say much. They're like Tiny. He probably knows everything that ever happened here, but he can't talk about everything he knows. The Big Island is not that big. Bigger than others, but not that big. What you say today comes back to you tomorrow, or next week. It doesn't have anywhere else to go but around and around and around."

"And a cloudburst put that fire out before it went too far."

She nods again, as if this has significance, looking older in the murky light, somehow farther away, as if she is about to leave him. He feels like the hitchhiker or the random seat mate on the long bus ride, someone you can afford to be intimate with because you know he's only passing through your life. Has this made it easier for her to talk the way they have been talking? And is he now the inept stranger who has stepped across some boundary of island gossip or island lore?

Tiny is running sound tests, checking levels. In his hands the mike stand is like a twig. Under red/blue gels he fills half the stage, his beard blue, his teeth white. The lights tint most of the club, giving Angel's face the gloss of porcelain.

"When there's more time," she says, "I'll have to tell you some stories."

"About what?"

Wherever she went, she has now come back. She shrugs. Her smile is so infectious, so full of mischief, they both laugh again, children with a secret.

"Pagan stories," she says. "About the nature signs."

"We still have some time."

She leans across the table and tells him about a hula master and teacher, a famous chanter known to all as Auntie Helen. A few years back she went into the hospital. She was very old, ninety, some people said. For ten days before she died, dry lightning cracked in the sky over Hilo. Everyone saw it, lightning in the blue and cloudless sky. Every day for ten days. Then on the day Auntie Helen died, the sky relaxed, and the rain came to cool the town.

The light in her eyes has changed again. Or so it seems. Whether it is a movement in the stage lights, or some other shifting in the room, he cannot gauge. He dares not glance away. Her voice has dropped again to its lower register, and her eyes look darker, as if the light now comes from farther in. This time she is not withdrawing. She is offering him the story.

"You believe things like that?" he says.

"You don't have to believe anything. It happened."

"I mean, you believe it's connected?"

"Tutu Helen was a powerful woman who had lived her whole life here, listening to the island and the sea and the forests."

A ripple moves across his skin, as every hair and hair fiber comes alive. He watches her face for some show of qualification, a crinkle, a softening of the dark light to tell him he can take this pagan story with a grain or two of salt. Her eyes do not change. If anything they grow darker. She is watching, testing his reaction. He tries a smile that has worked since childhood, his charmer's smile. It has no effect.

The current running through him breaks into a thousand needles, sprinkling his arms and legs and belly with a thousand sparks. His skin feels flammable. Is something going on inside the earth and in the air above the earth? Or does he somehow want it to be going on? And is he merely falling again for Angel and willing to agree to anything that might please and draw her toward him? He can not unravel it and doesn't care to. Not now. His heart is next to hers again, his heart is with Angel's and with her cousin Tiny and with the tall Hawaiian man he does not know. He wants to hear more from them about power and whatever seems to freight the atmosphere around the drilling rig with its invisible and incandescent charge.

Onstage white light is added to the reds and blues. Tiny snaps his fingers twice, and rhythm chords fill the room. The slack-key guitar comes in, followed by his own electric bass. His face is fierce and shadowed. His voice is like river water, a healing voice. He opens with a song about the mountain, Mauna Kea, the quiet inspiration of its snowy peaks, yet somehow heartbreak is in the air, a deep current of heartbreak for times gone by, along with a high note of celebration for all those things that last or come back to you, like the snow, like the seasons, like the reunion with the one you feared was gone forever. Once again the past and present merge with a tiny click.

This is what they used to do, hang around the clubs in Waikiki and listen to Hawaiian bands. This is the old time and the new, and Tiny's voice expresses it with a sound much like the sound they heard at noon, at the fence line, in the tall man's prayer to the rocks and the trees. In Tiny's song about the mountain they hear some echo of that chant, the way his words vibrate. The melody has a gospel ring, as do so many island songs, flowing out of old tunes shipped in by missionaries a hundred and seventy years ago. The harmonies are choral harmonies with Sunday organs ringing in the distance, but the deep lament swelling up from underground to catch along the edges of the throat, that sound goes back a hundred and seventy years times ten. And it is a lucky break for Angel and Travis to have this coming toward them, linking them to the noontime meeting and to other meetings long ago. Is Tiny's band playing their song? *Our song?* Yes. That's exactly what it is. *Our song* means some piece of background music you can't forget, the tape loop for a shared and long-lost time that comes alive again. The sound itself can seem to knit your ragtag life together.

It is a warm-up night for Tiny's band, a sneak preview in the middle of the week. They play a long first set, with other singers climbing on and off the stage, among them a round Hawaiian woman known for her rich and bluesy voice. When she and Tiny sing the final tune, it resonates with quivering harmonics, causing Travis's skin to buzz and his blood to race. After two beers and half a bottle of wine he is on overload.

"Come outside with me," he says.

"I can't. They'll be here any minute. I don't know where they are. They must be on Hawaiian time."

Desperate for any small foothold in her life tonight, her life tomorrow, he remembers the film he shot, film he would ordinarily send back to San Francisco, and she says sure, she can do it for him right away, negatives and prints.

"It's in my car. It's in my camera bag."

"You can bring it in the morning," she says warily, holding to the table like a guard rail.

"I'll do that too."

"Please, Travis. I can't walk outside with you. People here know me. It won't look right."

He pushes his chair back, as if to leave.

She doesn't move.

He says, "I have to ask you a personal question."

Her eyes are steady, neutral, waiting.

"It's about Roland."

"What about Roland?"

"That's my question."

"I told you, he's a friend."

"You said a close friend."

"Close enough."

"Does that mean . . . ?"

"I'm not very close to anyone, Travis, if that's what you're concerned about. I don't want to be. I hope you can understand that."

He doesn't. That is, he does not quite hear these words. They don't reach him. He leans toward her.

"I'm doing my work," she says. "Putting my life back together. My daughter just turned thirteen."

He is about to lean closer, about to try touching his lips to hers. Before he moves, she turns away.

"Don't, Travis. Please."

"I've thought about you a thousand times. Ten thousand times."

"And you're going to fly away again."

"I'm going to be here at least a week. I know that now."

"Then what?"

"A lot can happen in a week."

She can't look at him.

"I'm going crazy," he says.

He is burning. She is burning too. He knows it. When she turns to him this time her eyes are like coals. Her hair is lined with the thinnest blue flame. He also knows she is right. He finally hears her words, which have hung in the air above the table. After years of strain and confusion her life is starting to be orderly at last. He knows what that is like. He makes a vow, a silent vow not to touch her. Touching is what gets you into trouble. He will spend time with her, as much as she will allow, inside the globe of shimmering light they make, and as long as they do not touch each other they will be okay.

Familiar Voices,
Lyrics Far Away

He steps outside to get the film. When he returns, three people have joined her at the table. The others are expected soon. She introduces him as a friend in town on business, and now a customer too, showing the little cannisters around like trophies.

"Hey," says a husky fellow called Junior, laughing, "hey, the guy just landed, you already got him owing you some money."

"Don't let her overcharge you either," says his wife, Leilani, with a silky and sardonic smile.

It is jokes and small talk after that. He finds himself squeezed in close to a young woman named Brenda, Angel's neighbor, a nervous talker with a pretty face made hard by too much makeup, black accent lines along her eyelids and high color added to her swarthy cheeks. She is Portuguese and filipina, small, compact. Needles of short-cut black hair rise from her scalp. Her T-shirt says *Island Style*. She orders a Diet Pepsi, telling him she is a reformed alcoholic who hasn't had a drink in three years, "not in one thousand one hundred and ninety-seven days."

He likes Brenda, but he has to get out of here. The Angel/Travis spell has been broken. Maybe he should be disappointed, or annoyed. He isn't. He needs some distance. They both need it. Before the second set begins he is on his feet. With a glance at his watch he puts the blame on the time change, which seems to be the right thing to do. It allows them all to smile generous and releasing smiles. In the islands you can make allies this way, letting it be known that you too have at last surrendered to Hawaiian time or rubber time or travel time or the delayed sledgehammer of mainland time.

134

The sky is close and heavy, in between showers. The parking lot is mostly mud. He guides around new puddles, almost to his car, when he sees a figure lurking near it, a profile against the darker backdrop of thicket and hau trees. His first thought is Roland, or some thug sent by Roland to rough him up for lingering this long with Angel. He stops, looks around, sees no one else. The voice is low and urgent.

"Doyle, it's me."

"Brockman?"

"The girl at the hotel told me you might be here."

"Call me tomorrow."

"Can we talk?"

Headlights swing around a corner, angling toward the entrance to the lot. Travis thinks, Shit. "Get in," he says, as he opens the driver's side door. They sit in silence while in the rearview Travis watches the car park. Roland and two women cross the lot and mount the stairs and enter the club. He wears a shirt that emphasizes his shoulders. Watching the swagger, Travis thinks of a Golden Gloves boxer he once knew.

With a smirk in his voice Brockman says, "The press is here."

"You know that guy?"

"By reputation. He's the only one they have who can write."

"What does he write about?"

"He's on our side."

"Our side?"

"He doesn't trust Energy Source any more than we do."

"What do you mean, We?"

"I recognize you, man. You are not a claims adjuster. I know that's your job. But that's not who you are. You are a renegade. You're out here riding the bronco, just like me."

Travis shoves his key into the ignition. "It's been a long day. What specifically is on your mind?"

"I came over here to thank you."

Brockman wears the same T-shirt. In the club light his forehead is a blue-red dome.

"Since you stopped by the house I have been putting this and that together. Those letters I wrote, they showed up *after* the fire, right? I walked right into it."

Travis toys with the switch. Brockman reminds him of someone he doesn't want to think about. Yet all the drinking makes it easy to sit still and wait. It is more than the wine and the beer. One hour with Angel has left him stunned, immobilized.

"Walked into what?" Travis says.

"Think about what they're doing, Doyle. Some kind of insurance scam? Too easy. Either way, arson or an accident, it's all the same. They are still covered, right? It's not about insurance. It's about real estate. Sooner or later everything in the islands is about real estate. Prince is an old-fashioned speculator. It runs in the family. He has had his eye on a big parcel he wants to get surveyed, but he doesn't want anybody official to know about it, so he has to clear his access route with a couple of the medium-size dope growers back in there who work their crops in their quiet way and will cut your arms off if they don't know who you are. Western Sun has half this forest leased, as you probably know, but until they have a couple of wells on line, the land just sits there while all the things that have been happening keep on happening, the growers just keep on growing—"

"Hold it, Brockman. Hold it. That is not my area. Not at all. I am over here to do one thing and one thing only—"

"You have to have some background. Otherwise you are never going to get into the foreground. I know what I'm talking about. I used to have my own modest parcel of loco weed. That is why he came to me the first time, although he said it was because he knew about my pig traps, and with all the acreage they were leasing they could send a lot of business my way. This is how he works, you see. He will make you a little offer, to see how open you are to doing things his way. Take the first bite, you'll be hearing from him again. You mark my word. Before you know it, he'll be offering you something. Maybe he already has."

Travis looks at him. Brockman's eyes have a lonesome, famished, triumphant gleam.

"Am I right?"

"Maybe," Travis says. "Maybe not. I don't know yet."

"You see? Do I know what I'm talking about? Forewarned is forearmed, Doyle. A couple of days later two tickets to Honolulu just appear in my mailbox, and that's when I made a grave mistake. I used them. My kid's grandparents live there. We flew over for a weekend. Next thing I know he is feeling me out, looking for a kind of middle man. He doesn't want to be talking to these guys face to face, and he knows I know my way around the island. With all his moves back and forth he himself could be scheming to squeeze them out and start his own export import business on the side. You know what I mean? A transpacific weed merchant. I wouldn't put it past him. It scared the shit out of me, man. I told him so. I told him to keep the fuck out of my life, and that hurt his feelings. He has a very thin skin,

Mr. Ian Prince, a poor loser, and what you are seeing now is revenge pure and simple, setting me up as the guy who torched his shed. He knows I am on to him, and he knows I won't go to the cops."

"Why not?" Travis says. "They should be hearing this, not me."

"They'd *love* to know that somebody thinks I could qualify as a go-between. They watch every move I make. For all I know, they're in on it. They're in on everything else. Why do you think I stayed away from that rally today? fifteen people got arrested. I could have been one of them. They would love to have my ass on any kind of charge at all."

"I was there. I saw it happen."

"So I've heard. That's good. We need all the support we can get. The shit is about to hit the fan. That rally was just a start. It gave people a taste of what is possible. This weekend there is going to be a public hearing, to voice the pros and cons. This is where you and I working together can blow Prince's cover."

"Okay, Brockman, that's enough." With a shake of his head, Travis sits up straight. "Maybe you are riding the bronco. I am just over here to check out a fire. I appreciate your point of view, but a few more days and I am gone."

"Have you been listening to me? I'm telling you what is going *on*. I'm telling you why. All I'm asking you to do is show up."

Travis doesn't believe much of what he's heard. That is, he chooses not to. Brockman talks too much. Yet he keeps listening. Why? The voice. The voice pushes at him now, deeper and thicker, not louder, but closer.

"You are the investigator. All you do is tell them how you see it. They won't let us into the compound, not even to collect evidence on my own behalf. Others, of course, will speak out too, people who know me. But you have access.

You see what I'm getting at? This is a public hearing. Big shots from Honolulu will be there, plus all the locals. We set a little trap. You deliver Prince, because he will talk to you, he won't talk to me. Meanwhile I make sure my guy is there—"

"Your guy? What guy?"

"He'll be there with the aerials."

"Of what?"

138 "Don't worry, Doyle. When the time is right, you'll know. We're doing this in full view of the public, see. Later, if we *have* to, we go to the police. My guess is, once we confront Prince with the truth, he will freak out before our very eyes."

"The truth?"

"That they are lying, setting me up. These are deceitful people. The first step is to raise a question, and the question is, How deep does it run? If they are lying about this, what else are they lying about?"

A good question, Travis thinks. A half-assed and demented scheme, but a pretty good question, one he himself would like to know the answer to.

There is a smell in the car now, not a bad smell, a strong male smell that comes with the effort behind all the talking, as Brockman dreams this spontaneous trial and his own vindication. Travis knew someone like this in the service, a corporal, a talker, a schemer, always trying to talk you into things, and dangerous to be around because he was good at it. He had the knack for intuiting what you were almost in the mood for, had the knack for calling out your comradely sympathies. He made it difficult to say no. Saying no to that corporal was a failure of comradeship. Even when you did not feel particularly close to him, you had somehow failed the Eternal Principle of Comradeship.

Is Travis drawn to the vision of Ian Prince exposed and squirming for his transgressions? Or is he reminded of the corporal, who used to wear his hair shaved close, for the jungle climate? Travis wore it that way too. Maybe Brockman reminds him of himself. Maybe being with Brockman is like being in the service again, where men without women will think up half-assed schemes and sit around in vehicles trying them out on each other.

Fuzzed with drink, Travis does not agree or disagree. He asks him if he needs a ride. Brockman says his car is right across the street, but he makes no move to get out. For quite some time they sit in silence, in the semi-dark, with the blue-and-red glow from the lounge leaking into the Toyota, along with the strains of guitar chords and falsetto lyrics far away. It begins to rain again, and the music is drowned by the thunderous clatter of bullet drops on the thin metal roof and hood. Water pours down the windshield, and Travis is thinking of the corporal, the last time he saw him. He hears the voice again, a voice much like Brockman's, purring and insistent and seductive.

They were in a wet clearing inside an abandoned house where sheets of water poured over sloping eaves. Under there they stood looking through water like men half blind, and the corporal was saying over and over that anyone who feared death had never understood it. Just the two of them, as if inside a waterfall, and he repeated, almost whispering, "You hear me, Doyle? You hear what I am saying?"

Or is this Brockman's voice, seated next to him in the Hilo downpour. "Did you hear me, Doyle? Did you hear what I was saying?"

Travis can't tell. He doesn't want to turn and look, certain he will see the corporal and hear again the words that followed him out the door of the empty house and across the clearing as he headed for the road through the mud and high grass. Travis was sprinting and somewhere behind him the corporal was yelling, "Doyle, you fucker, come back here and listen to me! I am not afraid of it!"

The rain slacks off, stops as suddenly as it began. The clattering ends. The windshield drains and clears. The music from the club returns, and Brockman opens the door. With his John-the-Baptist smile he says, "You don't have to make up your mind now. We'll just take it one step at a time. Check with me tomorrow, okay? But early."

Travis watches him cross the lot and climb into his now rinsed and shiny white Dodge Dart and drive away, and he sits alone remembering the corporal, a demented man from New Mexico with a mustache and a shaved head. In those days they were all demented. Spinning out. The war was nearly over. Travis was sure, at twenty-one, he himself would be the last to die in the last few seconds before a cease-fire was declared. For days, for weeks, perhaps since the moment of his birth, he had been foreseeing his own death, imagining the many ways it could happen. It seemed right, at the time, that one of their own men should be his executioner, this fellow from his own unit, who could no longer tell friend from foe.

Travis ran past the clearing and listened until the corporal came rushing after him, leaping into the roadway to lob his grenade. "Doyle!" he bellowed, as if to make sure they both knew whose name it bore. And "Doyle!" again, causing him to stop and turn and watch, then dive, as the grenade arced. He still sees it now and then, usually in slow motion, an arc against the morning sky, a dark sun rising, a dark and distant sun, almost comforting to look at, a dozen years later, a memory he almost doesn't mind. He has learned to live with that. He can slow it down or speed it up or shut it off. He has found a place to put it. For a long time he blamed the grenade for the way his life was turning out. He blamed the corporal too. His blaming days are just about over. But still, he minds Brockman's voice. It has the ring of the corporal's and gives these memories a sound track he prefers not to hear. He will have to be wary around Brockman, the kind of fellow who can lead him somewhere. Brockman has doom in his eyes. At night you can see it.

He rolls his window down, and music from the club swells toward him, a plume of sound. Throbbing chants from ancient times ring underneath the congregational harmonies. Tiny and the woman are singing again, the sweet falsetto next to her contralto, singing in Hawaiian, breaking and bending notes, like blues singers reciting an old lament for the homeland.

Their Song

In the years when his mother's mother still lived with them she would sing from the same hymnbooks those old missionaries to Hawai'i had carried around the world. Songs that had been sung in the Big Island churches made of rainforest logs and blocks of coral were songs his mother and grandmother and sometimes Travis himself would sing on the Sunday mornings of his early childhood, though they were different when Grandma sang them by herself. Sitting on the porch of the big house there by the orchard, she could have been somewhere back in Oklahoma in the years before the families came west, with all the time in the world, secure in her knowledge that she was the Lord's child and a dutiful disciple of Jesus. Her daughter, Leona, had a good soprano voice admired by the congregation song leader, who would sometimes select a tune from the hymn book knowing she was there to hit the highest notes with confidence and carry along the quaverers and faint-of-throat. But Leona would never interrupt when her mother started humming on the porch, as if these melodies belonged to Grandma alone.

She was in her seventies then, her once-alto voice gone reedy, yet still sweet, thin and sweet and quiet, sometimes in tempo, sometimes slowing it down, when the words she sang took her somewhere else, her pure notes drifting back through the house, through the long hallway, toward the

outbuildings and out among the nearest trees where young
Travis already had the habit of appearing not to listen, the
words so harmless coming from her, like a trickle of clear
water in the morning air:

> Rock of ages, cleft for me,
> Let me hide myself in thee.
> Let the water and the blood
> From Thy wounded side which flowed
> Be of sin the double cure,
> Save from wrath and make me pure.

Tonight, while Travis sits in the Hilo parking lot with his
window down, Leona is driving home in her Land Rover,
two time zones across the water, and humming this song the
way her mother used to hum it long ago. She feels the need
to hear a tune that ties her to the warmer time, the family
time. With lights on high beam and her seat belt tight she
hums against the darkness, thinking of her boys who aren't
boys anymore, thinking she'll call Grover in the morning,
early, at his office, while his voice is fresh, and he'll be in the
mood to joke around for a couple of minutes, maybe invite
her out to lunch. She would call Travis too if she had any
clear idea of how to get hold of him. She can't bear the
sound of that message machine in his apartment, like the
FBI is listening in. Maybe Marge will know how to track
him down, though she doesn't enjoy talking to Marge these
days, and never cared for her all that much in the first place,
if the truth were known. Travis's choice, of course. There's
no point in getting into a squabble over something you can't
do anything about. What was it Hank Williams used to say?
"No need to worry 'cause it ain't gonna be all right nohow."

Part Three

Legends

Pele carried a digging stick, they say. Before she reached her present home she stopped at each island in the chain, each time intending to stay. With her stick she would scoop out a place on the earth and lay claim, fill it with fire, only to have the fire drenched by water rushing in or rising from below, the powerful waters controlled by her older sister, Na Maka o Kaha'i, goddess of the sea.

Pele stopped first in the far north at Nihoa, so old and worn down now it is nothing but a chip. From there she moved south to Ni'ihau and then Kaua'i, where tropic swamps have claimed the volcanic lowlands. On the next island, Oahu, Pele dug into the crater known as Diamond Head, releasing new lava, and angering Na Maka o Kaha'i. The two sisters soon were locked in battle. The water sister won, and Pele had to move farther south, this time to Maui, where they fought again, on the slopes of Haleakala, the House of the Sun, and again she lost. Her body died and her bones were scattered, but her spirit form rose up and moved across the channel to the Big Island, the most southerly, the newest and wildest, where her fires still burn.

The wisdom of this story, sung through the centuries, is borne out by geologists who say the Pacific Ocean covers a vast piece of crustal plate with a hot spot at its center. A magma leak. They say each island was formed while passing over the hot spot, lingering as the plate drifts north and west, an inch or two a year, maybe three hundred inches since Captain Cook first sighted the Big Island in 1778 and dropped anchor off Kealakekua Bay, maybe three hundred yards of drift since the first double-hulled canoes sailed up from the Marquesas and touched shore at South Point, where sailors piled lava rocks to express their thanks and sanctify the place fifty generations ago.

The magma leaks upward, they say, into a chamber below the great caldera where Pele makes her home. It boils under there, restless, probing, pushing, looking for somewhere else to go. No one knows precisely where or when it will next burst forth to spill and send out fiery rivers rumbling toward the sea. But day and night they watch it. The geologists watch and wait.

A couple of hours after Travis leaves the Blue Dolphin, a fellow working late at the Volcano Observatory, in the high country outside Hilo, notes on one of the many monitor screens a rush of activity in the magma chamber, a sudden swelling, then a deflation. Farther downslope, a few miles out along the eastern ridge, where the lava gushed less than twenty-four hours ago, there is another atypical fluctuation in the subsurface tremor, bigger this time, big enough to move his hand toward the phone to call the observatory director out of a sound sleep. He also puts in a call to Civil Defense.

While he finishes up his paperwork he keeps an eye on the screen. Tomorrow could be lively, it could be fountaining again, with some real movement. This is his guess. Every month or so, for quite some time, new lava has come pushing through in the form of flaming geysers, or as a black-orange mass that will slide from the end of a covered tube and make a puddle in the hills, or ooze downslope a while to astonish sightseers along the shoreline road. You can never predict such things. You can only report them when they happen, then measure and chart them. The volcano is fickle. As soon as you say, "Yes, now we see it, now we have it figured, and this is the pattern," the pattern will change.

Meanwhile, in his heart of hearts, how does he regard it, this geologist working late? Is this a sign that the slumbering lava may soon be on the move? Or is the blood of earth preparing once again to spill itself across the land? Or is Pele opening her blazing eyes to look around the island over which she holds dominion?

Later on, Travis will be having a drink with him and will hear him say that he does not like to be out alone on the lava beds at night.

"I have had to do that a couple of times, taking readings, you know, something we were observing around the clock. But it was too uncomfortable. I don't mean the rocks. I can sleep almost anywhere. I mean, it is occupied territory out there. You always have the feeling somebody is right behind you, watching you. It's like being in a dark alley with the sense that someone is following you, even though you *know* you're alone and there's nobody around for miles. You talk to Hawaiians about this, they will tell you it is Pele. Or they will say it is the spirit of somebody who might have got buried in the flow. Down toward Ka'u you can still see the footprints of the warriors who got caught during an eruption two hundred years ago, buried in the cinder fall. A hard-nosed scientist would more likely attribute anything you think you feel to the electromagnetic field up there. I don't know. I wouldn't necessarily put a name on it."

He will lean toward Travis then, with a conspiratorial grin. They will be sitting by the picture window in the bar at the hotel called Volcano House, on the rim of Kilauea Caldera, looking out at twilight shadows across the crater. He will glance to make sure no colleagues are within earshot.

"I'll tell you what it's like up here. It's like the stock market. There are dozens of us. We're all experts. Put our degrees end to end they stretch halfway around the perimeter road. We study the volcano twenty-four hours a day, every day. We have this whole island wired to monitors and computer banks and seismographs. We have charts on everything you can measure, from the top of Mauna Loa to the bottom of the sea, records going back to the day this observatory opened. And it is still a mystery. We still never know what it's going to do next. This does not stop us from making predictions, you understand. We are always making predictions and forecasts, based on all the data we accumulate. But there is still more we don't know than we know. I can relate to that. It makes as much sense to me as worshiping the ups and downs of the Dow Jones Industrial averages."

Her Way of Seeing

Angel's house is set back from the street and raised off the ground, a frame house surrounded by a rug of thick green grass. A track of red lava gravel borders the grass, leading past the house. Along the back edge of the property young royal palms are spaced like oversized fence posts. Everything glistens in sudden light, as a ponderous gray overhang slides apart, turns blue. Bougainvillea climbing over a carport is more than purple. Its thousand blossoms each make a separate purple flame. The only sound is a metallic drip, the last of the rain in a downspout.

A tiny jingle cuts through the dripping quiet, and a moment later Angel, bearing a coffee cup, steps out of her darkroom and into the kitchen, moving toward the message machine. She almost lifts the receiver, then waits.

"Good morning, Ms. Sakai. Are you there?" Pause. "This is Ian Prince." Pause.

She sips and listens to him postpone the trip he mapped out yesterday, a half-day helicopter tour to get an overview of what he called "our options." He didn't tell her what the options are or what he needs the photos for. She guessed it is the interisland cable route. She didn't ask. She didn't like talking to him. His voice had the sound of a taker, a man who made her feel as if he'd already optioned a piece of *her*. She is much relieved to hear that the trip has been called off, though she wonders now if she was wrong about him. Today he sounds different, more charitable. She turns the volume knob, listening.

"Don't give up on me. I'll be getting back to you sometime soon."

What does she hear there? Apology? Regret? Clickety click. A hum. As she steps back into her cubicle, the little red light begins to wink.

Fifteen minutes later the Toyota pulls up in front and out steps Travis. He crosses the grass, lingers by the bougainvillea waiting for he knows not what, until he spies a note tacked outside her door. He climbs the stair and reads, *T. Take your shoes off and come on in.*

Breakfast smells are in the air, toast, coffee, some kind of fruit. Through a half-open door he can see a bedroom, the daughter's room, judging by the clutter of snapshots and posters and the unmade bed. The front room is both office and studio, with a businesslike desk in one corner, some light stands, and a backdrop screen. He sees a wedding party gathered around a pulpit, the men in tuxedos and ilima leis, the women in violet gowns and orchids, the bride and groom heaped with broad-leafed maile. There is a graduation portrait, and a baby in diapers on a white sheet. There are clouds of mist rising from a waterfall, and many rocks, empty fields of rippling lava, close-ups of fissures, and folds like drapery.

The largest prints are mounted blowups of family album photos. One of these catches and holds him, a white-haired man, backed by the unpainted wall of a wooden house, with lush foliage pushing in from the side. He still has vigor. Travis sees it in his skin, in the radiance of his look. He gazes at the camera with a light much different from the healthy gleam in the eyes of those who mainly feel good about themselves, and different from the bright and piercing light in the eyes of the smart, ambitious executives who appear in Carlo's office, different from the eyes of eager kids. There is a forest in this man's eyes, an older, darker glow. Has Travis met him somewhere? He knows these eyes. It is an odd and centering kind of recognition, soothing, and so complete he does not hear the bare feet slide across the floor. When she says, "Good morning, Travis," his body jerks with shock.   153

She wears a T-shirt, walking shorts, looking cool and trim. He can barely speak.

"Did you take this picture?"

"Not that one. It was just a family shot I printed up."

"Who is it?"

"My great-uncle David. One day you should meet him."

"I'd like to. He has your qualities."

He can smell the coffee on her breath, a light clean smell. They look at each other. Being next to her makes his skin feel raw, exposed and tender. Later, when they talk about this day she will tell him she felt the same. 'Bodies do a lot of talking,' she will say. 'I think sometimes skin can actually speak to skin.'

"C'mon back," she says. "I've done the negatives."

"You're fast."

"I did them last night, so they'd be dry."

In the deep blue light of her darkroom they stand side by side, while she sets up the enlarger and brings an image into focus. She runs four negatives this way, prints four eight-by-tens, and moves them through the solution trays. They watch gray shapes rise from the glossy paper, the shed, the burnt rubble and charred equipment underneath the peaked roof, the long panels of new metal, silver against the corrugated sheets of smudged and smoky older roofing, stained and rusted from the weather.

"Pretty good," she says.

"My Touchmatic did the work. I take no credit."

"Does anyone else have pictures like this?"

"Energy Source sent us a folder full. Everything *but* the roof, I just realized. You see up here? Underneath these new sections? The support post is split at the top, splintered. And look there, around the splinters. Doesn't it look scorched? See these black flashes? No fire starting from the ground could do that kind of damage, or *only* that kind of damage. If it burned from the ground, the post would be down. But it's not. You see what I mean?"

As they lean together, light from an overhead lamp bounces up to line her chin, her cheeks. It's a small room, not much more than a closet, and he is trying not to be aroused, trying to keep his attention on the images, though his mind flashes forward, dreaming dreams.

Things his eyes missed in flashbulb haste the negatives are revealing now. If he wants to wrap up this case today, tomorrow, he can. From what he sees, no human hand set the fire. It was what they used to call an act of God, "an act no one could foresee or prevent, an accident due to natural causes" (*Investigation Handbook*). He has enough right in front of him to write it up, enclose the graphics, be out of here and on the loose. If his luck holds, they can be out of here and on the loose together. This is his dream.

He sees a very probable sequence depicted on her counter, how the blaze began, at the top, and how it spread. Sometime after the lightning struck, a long chunk of burned-through roof beam fell across some copper tubing that fed into a propane tank. Flames from the beam no doubt ignited leaking fuel, which could account for the explosion first reported as the cause.

And yet if such a reading is correct, how does it fit with what Brockman told him last night? How does it fit with Prince's vision of a saboteur at work? In the packet of "new documents," which Travis looked at over papaya and sausage in the coffee shop, there is nothing new—Xerox copies of the home-typed letters, a grainy photo of a Dodge Dart, various clippings, a court docket setting the arraignment date. Only the tone has changed. It feels like an indictment now, not an insurance claim. Given the testimony of these glossy prints, can it be anything but bad melodrama? It is embarrassing to read through. Prince appears to be obsessed, and Travis doesn't want to know why. Not now. Not this morning. He could go back to the office, throw photos on a desk, and shout at Connie. He could drive out to the drilling site and ask Clemson to his face who tacked on the roofing and what exactly are they trying to conceal? He could call Brockman, call Carlo. There are a lot of moves he could make today. But as they stand in her darkroom with the risky juices of desire trickling upward toward his belly, warmth and craving in the belly, apprehension in the heart, he knows he can put everything on hold.

"Why did you ask me to print these, Travis?"

"Things you said at the Blue Dolphin, I guess."

"You knew you had shots like this?"

"While we were talking it occurred to me that maybe I got lucky."

"But while you were taking them—"

"It was almost dark. I was shooting fast."

"Amazing detail, considering the light."

She shivers and hugs herself, pulls her elbows close, gazing at the wet prints, at him, at the prints. What gives her a rush of chicken skin, as if a blast of arctic air has just blown through her humid little vault? She already knows or believes she knows how the shed caught fire. The folks down that way, they all know. Uncle David knows. It is street knowledge, back-road knowledge. So why does she shiver? It is the proof made visible. Spots of black and gray on glossy paper. Plus the unlikely fact that Travis Doyle took the pictures and somehow brought them into her life.

She is shivering with questions. After all these years of silence, why is he standing in the room where she spends so many hours alone? Why now? And how can he get shots like these when no one but employees have been allowed past the fence? Is he, after all, a hireling of Western Sun playing some covert game?

It is too strange. They both feel strange. Travis knows she needs to be reassured. He can see it in her eyes, which are wonder-filled and wary, waiting. He does something he has never done, a small thing, but it looms large, since it involves betraying Carlo's trust and the great pride Carlo takes in protecting the privacy of his clients. Call it Carlo's Code of Honor. "You look. You ask," he has told Travis more than once. "You don't pass judgment. And above all you keep it to yourself." But Carlo is twenty-four hundred miles away, and receding fast.

"Why don't you keep the negatives," he says, "make some prints for yourself if you want. Legally they belong to Twenty Twenty. But somehow they are mine and not mine. Out of my hands. I don't know how to say this. Pictures of what the lightning did, maybe they belong to someone else. Does that make any sense? You're in touch with the people here. Maybe you can help me work this out."

"Are you reading minds now, Travis?"

"Why? What are you thinking?"

She tells him about Prince's call, her second thoughts and third thoughts, the job she needed and dreaded and now has been excused from, and how she will soon be driving out to ask uncle David about his double message. The idea of taking these new pictures along just came to her. "Tutu sees a lot that other people miss," she says.

In her view all these things are joined—the change of plan, the timing of Travis's arrival, the story his photos tell. Travis would call it luck, or happy chance. She would call it luck plus something else. She would never call it chance, and for him this will take some getting used to. But if it means he can have part of a day alone with her, he's glad to move another step closer to her way of seeing. He will be friendly to all the nature signs, the earth, the wind, the sun, the moon, the planetary bodies. He will not ask her to play the message back or ask where Prince called from, whether Maui or Hilo or somewhere else. It doesn't matter.

The cubicle has kept them side by side, arm to arm, now face to face. Brightness rising from the paper makes him blind. The lens of his life has opened by five f-stops, five times as much light pouring toward him and through him. He forgets where he is and how he arrived here. None of this matters. I am not that close to anyone, she said. But it isn't true. She is close to him, much closer than last night. Her eyes have become like the old man's eyes. Something has changed her view of what is possible. Something has filled them with the same forest light.

They smell coffee burning. She pushes the door open, steps into her kitchen and toward the stove, where she turns a knob. She is skittish, off her track. She tips the pot and spills some coffee and wipes it clean. She turns on the radio, searching for eruption news, which is not necessarily bad news. On the Big Island many see it as good news. They don't flee the lava, they rush toward it with cameras and binoculars. Tour buses make unscheduled loops along Chain of Craters Road. They hear a talk show host say that yesterday's lake is boiling again, geysering, and a new river has spilled out, meandering south and west in the general direction of the shoreline. By afternoon it may be visible from the road, Angel says, and maybe he should drive down to take a look. He tells her he would need someone to show him the way. Twilight is the best time to go, she says, or a little before. As the day wanes, the orange stripes grow brighter. At dusk you are looking at the colors of creation itself.

In this way they begin to plan a trip, though it doesn't take much planning. She wants to show him her island. It's what they both want, the kind of thing they used to do, when they were children. Borrow a car, sneak away, go for a drive. The case can wait. Prince can wait. The photos can wait, and whatever else she may have to do in the darkroom. All that can wait while they build a little time capsule and go back, go back, go back.

Angel's Tale

Beyond Hilo they follow the coast road north through sloping fields of sugar cane, curving around the broad skirts of Mauna Kea, where upland clouds are heavy. Offshore they see squalls moving across the water, columns of downpour floating toward the cliffs. He isn't sure what to make of them. One moment you are looking at an ominous gray wall driven over the choppy sea. The next it is a sheet of moving color, as the cloud parts miles ahead, slanting sunlight into the squall, making a rainbow curtain speeding toward you on invisible pontoons.

They ride for an hour, telling stories as they go, both ragged, talking about everything at once, catching up, spilling it out, as if this hour is all they have. He tells her stories about Marge and Carlo. She tells him stories about Walter and Marilyn. He yearns to reach across and touch her arm, just for the touching, for the way a touch can close the circuit, but dares not risk it. That is the difference between then and now, certain things they dare not do. There are many forms of contact, he tells himself, and perhaps we can keep it just like this, fine companions whose bodies know their limits. He has never regarded a woman in this way. Driving north with Angel by his side he can begin to imagine it, can tell himself that the pleasure of her company is already a lot. Perhaps enough.

She's been wanting to visit her family homestead, her great-grandfather's farm. A perfect place to start, she says, and from there head south again. From a lush river valley to the treeless rocky plain. From the very old to the very new. Puna, the district where the steam gathers and where the lava soon will flow, takes its name from the word for "spring" or source. The valley she wants to show him is called Waipi'o "curving water," made of lava that poured north toward the sea a million years ago or so, to harden and then be carved away.

Where the pavement ends on a high bluff, there is a clearing for cars and an observation railing. The wind feels wet. He can taste the sea in it and the approach of rain. It isn't a cold wind but it cuts right into him, and he wishes he had a jacket. He didn't even bring one from San Francisco. Side by side they stand in the blowing wind, looking down six hundred feet toward the valley floor, where a stream curves through leafy bottomland and past the beach into a narrow, surf-rimmed bay. Across the valley a headland meets the sea, a furrowed wall reminding him of the monumental cliffs at Big Sur, blunt and final. Beyond it lie more remote valleys you cannot drive to, though you can reach them by boat or by horse.

Waipi'o is still known for the tsunami that sent thirty feet of water two miles inland back in 1946, burying fields, trees, houses, graveyards. He can see how that might happen, how the valley could become for one terrible hour a fjord, a narrow bay. The Big Island is the most easterly in the chain, and this beach faces due north. Behind it the valley is a long throat perfectly positioned to drink in whatever might roll down from the Gulf of Alaska. Travis can understand why farmers drive in each morning to work their taro fields and head back for higher ground each night, the old plantation towns along the coast road. When you're there you feel that at any moment the water might return.

They have day packs, hats, walking shoes. You can't take in a vehicle without four-wheel drive, Angel says. The trail is so steep and pot-holed, lightweight compacts have been known to flip. The wind falls off as they descend the plunging cliff. Rainy wetness gives way to muggy wetness rising from clumps of banana trees and untamed bougainvillea and the silvery taro ponds. Soon the wind is gone, and with it goes the windy rushing in their ears. As they near the lowlands, but before the small local sounds begin to reach them—the trilling of the birds, the stream's ripple—they pass through a thick and soundless space like the insulating space between two sets of weather doors. While the air gains weight, the cliffs rise high around them, closing off the world above.

As it levels out, the trail becomes a rutted road. The soil everywhere is damp but only muddy where the road meets running water. It is a jungle track lined with a long low wall of black stones. The whole valley is laced with these lichen-spotted walls, she says, and some are very very old. Here and there a farmhouse can be seen holding its own against the vines and rain-fed growth, with a mud-spattered pickup next to a coco palm. Other houses stand locked and silent, surrounded by chain-link fence.

They take their time. They have plenty now, just the two of them, and she tells him that her father's father came from Japan. Her father's mother was Japanese Hawaiian. Her parents met in Hilo, where they went to school and where they decided early they did not want to work the land. But her mother, born on the upper road, spent a lot of her childhood in this valley, which was the home valley of her grandfather, that is, the second husband of her grandmother,

Angel's great-grandmother, Malama, who had first married a Welshman and then a Hawaiian man.

"Don't ask me for details," she says. "Nobody can get it right. My mother was a little bit of everything. It's chop suey. It's United Nations. By the time it gets to me I'm Hawaiian in one leg and maybe a hip"—slicing fingers across her waist—"from here down."

Half a mile in, where a smaller gorge forks away to the left, they stop to admire a famous falls. Water pours through two notches in a silhouetted slope, making two white ribbons against the wall of shadowed, brushy stone. They stand for a long time, held by the surging strips of white and the far-off muffled roar. A creek runs through the gorge to join the river, which empties into Waipi'o Bay. When she begins talking again, her voice is like the creek sound, cool and gentle, accenting an eery stillness.

"My great-grandfather was born down here in the 1870s, they say. His father's house was covered with grass, in the old style. But he wanted a wooden house. He felled the trees and cut his own lumber. He was a taro farmer. That's really all he knew, that and fishing—they all fished—and music. He was a singer, they say, a chanter. He knew the old chants, the kind that told the story of the region. I mean, he was a Hawaiian man of the old school, working taro ponds laid out a long time back. It is a root, you know, like turnips or potatoes, and you pull the roots, and you make poi. And that was his life. Until 1946, when the ocean came in. By that time he was alone. Everyone else had moved to Hilo. He was seventy-five, they say. His wife had passed away. He didn't want to move, and he didn't want to live in town, and he didn't want to be anybody's burden. He had chickens and a couple of pigs and a little garden. Maybe somebody rode by to warn him a tidal wave might be coming. Or maybe not. Maybe he had heard ahead of time and didn't believe it. Or maybe he had no fear. His son, my grandfather, was a commercial fisherman who used to say anybody who has no fear of the ocean will soon drown. Maybe the old man had lost his fear, or maybe he just didn't care anymore. I have imagined him climbing the stairs to the second story and looking out and realizing he would have to get up on the roof, then discovering too late that even the roof would not be high enough. He had to be outside somewhere, don't you think? Because they never did find his body. They found some porch furniture scattered around, and the whole house soaked and ruined."

They have come to an opening in one of the rock walls. It may once have been bracketed by gates. On either side, stones lie where they fell, grown over with grass. Beyond the wall, the faint memory of wheel tracks can be seen in the contour of the deep green grass. He follows her toward a mango tree whose limbs reach nearly to the ground. It is not the season for mangoes, but other fruit grows wild. There are guava trees rising from the thicket. Angel picks one and offers it to him and picks another and breaks it open, sucking at it while they look around.

He sees patches of a rock-bordered path. Underneath the mango and in among the creeping vines, scraps of rotting lumber tell him a house once stood here, probably some outbuildings. It is an overgrown glade teeming with its own wild silence. There is the silence you feel in an empty crater at high altitude, which is the absence of sound. This is the other kind, the silence that tells you something has been added.

"You see that mango?" she says at last. "It is over a hundred years old. When the tsunami came it was at least sixty, and those who rode down the next day looking for the old man, they found things hanging in the highest branches of that tree, which was higher than the house, even then. They found a woman's red bandanna up there, and pieces of jellyfish, and big gobs of seaweed. Can you believe it? At the top of this mango they found seaweed."

He looks up toward the higher branches and can almost see it hanging there, strands of seaweed that no doubt served as her great-grandfather's shroud. His neck hairs prickle. He feels the old man standing in their midst and feels the sea gathering around them. The white cloud cover, which has remained above the valley, is now luminous, no longer gray. They have been fortunate. The darkest thunderheads still hang far beyond the beach, and it occurs to him that what hovers over them is not cloud but the white roll of surf as seen from a reef looking upward at the underside of a broken wave.

His throat is parched. He rips off his day pack and extracts two wine glasses and the bottle of white they have brought along, the same brand they used to drink, packed in a plastic bag of ice cubes, and opens it, and pours.

"Was he a drinking man?" Travis says.

"He liked home brew, from what I hear."

"He wouldn't mind then if we raise a glass."

"It's the feeling that counts. You must do it with respect."

"I have plenty of respect, Angel. I have seen something. I hope I can describe it to you . . ."

His voice catches, his chest feels thick. He closes his eyes and waits, as if thinking a small prayer for the ancients who walk there. When he opens his eyes she is smiling with approval. She reaches her glass toward his, and they sip. Or rather, she sips. He gulps. Then he unrolls a poncho-tarp underneath one of the mango's ample limbs. They have brought along all the things they used to eat, crackers and salami, dill pickles, cold teriyaki chicken, sushi. A papaya for dessert.

Her eyes grow moist with hunger and with anticipation and with nostalgia. In the pearl-gray air her eyes and her skin seem illuminated. He wonders if the wine has tinted his perception, that first full glass on an empty stomach, giving her an aura that isn't there.

Under Water

The food and wine bring the old times back, and he asks her if she ever thinks about the day they met.

"Sure I do."

"In your mind is it vivid? The way we stood on the launch, heading out to see the *Arizona*? That's how I've remembered you, with the lagoon behind, like backdrop."

"Pretty romantic, Travis."

"Maybe I'm a romantic guy."

"You had your shirt off."

"I don't remember that."

"I do. I wish I had a picture. You had your T-shirt off and tied around your neck, and you were flexing for my benefit."

"I don't think that's true. I never did stuff like that."

"The thing is, it worked. I fell for it. I fell for your build. I didn't care who you were, where you came from, what you were doing in Honolulu."

"Why didn't you tell me that?"

"You already knew it."

"A built but callow youth? Is that what you're saying?"

"You took after your father. I remember him too."

"Why do you mention my father?"

"He was right next to you. And crying. Don't you remember that?"

"I remember your uncle was there, your uncle from Japan."

"They were all out there reliving the war, weren't they?"

"Yes, they were," and again his voice catches, as a picture stops his breath. Like a fuzzy slide it snaps into focus, and he sees his unremembered dream, sees it awake for the first time. He is on the bottom looking up, watching water move and the billowy curls of white dissolving. He sees himself flagellating like a strand of seaweed planted in the reef, as he holds on and considers never coming up. If the old man surrendered to water, if he stood on top of his house in this teeming glade and let the rolling water take him, that is no mystery to Travis. He knows that moment all too well. In green light he floats, waiting until the next wave breaks, and suddenly, quietly, as he stretches out next to Angel under the mango tree gazing up at the surf-colored clouds above Waipi'o Valley, he sees at last the face that has hovered in these dreams, wavering and blurred.

As if he has always known who it will be, he sees his father's face, and he finally sees where he has been standing all these years, looking up through blue-green water from the bottom of Pearl Harbor, with his father gazing down as if their tour launch was a glass-bottomed boat and Monty's face is somehow pressed against the glass watching Travis sway alone, yet not alone. They are all down there with him, the young men who settled to the bottom with the sinking of the ships, a sea-floor world of men in uniforms, eternally young and silent. He feels the tears his father wept back in 1968. He feels that he understands his father's life. But he does not know what to do with this feeling. Where has it come from? And why now? It swarms in his chest. His eyes are brimming. Her hand touches his. She has been watching his eyes.

167

Her mind too is wheeling back. "You know," she says, "I was so innocent then. Before my uncle went home to Japan he begged us all for forgiveness for what had happened during World War II. He begged my father, who was his nephew, and he begged my mother, and even me, though I didn't see how I had anything to forgive. It was years before it came clear to me why he had to do that."

"Forgiveness," Travis says, speaking a word he has never spoken. He has read it, and heard it, but hasn't said it out loud until this moment. The syllables burn inside his skull. As if released by the sound, his tears spring forth. Before he knows what hits him, he is sobbing.

"What's the matter?" Angel says.

"Nothing."

"Were you thinking about your father?"

"Yes."

"Has something happened to him."

"I'm all right."

"Tell me."

"He died last year."

This news fills her face with pain.

"I guess I should have told you sooner."

She looks away, and they sit there until his tears subside.

"It was an accident. No reason for it to happen. Highway 101. Some slob in a pickup came over the double line and hit him head on."

"I'm so sorry, Travis."

"He was always a good driver And he knew that road. He'd been driving it all his life. The other guy must have fallen asleep. He must have just loomed up out of nowhere . . ."

"Don't talk about it now, if you don't want to."

"I don't mind. I want to," he says, though he doesn't know what he means by this. What does he want to say?

He says, "You knew him."

"I remember him. I couldn't say I knew him. Not really."

"But you saw them there. You saw them all together. There's nobody I can talk to about this."

"Were you close? Had you been in close touch?"

"I wanted to be. I mean, I had been wanting to straighten out some things. I just waited too long."

"What kinds of things? What did you want to tell him?"

"While you were talking, I realized I have wanted . . ."

"Realized?"

"I have wanted for a long time to ask him to forgive me."

"For what?"

He has to think, to get it right. When the words come, they surprise him. His voice breaks.

"For blaming him."

Again she looks away and waits, and Travis see the launch again, sees himself the day they met and this time sees his brother, and the broad shoulders covered by his father's arm. They happened to be lined up that way—Montrose, Grover, Travis—watching circles of red and white carnations float above the turrets, when Monty threw an arm around his nearest son and pulled him close. Travis sees the hand clutching, bunching up the cloth of his brother's aloha shirt. By that summer the war was in full swing. Fellows Grover's age were draftable and leaving by the thousands every month. Maybe Montrose saw himself in uniform again and saw Grover as the son who might have to be the first to go. He had two arms, of course. Travis could have moved around to the farther side. Surely Montrose would have drawn him in. Why didn't Travis do it? Why didn't he move? Some teenage stubbornness, not wanting to concede. As Travis saw it then, his father was doing exactly what he always did, choosing the son who favored him. And whatever meaning the harbor had, Travis was suddenly outside it, outside the boundaries of that compulsive hug. He turned away from the famous memorial they had come to honor, and there was Angel, looking right into his face, as if waiting to be seen. Now she waits again, in the thick Waipi'o Valley air, her eyes averted, while Travis sees at last that something in himself let Montrose make that choice, allowed the father to choose the older brother once again.

The knowledge overwhelms him. He swallows hard and sucks in air. After a while he says, "What's going on, Angel? Something is going on."

"We're still good friends, that's what's going on. I've always felt that way about you, always knew that whenever we met again we would still be friends and could talk about anything. So whatever you do is okay. If you want to cry, I mean. Crying is okay."

"When I'm with you I feel things I didn't know I could feel. Whole pictures come into my head I never saw before."

"It's the same with me."

"What's happening?"

"You let me be a way I like to be," she says. "Not everyone does that. I'm not this way with everyone."

"What way?"

"The way I am with you."

"There's a little world we make when we're together," he says.

"Yes."

"So crying is okay."

"Yes. Laughing too."

"Or not saying anything about what made you cry."

"Yes," she says, "not talking is okay."

"Or sending silent messages."

"It's all okay."

They are silent for a long time. She gazes down at him with such penetration he cannot move. He feels naked, transparent, as if she already knows his history, all he has told her, and all he has yet to tell. The way her gaze lingers, he thinks she is about to mention his eye, and he wouldn't mind. That's how much he trusts her just now. He lost some sight there, nothing anyone would notice unless they knew him from an earlier time, as Angel does, having seen every part of him at close range, as he has seen every part of her. He imagines what he will say. A piece of shrapnel, he will say, hardly a sliver, from a grenade I actually watched coming toward me. I saw it coming and I dove, but in the wrong direction. I dove right toward it. Or maybe it was not the wrong direction. Maybe I meant to, and maybe we do everything that way, maybe you never dive in the wrong direction. You just dive.

171

He doesn't have to say any of this because she does not speak, looking at him in the same way he looks at her, observing things he will not necessarily mention. Not now. Under her right eyebrow a long thin scar. Around the perfect black ring of each pupil, the brown and glossy irises notched or seamed with threadlike fissures.

The touch of her fingertip against his cheekbone sends a current through him. She is pushing aside some wetness that has collected there, whether sweat or moisture spreading from his eyes he is not sure. Her fingers slide down his cheeks, draw a slow damp line along his jaw. He reaches up and guides them toward his mouth, kisses them, takes them in his teeth, feels her ease against him. He pulls her close, and their lips meet, tentative brushing. Of all his life's kisses, this is the most delicious, the first few moments of kissing Angel again, under the mango tree. If he once vowed not to touch her, that was in another lifetime. Their mouths open, tongues meet. From tongue to belly to hips and legs, their bodies remember the perfect fit. There is no resistance anywhere. They are lost inside the kissing. A few more seconds and they would be undressed, did they not now hear the stutter of an engine slowing down as if to cross the river.

She lifts her head.

"Sightseers," he says.

The vehicle makes a turn and seems suddenly upon them, its gears grinding. Four-wheel drive. The brakes squeal.

"They're stopping," she says.

He is kissing her throat, tongue along her luscious collarbone.

"They can hear us," she says.

"They're gone," he says, "they're already moving up the road."

In low, the whining gears recede, and soon there is no sound but a humming stillness. She relaxes against him, yielding her neck, with an upraised rolling of the chin, like a cat asking to be stroked. He is under her, seeing leaf-filled limbs above, and muted pearly light through the leaves. He unbuttons her shirt, his lips moving past buttonholes, one by one, taking his time, nothing but time now, as he savors each portion of flesh revealed. He feels her fingers against his scalp where no one but the lover and the barber ever touch you. Her hands slide into his hair. She pulls his head back and again presses her lips to his, a long full bold kiss. Her shirt peels away and falls behind her, then his shirt falls, and he chooses not to hear the voices coming toward them from the road. Their arms and chests are sliding with moisture, slick and slippery, their lips roaming everywhere, when the voices grow more distinct, a man and woman perhaps, though he cannot make out the words, just the flow of random conversation, moving closer.

Again Angel raises her head. Groping for her shirt, she rolls away from him and listens. Are they just outside the low stone wall?

"I can't believe anybody would stop right there."

"Goddam. Son of a bitch," he says.

Screened by limbs and foliage they lie on their bellies and listen to the shuffle of feet moving from the road with slow deliberate steps, pushing through the heavy grass. Other sounds recede, it seems, to amplify the whish and scratch of these footsteps. They move into the clearing, pause, then move away again.

After a while Angel sits up, slick, gleaming, gorgeous, her blouse open, hanging loose. From the silvery light of their little grove they look out into the empty clearing. They look at each other, listening to the insect buzz and far-off stream gurgle that closes in around the disappearing sound. Between their curiosity and their passion, a curtain falls. In the blood their unspent desire still runs. It gathers around them, desire on hold, held in check by . . . by what? By random hikers? By beach fishermen looking for access? By ancestors? Hers? His? Old underwater patriarchs? Or were these sounds that they had both imagined?

He wants to touch her breasts again, devour them. He knows she desires him in that same way, yet they cannot reach through this curtain. He thinks of those farmers who work their taro and at night climb out of the valley again. Are there other fears besides the fear of tidal waves? Waipi'o is said to be a ghostly place. Maybe the great-grandfather is in their midst today. Later Travis will learn that this is exactly how she reads what they are feeling—his spirit, somewhere among the voices floating around her family meadow. This has spooked her. It spooks them both.

"What's the matter, Travis?"

"I feel creepy."

"So do I."

"It's crowded, isn't it."

"And hot. I'd forgotten how hot it gets."

"Let's move farther in. Maybe we can find a cooler spot, away from the road."

She shakes her head. "It'll be hotter farther in, and we'll have mosquitoes too."

A line of large red ants has made it halfway across the tarp. As she speaks, one bites into his ankle. "Christ!" he shouts, slapping it away.

"I forgot about the bugs. They're everywhere out here."

"Then let's go back to town. What about your place?"

"Marilyn's around all afternoon."

"The Orchid Isle. I have a room, a great room with an ocean view."

She turns and gives him a sideways look. She likes the idea. It appeals to her sense of history. The first time they went looking for a place, in the middle of the day in that long-ago summer, after swimming offshore at Waikiki, touching and squeezing, they crept into one of the beach hotels and found an empty room.

He waits. But again she shakes her head. "People know me there. The woman at the desk, she knows my family. It wouldn't look right."

He reaches out, reaches through the curtain to touch her hair, the side of her neck. It wouldn't take much to ease down onto the ground again. He imagines doing it in the dirt with the ants and the stickers.

She stands up, steps back, buttoning her blouse, and murmurs, "We'll have another time, Travis."

This isn't coy. Her eyes are compassionate. Her smile is tender. He tries to match her smile, as if he too can let this opportunity pass. But he is thinking, Hey, the time is now, the time is perfect, the *place* is wrong. Once they are back on the road he will surely come up with something. Maybe he can sneak her into the Orchid Isle by the side door, if they have one, or the back door, just like old times.

They fold the tarp, repack the pack. They are halfway to the trailhead when a taro farmer gives them a ride on the bed of his half-ton truck. At the top Travis sees his Toyota parked, and remembers then what is locked in the trunk, zipped inside his zipper bag of documents and notes, above the metal well where the jack and the spare tire rest.

"Angel, how far is it to the leeward side?"

"From here, about an hour."

"Let's drive over there and check into something fancy."

She laughs. "Don't be crazy."

"I'm serious. I think I can get us a room."

"They cost so much. They're all so overpriced."

"I'm talking free."

She is interested again, intrigued, suspicious. Radar eyes drill into him.

"Which hotel?"

"The Manu Kona."

Her eyebrows lift.

"Have you been there?" he says.

"It just opened. Everybody's talking about it."

"Let's try it then. What the hell."

"I thought you didn't work for anyone."

"I don't. It's a little bonus that came along. A gift."

"A gift."

"These things come to you. A great gift you and I both deserve."

She is looking past him, weighing things, this against that. Nothing happens by coincidence, but you still have to weigh the gifts of life against the practicalities. She has not changed. Her look is one he remembers from the day they stood in neck-deep water. Across the flush in her young face there had moved a shadow of worry, as if a small cloud had covered the tropic sun. It was the shadow of duty, of family obligation, some errand she promised to run, or lesson she had to attend. She was not worried about getting caught inside. This did not occur to her. When the shadow passed, something reckless came into her eyes, and they were wading toward the beach to spend a wanton hour on the fourth floor of the Waikiki Surfside. They escaped without detection. When you are that age and running on hormones you don't think of all the ways your scheme can backfire. Thoughtlessness can be your downfall. It can also put you in a state of grace. In his memory it was a golden day, shimmering. He wants it again. So does Angel. The same look comes into her eyes, that reckless flash, as the worry shadow passes. He used to wait for this, her mischief look. It meant he could talk her into things. Another difference between then and now. All the same. All different. Talking her into things is now beside the point. A mere formality. She knows her mind, and his mind too. They both want that dream time back, when love was lust and no one had yet been wounded. They know better. They both know such times are gone forever. But when has knowing better stopped you from wanting something you cannot have, or that no longer exists, may never have existed at all except in the shining glow of memory?

"I have to pee," she says.

"Yes, good. I'll make a call."

Perfect timing. He doesn't want her to overhear the details. Is this deceitful? A form of lying? It doesn't seem so. It seems expedient.

They have a vacancy and, yes, a credit card will hold the room. His loins are heating up again, as his coupon swells to the width of a king-size bed. If there are strings attached, Travis doesn't feel them. What does he owe Ian Prince? His greater concern is that the gift is phony. But even then, so what? I'll just put it all on a card. Charge now, worry later. That's what credit cards are for. What the hell. Life is short, and she is willing, and now she is walking toward him across the slope of mowed grass with that delicious walk, the light swing of hips and shoulders loosened by the air she grew up in. She too has calls to make, one to neighbor Brenda, and one to her message phone telling Marilyn what to fix for dinner. As she nears the booth the wind lifts her dark hair and presses her shirt against her belly. The slope ends at a drop-off cliff, making her background the blunt green headland across the valley, with other headlands ranked beyond, each sheer face fringed at the bottom with silent surf. In her hair, in the laden sky, in the row of cliffs, in the broad sweep of moving water there is an element of wildness that catches him by the throat. He wants to meet her in the grass and twirl with her, and also stand forever to witness her stride across that terrain. He watches as long as he can bear it, then rushes forward and takes her in his arms in a great clumsy dance through the grass and wind and blowing mist.

A Burning River

At that end of the island you can travel from the windward to the leeward side in less than an hour. They open another bottle of good wine for the trip. She tells him how chancy this is, each time they sip, how many ways the local cops and courts can make their lives miserable. He tells her Chance is his middle name, keeps sipping. It's another link to the dream time, when they would circle O'ahu in his father's rented car, holding unmarked paper bags and scanning for patrol cars. They are nervous too, like teenagers drinking nervously, waiting for the miles to pass.

Between the mountain ranges there is nothing on the radio, so he starts singing "When I'm Sixty Four," a big song the year they met. Angel chimes in for a while, as they move around from song to song in this opera from their gypsy days, *Sergeant Pepper's Lonely Hearts Club Band*, laughing and drinking and shouting, "What would you think if I sang out of tune, would you stand up and walk out on me?" Travis could do the whole score, he has it all in his head, but her alto finally trails off.

"How do you know so many songs?" she says.

"I don't know that many."

"I've never met anyone who knows so many songs."

"I just sang every song I know."

"Good. I don't really feel like singing."

"What do you feel like?"

"Talk to me, Travis."

"I'm talking."

"Tell me what is on your mind."

"You. You alone. You are on my mind."

She is sitting close. Her hand moves across his shoulders, finger playing with his ear. "Maybe I already know that. Tell me something I don't already know."

"I was in Honolulu for a couple of weeks on my way back from overseas. Did I tell you that?"

"No, you didn't."

"I was on my way home for discharge. I almost called you. I kept thinking I should."

"What year was this?"

"'73."

"It's a good thing."

"I think so. I was out of my mind."

"For most of '73 I was pregnant, Travis. I was sick every day. I was fat."

"I can't imagine you ever being fat."

"It would have been terrible."

"Timing is everything, I guess."

"Just about everything, yes. Yes, indeed."

He does not want to tell her what else he has begun to think about and see. He only wants to see Angel and the road that takes them where they both want to go. He keeps his eyes on the road, while in his mind he sees another woman, another picture in this slide show triggered by Angel or by whatever she is doing to him, a woman whose eyes also smoldered with anticipation, a woman from another time, which was the worst time of his life, the year he got wounded and the year he came back home. It is a hard memory, cluttered with echoes and eerie repetitions. His veins feel cold and empty.

This woman's hair was also dark, and they made love the first time in a Waikiki hotel, and she too carried a camera, taking photographs of everything. It was back in the days when people officially changed their names, Betty to Moonstream, Ruth to Rainbow, Ralph to Ram. She went by Crystal. Her passport said Lorraine. The camera was her calling, Crystal said, though her photographs were never very good. She was a dabbler, a snapshot junkie. She dabbled in many things. Including men. She collected men. She collected Travis. He collected her. They brought out the worst in each other, and why does he have to be thinking of her now?

He says, "Sometimes I think you know it all before I say it."

"I just want to talk."

"I am talking."

"Don't overtestimate me—"

"Listen to me talk—"

"Or put me on a pedestal—"

"I am talking like a lovesick fool—"

"Or start thinking I'm someone I'm not."

"You don't want me to idolize and adore you?"

"I'm just a woman—"

"I object to that!"

"Someone you used to know."

"I don't agree with that at all! In the whole long, star-studded history of the world, there has never been another woman like you!"

"You're shouting, Travis."

"I have things to shout about!"

"Can you shout and drive at the same time?"

"I thought you said shouting was okay. Didn't you say that?"

"Of course I did. And not-shouting too."

"Then singing old songs is okay."

"Yes. And drinking in the car," she says, as she takes a pull from the bag.

"And spilling it down your chin."

"Yes, that's okay," she says, dragging a wrist across the dribble.

"And spilling your guts, if you have to."

"Or just talking to talk."

"And grabbing your hand for no reason," he says.

"Or your leg."

"Not now."

"And kissing your neck."

"Not now," he says, as the car swings wide.

They rave on like this, sipping and squeezing, trying to keep their hands off each other so he can drive. Past the ranch-country town of Waimea they head down the leeward slope, as the Kona coast comes into view, sprawling south, dry, and hazy from the dryness. The Big Island is sometimes likened to a continent, a mini-North America, with every kind of climate zone, empty deserts, pasture land for cattle, rain forest, frozen peaks, tanning beaches, crop lands with rusty plantation towns. As the slope bottoms out and they swing onto the coastal highway, it is like reentering southern California after a week in the high Sierras. There is traffic again. Not merely cars on the road, but traffic. American traffic. Travis feels pulled two ways. He hates the sight and sound of it, yet he is energized. He feels the addict's rush. In afternoon light it is Malibu traffic, airport traffic, hotel-bound and beachtime traffic, and they are snug and cruising in their rented Toyota with the radio picking up a local station, two more pleasure seekers following the asphalt strip laid across old lava.

Where an access road turns west toward the beach, black stones have been mortared into a setting for a small molded sign saying MANU KONA. They tail a stretch limo down a corridor of smooth-trunked royal palms interspersed with wooden replicas of Hawaiian temple gods. Kukaʻilimoku, the scowling god of war, stands with his knees bent, his fists clenched, his distended lips drawn back. As they near the crescent turnaround where arriving guests pull in, the carvings give way to marble and alabaster statuary, Greek gods, a Venus de Milo, a sphinx, the head of Nefertiti atop a Doric column. The entry is modeled after an Egyptian pyramid, with sides cut away to admit vehicles. In the shade of this pointed canopy, giant hapu ferns arc above the taxicabs. The limo glides in close to a carpeted walkway where a dark doorman presides, dressed in white jacket with braided epaulets, white slacks with gold striping, white shoes, white skipper's cap.

Travis pulls past the shuttle unloading bags and a vanful of new travelers who have just landed at the leeward airstrip. In the ten-minute zone he tries to sit very still. They've both had quite a bit to drink and until this moment have been in a fever to get to the room.

At last she says, "What are we doing?"

"I can't walk into the lobby with a hard-on."

"Well, I'm not going in there alone."

"I'm not suggesting that."

"I'm not going in there at all. Look at the way those people are dressed."

"Just help me think of something that will make it go down."

"How about that sphinx back there."

"It's weird, isn't it."

"It's depressing, Travis. A sphinx in Kona."

"That's good. Thank you. I'll think about the sphinx."

"And think about the bags."

"What bags?"

"How can we check into a place like this without bags?"

"We don't need bags."

"Maybe this isn't such a good idea." she says.

"What isn't?"

"Coming over here."

"Listen. Here's what happened. The airline lost our bags. Remember? They're coming in tomorrow, from Honolulu, on another plane, or we will goddamn well know the reason why."

Before she can speak again he gets out and opens the trunk and grabs his attaché case, using it for a groin shield as he walks past the towering, white-clad doorman and into the lobby.

It is breezy, with more ferns and palms and high-spouting tropical plants, orange birds-of-paradise, and pink bougainvillea hanging from somewhere high above. An inner garden is open to the sky, surrounding a Persian reflecting pool, long and oval and brilliantly blue. Just as he enters, the pool seems to explode. Twin fountains send misty trees of jet-powered water rising fifteen or twenty feet. A splashing clatter fills the air.

The registration desk, a long slab of white marble, looks out upon this pool. An arcade curves away to the left, rows of shops where golden bracelets from Singapore gleam under muted fluorescent lamps, next to eelskin wallets from Korea, and lace blouses from Manila, Malaysian pewter candlesticks, scarves of Japanese silk, fiji clamshells the size of a tub. A blonde and blue-eyed woman looks up with a familiar smile, a California beach girl smile, open and instant and sparkling and tan. He guesses she is over here for a year or two, wind-surfing after work.

"Welcome to the Big Island. How can I help you?"

He shows her his coupon.

"These aren't easy to come by," she says.

"Does that make me a VIP?"

She doesn't reply. As she punches in an entry, he watches her face assume the look of the screen watcher, a low-lidded, official and officious look. As her eyes follow the data, they become little terminals where printouts for the past and future begin to roll. His life's dossier has been called up and this unknown woman knows all his failings.

Still watching the screen, she says, "The management will be very pleased to know you're here, Mr. Doyle."

He doesn't like the sound of this. He doesn't need any attention from the management.

"No need to make a big thing out of it. Some peace and quiet, that's all we're hoping for."

Looking up at last, she says, "Oh, we can promise you that."

Her eyes, as blue as the Persian tile beyond her desk, direct his attention to a loading dock at the pool's far edge. A channel leads from there past shop windows and out into a system of causeways and lagoons. Guests who have already registered are stepping onto a long barge, to be carried to their rooms. The steersman's outfit is somehow both Polynesian and Venetian. He wears a sarong and waist sash, a bicep bracelet, a floppy cap of red velour. From one angle his craft looks like a gondola, from another an outrigger canoe. He stands at the stern with his hand on a wooden tiller, but the barge is motorized, held by unseen rubber wheels to an underwater track. He shifts a lever in the control box behind him and eases out into the channel.

When Travis tells her he has a car to park, she hands him a map and two coded plastic key cards. The place covers two hundred acres. Their room is in another building. "Feel free to use the barge at any time," she says.

There are six buildings, arranged along the shoreline, each four stories high, each with its own design motif—

Japanese, Thai, Tahitian—connected by looping waterways lined with palms and young banyans and leafy plants and more statuary from Asia and Africa and the Middle East. In a mini-jungle they see kangaroos and flamingoes and black and white zebras grazing. There are brush-tailed wallabies farther in, and ostriches preening under shade trees. The map calls this the Garden of Eden. One corner of the garden is a small mountain of molded concrete, where water cas- cades into a lagoon that feeds the causeway. They are crossing a bridge modeled after the Bridge of Sighs in Venice just as the gondola passes below them.

Angel says, "Stop the car."

She has her camera out for this. Travis leans on the horn and waves. When the floating guests wave back, she snaps a couple of shots. Someone calls, "Aloha."

"Can you believe that gondola?" she says.

"Is it gaudy?"

"It's beyond gaudy."

"But you're glad you're here," he says, "you love it."

"Do they have room service?"

"They always have room service."

"Who wouldn't love it?"

They are on the fourth floor of the Bali Tower, above a golf course bordered by a black field of mounded lava. There is a king-size bed with a fresh baby orchid on the cover, wall to wall plush carpet, climate control, a twenty-four-inch TV monitor with X-rated options, a pay-as-you-go refrigerated beverage cabinet, elegant bamboo furniture, and on the bamboo coffee table a small bowl of chocolate-covered strawberries along with a note of welcome from Doreen the housekeeper.

"They must like you at the office," Angel says.

Maybe this is a double-edged remark. He doesn't want to go into it just now. Neither does she. The excess and the opulence has worked on them as another kind of foreplay. It stirs the blood, rekindles the body heat, the call of the bodies, and the call of the enormous bed. He is reaching for her buttons, her waist, her skin.

"Let's try these first," she says.

She points the largest strawberry toward has mouth. He takes it in and feeds her one, and they look at each other, with the chocolate and the juice running over their lips. It is a theatrical move, one you would see in a film. Something about the strawberries and the room says, Be theatrical. They are standing next to a makeup counter, a marble ledge where a wide mirror is lined on four sides with large clear bulbs, giving it the look of an actor's dressing room. Her back is to the mirror when their juicy lips touch, explore lightly, then open in an urgent joining of tongues and berry sweetness.

As their clothes fall, he cannot help watching her shoulders in this dressing room mirror, her black hair hanging long against the skin. It is the wrong thing for him to be looking at, and he turns their bodies, but too late. It has taken him back again to the time he doesn't want to think about, the place he doesn't want to be. It takes him back to Honolulu and the first night he went to bed with the woman who called herself Crystal, in another hotel room with another mirror on the wall. She was a lady who liked to perform in front of mirrors. It comes clear to him now. In an instant he sees what it was about his sex partner and flesh mate for two manic months back in 1973. She was a performer, always onstage. She had to have the lights on and mirrors handy, and in her nightly show, was he simply a stand-in? A walk-on? No. In order to possess her body, he became like her. He too was a performer, both actor and audience, always watching their bodies as if foldouts had come to life.

He is saying, "Angel, Angel, Angel, I love you, I have always loved you."

But as they fall back onto the satiny bed, as her slender arms encircle him, he is thinking of Crystal, not because he wants to, not because he longs for her or loves her still. There was no love between them. He did not even like her much, and she did not like him. So why does she come to mind right now, in the midst of this otherwise perfect moment in the ultimate hotel room and cause him to soften? Why now? Why now? he asks, in an agony of self-loathing.

"What's happening?" Angel says.

"Just want to see if you're paying attention."

"Are you afraid?"

"I guess so."

"You didn't used to be."

"That was a long time ago."

"It's okay, Travis."

"Okay to be afraid?"

"Yes. Everything's okay."

She is kissing him. Her hand reaches down.

"I'm afraid too," she says.

"Of what?"

"I can't tell you that."

"Why not?"

"You'd know too much. You'd know everything about me."

"I want to know everything about you."

He raises his head and looks into her eyes, and he sees Crystal for the first time, along with every other woman he has known. He sees Rachel. He sees Francine. He sees the woman in the bar on Geary Street. He sees Marge. He understands what he failed to see during the five years they were together. As bodies go, Marge is more voluptuous than any of them. In sheer distribution of body parts few he has seen compare with her, in the flesh or in the magazines. Angel is not endowed that way. Yet she is more desirable. The first night he spent with Marge her eyes were bright with lust, a brightness he has seen many times. But they have never shone with the light he's seeing now. There are two flames that have to burn as one, the flame of the loins and the flame of the spirit. Before he saw this double light

in Angel's eyes he had no idea what could have been missing. All the different pairs of them—Crystal and Travis, Rachel and Travis, Marge and Travis—they were blind together. They were blocked, and stuck. With Angel something else is going on, something else has been released. In her. In him. In them. As they pause face to face, eye to eye, it fills him and carries him past excitement and desire. Her hands have revived him. When he enters her they both cry out, the groaning cries of unspeakable ecstasy. He wants it to last, but she is rolling under him, rolling her head, her tears are falling, she is calling his name. He can't see her. The world turns white. His body is a candle, a column of flame, a burning river of pure white light comes flooding through him, a burning river of purest white.

After Dark

They lie there for a while talking and touching, then doze off. He dreams he has entered a room where a woman watches him approach. She is someone he knows. If they have ever been intimate, something between them has gone wrong, pushed them apart. His entrance, his return, draws her toward him. Their bodies generate magnetic heat. He puts his arms around her. They stand pressed into a corner, in a long kiss that connects him to everything. He feels whole. In the dream he is not aware of it. Only when he wakes and a nameless foreboding grips him, in the instant after waking, does he recognize the pure thrill of eagerly kissing someone you are wild about and how this requires nothing else.

The phone rings, or has been ringing. His understanding of the dream falls between the first and second ring, a soft ripple of a ring coming from a white phone of the same marbled whiteness as the bedside stand. The sky outside is dark. The glass doors are open. Gauzy undercurtains billow back into the room. He doesn't know what time it is, doesn't care. Without moving head or body, he reaches and lifts the receiver, feeling invincible, in command of every feature of his world.

"Four oh six."

"Doyle, listen. This is John Brockman."

He places the receiver in its cradle and stares at the ceiling. He glances at Angel, who sleeps soundly, her honey shoulders smooth in the half light, her presence miraculous. The shock of the voice makes this suddenly clear. The voice alerts him, opens his eyes. She is the miracle he has long been searching for, and this moment is a miracle too, next to her, awake while she sleeps, with the luxury to gaze and

listen to her breathe. He does not want to talk to Brockman or think about how anyone can know where they are or ask who might have triggered this call. None of that. Only savor her. Look and savor. Life is short. A flick. A flutter. A click of the shutter.

Travis once met a poet who told him he did not write the words. Something spoke through him, the poet said, or poured through him from somewhere else. "I am just an instrument," he said. Later Travis met a medium who told him the same thing. She didn't speak the words, someone else spoke through her, and she too was just an instrument, a channel for all those voices living outside her, the invisible chorus. Later still he heard a fellow on the FM station out of Berkeley, a traveling lecturer with a vaguely British accent, say that we are not our thoughts. We inhabit a universe of thought, this fellow said, and they move through our brains, rather than originating there. As Travis listened, the thought moving through his brain went like this: It must be something on the order of light. Our eyes do not create light. Our eyes record light, so that the world I make contact with is visible to me. The world enters me along with the light.

On this first night of their reunion he begins to think of Angel as a form of light that has entered his life, making of his entire body and mind an eye, leaving pictures, releasing in him another way of knowing. Next to her, he has never felt more alive, more complete. This right here, he is thinking, this is it. Eternity. This must be the way eternity feels, this is surely how it looks. Two creatures side by side in the dark pool of endless night, lit from within. Don't be distracted, be here in bed, on the white sheets, with honey-shouldered Angel till the end of time . . .

When the phone rings again he lets it warble, a gentle sound, like seawater gurgling through the wires, receding, gurgling again. At the seventh gurgle Angel moves.

"Is that the phone?"

"I think so."

"Aren't you going to answer it?"

"I don't really want to."

After five more warbles she is awake. "Well, take it off the hook then."

He doesn't move. She is on her elbow, leaning across him. "My God, Travis. How can you stand it?"

"All right. All right."

He lifts the receiver and holds it to his ear and looks again at the ceiling.

"Hello?"

"Doyle, don't hang up until you hear what I have to say. Something has happened to our boy. I figured you should know."

"What are you talking about?"

"Just listen. A cop found his car this morning with the windows bashed in and the inside trashed. At first they figured somebody stole it and drove out there for the hell of it and dumped it, since certain locals consider any rental fair game."

"Dumped it where?"

"But Prince himself still has not reported it, and nobody knows where he is, and the next thing I know, a cop is standing in my yard asking me where I was last night. Though I didn't say so at the time, my gut feeling is we won't be seeing Mr. Ian Prince again. You get in too close to these backcountry guys with their crops to protect and pretty soon, well, you're just in too close."

"Who is it, Travis?"

"Room service."

"Yes, you got it right," Brockman says into his ear, the voice close, insistent, as if he is hunkering next to the bed, "coming straight into the room because you too are on the talk-to list. You had breakfast with him, right? I am in a position to help you, Doyle. We can help each other. I called your hotel and left a message. I called twice, then I called his number and told his secretary I was a clerk at the Orchid Isle with urgent messages. She told me this is a place you could possibly be. Forgive me if I'm interrupting anything, but we can save each other a lot of hassle just by telling the cops we were together last night. I was with you. You were with me. That's why I'm calling. They think I would stop at nothing to stir up shit for Western Sun. What they don't know is how that company is its own worst enemy."

"I'm going to hang up now. I appreciate the call—"

"You never got back to me about the meeting, Doyle. But it probably doesn't make any difference. Before long we'll all be out of the way. They don't want people like you and me hanging around this island. They want tourists who spend money and don't ask questions you're not supposed to ask. But I am not going anywhere until I make a statement. You cannot fight them with aloha. You have to fight fire with fire. I mean, literally. This afternoon I saw something. I want you to see it too. In fact, I am going to set this up. It changed my whole perspective. My friend Holiday took me up in his chopper, out over the flow, where you could see everything. You could see how it's creeping along about as wide as Wilshire Boulevard, and you know what's waiting out there in the distance, man? The derrick. The rig. Not right in the path, you understand. Not yet. The flow would miss it by a quarter of a mile. It is still a couple of days away, according to Holiday. But I saw how it could be possible to divert the flow! You get what I'm saying? People have done this before. With bombs. In Iceland they did it with power hoses and seawater. A couple of guys with dynamite could divert it from the course it's on and send lava down to cover the whole goddam site! I know my way around out there. Going after the pigs has taught me a lot—"

Travis hangs up and closes his eyes.

Angel says, "That wasn't room service."

He considers various lies and alibis. When he opens his eyes she is looking at him. He can already feel her blood slowing down, getting cooler. The ice woman wants to know who was on the phone.

"It was John Brockman."

"How would he know to call you here?"

He has to tell her. There is no way around it. That is, he can't think of one.

"He got the number from Energy Source."

Her eyes are cutting him into thin strips. She doesn't move, or speak.

"Please, Angel. Don't get the wrong idea."

"How did they know?"

"Know what?"

"Where he could find you?"

"They didn't."

"'I don't work for anybody.' Isn't that what you once said?"

"I know it looks bad . . ."

"It's sickening."

"It's not what it looks like."

"You lying son of a bitch."

"Listen—"

"Lying right into my face."

"It was a bribe."

"And you went for it."

"Ian Prince gave me the room."

"You bring me up here like a hooker."

"I wasn't going to use it."

"Stop! Stop! Don't make it worse than it already it. And stop looking at my chest!"

"Then put something on, for Christ sake!"

"I think I will. I think I'll get dressed and be on my way."

She pulls her top on first, her shorts. She grabs her sandals and her bag.

"What are you doing?"

"I'm going downstairs. I'm gone."

As she heads for the door he clutches her arm. Her face has filled with furious heat. He can feel it burning into his brow, his cheeks. Her eyes are like furnaces, and the air so hot and heavy neither one of them can breathe. He has to think through Brockman's call—how much can he believe? how much is invented?—but she is running down the corridor and he still leans against the wall with a nauseous weight across his chest and belly.

In the few moments it takes him to dress, she has stepped between the elevator doors. He catches up with her on the ground floor, in a promenade lined with jade buddhas and ancient mandala tapestries from Nepal.

"Angel! Hold it! Listen!"

She is running toward the lobby. A vanload of late travelers from the airport have just walked in. The broad marbled entryway is filled with flowered shirts and luggage and bellmen. In that same moment the twin fountains explode from the surface of the Persian reflecting pool, spewing twenty-foot towers.

He reaches for her elbow. Over the chatter of falling water he has to shout. "Angel! What are you doing?"

She jerks her arm free. "I'm calling a cab?"

"To where?"

He can't hear her reply. They are near the lobby doors now. Her eyes are wet with misery and rage.

"I can explain it! Will you listen to me for one minute?"

A bellman pauses to observe this exchange. Travis steps in closer, mouth to her hair, with an intense whisper. "You have to let me explain this. Come back up to the room. Please. For five minutes."

She can't speak. She won't speak. She stands rigid.

"If you don't believe what I tell you . . ." His arms fall loose. His hands dangle. "Well, okay. But give me five minutes. I'm begging you. If you go away now, like this . . . I'll die. I'll hang myself. *I'll drive my fucking car off the nearest cliff.*"

The fountains subside, and his prediction fills the lobby, bouncing off the marble flooring and the teakwood paneling behind the reception desk. There is a brief, fearful silence, followed by murmurs, turning heads. This time she allows his hand to remain on her arm, but only until they are alone inside the elevator's rising cubicle.

Her voice is tight, her eyes closed. "I am just going up there to get my camera. I forgot about that."

Lamely he says, "I'm sorry this had to happen."

"Do you know how humiliating it is, Travis? If you want somebody to hang around with you in a glitzy hotel, go back to Kuhio Avenue and pick up a streetgirl like every other mainland hustler does!"

The doors slide open. They have reached the fourth floor. An elderly pair in tropical dinner dress—white linen suit, high-collared mu'umu'u—step back as if the elevator is filled with noxious fumes. Like a longtime married couple keeping up appearances, Travis and Angel move past them in silence.

When the room door is shut she walks out onto the lanai and stands with both hands on the railing, stiff-armed. He waits behind her. She won't turn.

"Don't call me a mainland hustler."

"How do you think you look?"

"C'mon, Angel. We know each other better than that."

"We don't know anything. You don't know me. I don't know you. Who are you? What are you doing here? What am I doing here? Why don't I ever learn anything? You and John Brockman and the guys at Energy Source . . ."

"What is that supposed to mean?"

"Hawaii is your playground. You are all the same. You come and you go and you take what you want. It is so disappointing, Travis."

"I don't know these people. I just got here."

She turns now, her eyes hard and fierce, and shakes her head.

"Then how do we end up in this hotel?"

"That's what I have to explain."

"You know it's part of Western Sun."

"I didn't know that."

"Please don't lie to me."

"I'm not lying."

"All you have to do is look at the ashtrays. Or the napkins. All these little signs. Look. Right here along the border. 'A Subsidiary of Western Sun.' Aren't you an investigator? Aren't you supposed to notice things?"

"I didn't know that, Angel."

She stares at him and looks away.

"I don't know what else to tell you." he says.

He figures it is his stupidity that finally convinces her, his blindness, his failure to make the obvious connection.

Maybe the color rising into his face speaks the loudest truth. She looks up at him with lidded eyes, as if exhausted.

"I would really like to be able to trust someone," she says.

He moves her inside and sits her down in one of the upholstered chairs next to the bed and goes through it all, Prince's detective work, Connie's call, the claims and counter-claims, everything he knows up to this point, or thinks he knows, his vows not to touch her, then the craving in the loins that could not wait.

"My balls were aching, Angel. You have any idea what that is like?"

This draws from her the thinnest smile. But her voice is weary, heavy, her face haggard. "Before I die I would like to meet one man I believed I could trust."

The way she says this, the hopelessness, the cynicism, cuts through him like a sword.

"Okay. Okay, then. I want you to listen to one more thing. Will you do that?"

"Just be straight with me, Travis. Don't tell me A, then start doing B."

"I'm going to make a phone call. I want you to listen in on the bathroom extension."

"Who is it this time?"

Who's Paying

He dials Carlo's number, reversing the charges. As the voice comes floating on a transoceanic hiss Travis can see him alone in his cluttered office with his industrial view of the nighttime bridge, a pastrami sandwich unwrapped, half eaten.

"Travis, where are you?"

"I'm over here on the Big Island."

"Good. That's where I want you to be."

"How's life in San Francisco?"

"The same. How's our case coming along?"

"This may be the most fucked-up job you've ever sent me on."

"I was afraid of that. I had a feeling about this one."

"What kind of feeling?"

"I don't know. Something didn't smell right."

"Why didn't you mention that before I left?"

"There was nothing to mention. It was just a feeling, a fleeting thought."

"You should always share your feelings, Carlo."

"Is that what you called to tell me? Who's paying for this?"

"I need some guidance."

"I'm listening. But make it quick."

"Maybe the guy who filed the claim has disappeared."

"Why do you say maybe?"

Travis tells him what he's heard.

"And what do you think?" Carlo says.

"I think you should put somebody else on the case."

Carlo does not seem to hear this. "If you want my cold-blooded and professional opinion," he says, "this guy Prince is not the client. Western Sun is the client. A very big and influential client, I might add. The thing to do is get busy and find out what happened. But keep Twenty Twenty out of it. We are invisible. We just bear witness. And be nice to people. Whatever else, be diplomatic."

The situation is no longer as cut and dried as it once appeared from across the ocean, Travis tells him, noting the swell of local feeling, the pickup trucks, the electric storm, the two kinds of law spelled out by the tall Hawaiian man, and strange winds that can blow vital documents out a trailer door.

Carlo is so quiet Travis thinks they've lost the connection.

"You still there?"

"Is this all going into your report?"

"I don't know."

"Listen, Travis, maybe some numbers can help us think about this. Have you ever wondered how often lightning strikes somewhere on the planet Earth?"

"I still haven't told you the main reason I called—"

"At any given moment of the day or night there are something like two thousand thunderstorms rolling and cracking. In our line of work you can't afford to forget these things."

"—and please don't take this the wrong way . . ."

Above the low-level hiss in the line Travis hears a long intake of breath, as if Carlo is bracing himself.

"I guess I know what you're trying to say, and I have to remind you of what we're up against here in the office. You want some guidance, I would say back away for a day. Sit still somewhere. Go to the beach. Have you been to the beach? Treat yourself to a swim."

A tiny click tells him Angel has hung up her receiver.

"Hello?" says Carlo. "You there?"

"It's nothing personal," Travis says, "it has nothing to do with you as a person—"

Her finger depresses the button on Travis's receiver. He looks up. She's been crying. The dial tone comes on.

"Don't quit your job."

He moves to redial. She grabs his hand.

"I can find another job."

"I don't want you to do that. You don't have to do that."

"I want you to trust me."

"I do too."

"Do what?"

"Want me to trust you."

"But you don't."

"It's not just you . . ."

"I'm going to stay over here for a while."

"Don't say that."

"I mean it. I may never go back."

"Don't say that either."

"I thought you wanted me to stay for a while."

"I thought I did too."

"Now you don't."

She is standing between the sliding doors, with the night-lit golf course beyond.

"Maybe this is like a high school reunion."

"Shit, Angel."

"I'm sorry."

"That's a hell of a thing to say."

"I shouldn't have said it."

"Something we both had to get out of our systems. Is that it?"

"I don't know . . ."

"And now it's over. Is that it?"

That isn't it. She looks at him with eyes that ask questions he does not yet have answers for. She searches for the skin behind the skin, the look behind the look, a glance or gleam she can recognize, with the careful probing that can come into your face when a familiar person becomes a stranger. Later they will talk about this moment and she will tell him why she simply cannot speak.

"Almost anything could have sent me walking out the door again," she will tell him. "I was still very close to that. When you said, 'Now it's over,' that stopped me cold. Something was over. It wasn't us. What I could not see yet, but somehow knew, was that the past was over. The kids we used to be. After all those years. I couldn't tell you that, you see, because it would have meant . . . it seemed to me it would mean having to tell you not just how many times I had thought of you, but all the ways I had thought of you and had clung to those memories of how we were when we were kids, all the things we did, the ways we did them. When Walter and I lived in Daly City, a hundred times I almost called you, maybe a thousand times. I would touch the phone and think your name and think your number and think the address I had sent so many letters to from the islands and now it was just another hour down the coast. I probably shouldn't tell you this, but I used to imagine that we would run into each other somewhere. For all the years we lived there I would imagine it, in a coffee shop, or at fisherman's Wharf, or just walking along the street in some neighborhood. Why didn't I call you? I still don't know. Maybe I was afraid Walter would find out. Maybe I was afraid to hear about the war. Maybe I wanted you to always stay sixteen, my mainland heartthrob who would never change. Sometimes when you want to talk the most, you can't talk at all. That room we were in made it hard to talk. It was such a perfect setting, like somewhere out of the past, or out of some fantasy. I had put the Western Sun part out of mind, just to help the fantasy come true. Do you know

202   what I mean? Over there in Waipi'o, as soon as you mentioned the Manu Kona I flashed on who owns the place. I flashed on what you told me about your job. I couldn't believe you would actually *plan* something so transparent and sleazy sounding. But if you want to know the truth, I didn't really care just then. Everybody wants to come to a hotel like that, sooner or later, no matter who is running it. It's so seductive you can't resist. Right? When I yelled at you, I guess I was yelling at myself, despising myself, really, for being there at all. I wanted the hotel to go away, and I wanted to stay there on the fourth floor forever, just like I wanted you to go back to the mainland and leave me alone, and I wanted you to stay right there and never move. If you had touched me then I think I would have hit you. But you didn't. Instead you said, 'Let's order something. Let's have some food sent up.' Suddenly I was so hungry I was drooling. I knew it was too late to start back to Hilo. You had this insanely desperate look on your face which meant I could order anything, and I didn't ask who was paying for this because I didn't want to know. That is, I didn't want to hear it said out loud."

Night Sounds

He orders steak, with a double order of bluepoint oysters to start, and a bottle of good champagne. She orders swordfish and Caesar salad. When the waiter shows up in his tux, with the ice bucket and the food under silver lids, on a crisp white tablecloth, Travis asks him to roll his table out onto the lanai and move a couple of the bamboo chairs out there too.

They have donned the fluffy white guest robes from the walk-in closet. By the railing they pass morsels back and forth on silver forks, clinking tall slim glasses in little wordless toasts. A band is playing down below, a reggae band in one of the lounges. They hear loud applause, like the distant sounds from a party across a mountain lake. From time to time they hear nearby laughter and raucous noise from another lanai somewhere farther along this side of the Bali Tower. These sounds are punctuated by the far-off pock of tennis balls from one of the courts. They can see the lights and hear the pocks, but trees screen the courts and the players.

It is almost like a second honeymoon, as if they have never been apart. Somehow they have been together all these years, and this is a kind of anniversary party where old vows are being reconsidered.

She raises a glass. "Thank you, Travis."

"You're welcome."

"For bringing me here."

He feels large and lofty, as if by accepting the gift of this room he created its many embellishments. He says, "It's the least I could do."

"Walter and I went to Las Vegas a couple of times, and he would get deals on rooms, with the company. But it was never anything like this."

"Good. I want you to forget everything about Walter."

"I am seeing some things, you know."

"Such as?"

Her lips move toward a thoughtful smile. "They say this whole side of the island is going to end up like Waikiki."

"Disneyland would be closer to it. Ringling Brothers, Barnum and Bailey."

"Is it the wrong time to talk about this?"

"We can talk about anything we want."

"Maybe we should just sit here and celebrate."

"That's what we're doing," he says, as he pours out some more of the bubbly. He is happy. He can't imagine being happier. He doesn't care what they talk about.

"To us," he says.

"Yes. To us."

She sips and laughs a helpless laugh. "It's like being behind enemy lines."

"Why do you say that?"

"Doesn't it feel like we're getting away with something?"

"I guess it does, yes. But who is the enemy?"

He wants this to be a playful question. Angel seems to take it seriously. She looks at him again, then looks away, as if regretting how she sounded, or perhaps regretting the timing.

"Maybe enemy isn't the word," she says

He waits. She doesn't continue, and that is okay. He is content to sit and sip and look out into the night. The reggae band has shut down. From the Garden of Eden they hear zebras braying into the darkness. Below them, soft lamps light the Roman statuary and the manicured foliage along the causeways and lagoons, while farther out, higher lamps give the golf course the look of a broad jagged runway for late travelers who need plenty of room to land.   205

Underneath the rustling of the nearest palms, Angel is hearing night sounds of her own, among them the voice of a fellow interviewed on local radio the previous week, a Japanese gardener forced to sell his nursery when fertile valley land on Maui was rezoned for condos, another shopping mall, a golf course. "Where you folks gonna get the flowers?" he asked in his soft, sad voice. "The lei suppose to be a symbol for aloha. But where you folks gonna get flowers if all the soil gets covered up with fairways and hotels?"

She is hearing the voice of her cousin Tiny, who worked on the Manu Kona when they were laying the foundation. It was a great break for him at a time when there was no work around Hilo. He moved over to this side. He couldn't afford to rent anything close to the construction site. Resort plans had sent the land and housing costs soaring. So he bunked with relatives forty miles up the coast and commuted every day. Tiny had never thought of himself as a commuter. His father was a fisherman. His grandfather was a fisherman and a farmer with a house right on the land he worked. But Tiny didn't complain. He needed the money. On his home island, where his people had already lived for a thousand years when Magellan crossed the Pacific, Tiny became a commuter in order to make enough money to pay for the gasoline he burned driving back and forth to work and to maintain his pickup and feed his kids.

As she sits here in a fluffy robe with the Manu Kona logo next to her lapel, Angel is seeing and hearing what Tiny talked about. Behind enemy lines she feels like a spy, making discoveries and taking notes. One thing about the Big Island, it is just big enough that it takes an effort or special occasion to get from one side to the other. People who inhabit the windward side listen to the radio and read the paper and shake their heads about news they hear from the leeward side, and vice versa, as if it is another country with its own strange and dubious habits. She has not seen Kona in twenty years. She has heard stories. Now her eyes and ears are learning what his happened along this shoreline, where the condo towers run for miles, and all that follows in their wake, the gas-and-go's, the beachtown boutiques, the fast food corners, the intersections thick with vans and rented sedans.

When she speaks again, perhaps she is answering Travis's question. Perhaps not. It is just one word. "Listen." He knows what she means. He has been hearing it too, the low steady roar of a generator, or bank of air conditioners, and wondering if this means they were given one of the low-budget rooms, within earshot of a power supply. They wouldn't have noticed it until the band shut down and the last party ended. But it has been here all along, a rumbling growl from the roof above, or perhaps from the side of the tower, perhaps several generators humming along through the balmy Hawaiian night, just as they hummed all through the day.

It is the humming call of the great engine that fuels and feeds the vast resort, powering the Muzak in the elevators and the lamps along the causeway and the launches and the TV sets and the late-night VCR's and the mini-fridges keeping tomorrow's drinks cool, and the Jacuzzi pumps in the numerous hot tubs and the pumps to circulate the water so it will not stagnate in the landlocked and concrete-lined lagoons and the pumps that trigger the geysers in the Persian reflecting pool. Travis, listening, cannot help but wonder where so much juice is coming from, on this dry and riverless shoreline, way out here at the edge of the world's most isolated island chain.

207

Volcano Country

As Travis and Angel finish off the champagne and bask in the evening breeze on the fourth floor of the Bali Tower, John Brockman dozes fitfully in his kipuka near the southern shore, and the observatory geologist working late again takes data from his bank of monitors that will dovetail with some recent numbers from the Phillipines. Around 4 A.M. Dan Clemson rolls out of his cot and puts a call in to Houston, Texas, four times zones away, to propose a change in the drilling schedule until they know which way the lava's going to go. A few minutes later there is a crack, a lurching in the earth, somewhere south of Hilo, and Tiny Kulima's wife, already awake, turns to him and says, "What was that?" while Tutu David, alone in his dark cottage on the outskirts of town, sits up and says aloud, to no one, "What was that?" Then it is dawn all over the island, the sky semiviolet, layered with a lemon light, and they are waking in the corner room of the ultimate resort that has harbored them and bonded them and seduced them, and Travis, waking up in Angel's arms, is swimming in his desire and in his luck.

In the light they swim together and make love again, minus the fever and uncertainty. This time he is swollen with certainty. They giggle a lot and remember things they used to do, with nothing in their way. They use both beds, the upholstered chairs, the deep carpets. They take a long shower and dry each other off, lovers again, or trying to be, joking, touching. They order breakfast, eggs Benedict, guava juice, kona coffee, and talk about staying. The room comps say two nights. Has something actually happened to Prince—can even half of Brockman's account be true?— and was this little gift his last bequest? Travis doesn't want to dwell on that, not yet, not while the aromas of hollandaise and strong coffee float across the lanai. He prefers to see this as the chance of a lifetime, and he knows Angel is tempted. He watches her eyes, hoping the little frown of worry will flash again with reckless approval. But she is thinking of Marilyn, the daughter who will be wondering where Mom has gone. She is thinking of her Honda, left overnight in a supermarket lot. She is thinking of her island, what is happening to her island. Something's rising in the blood. So they check out of the Hotel Overkill and take the coast road south, to buy themselves an extra hour or two together. By this route they can complete the circuit they now call "Sakai's Round-the-Island Tour," which started as a kind of honeymoon and is going to end up like a divorce.

Later he will ask himself how one day can be so luscious and the next so shadowy, so layered and lined with shadow. He will come to see it as a feature of all the lava that surrounds their travels, or the dark fires hidden underneath the lava. Gradually this is what Travis will learn about volcano country. The lava works on everyone who remains there for long. It is the main thing going on, whether aboveground and visible or belowground and invisible, just as in New Mexico the desert is what's going on. You look at it, you think about it, you talk about it, you move across it. Before you have entered the desert, the desert is already entering you.

Another hotel, a twin, is going up just beyond the Manu Kona's access road. He has to stop while Angel takes the backdrop photo. Both sites have been hacked from sloping lava. Both are bordered by the wall they saw from their room, a wall that marks the mile-wide cut across this plain. Travis thinks of surf-damaged houses Carlo once sent him to look at, south of San Francisco, houses built so close to the median tide line the owners had to pile up tons of rock to protect their properties from the in-rush of winter surges. The sheared-off black wall has that look, as if a tidal wave came rolling down from Mauna Loa and froze at the edge of these verdant lawns and the first row of walkway lamps.

Heading south across the fields of rock they reach Kailua, the largest of the leeward towns, once an oasis marked by palms, a harbor town, once Hawai'i's royal town, home base for Kamehameha I, who retired here after subduing the chiefs of all the islands to create his mid-Pacific kingdom. From above, from the coast road as it climbs, they see what Kailua has become. Against the ocean's glitter they see far-off tiny cranes at work, and silhouetted webs of scaffolding, filling in what gaps remain in the long frontage strip. Nothing new, in the history of the world. But in Angel's history it's another shock. She calls it a sacrilege. They should leave this island alone, she says. "Give them Honolulu. Give them Lahaina. Why can't the Big Island be a sanctuary?"

Some people already see it that way, says Travis, sun lovers who fly in from the cold and heartless cities, who are down there right now on decks and beaches and recuperating around the pools.

She gives him a sour look. She is not thinking of visitors. She is thinking of islanders and hearing stories again, about families who can't afford the shoreline now. Only corporations can afford it, or time-share investors from L.A. and Tokyo. People whose families have inhabited these shores for twenty generations can no longer pay the taxes. But their

problems and their losses are obscured by the income from
the green fees and the generous tips left behind by travelers,
like the generous tip Travis left behind on the silver breakfast
tray.

Looping wide to skirt Mauna Loa's southern flank, they
stop again for photos and ponder the lava, the glacier-size,
sprawling mass. They cross the flow of 1926, which forked
above the fishing village of Milol'i, sparing the house of a
man who spread ti leaves across his yard and ran up the
mountain with a squealing pig and threw it into the
advancing stream. They cross the flows of 1907, 1950, 1968,
and 1887 and enter the district called Ka'u, lonesome miles
and heaps of seldom-watered gray-black rock.

Raw and uneroded terrain comes spilling toward them as
they make the steady climb, and Angel tells him the story of
legendary footprints out in the middle of this desert, pressed
into a layer of hardened ash. They mark the path of soldiers
fleeing an explosion back in 1790, during the days when
Kamehameha was starting his campaign. An opposing chief
of great reknown was leading an army across the island to
do battle, when Kilauea erupted, ten miles away. Though the
soldiers ran, many were trapped and buried in the shower
of ash and fiery debris. For Kamehameha the eruption was
a sign that the lost troops were on the wrong side, that Pele
was with him and his cause was honorable.

Into Angel's voice has come a sound he can't identify. She
asks him to promise her something.

"If you're ever roaming around in places like this, Travis,
it's important to ask permission. It all belongs to her, you
know. If you tell her you come with respect, she'll watch over
you. But it takes your full attention. I'm very serious now.
You can't fool around out here."

Is this advice? Is it a warning? Or some kind of scolding
in advance? Her voice puts him on guard and puts new

distance between them. He looks at her, but she looks out the window at the lava, as if he has already made a promise and broken it. He does not yet know how close they are to Pele's home or what it will mean to her to see the firepit again.

The plains of Ka'u border the southern district called Puna, where the island's reservoir of magma lives. Halfway around the crater rim they park and hike out along an abandoned strip of asphalt, once part of a perimeter road. A few years back large chunks of this roadbed broke off and fell into the crater, shaken loose by tremors. Trenches opened in the asphalt, little rift zones. Where cars once traveled, wide potholes make untended gardens swelling green below the grainy surface.

They stop at a railing of weathered iron pipe and look across the skillet-shaped caldera. Its broad floor is a gray sea. Beyond the farther rim Mauna Loa humps smooth and tawny. At four thousand feet the oxygen gets thinner, but something has thickened the air. Whether it is coming from Angel or from the crater he cannot tell. They stand side by side yet seem to be moving farther apart, as the silence of this place feeds a silence that grows between them. He will soon learn that the magma is working overtime again, percolating downslope, pushing, probing, preparing to spring forth again, as it has done for the past three nights just a few miles south and east. It adds to the atmosphere some urgency that works on both of them. On Travis, in one way. On Angel, in another way. She is drawn into it. He is pushed away, or pushed above it.

This is his first volcano, except for what he's seen in reruns of *The Last Days of Pompeii* and the coverage of Mount Saint Helens. Does he expect a mushroom cloud, a Vesuvius of the Pacific, with the lid blown off and the old warriors of 1790 forever running for their lives? On this day, only the wavering steam leaks upward to remind him of what bubbles underneath. It is a sea floor of lava broken by pits and crevices, a wide and seared and ghostly place, silent and still, yet never at rest. A sun-covering cloud turns half the lava a darker gray. The shadow resembles a continent. Other shadows follow, and with three or four floating on its surface, the caldera becomes a map of the world at an earlier time. Eons pass, as they move along and change their shapes and float apart. Then brilliant sunlight fills the bowl. The wind falls off. From the wooded cliffs below come the trillings of the forest birds. Their tiny calls rise through the uncanny emptiness, and something comes clear to him. He thinks he glimpses the island's underside, with all its tubes and layers.

He sees the streaked and lunar bowl, and below that the chamber where the magma waits and sends its arms and creepers out through subterrenean channels, and below that the great boiler room as wide as the island, filled with steam, feeling the pressure of the island and the pressure of the all-surrounding sea. Into that reservoir the driller's pipe will soon descend to tap the steam and lift it, convert it, squeeze it into wires that will take the power north and west, borne up by hundreds of cable towers, around Mauna Kea, past Waipi'o, across the old Kohala Range, then into the channel between the islands, up and out again to cross Maui's southern shore, underwater past Moloka'i, and on to Honolulu, the metropolis. five hundred megawatts is the long-range plan, enough to light up three Honolulus. Does he approve? Or disapprove? It's too soon to say. Imagining it for the first time he regards it for a while, as if from overhead, as if hanging from a hot-air balloon, and he has to admire the logic of it all, the neat techno-logic of the engineers and drillers.

That is the difference between the two of them today. In seconds he can float away and dream about the ring of fire and see the vast zigzagging pattern that encircles the Pacific and see this island at its center with a plumbing system to tap the sacred furnace. In his mind he will soon weigh the ironies and in theory be offended. But Angel feels this in her body, like an early appendicitis twinge.

She has been gazing toward the firepit where the ashes of her great-grandmother were strewn twenty years ago. From their vantage point, Halema'uma'u is a dark smudge in the lighter gray, three miles across the crater, a hollow at the edge of this scorched and steaming ring. She knows it is one place she cannot take him, to the lip of Pele's home and Malama's final resting place. Tourists stop there every day, of course, by the hundreds, by the carloads and the busloads. But for Angel this is not "a site." She will never take him there. Inside her is a place where the great-grandmother's flame resides, with the flames of all the mothers before her whose bones were sent back to the source. And to this place Travis cannot go. He can visit Halema'uma'u on his own, any time he chooses, to pay his respects to whatever hovers in the air and rises from the rocks. But he can't go there with Angel. They will never talk about it. They will talk around it, and he will take it personally at first, until he learns that it's a pilgrimage she has to make alone. In the end he will love her more for this, love her more for the place she will not take him, though he cannot say that or see that as they stand together on the precipice.

She is one-fourth Hawaiian. Today the fourth part of her blood speaks loudest. She has seen where Pele's juice will be spent, and it makes her belly hurt. The wide drill bit that tomorrow or the next day will make its first cut is preparing to enter *her*. This is what her body says. In advance she feels the probe, she feels violated. But by what? By the bit itself? By the six thousand feet of nine-inch pipe? By the rig that overwhelmed the forest skyline? By the island-hopping cable? By the high-rent hotels? By the visitors who see these islands as a great recreation zone, who come and go and take what they want and will now use Pele's steam, if it is offered, without a second thought?

Travis has moved his eyes from the crater to her face. He has never desired anyone the way he desires her right now, whatever this may mean—the way she stands, her look, her heart, her chiseled silence, wherever she will or will not take him, wherever they may take each other. He feels cursed with lust and longing and fear of this woman he thought he knew, once, eighteen years ago. Now, in her face, in her eyes he sees something as stark and riveting as the aspect of the caldera itself. On the other side of her anger there is a place where that same fierce energy lives. In the Blue Dolphin Lounge it almost looked like passion. What he sees this afternoon is another kind of fire, coals blown to new life, coals glowing black.

All along the way she has been snapping photos. The camera hangs around her neck, with its lens at her solar plexus like a large third eye, three eyes holding him, and she is Angel turned inside out, as if her image has been polarized, the lights and shades reversed. He feels himself teetering. It's hard to look at her, and hard to look away. The crater below them is wide and still and beckoning, and a voice somewhere says, Step back, step back! But he can't do it, he can't move. He closes his eyes. A yawning darkness opens around him, a windy, humid vault, and he is tumbling through it, in a free fall, loose and tumbling.

Travis's Tale

They have crossed the line where dry meets wet, a mini-Continental Divide. Now 'ohi'a trees border both sides of the road, the slender, shaggy, high-country survivors that feed on rock and air and water. 'Ohi'a bark is the color of ashes, gray-brown and rough, as if dusted daily with gray volcanic ash. Atop each trunk a dusty bouquet of gnarled limbs sends leaves fanning upward and outward, each leaf small and oval, like those of the dollar eucalyptus, and in among the foliage you see little beacons called *lehua*, said to be Pele's flower. As they start down the windward slope toward Hilo, these rain forest eyes watch them pass, the anemonelike lehua blossoms, as red as the lava used to be.

Travis is shivering, as if from dampness. They have entered a heavy mist. He strains to see past the wiper's sweep, his mind racing, his voice at the edge of speech, the edge of a shout, a cry, an accusation, a flood of everything pushing to come out.

"Are you upset?" he says.

"Why? Are you?"

He almost says, I'm dying. Aloud he says, "I'm thinking. I'm watching the road. This fog is something."

"You're not here."

"I'm here."

"You're just sitting here."

"Didn't we say not-talking is okay?"

"Talking is okay too."

"It's not easy."

"Talking?"

"Being with you."

"Did you think it would be easy?"

"I didn't know it would be like this."

"Like what?" she says. "Give me an example. What is it like to be with me?"

"I'll tell you later."

"Tell me now. Nobody ever tells me things like that."

"You're not the same."

"The same as what?"

"You know what I mean."

"Why should I be the same?" Her voice is heating up. "Nobody is the same!"

"I can't talk about it."

"Then let's talk about something else."

"What?"

"Things you said."

"When?"

"In the car. This morning."

"What did I say?"

"How all the people crowding up the island have a right to be here."

"I didn't say that."

"'Their sanctuary,' you said."

"I said *they* see it that way."

"How come everybody from the mainland thinks they have a right to come over here—"

"Don't start that again."

"—when you don't understand anything at all about what is going on!"

"Did I ever say . . . ? I don't claim to know what's going on!"

"No, you don't! You don't know shit about what's going on! You're living in a dream world!"

"Shut up, Angel! Just shut the fuck up for a while!"

She lunges at him, pounding with her fists on his arm and shoulders. *"Damn* you, Travis! What are you doing here?"

"Hey, cut it out! I have to drive!"

"Why are you here?" she cries, pounding on him. "Why did you come back? I don't want to have to deal with this!"

"Neither do I! You're crazy! Get away from me!"

He shoves her across the seat, shoves harder than he means to. The car careens over the center line, as two fuzzy headlights come over a rise. They swerve back to the right. The other driver's honk recedes into the fog. When Travis finally straightens out, his heart is thumping.

"Christ, Angel. What's the matter with you?"

She sits against the far door, staring straight ahead. After a while she says, "We can't do this, Travis. You know we can't."

"No, I don't know that."

"Once we get back to Hilo . . . it's going to be impossible."

"So it's good-bye at the supermarket and drive away forever. Is that what I'm hearing?"

As if surrounded by insects, she shakes her head, though whether it means no to the question, or no to things in general, he isn't sure.

"Listen," he says, "I want to tell you something."

She waits, watching the mist.

"There are some things you should know about me."

"Yes."

"Quite a few years ago I came through Honolulu. I was there for two weeks."

"Yes, I know."

"I almost called you. A dozen times I lifted a receiver somewhere, then set it back down again."

"You told me that."

"But you don't know what I was doing there."

"You were out of your mind, you said."

"And you were pregnant."

"That's right. That was the year. Nine-teen sev-en-ty-three." She dwells on each syllable.

His movies are running now, old stories he has not intended to tell, like meeting the woman in the Geary Street bar, though these are different, lurking under that one, and it will not be the first time he has told them. Some nights when he woke up sweating and and couldn't sleep, he would tell things to Marge. He would watch her eyes spring open and doze again while he babbled at her in the darkness of their apartment in the city, stories she grew weary of, stories from the dark time she could do nothing about. Between Travis and Marge they would hang in the air like clouds.

He starts with the story of his eye, the grenade, the deranged corporal who tried to do him in, and the season of blindness under white bandages, ending this the way he rehearsed it. "I dove in the wrong direction, you know. I dove right toward it, though maybe it wasn't wrong. Maybe you never dive in the wrong direction."

He feels her fingers on his cheekbone, reaching through the dark space, but without the softness of touch that sends sparks falling across his skin. Cold from the dampness gathering inside the car, her fingers make him shiver. Like a blind person she taps around the socket and says, "Yes, yes," half agreement, half question, as if she already knows these things, or by methodical touching she has verified his account.

The corporal, he tells her, used to boast that one day they would steal a plane and fly out together, get back to the states. They would take it to the Phillipines. After that, the corporal would say, "we'll be home free." He had never flown anything, but one night the corporal could wait no longer. He climbed into a plane they used for light cargo and got it started and taxied out into the predawn, fooling around with the controls as he dreamed his final journey. He picked up quite a bit of speed, but he never got off the ground. He plunged on past the runway and smashed into a grove of trees, where the plane caught fire and exploded.

This time Angel doesn't speak. Has he gone too far? A voice behind his voice has been saying, Why are you doing this? Don't you ever learn a goddamn thing? But he can't stop yet. He wants her to know that he too has a crater in his life, a pit where murky fires smolder.

He fills the silence with more words, nervous memories, quoting from the New Testament, telling her how he went all the way back to the Acts of the Apostles, hoping the lessons there would somehow justify his life, how on the way home he read with envy chapter 2. Jesus has already died and been resurrected, and his disciples have gathered in Jerusalem:

> And suddenly there came a sound from heaven as of a rushing mighty wind, and it filled all the house where they were sitting. And there appeared unto them cloven tongues like as of fire, and it sat upon each of them. And they were all filled with the Holy Ghost, and began to speak with other tongues as the Spirit gave them utterance.

Reading this Travis saw a flame resting on the head of each Apostle. He heard the sounds as they spoke in other tongues. He wanted to be there among them, in a transcendant state, rather than on a MATS flight heading back to the hostile and war-divided country of his birth. He wanted to be the master of an unknown language.

Later that same day he was sitting in an open bar on one of the side streets of Waikiki, beginning two weeks of rest and recoup, when he found himself next to a man with an idea for a film. After they talked and sipped for half an hour he offered Travis the lead. It was going to be an adult film, rated double X, about two people who meet at a gospel revival, and this appealed to him. Revival was on his mind.

The director/cameraman wanted to shoot the love scenes first. As Travis walked naked onto this fellow's "set," he was introduced to a desperately beautiful young woman who said she would tell him her name after they were better acquainted. She too was a first-time performer, aroused by the whirring cameras. Travis was not aroused. He couldn't get it up.

To Angel he says, "My life as a porn star lasted about eight minutes."

She doesn't like this story. It repels her. Travis doesn't like it either. Telling it feels sleazy.

"That sounds like Waikiki," she says.

Her eyes are dissecting him. "This woman, what about her? Who was she? Was she local?"

"I think she came from Texas . . ." And he almost says her name. That is, he comes very close to calling Angel by that name, but catches his tongue, as his voice catches on the fear of what he's almost done, the surprise of it, mixing Angel and Crystal once again. Aren't they opposite in every way? Crystal almost consumed him. A predator. Perhaps a witch. That's how he came to think of her.

He falls silent, driving the long, wet downhill road as if alone, while the movie keeps running, scenes he is afraid to speak, or think, imagining that Angel can see what he is seeing—the union of their naked sculptured bodies, and the eager, depraved, and tortured face of the cameraman.

Travis told Crystal that if she would put her clothes back on and quit this picture he would take her to the Royal Hawaiian Hotel for dinner. In the elevator the way she stood next to him made him feel strong, and vengeful. He told her he'd forgotten his wallet, and would she wait downstairs. In the room again he punched out the cameraman, broke his nose, smashed his lenses against the wall, lingered to watch him bleed and weep, never mentioning this to Crystal or to anyone else, though she continued to have that effect on him.

Her lips alone were an aphrodisiac. Full and bruised-looking, as if recently hurt by small bites and pressures she had tried to conceal with dark lipstick and had not quite concealed. It was easy to believe she did this by design, as if to advertise that she had been roughly treated. The near-bruises called out a roughness. To that list of lips and teeth that may have left their marks on her, he wanted to add his own, and she never protested, never pulled back or cried out, "Stop it," or "That hurts," or "God, Travis, is gentle anywhere in your vocabulary?"

As they spent that night together and the next and the next, she would call forth bursts of angry power, in the elevator, in the bed, and he would have to take some part of her body. They both liked it that way. He didn't hit her. He has never hit a a woman. He used her roughly. Repeatedly. They used each other. They took bedroom pictures of each other and blew them up and tacked them to the wall. "Lovers" would not be the word to describe what they became. The so-called director of that adult film that never got made, he knew more about them than they knew about themselves.

When Travis invited her to fly home with him, he only half meant it. He hoped she would take it as a joke. But she was on the loose—a photojournalist between assignments,

she called herself—twenty-two and in the mood for anything. He has regretted it a thousand times. There is a long
list of regrets from that dark season of his life. The worst
part of crossing the ocean was what happened after he got
home. He needed resources to make it through such a year.
He needed to be grounded somewhere. But in those days
Travis was spinning. He had become some kind of magnet
for stray particles and demon/comrades and desperadoes.
They are still with him. They always will be. Certain
memories are like that, like the plastic containers you can
bury but never get rid of. Nonbiodegradable.

When Crystal died he did not miss her. Years would have
to pass before her memory triggered tears. So why did he
avenge her death? He knew the fellow who took her life,
knew him better than he cared to know anyone. In junior
high they played two-man basketball in a backyard league.
They once started a rock and roll band, two guitars, bass,
and drums, which fell apart because this fellow had to be the
lead singer. He could play a lot of bass but he didn't know
the difference between singing and yelling. "Loud does not
mean good!" Travis shouted at him more than once. It was
so painful it could crack them up, the way this frantic voice
would demolish a rehearsal. The fellow had been crazy all
along. They just didn't know enough to see it.

In the secret address book of old alliances, Travis calls
him Deathwish. That was not his name, but that was the
effect he had. While Travis was overseas the crazy bassist
became a monster, holed up in a cabin outside town, a
hermit losing weight on a macrobiotic diet, doing acid,
reading Tarot, unraveling in his own monastic way, his table
cluttered with pages ripped from Genesis and Exodus and
Butler's *Lives of the Saints* and articles about Aztec ceremonial rites. These "readings" had persuaded him that
certain acts of sacrifice were needed from time to time to

right old wrongs against God and the natural order. If Deathwish had kept this view to himself, no one would have minded much. He would have been numbered among the many sad and silent casualties of the war at home. But he couldn't keep this theory to himself. He had to test it.

He started choosing victims at random. Women mostly. The last one happened to be Crystal the Explorer, who should have known better. She had seen where Deathwish lived. Why did she climb into his car and let him drive her into the hills? Travis still gets queasy when he thinks about it, wishing he had known enough to warn her. He was blind, of course. They were all blind, and of all his dark days this was the darkest.

After Deathwish smothered her and buried her body in its hasty and shallow grave, he came looking for Travis, his long-lost boyhood pal, to tell him all he had done. To brag? No. To rile. To prod. To taunt. And Travis? This sickens him the most, when he thinks about it—Travis listened to the taunts. He let Deathwish enflame him with the words and perverse details.

They were drinking in town. Then they were driving. They were in the forest when the knife was pulled, when Travis swung the chunk of ragged fencing and caught his shoulder. When Travis swung again the knife fell, and Travis recovered it and lifted it, circling, but not ready for the lunge that brought Deathwish in so close he could feel stale breath upon his cheeks and hear a snag of phlegm clicking in his throat. The eager heart found the blade then, seeking it, just as the blade sought out the heart, or so it seemed to Travis at the time.

He could not see much of anything before or after the stuck body dropped. He has no image of the knife moving, the night was so complete, under looming redwoods. But he can still see the two of them like darker silhouettes, dancing around the invisible blade, both hoping to die. Travis knows that much about what happened. He was ready to die. The official verdict was self-defense, but it had seemed to Travis a fine year, a fine week, a fine night for dying.

Now, in the car with Angel, he is ready once again. He doesn't know how this death will differ from the others. Because he cannot yet tell the difference, old deaths are coming toward him. Behind the wheel he is running with sweat. How long have they been driving? An oppressive silence has filled the car like steam. As they near Hilo the rain increases and multiplies, and he is thankful for the din, the pelting. In the near-dark they splash through road-wide puddles. His drenched windshield turns car lights into flashing shards. In the supermarket lot he does not turn off the engine. He wants all the noise he can get, engine, roof racket, wiper swish, puddle splash from wheels of passing shoppers. She wants out of there.

"I have to go," she says.

"Me too."

They sit regarding each other as if in a fever, both damp, gleaming with moisture. In the splintered light they both see strangers. They are both on the edge of trembling fear, wondering how they have arrived in such a place at such a time with such a person.

She runs to her car. While she unlocks her door he sees her hunch against the downpour. Through streaked and dripping glass he watches her shoulders close in against the rain.

Medeiros

He plans to have a drink at the Orchid Isle and try not to think about his life. Maybe two drinks. Or three. By the time he finds an empty stall in the hotel lot the rain has stopped, the way it does in Hilo, as if a celestial shower faucet has been turned on and off. A desk clerk nods toward the shadowy lanai where a large man is rising from one of the rattan sofas. He wears a pressed aloha shirt, slacks, has a pleasant smile that says I hope we can keep this pleasant. His hair is dark and wavy, a very elegant man. Thick arms hang at his sides as he waits for Travis to approach.

It is Lt. Tom Medeiros, county police, wondering if he has a few minutes. Travis offers to buy him a drink.

"Not on duty," he says, "but I don't mind if you have something."

The cocktail waitress happens to be Linda, dressed for night duty.

"Linda," Travis says, "I thought you worked in the coffee shop."

"My friend let me trade shifts. Tomorrow's a big luau for my mom and dad." She's happy about this, shrugging and smiling.

"Anniversary?" Medeiros says.

"Forty years."

"Long time already."

"You folks know each other?" she asks, with a back-and-forth glance.

"We're starting to."

Travis says, "I guess I'll have the usual."

"Scrambled eggs?" says Linda with her kidder's grin. "Papaya?"

"Maybe a Heineken's on the side."

"I'll be right back."

"She likes you," Medeiros says.

"She's a sweetheart. She must like everybody."

He shakes his head. "Some people she won't talk to. Touchy. Very particular. You seem to make an impression around here."

It's a loaded remark. Travis waits to see how he means it. They are leaning back into the sofa, looking across a fern-lined carp pool, and it feels, at the start, as if they are fellow investigators swapping data. Travis welcomes the diversion, anything to take his mind off Angel. But he is watchful. Medeiros knows something, has something on him, or thinks he does. The subject is Ian Prince, whereabouts still unknown.

There was no sign of bodily harm, Medeiros tells him, no blood or hair or scraps of clothing, just the damage to the car itself, the shattered glass, torn seats, wheels gone. The kids who trashed it are local punks who wouldn't know one rental from another, and now they say they didn't drive it. They found it there, made several passes before they struck. The sheriff's helicopter has scanned terrain on both sides of the highway and seen nothing but what you always see out that way. Old lava. It's an empty stretch of the southern shoreline and it's all lava, Medeiros says, from the mountains to the sea.

"Were the keys in the ignition?"

"They were, yes."

The Heineken's arrives, and Travis takes a long sip. "So maybe they found it there, or maybe they drove it there from someplace else. They could have found it anywhere. Right?"

Medeiros pulls from his trousers pocket a handheld tape recorder with a cassette already inserted. "His secretary passed this on to me. She found it on his desk when she opened the office yesterday morning. Some notes and letters he was dictating. All routine. Until we get to the end."

He presses PLAY and a voice comes into the lanai, low-pitched and weary, as if late at night on a long-distance connection:

> . . . *no letterhead on that one, Connie. It's personal. And don't type my name at the bottom. It should feel like a personal note. And . . . wait a minute now. What is this? . . . Somebody's pulling up out in front . . . the fellow from San Francisco? What's he doing here? Damnit. I need more time . . .* (Chair scrape. Mike noise. Click.)

Medeiros lets the empty tape run awhile. Travis tries to imagine Prince inside the office, recorder in hand, watching him mount the stairs. He sees the picture window, the venetian blinds. Was he right there? Behind the blinds? Two feet away and peering out?

"Was he right?" Medeiros says. "Was it you?"

"Sure it was me. I was coming by to pick up some paperwork. She left it in the slot outside."

"What kind of panerwork?"

"Stuff about the claim. You want to see it?"

He shakes his head. "Then what?"

"I drove away."

"And when you drove away, where was Prince? In your car? In another car?"

"Hey. If he was inside his office, I didn't know about it."

"You didn't see him? You didn't talk?"

"The lights were off. It must have been seven-thirty. The door was closed. The 'Returning Soon' sign was on the door."

Medeiros seems amused. He blinks a couple of times. "Okay. What next? You picked up your paperwork . . ."

Travis retraces all his moves. Why try to fake it? He could delete the encounter at the Blue Dolphin, but he is sure Brockman already made the most of this, his cover story.

"So you met John Brockman outside the club."

"We didn't *meet*. That is, it wasn't planned. He was out there, standing by my car."

"One of Prince's trusted allies," Medeiros adds, with a friendly little smile.

"You know Brockman?"

"A lot of people know him."

"Then you know what kind of a guy he is. He's been following me around. I didn't seek him out, believe me. I am just over here trying to do my job."

"Was it part of your job to be down in Puna day before yesterday lined up with all the agitators?"

From his shirt pocket Medeiros withdraws a four-by-five snapshot in a glassene packet. There is Dan Clemson with his hands on his hips, looking like the angry plantation owner in a union movie, and there is Travis in dark glasses and Jack London hat. Angel had the only camera he saw, but this shot came from another part of the crowd, cropped so you could get the impression that Travis had organized the march.

"Adjusters don't usually take sides."

"How could I take sides? I don't know enough to take sides. I've got my hands full trying to check out a claim."

"Do you mind if I ask how that's coming along?"

"It's coming along fine. I just can't talk about it yet."

"Our fire department says the probable cause was a propane tank. You've seen their report?"

"I've seen that part quoted."

"You don't agree."

"There are other opinions."

"What was Prince's opinion?"

"Are you using the past tense?"

"What *is* his opinion?"

"You think he's history?"

230   "I was hoping you might be able to shed some light on that."

"Look, lieutenant, what is this? You think I did something to Ian Prince? I don't even know Ian Prince. I've talked to him twice in my life."

"From what we can tell right now, before whatever happened happened, you were the last one to see him."

"Maybe he saw me. I didn't see him. I didn't know he was in his office."

"He was just sitting there dictating letters in the dark."

"That's the way it looks. He wasn't supposed to be there. He was supposed to be on Maui. Right? Gone for a couple of days. Prince is the guy with the things to hide, not me."

Medeiros gazes out across the carp pool, inhales quietly a few times.

"I've been told he was at the drilling site on the night that fire started."

"According to who?"

"Word of mouth," Medeiros says. "Evidently he was out there by himself."

"In the rain?"

"And in the dark."

"Doing what?"

"You tell me. Maybe he likes it in the dark."

A glint of satisfaction shows in the lieutenant's eyes. It is hard to tell how much he knows, how much he's fishing for. At last he stands up and steps out away from the sofa.

"I don't know what you're doing on this island, Doyle. It doesn't fit together. But I'll find out. So just be warned. Be careful. And do me a favor. Stay away from Evangeline Sakai. You have good taste there, but bad judgment."

"What do you mean by that?"

"I mean she's taken. Roland Fernandez is like a younger brother to me. He finds out how much time you are spending with her, I don't know what would happen. I probably do know. But I don't want to go into it. I would just rather not see his feelings hurt. I don't want any harm to come to Evangeline either."

"There's no need to bring her into this."

"That's right," he says, with a farewell nod.

As he watches Medeiros move through the lobby, it occurs to Travis that there is a softness around this man. The material of his shirt is softly textured cotton. The gray slacks are some kind of lightweight wool, the kind that breathes. He takes his time talking and walking. He does not sweat. His skin has a velvet quality, remarkable for a guy his age, midforties, Travis figures. He is very sure of himself. He has the gentle manner of a large man with great strength he prefers not to use unless he has to. Travis guesses he played tackle in high school and broke someone's hand or leg and still regrets it.

Ancient Mirrors

He sits staring at the pool where fat carp glide in and out of view, their shapes distorted by the competing light, half of it from shaded lamps, half from the night sky above the bay. He is observing the route of one long black-and-white creature when it stops in front of him, with softly undulating fins, caught between the shadings on the surface of the water, so that the whites sometimes look black, and the blacks white.

He gazes so long, this hovering fish becomes like the word you repeat and repeat and roll around on your tongue until it loses all meaning, then seems to contain all meaning. The blacks and whites reverse and reverse again, changing polarity the way Angel changed before his eyes. It sends him wheeling back, imagining there could be another way to read the past few days. He tries to remember how she looked this afternoon, and can't. He can only remember his helpless sense of teetering, tumbling, and hasn't he done all this before? A woman with a camera? Trying to take him somewhere he doesn't want to go? A hotel night? Perhaps another body waiting? It isn't what Medeiros said that scares him. It's the specter of an unseen net and the chance that this is Angel's doing. If their lives are linked in strange and unchartable ways, could she have lured him toward that rally? Why did she choose the Blue Dolphin Lounge? And is it Angel then? Or is it this island world she lives in now, with its web of pagan stories? Is she somehow entrapping him? Or could he be entrapping himself again? Suppose there is a pattern that he himself creates, something about the people he selects, or who select him, no matter where he goes? In the humid breeze across the lanai of the Orchid Isle Hotel he swims among the eery correspondences, watching fat carp swim in and out of mottled, double light.

A cold wind blows through his veins again, and he shivers with the certainty that Angel and Crystal are one and the same, Angel and Crystal and Rachel and Marge, all the women he has ever known are versions of the same woman, one he has chosen time and time again, before and after the grenade, before and after his vision was splintered by the shrapnel chip. Isn't she too another version of the woman who will bring out the worst, who will turn on you when you least expect it?

Linda stops to pick up an empty, handing him an envelope labeled WHILE YOU WERE OUT. "You forgot to pick up your messages," she says.

He asks her if she can bring him a sandwich and another beer. There isn't supposed to be any food on the lanai, she tells him, but she'll see what she can do. He says, "You have a minute?"

"Maybe half a minute."

"Sit down here on the couch."

She shrugs, with a quick and careful smile. "Duty calls."

He sees one couple having a drink across the lobby. A glance tells him the restaurant is nearly empty. He scoots over. "C'mon, Linda, take a break. Talk to me. Tell me something."

Her face changes, or rather, in her face, he sees himself. He is no longer a customer. He is a man alone in the early evening, a needful man who for one reason or another has come to the attention of the local cops. Around her customer-pleasing smile, around her thirty-seven-year-old eyes all the burdens of her life show through, her family cares, her no-surplus income, her fear that he might raise his voice or be waiting outside when she gets off work. He feels close to Linda, very close. They are marooned together on this little raft that resembles the lanai of a small hotel. When she walks away he feels totally abandoned.

Somewhere a trio has started to play, acoustic bass, ukulele strumming, lonesome whine of the steel guitar. Floating on the trade winds the sound is so poignant, so sentimental, he longs to hear Angel's voice. He does not care which kind of woman she is. A yearning grabs him that is nearly unbearable. He can almost hear her speaking, as if he wears headphones that have picked up the faintest signal. He has a good reason to call, he tells himself. If Medeiros is right, if Prince was out there when the fire began, this report he thought was all sewed up may now have come unraveled. He needs to look one more time at his photos of the shed.

But it's too soon for that. Too soon. Too soon. first, check the messages.

Here's one from Carlo: "What gives, Travis? Did you hang up on me? Were we cut off?"

Here's one from Brockman, accompanied by two Polaroid shots of a lava flow from high above, stripes of orange against the black: "So far, so good. If you want to see more, meet me Saturday, 3 P.M. Holiday Air."

The message from Prince is the one that holds him, called in yesterday at 8:45 A.M., which would have been before they found his car but after he left his voice on the tape now snug in the pocket of Tom Medeiros. Travis sees the porch again, the dark-rose sky. He sees himself outside, the pulled venetian blinds. Could Prince have been sitting there alone, peering through the slats? The thought of it grips him, the odd and invisible intimacy of such a moment. It repels him, and it beguiles him. What was Prince doing there? What was he looking at? Or looking for? What was he thinking of? Where did he go next? And why does Travis care?

"We seem to be missing each other. I hope you enjoy the Manu Kona. Please call this number as soon as you can. I have some news."

Why should Travis be giving a damn about this man who gave him bad directions and once offered him a bribe and ordered a breakfast he never intended to eat? Medeiros doesn't have a case. At most, a semi-case. A car was ripped off here and trashed there.

He doesn't recognize the number, or the voice. For some reason, he expected a man. It's a woman. Not Connie.

"This is Travis Doyle."

"Yes, Mr. Doyle. How can I help you?"

"I hope it's not too late."

"That's all right."

"I'm trying to reach Mr. Prince."

"Yes. He told me you might be calling."

"Is he there?"

"He was here a couple of days ago. I haven't seen him since."

"Did he say where he was going?"

"Back to the Big Island, I believe."

"Isn't this a Big Island number?"

"It's a Maui number."

"You're his therapist, then."

"He said he was hoping to meet you."

"When? Where?"

"At the drilling site, he said. It would have been yesterday. Late afternoon."

"Did he say why?"

"It was a matter of insurance, he said."

"Insurance."

"Yes. But I gather you missed him."

"I just picked up this message."

"That's too bad. I've been waiting to hear."

"Hear what?"

"Something. How he's doing."

"So you've known him for a while."

"Much longer than I expected to."

He wants her to continue. She has a soothing voice, even while on guard, a voice he wants to hear more from.

"Is that all?"

"Were you expecting more?"

"Why didn't he leave this message with Connie?"

"Maybe she isn't happy there. I'm just guessing. I think she took the morning off."

"So he wasn't calling from the office."

"I'm not very comfortable talking with police."

"Did he tell you I was police?"

"He said you're an investigator."

"I'm a claims adjuster."

He knows this sounds to her like the same thing. He doesn't want her to hang up. He tells her about the car and where they found it.

This gets her attention. "They're sure it was his?"

"It's the compact he leases from Alamo."

For a while she is silent. At last she says, "What do you think happened?"

"Maybe nothing. A stolen car."

"But he hasn't been seen, and he hasn't reported it?"

"Not yet."

Another silence.

"Still here?" he says.

"I have some water boiling."

"You want to go turn it down?"

"Are we finished?"

"Is there something more you can tell me?"

"Not on the phone."

"Is there something more I can tell you?"

He thinks he hears a slow, measured exhale, though maybe it's her kettle exhaling in the background. He says, "Do you ever get to the Big Island?"

"Once or twice a year."

"Suppose I flew to Maui."

"It would depend on when."

"It wouldn't be to talk about insurance."

"I would hope not."

"This is going to sound strange."

"Some days everything is strange."

"I don't quite know how to express this."

"Say it any way you can."

"It's about Ian Prince, and yet . . ."

"There's something else?"

"I guess you could say I'm at a point . . ."

This time it is a waiting silence, a long and unconditional and permission-giving silence.

"You're at a point?"

"I need . . ."

"What?"

"You probably . . ."

"Just say it."

"You probably hear people say this all the time."

"I sound like someone you could talk to?"

Let's think of it as a consultation, he says, at the going rate. After a pause she says he's lucky, someone has canceled, and there's a spot tomorrow morning early, if he can promise to be on time.

He promises, figuring he can catch an early flight, only to find out, three calls later, that all the airlines are booked solid until midafternoon. "But there's one more flight out tonight," says the velvety voice from Aloha Air, "and we still have plenty of room."

An hour later he is bound for Maui on a DC-8, the pilot swinging south from the airport toward the rift zone, taking it upon himself to loop in close so they can see the churning pool. It spills out into the black of night, mushy molten matter piped up from somewhere to heap and spread across older lava and roll into the 'ohi'a groves. Two broad stripes are oozing downslope, just as Brockman photographed them, one toward the shoreline, one more or less on an inland route. Yes, the drilling rig would be out in front of it, he is right about that part. And Travis can imagine himself out there too, dancing along the burning edge.

As they complete the swing, heading north again toward the flight path, a few trees turn to flame, making tiny sparks far below. He wishes he could hover there to gaze a while longer at the ancient mirror that holds him mesmerized, as flames of every size will do, from flaming rivers to the dots sparkling in the night sky above the plane. In the summertime campground you can always find orange light flickering across the faces of the rings of musing campers. On the freeway where a car is burning in the emergency lane, you forget for a moment the meeting you were rushing to and slow down to contemplate the scene. You almost stop, but a horn honks and away you go, feeling rushed, vaguely cheated, as Travis feels cheated by the Maui-bound turning of the jet. In Hawai'i, when the rift zone opens, helicopter pilots work day and night. Ten thousand photographers appear, with ten million dollars' worth of high-speed equipment, to catch it on film or on video, to take away with them for replay later on, making of each far-flung living room and VCR a fireplace, a place of fire, where they can sit and gaze again.

Conquistadors

The next morning, while Travis checks out of his Kahului motel, heading into the cane fields that sprawl between Maui's two mountain knobs, John Brockman is on his way to Honolulu, where he knows someone who knows someone who trades in explosives. Shopping on the Big Island would be too risky, with people watching his every move. He needs something fast that can't be traced. He also needs financing. For purposes of persuasion he carries in his bag half a dozen aerials of lava on the move. He will be looking up one of his old connections, someone "in the syndicate." That's what he is telling himself. He hasn't thought this part through. He has brought along his daughter, who sits beside him drawing mustaches on the faces of all the men pictured in the in-flight magazine. He is going to drop her off in Pearl City with the parents of his estranged wife. This much he knows. And after that?

As they leave Moloka'i behind, as Diamond Head comes into view, he is calculating that two guys with explosives and a timer can take out this one long low embankment of curling rock, throw down enough debris to divert the flow and send it through a new channel the blast will open up. If he can't get to the embankment in time, if something stops him, he has a backup plan. He will blow a hole in the access road to the drilling site, so the vehicles and the equipment can't escape. People can escape, but not equipment. Either way he will be keeping Pele on her path—which is why he can't ask anyone local to come in on such a manuever. Who would consider blowing up one part of Pele's body to save another part? The fact is, they will not blow up anything to save anything else. It is out of character. Sabotage is not the island way, Brockman thinks. If you ask a Hawaiian he will probably say, That is the white man's way, and when you use the white man's way you become like him and you lose the very thing you are trying to preserve.

But look what happens, says Brockman to himself, they lose anyway. They have been losing since the day Captain Cook showed up. In the last two hundred years the only Hawaiian who won big was King Kamehameha the Great, when he defeated all the other chiefs and united the islands. But how did he do it? He had British weapons. Don't forget the British sailors who knew a good thing when they saw it and jumped ship and brought along a few pieces of artillery, which none of the other chiefs had, so Kamehameha could move in with superior firepower. Isn't that the whole history of the fucking world? Aloha by itself just does not get it. Not in this day and age. You have to have aloha plus superior firepower. Maybe that is what I have to offer, maybe that is how I can make a contribution here. With a few people like me around, the locals don't have to risk becoming white. I can fight fire with fire because I am already white. I am already a conquistador. It's in my blood. So why not use it for a good cause instead of for a shitty cause? Just get on in there. Nobody needs to know who, or why. It's not about publicity. You don't go public. You wear gloves, and running shoes. Go in and divert the flow, cowboy style, aim it for the rig. It's going to be good for Hawai'i, and it's not even illegal. That's open land out there, mostly rocks. No property to wreck. Somewhere somebody has to draw the fucking line, before the Big Island ends up looking like Bakersfield. We already have Bakersfield, for christ sake! We know what that is like. We already have Galveston! We already have Mexico City! We already have L.A. . . .

Weeks later Travis will learn that in the neighborhood of Brockman's youth there had been a friend whose father used to backpack into the eastern side of the Sierra Nevada range, favoring trailheads you reached via Bishop and Independence, at the upper end of the Owens Valley. This revered surrogate father took young Jack along on two or three such outings, a memory that still brings wetness to his eyes. Brockman is like the lover who has been repeatedly rejected. He will never forgive Los Angeles, the city of his birth, for betraying him.

"Do you know the Owens Valley, Doyle?" he will ask.

"I have been through there. Highway 395?"

"Then you must know about the Owens Valley Project. Look back into that fiasco, you hear the same thing they are saying here. Are we going to grow and be an economic force? Then we need to figure out how to electrify this steam and move it north so Honolulu can achieve its great potential as a crossroads of the Pacific. It's the Owens Valley all over again. It's William Mulholland selling the idea that the future depends on tapping into a water supply two hundred miles away. We could have a great city here, he used to say. Too bad we're out in this semiarid bowl where there is nothing wet enough to qualify as an annual rainfall, and there aren't even any rivers flowing all year round. What we need to do is aim a little water in our direction. So off they go, across a couple of mountain ranges to drain the Owens Valley and turn a rich farming region into a total desert, and when the Owens Lake goes dry they run the pipe another hundred miles north, up to Mono, one of the rare treasures of the eleven western states, but now Mono is dropping by two or three inches every year, so they will pump that lake dry too and wreck the breeding ground for all the coastal seagulls, but that is okay because everybody knows people are more important than seagulls, and then they will run the pipe north into Oregon, or Washington. You hear talk now about the Columbia River and how there ought to be a way for L.A. to get a piece of *that!*"

"My question, Doyle, is what do you get by moving so much water from where it belongs to where it doesn't belong? Maybe it sounded like a great idea seventy-five years ago. But what you get, along with the water, is enough concrete to cover Rhode Island, and streets filling up with hookers and killers and addicts and overflow anxiety and you get air that doesn't deserve the name. You ever been there during a smog alert? They pull school kids in off the playground. My last job was in a hospital. I was an orderly. On the night I quit, I was working late in Emergency. This woman was wheeled in, she had been knifed in the parking lot outside a 7-Eleven. Big gashes in the chest and back. Dead on arrival. Drugs were a factor. So they had to do an autopsy to determine the actual cause, and the coroner told me later, 'She must have been from out of town.' I said to the coroner, 'Why do you sat that?' 'Her lungs,' he said. 'Her lungs are clean.'"

Like Almost-Lovers

She is around forty, pale blue eyes, ash blonde hair in a thick braid, with a melancholy sweetness about her, a large woman, ample and billowing, wearing a caftan. "Therapist" was Connie's word, he realizes. A framed wall certificate says *Counselor*. From the look of things, she could use the money. Her office is a glassed-in veranda. She works out of a bungalow with a view west across the lower slope of the old volcano, Haleakala.

She has a welcoming, talk-to-me manner, and he finds himself telling her what happened as he stepped off the plane last night. The air had changed, it was somehow lighter, with a feathery lightness, and this wasn't a change in humidity. It was actually atmospheric. As he stood on the runway, he says, a thick robe fell from his shoulders—a remark that seems to open a door.

They look out toward the dormant crater, as smoothly coned as Shasta or Fuji. fifteen years have taught her, she says, that each of these islands has its own character, its own mystique. *Maui no ka oi*, the bumper stickers say, *Maui is indeed the best*. What does that mean? she asks. For her, a Buddha island. Wise. Serene. Hawaii is much bigger, but also much younger. Raw and unpredictable. Maui is romantic, she says. The Big Island is passionate, with an unruly spirit that can make you do unruly things.

"Can we talk about that?" says Travis.

"We can talk about anything we like."

She steps to a two-burner hot plate on a narrow counter where cups and saucers and pitchers and a pot have been set out. "I'm going to fix some tea. Would you like a cup of tea?"

"Yes, thanks."

"I have all kinds of herbal, ginseng, Earl Grey too, and Lipton's."

"Earl Grey sounds good."

She tells him then that she and Prince were married once, for a couple of years. They met in college and went together for quite a while. She moved to the islands after they split up, and until the company started sending him over here, they'd been long out of touch. If Prince were a client, she says, she probably wouldn't be talking to Travis at all. But he isn't a client. He is a kind of ghost from another life.

"He tells me I'm the only one who ever understood him."

"You think that's true?"

"Maybe I'm the only one who tried."

"Is he married now?"

"Twice was enough, I think. He's too difficult to live with. He keeps too much hidden away. I used to think he was just a very private man."

"You don't think that now?"

She is moving toward him with the tea service, her smile tentative, as if she perhaps said more than she intended to. "I still don't know exactly what you're doing here."

He almost says, I think I'm going blind again, but waits, and watches her set a cup and saucer on the little table next to his chair. As she bends to pour, the soft pungent scent of steaming tea joins another scent. It puffs from her bosom, a delicate mix of powder and perspiration. She glances up at him, a glint of amusement in her eyes, a character-reading glance, female to male. They are alone in the house, alone in the world, faces just inches apart. She wears no makeup. Her cheeks are smooth, like peaches, unblemished, even at close range. He would like to stroke her cheek, or touch her arm, the way Prince might have done fifteen years ago, the casually familiar touch of the husband. He comes very close. His need is strong just now, suspended between the unknown and the known, and craving contact.

She steps back, to sit again, sipping and watching him through wisps of steam. He feels curiously unpressured, unhurried, even though he only has an hour of her time. Less than an hour. Fifty minutes.

"I don't ordinarily investigate fires," he says, describing the various accounts he's heard, and then the breakfast in the coffee shop, his impression of a man distracted, contradictory and ill at ease.

Leaning toward him through the steam she says, "Please continue. I haven't met anyone else who knows this part of his life."

"I wouldn't say I know him. We only met that once."

"It's news to me, whatever he said or did."

He starts again, and now he is telling both stories at once, Prince's story intermingling with Travis's, as the whole week-long saga comes tumbling out, how they met on his second day back in the islands, then meeting up with Angel after all these years, the mysteries, the family histories. The talking purges him, talking it through, and she listens well, with the eyes and ears of a counselor and also like the parent who listens to some story about a grown son long gone from home, listening for news from a part of her past or a part of herself she has been hoping one day to comprehend.

"Pardon me for interrupting," she says at last, "but I have to say that you remind me a bit of Ian. Perhaps it's where you're sitting. When he was younger, before he put on so much weight, he resembled you. The other day he sat right there and held his hand out and asked if I thought he was losing his mind. And I was like a fortune teller staring at his hand while he told me things he's never talked about with anyone, or so he said."

"What kinds of things?" says Travis, as if he is now the counselor and she the counselee.

She begins to describe the visit, how he didn't call ahead this time, walked in unannounced, as if they had never stopped living together and he had just been down to the corner to buy a loaf of bread. She wants to talk about it all, unburden herself to Travis, as he unburdened himself to her. They are both startled by a screen door's slam.

She glances at the clock. Her face fills with disappointment. "Oh my goodness. One of my regulars is here."

"Maybe I can hang around. Or come back later."

"Yes. Or call." She's flipping pages in an appointment book. "That would be better. Tonight, if you can. Or tomorrow."

In the matted front room a young woman sits reading, her dark face swollen with a rash. On the porch outside the counselor tells him he doesn't owe her anything. She owes him, she says, for flying all this way. He writes a check out anyhow, and they hug like almost-lovers, both wishing for something more, hold each other for quite some time, as if he is about to fly halfway around the globe. Almost as an afterthought, as if this hug has been a final test, she tells him she referred Prince to someone else, a *kupuna*, an elder, a man known to be wise in Hawaiian ways, as she often does when a case involves what she calls "local matters."

"It was all I could think of to do, and I can't guarantee that he followed my advice. He seemed calm enough, but he may or may not have been listening. And this man could refuse to see him, you know. The old fellow doesn't have a phone, won't make appointments. You have to find his house and hope he feels like talking. I know that may sound . . . unorthodox. But out here you can't always go by the book."

"So when he called yesterday, he had maybe seen this guy, or maybe not?"

"I wish I knew."

"I'm not sure I get this. Why did you send him to an elder?"

As he searches her face, she smiles with sudden apology. "What's wrong with me? Of course you don't get it. This is the part you need to know."

Deciding then to tell him much more than she has time to tell, she guides him back inside and calls the waiting woman with the face rash to join them for a cup of tea, since this is going to be the kind of story all islanders love to hear. She needs to tell it now, this morning. She has already tracked down the geologist, by phone, just as Travis, who will be back in Hilo in time for lunch, will soon track down old library files of the *Tribune Herald* to confirm the dates. He will find there a detail map, along with photos of the eruption. Later on he will hear other, more apocryphal versions of what occurred, but the tale told by the counselsor from the Buddha slope of Haleakala is the one that will stick with him.

Between the mountain and where he sits, baby orchids hang against the veranda window. This time he notices that her whole room is filled with potted orchids, their slender arms translucent. A few of these arch so far up and over, the filament blossoms seem detached, afloat. They are tiny white-and-purple shrimp cruising next to the glass. From time to time he is underwater with the shrimp, whenever he looks out the window toward the crater that rises from the ocean floor to ten thousand feet, old fire fountain soaring from the sea. He is a bottom fish, settling, settling, and he almost sees the face again, peering down through shafts of undulating light, the eyes blue-green. Just a glimpse. His underwater dream.

Prince's Tale

The summer before he started college, Ian went traveling with his father. Western Sun was years away from becoming a multinational conglomerate. His father was an aggressive vice president for corporate expansion, planning ahead, looking around the Pacific for investment opportunities. Colleagues in Honolulu were advising him to buy into some land not far from where a fissure had recently opened, south and east of Kilauea. The father was intrigued, but he wanted a closer look. He had seen the Big Island before. It was seventeen-year-old Ian's first trip.

They hired a geologist who arranged to guide them out across a section of the newest flow. Lava had been pouring over the lip of a mesalike precipice, rolling from there across the coastal plain and into the sea. Their destination was a steam plume that swelled up from the shoreline a mile past the end of the road. They wore the orange vests that would identify them as "official observers." Murky clouds hovered above the horizon, perhaps a storm system moving in, but slowly, and in the distance, sharpening the pleasure of the blue sky overhead and the tropic stillness of the sultry air.

A quarter of a mile from the plume they came upon a small bundle wrapped in shiny green ti leaves. There was nothing else around but slabs of broken lava.

"Could be gin," the geologist said.

"What do you mean, gin?" said the father.

"It's an offering. You find them out here from time to time."

"What kind of offering?"

"They say Pele likes gin, though it's not always that. It could be damn near anything. People charter light planes and drop things into the moving flow. Sometimes they'll hike out as close as they can get and leave something."

"Well, what say, Ian?" said the father with a laugh. "Let's take a look."

"I wouldn't," the geologist said.

"A bottle of gin?"

"Whatever it is, just let it be."

"Nonsense. C'mon, Ian, let's look into this."

Hunkering, Ian unwrapped the layers of leaves and found a quart of Gilbey's with the price tag still on the bottle, and wrapped around the bottle a necklace of polished nuts called kukui, polished to a dark glow.

"I'll be damned," said the son, sounding much like the father. "A quart of gin out here by itself on the most godforsaken pile of rocks in the whole Pacific Ocean."

"It's a gift," said the father, "it's a sign of welcome."

He made this a mock proclamation. He set one booted foot on a dark hump, like Balboa after crossing the Isthmus of Panama. "What do you say, Ian? A drink to the moment? To our great good luck?"

"If I were you," the geologist said, "I'd just wrap it up again."

"What's the matter, man? Not thirsty?"

"We have a full canteen. Back at the house there's everything in the world to drink. I'll fix gin and tonics until midnight, if you want."

"I suppose you're telling me it's cursed."

250

"I don't like the word 'curse.' I don't like 'superstitious' either. I'm just telling you I've been here awhile, and I have seen things happen that are hard to explain. You can drink that gin if you have to. And you can say there's a geologist who has been out here too long for his own good. I just wouldn't open that bottle or disturb that necklace if I were you."

His father unscrewed the cap and passed the bottle to Ian, whose eyes had been darting back and forth. He agreed with the geologist that it was a bad idea. If nothing else, 9:30 A.M. was the wrong time of day to be drinking warm gin from the bottle. But his father had made it a test of something. Manhood. Common sense. So Ian swallowed a small swallow and handed it to his father, who then offered it to the geologist, who shook his head with a pained smile. The father tipped it for a very long swallow that ended with a shiver of his head and neck and a satisfied, breathy "Aaaaaahhh."

He screwed the cap on and stuffed the bottle and the necklace of kukui nuts into Ian's day pack. The geologist was in a hurry now, urging them forward, perhaps because the heavy clouds were suddenly larger. Near the plume, the air temperature jumped about twenty degrees. The ground was much warmer. From the shoreline cliff an orange stream spilled into the surge. Steam churning upward became a tumbling cloud of white, rising toward a sky that was half blue and half gray shreds from the storm system's advancing edge. The steam poured back against slick black cliffs made of last month's flow, or perhaps last night's.

When you're that close to the planet's cutting edge something draws you toward it. You want to stand as close as you can get. They all three felt it, the geologist, the youth, and the cynic father too. So intent were they on creeping forward under the plume's gauzy and drenching mist, the offshore crack of lightning took them by surprise. A crooked bolt split the vaulting thundercloud. Ian lost his footing. His boot slid past a jagged edge and touched a soft place where a thin chunk of crust gave away. He saw a red stripe showing through the rock. His boot seemed to float in a seeping redness. He lunged. His right hand took the fall and found another thin spot in the crust and broke through into searing heat. He screamed and rolled clear, his palm scorched, his boot smoking.

In the emergency room at Hilo Community, the geologist told Ian he was lucky. A friend of his had almost lost his legs stepping through crust like that, in up to his knees before they pulled him out.

"The odd thing was, his feet were okay. The boots saved his feet, except for the eyelets. He still has eyelet scars on both feet, two lines of white dots where lava burned the laces out."

He did not mention Pele, or the bottle, or the necklace, but the father did, jokingly, after the geologist left, and then again in the days that followed, while the hand was healing, and from time to time in the years that followed.

"Old Ian," his father would say, "he was listening so hard to that rock hopper he must have believed him, because that is how these hexes and mojo deals work, isn't it? You have to be a believer before they can have any effect on you. As for me," the father would tell the table full of amused after-dinner guests, "as for Toby Prince, he turned that quart of Gilbey's into several fine martinis, and he is here to tell you that the sky has not yet fallen, and gin is gin wherever you find it," holding high his crossed forefingers as if to ward off all forms of sorcery.

When Ian was among the listeners at such a gathering, he would laugh with everyone else. Sometimes he would hold up his right hand, with the palm close to his chest, so others could see the living evidence of that day, and the truth of Toby's story, see the scars along the insides of the fingers, curling up beside the thumb, beside his wrist, curling like small white flames. He seldom showed the palm. The skin had grown back without the lines a palmist might read, but with something in place of the lines, an odd shiny contour in the scar tissue. In certain light he believed he could make out the profile of a woman's head, a long-haired woman. Sometimes it wasn't there. It depended on the light, on the season, on the temperature of his skin.

Tutu David

That same morning, while Travis was shaving, while John Brockman was en route to Honolulu, while Angel was in her studio printing blowups, while Dan Clemson was on the phone again, telling Houston he had been instructed by Civil Defense to be prepared to evacuate the site, Tutu David woke up thinking about the days when he was ten years old, living on the Kona side with his mother's brother in a village that has long since disappeared. The air reminded him, as if the sun's light were passing through the thinnest filmy filter. He remembered the night when he stood with his uncle and watched the lava come down from Mauna Loa.

It was like the first edge of a rising sun. They watched it slide over a cliff and drop, and then it was like a glowing waterfall. They watched it move closer, until it looked as if it might be heading for his uncle's house. They ran up the hill and laid out ti leaves. Outside the house his uncle's wife was chanting and praying. His uncle was praying. But the lava kept coming, rolling past most of the village and across his uncle's yard. They had to stand and watch the house catch fire and burn. It wasn't easy to do that, because it was their house, on ancient family land, and many things were left inside. But David was not afraid that night. Ten years old and watching the house burn down, he felt great sadness for his family, but he had no fear because his uncle had no fear. His uncle prayed, and she decided to take the house anyway, and without question he accepted that. He knew he could build another house, and he did.

In David's long life he has learned to fear and mistrust many things. He fears the men in Japan and in California who want to cover his island with concrete and asphalt and golf courses and parking lots. He fears the generals who send tanks and missile launchers to practice war in the saddle land between the craters, and he fears the admirals who have sent so many ships and planes from Pearl Harbor and Hickam to bomb and strafe the lonely island of Kaho'olawe. But he has never feared the lava. His uncle used to call it Pele's tongue, the tongue coming out of the mouth of Pele singing the song only she can sing.

Now he fixes himself some breakfast and takes his coffee out onto the porch and sits looking at the color of the sky, looking south where the blue takes on a smoky tinge. He sits all morning, thinking about his uncle, and about other folks on his mother's side, thinking of his mother, Malama, the way she was drinking at the end, the way she would raise her voice, this woman who was always so soft-spoken, accusing him and accusing her father, even when the father was no longer there, long dead, but still she spoke to him and warned him not to criticize and talk behind her back. Sometimes she would be accusing all three of them at once, David, her oldest son, and David's father, her second husband, who has Hawaiian, and the first husband too, who died before David was born, a man from Wales, the one who made her stop speaking in Hawaiian and would never let her dance.

What a dancer she was, that Malama! His mother. And what a blessing for her when husband number one started drinking at lunchtime on a day when they were clearing out the irrigation ditches up Honoka'a way. He was the foreman of the crew and known to be a man who could hold his liquor, so when he came back to work drunk that afternoon nobody noticed it, or nobody cared, until he took a wrong step and fell into the ditch and landed on his head and drowned. That's when Malama started dancing again, in the old style called *kahiko*, with just a drum and the *mele*, the chanter's song. When she married again she married a Hawaiian man who would let her dance. She had power in those days. What power his mother had in the days when she was dancing! Even after the drinking, she did not lose it. He remembers the day she came to him and told him he must say the chant for the young cousin whose baby was about to be born. He remembers his fear. It was a chant David had done only once, a chant he learned years earlier from a very old Hawaiian man in the district, whose voice was so thin and raspy the words would sometimes fade away. David feared he had forgotten this chant, that it had been lost from disuse. His mother, Malama, looked at him hard and said, "The words will come. The words will come." And she was right. When they gathered around the belly of the woman, the words came, the way the notes of a song will stay in your fingers even though you have not touched the guitar for ten years or twenty. He began to speak, and the chant came forth as if from some other body, as if the old man with the raspy voice were with them in the room.

As he sits on his porch alone he hears the words, and he speaks them again, softly, a ragged sound from low in his chest, the sound he chanted to Angel a month before she was born. Somehow the words squeeze the years together. He moves his head and sees the full-grown niece sitting next to him in the shade. He looks again and knows he will have to wait a while longer to see her there. He listens until he hears again his mother's voice, talking about the early times and the village she grew up in, a place which is now just a name on the map. So many died there, the survivors moved away. It was a terrible thing, she told him, to move away from the place where your ancestors have lived for centuries. "When Captain Cook brought his ships to Kealakekua," she used to say, "we were half a million people. Half a million! But by the time I was a girl, in all these islands you could not find fifty thousand Hawaiians. After so many years we should have multiplied. People always multiply. But not us. We went the other way. In a hundred years we went from half a million down to fifty thousand."

257

Greed stole our land away, she used to say, diseases stole away our bodies. Syphilis. Measles. Smallpox. Cholera. Whooping cough. Things you don't want to think about or talk about. But Malama would talk, and she would ask, What did that do to the heart of the people, so many deaths? What did that do to the spirit? The Americans were smart, she used to say, to wait until 1893 to take the government from Hawaii's queen. If they tried to do this in the early days, it would have been too bloody, with so many to subdue. With only fifty thousand left, whose hearts were heavy with loss, well, what better time for the Americans to take control. Not a shot was fired. The haole men from overseas walked into Iolani Palace in Honolulu and overpowered the queen.

When David was a youngster he saw her in parades, Lili'uokalani, in a carriage drawn by horses, wearing a high-necked dress like the queens of England wore. *Ka lani*— very high chief, exalted, noble. *Lili'u*—a scorching, a burning, or pain in the eyes. This was after she had been held captive in her palace for a year, and after she had been released. In the days after Hawai'i became a territory of the United States, and she lived on as the queen without a country, she would ride through downtown Honolulu, where Malama had sent him to go to school. His mother and his father wanted him to learn to read and write English, to learn the ways of the conqueror, so he would have a chance in the world, and he learned those ways well enough to know he did not like them much. He lived in Honolulu for many years. He also lived in San Francisco, when his wife was still alive. They sometimes performed together there, as singer and dancer. Before World War II, when Hawaiian music was at the top of the charts, David and his wife managed a night club in the old International Settlement. During this time he looked into the haole mind, and the more he looked, the more he trusted his Hawaiian mind. After his father died, in the tidal wave of 1946, David came back to the Big Island. Since then he has not left, not even to visit Maui, right across the channel.

This elderly cottage is much like the one he grew up in, nothing fancy, plain and comfortable, with a porch, papaya trees, ginger in the yard, and a son living down the road to keep an eye on him. Nowadays Hilo seems strange and foreign, too many malls and video games, a faraway place he visits less and less. But there is no need to move around much. People come to him, more than he cares to talk to. Cars arrive outside his fence, and he waits to see who steps out and what they want and whether or not he should speak to them, sometimes family, sometimes strangers, sometimes Hawaiians, sometimes Japanese, sometimes local haoles, once in a while a haole from the mainland like the blond and red-faced man who stopped his car in the middle of the road two days ago, or maybe three days now. He came walking across the yard carrying a six-pack of lime soda and a white box from the bakery with a lilikoi cream pie.

The woman on Maui had told him lilikoi pie was the old man's favorite, which it is, though not many know it. So he accepted the pie and held the box in his lap and told the visitor to come in under the porch, out of the sun, sit down and have a lime soda. He felt sorry for this sweating and overweight haole man. He watched the hands, which rolled over one another and would not stay still.

He told the man to sit with him and listen. "Nobody listens any more. Always turning something on. Get lonely, turn the TV on. In a hurry, turn on the microwave. Get anxious, turn on the rock and roll. What about turning something off? Turn off everything. Listen for a while. It's simple to do. We forgot how."

They sat in the shade until Tutu, who had been listening to the fronds overhead, finally asked the man, whose eyes were roaming like his hands, "What do you hear?"

"My heart. It's beating like a drum."

"What does it tell you?"

He listened then to the story of an offering taken from the rocks many years ago, near the site of a new eruption.

When the man finished, Tutu sat thinking of all the things haoles have taken, large and small things. He thought of scolding this man for waiting so long, then decided no. His fear was great. Simply tell him what to do, and leave it up to him to do it. Maybe he would learn something. Maybe not.

"Let me see your hand," he said.

The man held it out, palm down. Tutu touched it, turned it over, felt the smooth white scar, felt the heat. He held the hand in both of his.

"You remember the place?"

"I'm sure I do."

"Go to that place again, wherever it is, and make your peace."

"How do I do it? How do I make my peace?"

"Whatever you took away, put 'em back."

"It was a necklace made of nuts."

"Kukui nuts? Black?"

"Yes."

"You still got 'em?"

"In Hilo, in my apartment. There was a bottle of gin too."

"Oh."

"What's the matter?"

"I'm not sure about the gin, where that got started. But take 'em all back. The kukui. The gin. Maybe some flowers too. Anthuriums are pretty good. They last. Wrap em up in ti leaf. Do it with respect. Ask forgiveness."

"What do I say? How do I ask? Out loud?"

"Of course, out loud," said Tutu, with a hint of indignation. "Use your voice. Speak with your voice and with your heart."

The man offered money then. "Please come with me, and tell me what to say."

Tutu shook his head. "I'm too old to go out there. You do this by yourself. Hawaiian, English, Japanese, filipino, whatever. Speak the words from your heart, and she will hear you."

That is what he told the man, two days ago, or three. Whether or not the man took this advice, he may never know. Sometimes they come back to him, sometimes not. He sits and waits and watches the road to see who is coming next, and now another car coasts to a stop. He is pleased to see Angel, pleased but not surprised, nor will he be surprised to hear her say the pool of lava in the mountains has overflowed. David will tell her the woman in the long red dress came by again, yesterday afternoon. She stood at his gate again, called out again, and this time she smiled a seductive smile. "Think she was flirting with me, sister."

The Men in Her Life

Angel has picked up some *manapua* from the Chinese grocery store, soft-cooked dumplings filled with spicy meat. Tutu puts his hand inside the bag. "Still warm, sister. We better eat 'em up."

"Unless you want to save them for dinner."

"Dinner!" he says, as if the idea disgusts him. "I never eat dinner! I only eat lunch. C'mon"

She brings out plates and forks and sets them on his little porch table, but they don't use them. They sit in the shade munching and grinning. For a while they don't talk. Eating is enough. Eating is being alive. The old man makes her happy, the way he savors every bite. The food makes her happy. She hasn't eaten breakfast.

As she chomps into her third dumpling she realizes she didn't eat dinner last night, even though she started to cook, put some water on the stove, watched it boil, dropped the noodles in. Guilt killed her appetite. Walking out of the rain into her dark living room, she found Marilyn face down on the couch, gangly legs drawn up, brown arm dangling from the T-shirt. For one breathless second Marilyn looked dead, the moment Angel has breathed away a thousand times. In the line of her daughter's jaw she saw her own mother, wondered if her mother had known this fear. She stood still, gazing down, until one eyelid lifted.

The daughter spoke with a mother's reprimanding voice. "Where were you?"

"I'm sorry, honey. Did you get my message?"

"Were you with your old boyfriend?"

"What are you talking about?"

"Brenda said some old boyfriend showed up in town."

"Listen, Marilyn, please listen carefully. Whatever anyone else has told you, and whatever I tell you about the last couple of days, please, please, please keep it to yourself. People in this town talk too much. You know that."

"Did you stay overnight with him?"

Angel fell into the upholstered chair, felt her body unravel. Her eyes were raw.

"I'll tell you everything that happened, okay? I really will. But not right now. I'm feeling pretty ragged, if you want to know the truth."

Marilyn swung around and sat up with head cocked, a sidelong glance, a lowering of the lids, a look Angel would recognize anywhere, exactly how she herself looks when someone is holding out on her.

"Any messages?"

"Nothing for me. A lot for you, I think. The red light is blinking away. Roland was talking on the machine when I came in."

"About what?"

"Just checking in, he said."

"That sounds like Roland."

"You never stay overnight with Roland."

"That's right."

"Why not?"

"It's none of your business. Just tell me what's been going on around here. What did you do yesterday?"

"We went out for pizza after volleyball is about all that happened."

"Did you come straight home?"

"I don't have to tell you if you're not going to tell me what you did."

"Okay, forget it."

"You didn't even call this afternoon. I thought you'd be back by the time I got home." The daughter became the mother again, accusing, pleading.

"I said I'm sorry. I thought I'd be home too, a lot sooner than this."

"Hey, have you been crying?"

"Why? Are my eyes red?"

"What's the matter, Mom?"

"It's the driving, I think. The lights coming at you in the rain. How about dinner? You hungry?"

The daughter's smooth and innocent forehead had creased with lines of concern. "No."

"You're never hungry. When do you eat?"

Marilyn sprang to her feet, as if a siren had gone off outside. "I'm going to use the phone, okay?"

"I'm going to fix something, I don't know what."

"I have to call Rebecca."

"Sure," said Angel to the empty room.

She listened until the murmuring began, the murmur of fast-breaking teenage news, wondering why Marilyn never eats what's fixed for her, dabs at it maybe, or slips into the kitchen and picks bits from the pan or skillet, then eats somewhere else, later, or earlier, at the wrong time, spending money on things she shouldn't eat. Something like a pregnant woman, angel thought, that moody craving. She looked again at Marilyn, legs splayed across the floor.

Low-pitched chatter filled the house, not with words, but with its urgent tumble. She heard her own voice there so many years ago. Half listening she wondered if anything had changed. Here was the daughter in the kitchen conspiring with Rebecca about the boys in their lives. Here was the mother exhausted in the living room, brooding about the men in her life, still not sure what she wants, wondering if she's always kept them at a distance, flipping back through the mind's album of long-lost boyfriends, in high school, in junior high, her legs as skinny as Marilyn's yet promising something to Bennie and Kimo and Junior and Leonard, kissing and teasing and chasing, being chased, always glad to get away, as she finally got away from Walter. Whatever went wrong, was he the only one at fault? Could she have given more? Trusted more? Helped him see himself with clearer eyes and see her with clearer eyes? The answer is always no, she could not have done that, or wouldn't have, didn't yet know how or know herself well enough to be that clever a wife.

With Walter she built walls around herself. He tried to break them down with money, with possessions and promotions, and the walls grew thicker with all the things he piled there. Were they like the walls around her mother, who has found a way to spend thirty-five years with one man, yet always keep him at arm's length? Is this yet another lesson from the woman who has taught her so much? Whatever holds her mother and father together, it hasn't been love. Angel would never call it love. Maybe loyalty. Or duty. Or some old pact of mutual survival inherited from plantation days. Could this be why she's drawn to Roland? He looks like Walter, same mustache, same nose and thick eyebrows. In manner he is like her father, that gruff habit of leaning on the steering wheel and answering with grunts. Roland is crazy about her, in a fatherly and protective way, strong, mostly silent, good at what he does, the right fellow to get her through this careful season of her life, ready to rotate the tires on her Honda, haul a load of palm fronds to the dump. There is no doubt he wants to own her, the way Walter wanted to. But Roland is convenient. He is always there. He landed her first freelance assignment with the paper. Because she is thought to be his, other males now keep their distance. She can have as much or as little of him as she desires, as long as he looks good when they're seen together, appears to be in command of the female at his side. Like Walter. It is a juggling act, but one she understands now and agrees to. Why? It has been convenient. With Roland there is a role she'll play in exchange for the peace of mind that comes from knowing no other men on the island will trouble her. This lets her live an orderly life. And isn't that what she came here seeking? Order? Clarity? Serenity? Control? Sometimes she can imagine spending more than a season with Roland. She can imagine spending dutiful years together, while keeping him at bay.

Alone in her living room a shiver ran through her, as she realized she had been imagining this for weeks. If Travis had been next to her just then, she might have blurted it out. She might have reached for his hand and placed it on her forearm, so he could feel her chicken skin quiver of narrow escape. But he was across town in the hotel lobby talking to Linda the waitress. About the time he watched Linda walk away from his lonesome eyes, Angel began to ponder how he had so easily passed through her shield. Here was Travis Doyle coming back from another time zone to disarm her, and she had let him in closer than anyone since . . . since who? . . . since Travis?

"I'm not this way with everyone," she had said. But why? What is going on? Can she talk about it? Talk it out? Who with? With Roland? Marilyn? Mama? Brenda, maybe. If Marilyn weren't hogging the phone, she would have called the Orchid Isle. She didn't care what happened. Travis had frightened her, yet she could barely keep from calling him. This was the thing: he would tell her what was on his mind.

Or try to. He would listen in a way Roland never did. Roland holds his head as if listening, but she is never sure. His stories, when he talks, are like Walter's stories of victory and triumph over long odds, deals he has closed, assignments he has landed, golf games he narrowly won. Roland would never tell her what Travis told her as they drove down the hill toward Hilo. It had chilled her, the way he became just then, his face a kind of death mask, with light bouncing back into the car from the fog and mist. A shell grew up around him, around them both, as he sat behind the wheel and she sat frozen next to him, caught inside the shell, a place she did not want to be. But what had really frightened her? Was it Travis? Or the pictures she had seen, then tried not to see?"

Listening to the story of how he dived at the shrapnel and the story of the corporal who crashed into the trees and burned, she relived the days when she too dreamed of dying and the various ways she would do it and of the anguish this would heap all over Walter. *See how miserable you have made me? See what you went and made me do?* Her dream of retribution came and went and came and went until three months after the second time she got pregnant—a stupid mistake, They had been to a party and came home drunk, both of them, and there had been no love that night, or tenderness, just their bodies lunging in the Reno dark. For weeks whe went back and forth about aborting. She imagined driving to the coast, wading into the surf and swimming for the horizon, swimming until she disappeared, as a great-aunt somewhere in Japan had disappeared. One night she waited until his snores had told her he would sleep till dawn. She lifted the keys from his trousers pocket and crept out to the carport where he kept his BMW and eased it onto the desert highway heading north and east across Nevada, with her foot heavy on the pedal. She turned the lights off and sped into darkness, imagining she would hit something, or that something would hit her, a train, a truck, another heedless driver on the run. She was half an hour out when a figure appeared in the middle of the roadway, or so it seemed, a human figure walking toward her. She stomped the brake and went into a screaming skid, a long sliding turn of a skid across the predawn lanes that left her sitting alone in the empty desert, nauseous, with a pounding heart and bulging eyes, looking back the way she had come.

Three days later she miscarried. The new life spilled out of her like a small red fish determined to swim in the wrong direction.

What would Travis think of that? Could she tell him such a story? Would she ever have the chance to, now? At the crater's edge, what took hold of her? Who was there inside her chest, inside her eyes? As they drove across the island the hum had stayed inside her ears, the late-night hum of the pumping system. In her mind she saw mini-turbo dryers blowing in front of all the dressing room counters lined with theatrical lights in all the hotels that line the shores of all the islands, and in all the Manu Konas waiting to be built. It made her belly hurt, stabbed her like a needle and filled her with a tight insistent buzzing she did not understand. It put her on the road to Tutu David's house, although she isn't able to say quite why. She has no words to ask him where to put this buzzing.

The bag is empty.

Tutu sits back satisfied and pats his belt. "Manapua hits the spot."

"There's none left for later. I'll go pick up some more."

"No, no, sister. You sit still. Look like you need to sit. You been on the move."

"Yesterday I was over on the Kona side."

"Kona," he says. "I was just thinking about Kona."

"My first time over that way since high school."

"I lived in south Kona with my uncle once. I ever tell you about those days?"

"You wouldn't recognize the place, it's so built up."

He shakes his head and laughs a soft laugh, pulling a hand across his face. "Get to be my age, you don't recognize nothing."

"It's changing too fast."

"Pretty soon, maybe no more Hawai'i, you know. Only rocks sticking up through the water, rocks with cars and TV sets on top."

"Don't talk like that."

"Can't drive around no more. I don't want to look at it."

He is gazing south toward the filmy sky. After a while he says, "Maybe we got a few years left. Not too many. All that stuff you see in Kona, long time they been planning it. Who knows what they're planning now. They don't tell you, but they plan, plan, plan. I know some of 'em, sister. I grew up with 'em. We went to the same school. Banking guys with that kind of money. I still know 'em. Last year, maybe Christmas time, we went to a big luau in Kohala, lot of folks came, young folks, old-timers. When the dancer comes out everybody loves it because she dance the old style, the way Malama used to dance, the kind that makes you weep when it brings back the things you never see no more, except in the dance. You know . . . feeling for the land, and how the islands use to be . . ."

His voice gets softer, lighter. Small tears hang at the corners of his eyes, beads of clinging water, not rolling or dripping, nor is there any frowning or squeezing of the face. When he speaks again, the words seem smaller, as if obstructed.

"Some of these guys up there, sister . . ."

"Don't talk, Tutu. We can just sit. I brought along some pictures. We can look at those."

He waves his hand in front of his chest. "Local guys, with lots of money. I watch their eyes, and they are weeping too. They don't remember what they did to sell away the things that never can come back. Too hard to do that while you watch the dancer and listen to the songs. They shake their heads and later they come up to the dancer, with their eyes shining and hearts full, and put their arms around her and give her a lei and a kiss the way folks used to kiss Malama to thank her for such a beautiful dance. And after they dry their eyes they tell you, Now we need more electricity so the time has come to take the power from down underneath the island. We took everything else on top, now we going down below. But when I look at what they do with the power they already have, I say, Why should Pele let them take it? Can you tell me, sister? Do they deserve it? They got nuclear. What do they do with that? You think you can trust them with her power?"

These words are whispered, as if strained through gravel.

"Did you drink your medicine today?"

He coughs a small, quiet cough. Again he waves his hand, as if to wave away the question.

"People come here, they take, they take, they take. What they don't know is, she can take it back any time she want."

He tells her then about the blond and red-faced man from the mainland who parked in the middle of the road two days ago or three and walked into the yard with a lilikoi cream pie.

When he has told her the whole story, he shakes his head with a sound somewhere between a chuckle and a choke and touches the base of his throat, pushing at the place that has bothered him for months, maybe longer, bothering him the first time Angel came out to visit. Tiny's wife says it is his thyroid swelling up, and if he isn't going to take his medicine, what can he expect. Angel knows it runs deeper than the medicine can reach. Today she knows what she felt at the crater's edge, a sound coming through her she had no way to voice. When Tutu's throat closes around his words, she feels it like a hand around her own neck.

270   She looks at him, her great-uncle on her mother's side. He has the kind of voice they call *nahe nahe*, soft and smooth, the way old folks talk. Even when they talk English it has the old Hawaiian flavor, and the gentle flow of brook water. In the very softness of his nahe nahe voice she hears what she came looking for. It is not in the story he told. It is in the sound and in what lives underneath the sound, the unvoiced grief and rage that gets stuck somewhere below the tongue.

His whispery rasp has taught her something about sitting still. She has been avoiding certain things, certain places. And why has she done that? Part of her agrees with the old man's silences. Part of her agrees that you do not go to hearings, or join committees, or march along the road with placards. You speak in private, but you don't speak out. Don't get entangled with the system that has betrayed the island people time and time again. Keep your distance, perserve the quality of your spirit, trust in Pele to decide what's best.

Her mother in Honolulu would be comfortable with this, her mother who holds so much inside. Her father too, he would agree, except for the part about Pele. How many times has she heard Papa say, *Shi kata ganai*, It must be done, it cannot be helped, shrugging, smiling, turning back to his flowerbeds, after calling downtown to find out why the sewer assessment went up again, for no apparent reason, after chatting for five minutes with someone in Civil Service who had fought by his side in Europe when they were both twenty years old. *Shi kata ganai.* They have us right where they want us.

Yes, part of her has learned these lessons, while another part is ready now to . . . eager now to . . . what?

The answer is in the voice of the old man who has spent a lifetime watching people land on his island and take things that do not belong to them. Somehow, what he feels must be spoken. And he will never do it, she knows, not in public. That has never been his way. There is no point in suggesting it. "You are an elder," she might say. "If you speak out, everyone will listen." She can hear his reply. "Haoles run meetings. And Japanese. Nobody else can get a word in!" But maybe she can do this for him. Maybe she can go to the hearing and start at the beginning. When is it? Tomorrow? Or today? Wasn't there a story in the paper? *Stop taking things that don't belong to you,* she will say to the delegates from Honolulu and Tokyo and L.A. and Houston. *Whatever they may be, stop it! Just stop it.*

In her mind this is a shout, a scream that turns her hands wet and cold. Angel has never spoken out. In her student days she never ran for office or sat on a committee. In classes she kept good notes and kept her silence. At home with her mother she talked story. They talk story all the time, with relatives and friends. Talking is one thing. Speaking is something else. Speaking out. Maybe that's why she chose photography, a line of work that lets you watch, be present, bear witness, but keep your silence and stand apart.

She reaches into her bag and pulls out an envelope, glossy eight-by-tens of the ruined equipment shed, with multiples of one print she blew up to eleven by seventeen.

"I brought this for you to look at."

He puts on his rimless spectacles and leans toward the table where she is spreading out half a dozen shots.

"How come I know this place?"

"It's where they're getting ready to drill."

"Looks like lightning hit the timbers, right up here."

"Don't talk for a while, just look. I can leave them. Next time, you tell me what you see."

With a wink he says, "Maybe show 'em to the guys downtown."

"I'd like to do that."

"Let 'em know Pele got her eye on them."

"You think that's what it is?"

"Could be. Never know. Her way is fire. Sometime she come. Sometime not. Look to you like this shed is still burning?"

"What do you mean?"

"Light coming under the roof looks like it's all shining back at you. Who took 'em, sister? You?"

A car comes into view, creeping along the narrow road, the driver checking both sides for numbers, names. Before he sees them sitting there, back from the road and shaded by the overhang, Angel recognizes the car, or thinks she does, but tells herself it could be anyone, the world is full of red Toyotas.

When she sees him peering past the hedges and profusion of vines and tree trunks, her head, her body fills with a giddy hum of disbelief. How can Travis come driving up the road at the exact moment she is about to utter his name and while his pictures are being spread across the table? It is the hum she felt last night after she stepped away from the water boiling on her stove and into her darkroom, remembering the negatives they'd left in the enlarger.

A Second World

He sees them side by side as if waiting for him, some kind of tribunal, the old man in his jeans, his white shirt, the woman—and who is she? his Pacific dream girl? someone from an older dream?—lifting a hand as if to shade her eyes against a blinding glare. He stops at the side of the road, and they are poised like that, wary strangers meeting on a trail through the wilderness with no one else around for miles.

She murmurs something, then rises and steps off the porch, floating toward him across cropped grass. He doesn't know what to expect. He can barely move. If the ground opened under him he would not be surprised. She speaks with a conspirator's voice, almost annoyed, as if they are supposed to be meeting somewhere else.

"What are you doing here?"

"I think I'm looking for that fellow on the porch."

"My great-uncle?"

"Is he Tutu?"

"Yes."

"Tutu David?"

"Yes."

"Then he's the one."

"But why?"

"I don't know."

"You don't know what?"

"I do know. But . . ."

"What's the matter, Travis?"

"Something else is happening."

"What is it then? What else?"

Her eyes are so dark, so wide, the air so full he feels intoxicated.

"How could I know he was your uncle?"

"Who told you how to get here?"

"I flew to Maui."

"When?"

"It was a hunch, an impulse."

"What's in that box?"

"A lilikoi pie."

He tries to explain his junket, bunching details, scraps of talk, as if time is running out, though everything says the opposite. The thick stillness, the curve of fronds, the silent bursting of red hibiscus next to the porch, all say time is an invisible flower holding you forever in its vast cup of soaring petals and there is no need to hurry because there is nowhere to go. Tutu David sits like a patriarch, a brown ruler in faded jeans and pressed shirt on his straight-back wooden chair. He watches them talking, not listening, since he's too far away. Watching.

Angel shakes her head. "This is too much."

"What is?"

"Ian Prince was out here talking story with my uncle. Now you. I can't believe this."

She tells him what she just heard and what the old man told Prince to do. Once again she knows what Travis needs to know, can answer a question before he asks. It could be the day she first appeared next to him in the launch heading out to the *Arizona* memorial. At the very look of her hair, her shirt, her legs, he feels that awe and craving. It comes with the dread that poured through him when they met again in Puna. Is this the woman who took him to the crater? Maybe not. In the lush and liquid air of sea level, her eyes are forest eyes again, not caves of glowing darkness.

She has dropped her voice, talk/whispering, as if to avoid unseen listeners. The sound is addictive. He wants to be with her, but somewhere else. He wants to move, but his legs feel rooted. He shows her the map he copied from an old *Tribune Herald*, with a circled **X** out near the shoreline of a lava plain that looks to be three or four miles across.

"I think I 'm heading down this way."

Frowning, warning, like the desk clerk at the Orchid Isle the night he told her he was looking for the Blue Dolphin Lounge, she wags her head again. "Not by yourself."

"What do you mean?"

"It's like swimming in the ocean by yourself."

"To look around. It won't take long."

She studies the map. "You don't know the roads. You probably can't get in there now—"

"Why not?"

"—this close to the new eruption. Why is it important?"

"I have to get this lieutenant off my back. I have to talk to Prince again, find out what else he knows, before I wrap things up."

"And two days later you think he's still somewhere on the lava?"

"I have to check it out, that's all. Nobody else has seen him yet. Or heard a word." He touches his hat brim in what he thinks will be a mood-lightening imitation of an old-time detective. "Just doing my job, ma'am."

It doesn't work. They look into each other's eyes like two hypnotists trying to cast spells, or break spells. For a while he loses all powers of speech, all track of time. He imagines her by his side. He has a vision of the two of them crossing a field both black and red, walking and bounding and lunging and plunging. From inside this vision he says, "You could come with me."

Again her head says no.

"If we leave right now," he says, "we'll have most of the afternoon."

"Maybe tomorrow."

"I'm kind of on a roll. You know what it's like when you're on a roll."

"There's somewhere I have to be, Travis."

He waits, thinking she will tell him. From the way she turns to look at the old man it could be some family duty holding her, but maybe not. Maybe it is the soft farewell, the Goodbye-Travis-this-has-gone-about-far-enough.

"As long as you're here, come up and meet Tutu."

"Should I trouble him with this? I don't think I need to."

"More trouble if you drive away without speaking. You can't do that. It leaves bad feeling. Say hello. He won't hurt you. Isn't that pie for him?"

She has already turned, walking back across the grass. He's trembling, watching her hips, the hair against her shoulders, the way her feet spread with each languid step. Standing at the border of Tutu's property, with the big square pastry box under his arm, Travis is sick with desire and sure that if he follows her he will be crossing some threshold and there will be no return, and he is right. He is about to enter a place he has never been. Later he will come to think of it as a second world, which is always running parallel to the obvious world of highways and resorts and shopping malls and parking lots and vending machines and offices. Somewhere between his rented car and the rundown porch he crosses into a realm presided over by a kind of man he has never met. He has never known a man of this age and history. Tutu David is the brown stranger, his skin dark, his hair white, his little house old, in need of paint. Whatever emanates from him reaches into the space around his house, giving it the stillness of air before a sudden rain.

Angel sits down and pulls her chair in close and begins to explain who Travis is. Tutu raises a hand, a palm toward her, as if to say, Enough. Travis now stands at the top step, one foot on the porch. With a glance Tutu takes him in.

"This man a friend of yours?"

His voice gives the question great weight, soft but broad with authority, like a magistrate asking for an opinion that will be recorded for all time, as if her reply will go into the record book of their lives. He has the eyes you cannot lie to. David already knows the answer to what he asks. The asking is not to produce information but to call forth the words, the validating words.

Travis sees her face change. A screen falls away. Her answer has as much weight as the question.

"Yes, Tutu, he is. From a long way back."

She looks at Travis, as if for first time, and his screen falls too, or rather, one deep layer of his guardedness dissolves, as this old union is renewed again, reconfirmed: Yes, Tutu, this man is in my life, and I am in his life, but please don't ask what that means, or where it is going to lead.

Tutu nods. "Coming from the mainland?"

"San Francisco," Travis says, as he sets down the pastry box. "Just me, that is. Not the pie."

"*Mahalo*. Thank you." Tutu's face opens, emitting warmth. He lifts the lid to peek inside. "I used to work over there. I had a nightclub once. Come. Sit. You want something cool? I got lime soda."

Angel brings out three frosty bottles and they sit around the table where his photos are still spread. David touches his throat. "If I talk funny it's nothing to think about. Some-times I get a close feeling right in here. Maybe it's all this stuff in the air. What you call it, sister?"

"Vog."

"Vog," he says, with a little cough.

"It means volcano smog."

"This lady in Hilo wrote a letter to the paper telling the health department to do something about the vog. Bringing tears to her eyes and all that. Somebody ought to tell her the volcano was here first. She don't like it, nobody asking her to stay."

He glances at Travis, who says, "It sounds like the people who get mad at sharks for swimming too close to shore."

David likes this. He nods again, "That's right. Who owns the water? Who owns the air? Who owns the fire?"

The vog-tinted sky reminds Travis of the flight to Maui, the lava pool, the spilling orange rivers. "I've never seen anything like it," he tells them, "two streams, everything alive out there."

The old man's eyes glisten. "Two streams. Think of that! Thank you for telling us . . ." He wants to say his visitor's name but has forgotten it.

"Travis took these pictures, Tutu."

He slips his spectacles on again, looks down, then looks up with what seems to be more interest.

"How you get a shot like this, so much light, with the sun gone and almost dark?"

"I guess it was the built-in flash."

Tutu waves a hand across his face, rejecting this idea. "Look like the shed is still on fire. See?"

As they all lean over the table, Travis sees the clearing again. He remembers where he stood, half crouched. It was the end of a roll, and he framed what he thought to be the perfect shot, the derrick rising beyond scorched timbers. At the last instant he changed the angle, bent his knees, raised his elbow, as if a hand had touched his arm to tilt the camera. The fire-split beam came into the viewfinder, while the two silver panels turned molten. The soft and dusky sky seemed to spread, or open, as if trees had leaned aside and the darkening grove itself became a lens, a glowing ring.

In this enlargement you can see how light bouncing off the silvered panels of new metal ignited the air. From back behind the timbers comes the faintest shining. And with that shine comes something else. Another photo is floating toward his memory, from much farther back, with another glow. It is a pre-echo, an early warning signal from within. Hawaiians have a word for it, a word now used by Tutu David to describe the hint of fire hidden in the picture they are studying.

"You're right, Tutu," Angel says. "It looks that way. Some kind of light. But why?"

"Can't always tell," he says. "*Ho'o-ai-lona*. The sign we don't yet know the meaning for."

He takes off his spectacles and holds Travis with a long and probing gaze.

"You working for these people?"

"I used to."

"No more?"

"No more."

"Then . . . why are you here?"

It is another question that requires a truthful answer, or several answers at once. Why are you sitting in this chair? Why are you here in the islands? Why are you *still* in these islands? Why are you alive and on the earth?

He cannot fake it, or slip around it. He has to search his heart. He has been thinking he will ask for more details about Prince—what kind of car? what time of day?—but Travis already knows as much as he needs to know, and such niggling facts seem beside the point, perhaps a form of insult. Everything he has been doing these past few days appear to him to be beside the point, all prologue and preparation for stepping onto Tutu David's porch. Who does he see now in the old man's face? Who watches through Tutu's eyes?

"I've been wanting to meet you," he says at last. "Angel told me about you."

He looks at Travis as if trying to place him, which is how Travis looks at the old man. He feels he has known Tutu David for a long time, or somehow knew in advance he'd be sitting across from him like this. He saw the photo in Angel's gallery of family portraits, and he has been to Waipi'o, where Tutu's father's house once stood. Is this what calls to him? The fatherly ties? Months later he and Angel will talk about this day, and she will say, "I want it to be true, Travis. I want there to be a place in each of us where they all live."

"They?"

"The elders. The fathers. And the mothers. And the young ones too. The unborn infants. And all the children we used to be."

The way Tutu watches him has brought to mind his father, or rather, he reminds Travis of how his father had never been. Is Tutu then the elder Travis wishes he had known? A man you can talk to? A man who will talk to you? Tutu is both fatherly and the opposite of that. He is the ancient, and he is the child.

From his old man's face comes a boyish question. "You must know Angel a long time, yeah? Nobody calls her that any more. Hey sister, how come they used to call you Angel?"

"Papa used to. After I got married I thought Evangeline sounded more . . . I don't know . . . sophisticated."

"How about Travis? Who named you that?"

"It was my grandfather's name. On my mother's side. It was my mother's idea, I guess."

"And your father?" Tutu says

"That's my middle name. Montrose."

Angel says, "I didn't know you had a middle name."

"I never use it."

As if testing the sound she says, "Travis Montrose Doyle."

"Maybe I should start using it."

"It's good to use your father's name," the old man says.

In his mind Travis speaks it—*Montrose*—and in his chest he feels a softening then, a surrendering. The center of his chest grows larger, spreads wide and empty, opening, like a bowl, waiting, a shining bowl that is filled with sudden light.

"My father's name was David, just like me. Comes from the Old Testament. Whenever I say it, makes me think of him, reminds me where he is, and I can talk with him."

"How do you talk with him?" Travis says.

"He went away a long time ago. But he's still right here, you know. It's not hard to talk with the old folks. You just got to sit still and listen. My mother, my father, they're both right here. They're my good friends too."

Tutu's gaze is warm-spirited, deeply gentle, making Travis feel wise and patient, at ease. Years go flowing by like the stream that runs through Waipi'o Valley where he saw his father's face come through the water and where he wept his father's tears. In the quiet shade he sees the face again. This time he sees the photograph he has seen ten thousand times and yet has never seen until today, the one hanging in their hallway at home, his father at the end of World War II. This is what Travis almost saw in the muted glow of the print right here on the table—his father standing at the shoreline, self-satisfied, a bashful conqueror, with one knee cocked to feature the perfect crease in his summer tans. Behind his young face, glare leaps off the water, as if the old lagoon still burns.

In the incandescence of this moment their two lives—his father's and his—come together with a soundless click. He sees the photo, and somewhere nearby stands Montrose Doyle after twenty-three more years have passed, on the launch the day they motored out there to contemplate the aftermath of war. His father's youth comes clear to him, the unvoiced fear of troopship days and the exuberance of survival with its underside of anguish for the readiness of young men to rush away to battle, never remembering the lessons that are learned and forgotten and learned and forgotten. A low flame has spread from inside his head throughout his body. It is the quietest kind of recognition. Nothing moves, neither hand nor eye, nothing but some microscopic portal in the brain, and a slumbering perception blooms.

During the half minute or so that Travis gazes into the old man's face, a cellular window is thrown open, and his father's life enters his; or rather, Travis sees how it has lived within him, invisible form made visible, the father living inside the son. Thirty-four years old and sitting on the porch in the thick translucent breeze of early afternoon, he has half a minute of clarity, half a minute of pure and perfect peace.

Tutu's hands have reached across the table. Travis would like to take them both, but one is extended toward Angel, so they link all six to make a triangle. Her eyes are closed. The touch of her palm is like touching a bare wire. It burns through him as they wait, expecting the old man to speak.

At last Travis says, "There's so much around us, it's like a current, a power in the air. I think I'm going to stay right here forever."

Tutu's lips make small movements, which could be voice-less speech or just the tremblings of age. His voice is frail, when he finally speaks, wavering, coming from afar, but his hands are firm, the palms ridged with calluses. His eyes are lowered. Are they taking in the photographs? Travis can't tell.

"Always," Tutu says. "Always power in the air. In the fire too. In the 'aina, in the earth. The earth and everywhere, yeah? Don't have to be cut off from that, you know. Or sitting here. It's up to you. It's up to you. It's inside you, to be let out. We let it sleep too much".

After a while his grip relaxes. He leans back into his chair and takes a long pull of lime soda. The southern sky is a shade or two denser, screening the sun. They talk again about the eruption, and this kindles Tutu's appetite. He remembers the pie. Angel cuts three pieces, finds some plates. While they dig in, he says, "Good. *Mahalo*, Travis, thank you." Chewing, grinning, he remembers someone else coming by with a lilikoi pie, the sweating haole who parked in the middle of the road, though Tutu speaks as if this happened a long time ago.

"Maybe you remind me of him." David begins to giggle. "Could be that's how I know you. Or maybe you remind me of me a little bit, when I was living over there." He laughs softly, at himself, at all forms of foolishness. "Always in a hurry. Move move move. Busy busy busy."

Toward the end of his soft dry laugh David's eyes grow heavy. His chin falls upon his chest and the white head lolls. Travis doesn't want to move. In David's presence they are blessed. Once one of them moves, who knows what will happen? Who really knows if he has brought them together again, or brought them to the edge of another parting? Travis could stay here for hours, for days, in the eternal shade of the old man's porch. For the first time in years, perhaps for the first time in his life, he knows exactly where he is.

Part Four

 Man born for the narrow stream, woman for the broad stream.
Born was the stingray, living in the sea,
Guarded by the Stormy-petrel living on the land.

Man for the narrow stream, woman for the broad stream.
Born was the Sea-swallow, living at sea,
Guarded by the Hawk living on land.—from The Kumulipo,
a Hawaiian creation chant

Fathers and Sons

In the Hawaiian Islands two great fires are always burning. The younger fire burns at the edge of Honolulu, where clouds of black and orange flame boil upward from the ships trapped inside the circle of the old lagoon. Thirty, forty, fifty years go by, and still we watch them. At the USS Arizona Memorial Visitors Center, the clouds boil every half hour or so, a dozen times a day, in the theater built to show the background film. Two million visitors a year converge and mingle, they say, from both sides of the ocean, from Tokyo and Osaka and Hiroshima, from Seattle and Chicago and New York. Day after day they watch the flames, then motor out to the burnt and twisted spirit ship, read the names, and toss their leis toward the fires of history Travis's father visited twice and carried within him throughout his life. If you had asked Montrose to name a day that stood out above all others, he would not have said the day he met his wife, or the day they married, or the day his first son was born, or his second son, or the day he hiked to the top of Half Dome with the whole Sierra Nevada range around him. He would have glanced away and thought a moment and said, 'December seventh, 1941.' He would have let this sink in, and with a sly, ironic grin he would have said it had something to do with hearing the news on the radio.

"In the days before TV," he once told Travis, *"you did not look at the news. You listened to the news. You could look anywhere you wanted. I know it made a difference in the way you remembered things."*

Montrose was fifteen at the time, almost sixteen. He didn't really know where Pearl was or where Japan was. Those places had no meaning for him. Bombing had no meaning for him. He had never seen an aircraft carrier or a bomb or a place that had been hit by one. What he saw that day was his own father's eyes.

"You remember how your grandad used to look?" he said to Travis. *"His leathery old stoic face had been weathered and set long before he ever left Texas, and it never showed much of anything one way or the other. Hold it in, was his motto. But that day, that Sunday—and I recall it was around noon because we had just come home from church, sitting by the radio right here in the kitchen—that day his face looked like someone had just told him he had two weeks to live. That is what stayed with me and chilled my heart. Your grandad was never a man you could ruffle. It was later that the news itself sank in, and I decided to enlist."*

When his troopship stopped the second time in Honolulu, steaming home, Montrose made a pilgrimage out to the harbor where the war began. He had seen a dozen versions of the smoky plumage rising and the ruined fleet. He wanted to see the wreckage, and seeing it confirmed all his reasons for joining when he did. He passed his camera to a buddy and struck a pose.

As a kid Travis walked past this picture a dozen times a day. He never stopped to study it, any more than he would have stopped to study the grain in the redwood paneling. But it had a subliminal and lasting effect. He inherited something from that pose and that grin and what it seemed to say about war. He too crossed the Pacific, when his time came, to be wounded in the jungle, and he too stopped for rest and recoup in Honolulu, though he had no picture taken. By that time, in his view, there was nothing to commemorate. It still amazes Travis that he was the one to enlist, while his brother Grover did C.O. time back home. Grover is the most military-looking person he knows, with his Marine Corps jaw and the two rifles and handgun he keeps and cleans with great ceremony. Travis has never cared much for weapons. He still doesn't own one. It was not about weapons. Another impulse had been passed on to him, something like a passion, a long-smoldering West Texas form of subdued passion that was never voiced yet somehow was transmitted. Leona will say exactly what is on her mind, say all of it and then some. From his father, Travis had to get most things by osmosis, from a kind of male-to-male telegraphy, from the gaze in that hallway snapshot, blown up and framed, memento from his father's glory days, the photo Travis grew up seeing and not seeing, taken on a day when everything had a vivid edge, as if lined with aura light. The cocky pose and kicked-back overseas cap are set against the wreckage of battleships and carriers, their turrets poking through burnished water, and beyond them the luscious peaks.

The Pilot's Tale

🌸 From Tutu's place he heads now toward the older fire, listening to the radio for news of flow projections and which routes are closed or threatened. With half the afternoon gone he can't get himself stuck in a roadblock. Near the turnoff to the airport, Lyman field, he sees a small sign advertising charter flights. Does he recognize the name? Holiday Air? Brockman's pal. He checks his watch. What did Brockman have in mind? You never know. With him an observation flight could lead anywhere. A lot depends on Holiday, of course, thinks Travis, swinging left. A good pilot could save him hours of road and hiking time.

Between the main terminal and the runway he spots the shed. Inside, Holiday is leaning on a counter, filling in some entries on a clipboard. He wears coveralls and sports a thick red mustache. He raises his eyes, then glances at a wall clock with disapproval. Travis figures him to be in his late thirties, though he looks fifty.

"You Travis Doyle?"

"I am, yes."

Disgust is in his voice. "Jack said you might be showing up."

"Is he here?"

"As of an hour ago he was sup*posed* to be here. So were you. I imagine he is still in Honolulu, which is where he called from."

"He said three o'clock."

"Typical."

"He tell you where we're going?"

"All he said was Puna. Where everybody's going, of course."

When Holiday steps out from behind the counter, Travis can see he is built like a jockey, light and lean, wiry, eager to move. He is also feeling sorry for himself. Holiday Air consists of a closet-size office with a message machine and one helicopter parked outside the shed on a narrow asphalt strip. His sometime assistant still has not come back from lunch. He has already turned away two parties hoping to fly out for an overview of the flow, and there has been no word from Brockman, no cancelation, nor have any of the flights from Honolulu been delayed.

"Has he paid for the flight?" Travis says.

Holiday glances toward the field, as if distracted by a plane, though the runway is empty. "Originally we were calling it a favor."

"What's your fee?"

"It wouldn't have to be full price."

"I'll cover it."

"Fuel these days is out of sight."

"Let's roll," says Travis. "If we don't move now, we'll lose the best light."

"You flown in one of these before?"

"Once or twice."

"We won't be out there long, I hope you understand. I have people coming in at six."

"That's fine."

"What about Jack?"

"If he's not here now, he won't be."

Holiday leads him out to the plane, opens the door. "What about all this shit he asked me to bring along?"

In a pile behind the seats Travis sees ropes, flares, boots, a jacket. "Sure, that looks like it'll do just fine."

With a dubious smile Holiday says, "You still into checking out pig runs and where he sets the traps?"

Pig traps, Travis thinks. What is Brockman trying to pull? "Let's forget that," he says. "Today I'd rather hug the coastline, if it's all the same to you."

Holiday watches him climb in. He seems to like taking orders. "Sure," he says, "that's a prettier way to go."

Cruising south they hang offshore where blue water meets slick black rock, scarps and slabs and islets of rock. The crooked line between the colors is fringed with white, where water foams against the land, white dissolving back into deepest blue that spreads beyond the curve of earth. Inland the summit of Mauna Loa shows dimly through a pale voggy haze. From the air Travis can see how lava has laid broad rivers of rock through green vegetation, or sometimes rolled across rocky plains of lighter gray. He is scanning for this kind of terrain, a flow that has crossed an older flow and found its way to the sea.

As they near just such a stretch of shoreline, Holiday pulls his dark glasses off and squints downcoast. A couple of miles farther along, a cloud of white is billowing higher than his plane is flying.

"Hey, this is brand new!" he says, excited.

"What's happening?"

"A new flow came across the road this morning—in a minute you'll see where the white line just vanishes—but it wasn't hitting the water yet."

On the surface nothing moves. Lava is flowing underneath the morning's layer, winding along through tubes and tunnels from farther inland, finally breaking forth above the surf, turning the nearest water turquoise. Out beyond the churn, a turquoise fan ends sharply where it meets deepwater blue.

On the far side of the cloud they can see where the road used to continue along the coast. The divider line ends at a mound of black. Farther back, half a mile or so, cars are parked, rangers' cars, county cars, tourist cars and vans. They see people scattered along a barrier of yellow tape strung like string across the barren rock.

They fly above the cars, then swing wide over the water. Heading back the way they came, they can see how heat from the spill shapes surface steam into a broad and windblown **V**. From offshore the high plume rises against distant slopes, where a curving streak of orange can be seen. If they had more time, says Holiday, sounding like the guide he often is, they could take a pass over the second flow. It's out of sight beyond the ridge and still moving through 'ohi'a forest, setting trees on fire. "Hell of a thing to watch," he shouts. "You don't usually get so much all at once. It'll be better tonight. Things you can't see in the daytime will brighten up at night, like stars."

As they pass, for the second time, a curve of coast that seems to match the curve on his Xeroxed map, Travis reaches back for Holiday's binoculars. Peering down, scanning, he sees something out there by itself, a shoulder bag anyone might have spotted if they'd been looking, but this is not where police had looked. Prince's car was found ten miles farther down. He hands the glasses to Holiday and asks him what he sees.

"Some kind of blue bag, a backpack. fishermen leaves things lying around."

He has looped again, as if to return toward the plume.
Travis tells him to hover.

"Somebody's down there."

"I doubt that."

"Take a look."

"Where?"

"Next to that long deep crack."

Holiday looks and says, "Shit."

"Isn't that a tennis shoe? Part of a trouser leg?"

"We'll have to call this in."

"How hard is it to land out here?"

"You kidding me?"

"Somebody's down there hurt."

"I am not a rescue squad."

"Maybe dead."

"The county does that. They can be out here in no time."

He talks code numbers into his hand mike. A scratchy
voice comes back telling him the rescue unit is on a call and
could be tied up for an hour or more. Something happened
at the drilling site. Everyone was called up there. Two men
have to be flown out. The voice says, "It was an earthquake."

"How big?"

"That's all we know right now. Tell me where you were,
and keep in touch."

He switches it off. "Keep in touch. Holy fuck! What is
that supposed to mean?"

"It means you have to land."

"Son of a bitch! What are we doing way the hell over here
anyhow? I don't need this! I land down there they'll fine my
ass."

"It's an emergency. Who can fault you for an emergency
landing?"

"Bureaucrats can always figure a way, believe me."

They are close to shore, where a narrow strip of black sand shows. Travis asks him if he can set it down on the sand.

"I can lose my fucking license landing out here!"

"Jesus Christ, Holiday! Your license! Somebody could still be alive down there!"

He doesn't react. Travis points to the distant plume, now drifting with an onshore breeze, making a wall of mist between the chopper and whoever might be gathered down that way. "Who can see us? They're all watching the boil. You had to touch down for five minutes. It was a matter of life and death."

Holiday looks at him with harried eyes, his voice mournful, low. "Life and death. Don't tell me about life and death, Doyle. I have airlifted more dead guys than you can fucking count. I don't do that anymore. Six o'clock I got customers coming in for a flyover. If somebody is dead, you are on your own. You got that?"

The pilot's face is a map of old losses. Travis doesn't want to rush him. "All right," he says, "I got that. I'll be grateful if you can put me close enough to jump out the door."

Everywhere but the sandy strip is rough, broken, split with fissures, knobs, and folds, and here and there a fractured mound, as if giant fists have tried to punch up from below.

"Goddamn cocksucking dumbshit way out here alone deserves to be frying on the fucking rocks . . ."

This is Holiday's mantra as he eases the chopper down onto a broad slab about twenty-five yards from the foot and the leg, which are raised as if frozen midway through a kick. He doesn't say anything or look at Travis. He cuts the engine. They both jump out into the sudden silence and run over there, hopping from rock to rock, and find Ian Prince lodged into a narrow crevice where a slab has split.

Most of him is hooded by a curling overhang. Lava has formed a crescent like the half moon ridge of bone above an eye. Prince lies under it, with one hip and shoulder wedged. He's larger than Travis remembers. The body has begun to swell. With the foot out, and one arm back against the ledge, it looks as if he could have slid or drawn himself into this fissure, almost as if he chose the spot.

There is no sign of a fall, no abrasions visible, no cuts or signs of blows or beating. His contorted face and bent-back arm suggest a heart attack, which is Holiday's first guess. He is a volunteer fireman, he says. These days half the calls are heart attack calls.

It is a rugged couple of miles from the end of the paved road to the slab where they've landed. Prince most likely had hiked out in the double heat of the tropic sun, a heat that presses upon you from above and rises toward you from the heat-gathering stone. From what they can see he carried no water.

They step back from the crevice and from the smell.

Travis says, "Should we try to get him out of there?"

"No reason to. He's not in the sun. Leave it for the rescue people. They'll have a sling. Let's just cover up his face. I can't stand the sight. Why do I think I recognize this guy?"

"I recognize him too."

"From where?"

"I think we met in Hilo."

Holiday shakes his head, as if to say that isn't it, or perhaps to say this is more than he can handle. They start toward the plane, to get something for the face, walking into the wind, which is warm and strong enough to make you squint.

With the fuselage for a screen Holiday pulls out a Camels package and withdraws a perfectly rolled joint, holds it to his lips and strikes a match.

"I never smoke on the job . . ."

He lights it and takes a long hit and passes it.

"Neither do I," says Travis, as he takes a hit and passes it back.

"But Jesus Christ. I didn't expect anything like this."

Holiday takes another hit and holds it and exhales and closes his eyes and waits. He opens his eyes and says, "What's your line of work, Doyle?"

"At the moment, insurance."

Holiday nods, as if this explains something, as if they have run into each other at a wake and are now obliged to get acquainted. His smile is ironic. "And how do you know Brockman? I don't imagine this is exactly what you guys had in mind?"

"I wouldn't want to say what Brockman had in mind. I don't know him all that well."

"But you were meeting him today."

"I think he was hoping I would be there, yes."

The wasted eyes take this in, puzzled, then suspicious. Travis tells him why he first went looking for Brockman and how the calls and messages started following him around the island.

"Wait a minute . . ." Holiday almost looks amused. "You mean Jack isn't really in this movie?"

"Not today."

"It's just you and me? Out here on the fucking rocks?"

"You and me and . . ." Travis nods toward the corpse.

This strikes Holiday funny. He starts laughing, a low giggle that rises to a wild careening howl. They are both laughing, snorting and cackling and staggering with demented roars that are swallowed by the wind and carried away across the miles of windy plain. Then Holiday is laughing and weeping at the same time, blinking back sudden tears, waving long grimy fingers at his face.

"I'm sorry, man."

"You okay?"

"I'm really sorry."

He wipes his eyes. Travis studies the rock for a while. They both gaze into the distance, mourners at a graveside. Eventually they each take another hit. If Travis had reason to be secretive about what he knows or does not know, he has forgotten it. In the spirit of comradeship he tells Holiday some of Prince's story and how a long-smoldering fear could be what drew him back to this fateful spot. Holiday begins to pace, as if he has trouble accepting this, or absorbing it. He swings his arms and pulls at his mustache, muttering, muttering, and suddenly he's describing how things looked at the compound on the night the shed got hit. Holiday was driving the fire truck, he says. By the time they pulled in, the fire was out, along with the power and the phones, everything out and dripping and quiet, the place apparently abandoned.

"This may sound far-fetched, Doyle, and off the wall, but the first time I saw that poor bastard he was standing alone in the dark in his walking shorts. His head was tilted back like a guy waiting for the rain to wash him off. It was weird, of course, because the rain had stopped, but he wasn't moving, like he had been standing there for who knows how long. What I would call quiet shock. I asked him if he was okay, and he said yes he was okay. Maybe he'd been crying. It looked that way. His face was all wet. I couldn't stand it, man. He was going through something. I hate to see a guy like that, because it sets me off. It's just knowing the stuff anybody has to go through, and usually you go through it alone, I don't care what the fuck it is. Most of the time I don't want to know. That night I didn't want to know. I didn't ask him. I didn't fucking want to go into it. I am not a psychologist. We got him up into the cab where it was warm, gave him some coffee, and took him into town. By that time he was talking, you see, talking about weather. We all told weather stories. There was nothing to do about the shed but let it dry out, so we drove back and talked about the powers of rain and various strange stormy things we had heard about or seen. He wouldn't let us take him anywhere but back to his apartment, although I felt like shit, even at the time. He needed somebody keeping an eye on him, and now look where he ends up, out here at the edge of fucking nowhere and dead as a doornail."

His voice is soft, almost a whisper, yet panicky. He looks ready to break into a desperate run. The sight of Prince's bloated figure has filled him with confusion and regret.

"How do I get mixed up in something like this? It's not good for my business to be seen standing around with dead bodies . . ."

Now there is accusation in his eyes, as if Travis has forced all this upon him.

"You should take off then," Travis says. "Get going."

"I mean, what the fuck are you telling me? He was freaked by the electric storm? So he came out to fix some kind of *kapu*? I can't stay here, man. I hate that voodoo shit."

"There's nothing holding you," Travis says. "Really."

"What're you gonna do?"

"It only takes one guy to flag in the rescue unit. Go meet your customers. How much time do you have?"

He can see relief rising up through Holiday's body, to lift the shoulders and raise the hangdog chin. Rebirth in the body. In the eyes, a plea. "I wouldn't want to leave you out by yourself."

"We still have two hours of daylight, don't we? If I have to walk, the end of the road is . . ."

"As the crow flies, two miles, or a little less. But still . . . the vibes, man . . ."

With a guilty glance at his watch, Holiday says anything could happen, anything at all. He starts pulling gear out of the chopper, handing it over as if he owes these things to Travis, a down jacket, a ready light, a couple of flares, marker dye, heavy boots, a hard hat, a canteen. These were the items Brockman said they'd need, though Holiday still is not clear why.

"You know what it is about Jack? He is a crisis addict. If there isn't a crisis he invents one, and he sucks you into it. He calls up long distance asking for all this shit, like there is going to be an assault on Mount Everest, all at the last minute, in a big-ass rush. Then what happens? He doesn't show. This is the last time I listen to that son of a bitch, I swear to God. How do those boots feel?"

"Snug," says Travis, pulling the laces tight. "Just right."

"Sure you'll be okay?"

"Absolutely. I'll get this stuff back to you."

"No rush. You know where I am."

Travis stands up, testing his feet inside the boots. He reaches for his wallet.

Holiday pushes two hands toward him. "No, no, no, no."

"Will two hundred cover it?"

"I wouldn't take a nickel."

"One fifty."

"Leaving you out here by yourself? I already feel like a turd."

"Just keep on top of the dispatcher. Don't let them forget we're here."

Travis watches him lift off. From twenty-five feet up he turns once, looking back, his eyes pouched, layered with relief and self-doubt and gratitude and perhaps elation. His wave is from an old barnstorming movie, a stiff-armed salute he might have practiced in front of a mirror. The helicopter rises and veers out over the water, getting smaller, small as a dragonfly.

It is silent again, a silence accented by the steady breeze that has nothing in its way, nothing to rustle or rattle, no chapparal, no fence posts or garden gates, nothing but the stone, and Travis standing there, listening.

Heat

The sun is halfway down the sky, spreading shadows, adding another shade of gray-black to the heaps and ripples. In this empty terrain, Prince's shoulder bag stands out like a tiny stranded creature, a fallen blue bird. Travis walks over to retrieve it, thinking he will use it to cover the face. In his eagerness to light up, Holiday forgot that.

Near the hat he spots two offerings, a thick packet wrapped in ti leaves and a bundle of anthuriums, once red, now brown-edged and blotched with pinkish white after two days in the sun. The ti leaves contain a wrinkled paper bag, and inside the bag an unopened quart of Gilbey's gin, and around the bottle and bag there is an old necklace of the type that dancers sometimes wear, made of nuts that fall from the kukui tree. Each one is about the size of a small plum, dark and smooth and hard and almost indestructible. Years ago someone had gathered these and strung them, and Prince had kept the necklace as a souvenir of his brush with fire, as a trophy, maybe as an amulet. He had brought it along to hang in his Hilo apartment, he told the counsellor, "because I like having it around."

Now the offerings stand alone on the shadowy rock, at the outer edge of this curve of coast. A presunset yellow tints the sky and tints the leaves.

With prickling skin Travis picks up the shoulder bag, walks back, and hunkers near the fissure. Before he covers the face he looks down at Ian Prince, a man cursed as much by weight as he was by lightning. He remembers the way he walked, as if proud of his girth, advertising it a bit, not one to be bullied by some no-nonsense soybean and salt-free approach to health. He can see the hand thrown up against the rock, palm out, white from the scarring, all lines erased, and the white scars licking along the edges of four bent fingers and the thumb. He sees no picture there, nothing you could call a woman's profile, perhaps because all life has, by this time, drained away. Or perhaps, whatever Prince saw and carried hidden in his pocket, in the turned palm, was only revealed by the heat of his life, the warmth of his blood, or by the blood his very fear would send to color his extremities.

Travis imagines him hiking out here in the midday heat, packing his offerings to propitiate the powers that be, following Tutu's instructions, searching for the spot where they found the sack so many years earlier, turning red under the sun, his scalp blistering when his cap slid off. From the packet and the flowers to his final resting place is about fifty yards, but in the opposite direction from the road and roadblock, as if he had at last recognized something and decided on a spot, and then had lost his bearings. By that time he may have been feeling the effects of dehydration, seeing things, hearing things. What got him then? The heat? The kapu? A little bit of both?

These old Hawaiian warnings, Travis will never know quite how to account for them. In the islands they are as real as gossip or the weather forecast. Everyone has a story. When you're back on the mainland it is not easy to talk about. People look at you the way members of the Royal

Academy must have looked at the first British foreign office regulars returning from India with tales of snake charmers and yogis who could emerge alive after twenty-one days in an airtight casket. But Travis will never pass judgment on Ian Prince and whatever visions he carried to his open grave. After he has been out here for another hour, in the wind, alone, he begins to feel the presence of . . . what? Old

spirits? The ancient beasts who lurk forever in the bogs and caverns of the night?

As the sun drops, as darkness looms, it is less and less a mystery to Travis why he has come chasing after this sad and tormented man. He is an investigator on the trail of evidence. But evidence of what? What was it Clemson said about the driller's lure? Evidence of things not seen? Yes, that is getting close. Here is Prince, haunted by the power of an imprint left on his palm by some strange chemistry of rock and flame and flesh. A random pattern, if it was there at all, and yet it worked on him, clung to him as the atmosphere of the island can gather and cling, the shadow of a field of force outside the reach of logic or light meters. Travis begins to think of Prince as a man he might have been. The fire is a mirror. Is Ian Prince a mirror too? Some kind of shadow brother?

He stands up to stretch his legs and listen again for the county's helicopter. He hears no engine sound, nor does he see in the distance anything resembling a dragonfly. The sun is close to the horizon, and the color of the steam plume is gradually changing, from white to cotton candy to salmon, taking color from the sky and from the water below the sky and from what spills into the water. Farther inland and upland orange stripes grow brighter. He notices then a small red ring, much nearer than any other show of fire. It has seemingly risen out of nowhere, maybe two hundred yards away the glowing tip of a tongue of lava that has recently pushed to the surface, now licking a path across the rock, licking and slipping.

He watches its progress, fascinated, uncertain what to do, whether to flee or wait. He switches on the ready light and starts toward it, picking his way, until he is close enough to see that this is just a trickle, as streams of lava go, a creek of lava about ten feet wide, moving across terrain so flat there seems to be no pull of gravity, but a willful forward motion, such as you see in a caterpillar that has no wings or tail or visible legs to propel it, yet somehow moves of its own volition.

It is slithering more or less in the direction of the crevice where Prince lies wedged, in a slow, oozing pattern that spreads and narrows and spreads again, as it passes outcroppings and low barriers of folded rock. He paces off the distance, tries to calculate the rate of flow and figures that even if it does not stop, they still have an hour before there will be anything to worry about.

He watches it move, a newborn earthen creature with a life of its own, giving off heat like a wood stove, hissing and crackling softly, a form of speech he might be able to interpret, if he stepped a little closer and shoved his face and eyes and ears right into the waves of heat.

Words

Outside the school's multi-purpose room, a dozen people gang around the open double doors. Angel runs from her car and joins them. She snaps water off her hands, throws away the soggy newspaper she used for cover. It is raining again, windless acre-feet of straight-down rain. A woman grins at her with a head shake, a flash of amazement, as if the rain, which comes every day, has taken them all by surprise. It is a vulnerable grin, reminding Angel that these are mostly local people, concerned, confused, curious, troubled, and feeling as far removed as she does from Honolulu and the dignitaries flying in. She feels she understands what's in the air, her life in sync with other lives. She feels inspired now, and her fear is not a bad fear. This thick knot below her chest is like stage fright. Yes, something is going to happen today, and she is moving toward it, moving into it.

As she slips through the doorway and joins the line of listeners pressed against the back wall, a tanned and confident woman is taking the microphone. She has a golfer's tan, smooth and seamless, her hair sun-tinted. Angel doesn't hear the words. Not yet. She hears the smooth, compelling tone. She envies it. Then she sees black hair halfway down the back of Roland's neck, where he sits in a roped-off block of chairs reserved for the press. She has not yet returned his call, until now she hasn't thought of it. What should she tell him? His eyes will soon be asking why. She sees the long glance of the young and handsome county supervisor, up there at the front table, noting her arrival. Chinese. Yee. Chinese plus something else. Hawaiian. Last month at a city hall reception he confessed to her that he thinks geothermal is the wrong way to go. "All the megawatts they say we'll get from the steam we can get by doing better with what's already in place, and it won't cost us half as much. Think of where else we could put four billion dollars." *Where else*, she thought, with a tentative smile. *Where else. Where else.* Twice since then he has called about lunch, leaving long and detailed messages.

". . . it's our children we're talking about," the tan woman says. "Without a viable source of local energy you hamper growth. You all know what happens. Our young people drift away. My kids grew up on this island. I want them to see opportunities here that encourage them to stay."

Children, thinks Angel, who was a child when she left the Big Island and still a child when she left for the mainland, and now she is back, she is back, she is back.

Nodding toward the applause, this woman takes her seat at the front table, behind a printed card that says HILO DISTRICT BOARD OF REALTORS. Next to her sits a man Angel recognizes as the Chamber of Commerce president. She recognizes a state senator whose photo is often in the paper. She recognizes the chairman, even though she has never before seen his face, a Japanese American man of the World War II generation who reminds Angel of her father, perhaps finishing out his thirty years, somewhere in the state's Department of Business and Economic Development. He wears hornrims, a short-sleeve white shirt, pressed khaki trousers. Introducing the next speaker, he sounds tight with resentment. Angel knows that if her father held such a job

307

he would consider it a waste of time and public money to be paying someone like himself, who has a desk back in Honolulu piled with better things to do, paying him the airfare and per diem and the car rental and paying out whatever it cost to run a sound system and to light this room to conduct yet another debate on a project so clearly good for the future of the islands.

308   An elderly man has reached the podium. He lives in a retirement compound two miles from the drilling site, a Caucasian man who has come to speak for the South Puna Residential Coalition. He wears a red-and-yellow aloha shirt that hangs from shoulders frail with age. From the way he walks Angel can tell his neck hurts, his knees hurt. He has been sitting too long. The meeting started forty-five minutes late. He was up all night, he says, with some of his colleagues, drafting a new position paper. For a while SPRC lined up in favor of the drilling, persuaded that a short-term nuisance would lead to lower monthly bills. But a small story on page 10 of yesterday's *Advertiser* predicts that most of these development costs will sooner or later be passed along to consumers. A spokesman for Hawaiian Electric is quoted as saying, "There is no free lunch."

The man in the aloha shirt is so angry he cannot finish his sentences. His whole life is running through his mind at once, the words and the years colliding. Back in Ohio, later in Michigan, he lived close to factories and smokestacks and wants no more of that. He knows about hydrogen sulfide too, the stink of it. He knows something about the legal limits on emissions, how many parts per billion. He has studied the reports because his wife's bronchial tubes have been inflamed ever since they moved to Puna. Add to that the trucks rumbling back and forth carrying pipes, carrying water.

Naked, Angel thinks, he feels naked, unprotected. Her heart is with him. He is not a cultivated speaker. She can't follow all he says. Being up there terrifies him, but his rage runs so deep he somehow staggered to the mike. Now many hands are in the air, supporters' hands, detractors and challengers. He waves them away. He is staggering down the center aisle again, when the room begins to quiver. Did his lunging, off-balance steps loosen something in the floor?

He falls into his seat, and rows of heads turn, questioning eyes turn toward him, toward one another. When the room is still again, uneasy laughter ripples through the crowd, much like the tremor that rippled through the earth beneath the school.

Gloomily the chairman says, "I told you folks today was a wrong day for the hearing."

This triggers a larger, more nervous laugh, another trembling ripple. When it subsides he introduces the last of the scheduled speakers, Dan Clemson, whose name was added this morning, as one who can bring the community up to date. Clemson doesn't like this role. Someone talked him into it, the Western Sun attorney, the only man wearing a coat. He too is a Texan. He wears a lightweight leisure suit, beige, tailored, with subtle stitching along the lapels and pocket edges. In this room full of loose shirts and loose trousers and shorts and slippers, his coat gives the attorney an authoritative look. Clemson wears another kind of authority. Mud darkens his boots and his jeans. His eyes are raw. He has the bluff, haggard manner of an infantry captain who has stepped off the battlefield into a press conference full of scribblers. These two have been arguing all morning, face to face, after a week of shouting into telephones. The attorney's first concern is their contract with the state, to deliver so many megawatts by such and such a date, and the fines they'll have to pay for defaults and delays. Clemson's first concern is the rig itself, a half-million-dollar piece of machinery, and the welfare of his crew. They hate each other's guts, but they have come to the hearing together to offer a united front.

Clemson leans his forearms on the podium as if he is so weary he might collapse without it. The new release of lava has changed their plans, he says. Though it is not yet a direct threat, their start date has been postponed until they know more. They are on alert status, along with some of the road crews, and would be much happier without a meeting to attend this afternoon. As for contingency plans, yes, once the reservoir of steam is tapped, a concrete barrier will be installed to divert any future lava. Eventually they will be prepared to cap the well, so that if it's ever covered they can drill down through new rock to reactivate the well.

"first, of course, we have to find the steam. And we are ready now to start drilling, as soon as the coast is clear."

He keeps it short, eager to escape. A few hands go up. Clemson glances at the attorney, who glances at the chairman, who says, "He has to get back to work. Please save your questions until we start the public testimony."

The hopeful hands fall. The chairman checks his notes. As Clemson takes his first step away from the microphone, Angel hears a soft and familiar voice coming from a great distance.

"If the well hole gets covered over with lava, maybe you should leave it that way."

Heads swivel toward the rear. The chairman looks up, annoyed. The state senator who flew in from Honolulu with the chairman, he looks up, and the young supervisor who organized this hearing, and the Chamber of Commerce president, and the woman from the Hilo Board of Realtors, whose eyebrows rise in mild disapproval. Are they looking at Angel? Under lights that now seem brighter, harsh, surreal, she feels exposed, suspended above the floor from invisible strings, or perhaps held aloft, pinned, by the hard challenge of Dan Clemson's blue eyes.

The chairman says, "Please hold your comments . . ."

When the soft voice continues, Angel knows it is hers, though it still sounds distant, enclosed, speaking from a room down the hall.

"How come you folks never listen?"

Clemson's big voice says, "That's about all we *are* doing. That's what this whole meeting is about."

"You only listen to words," she says.

"You're speaking out of turn," says the chairman, with fatherly impatience, as the murmurring begins.

"And then you only answer with words."

The chairman, who longs for a gavel, brings his hand down flat. "A lot of people here want to speak. They have come to speak. We have to proceed in an orderly manner."

"You should listen to the island," Angel says. "It is calling out to you. It is calling out to all of us. All of us. But who is listening?"

Color is rising in Clemson's face, his ears, his burly neck. "Mr. Chairman, I don't have time for this."

Angel moves along the center aisle, looking at the chairman the way she looks at her father, directly into his eyes, with a little smile that says, "Forgive me, I know you want to maintain control here, but this is something I have to do." Her look, her smile, the steadiness of her gaze, leaves him speechless for the time it takes her to reach the mike, where she turns to face the room, astounded to find herself there, beyond fear, drenched in some kind of searing theatrical light, with so many eyes waiting.

She brought along her envelope of prints and now holds aloft the eleven-by-seventeen blowup. "When this old shed caught fire down at the drill site, they said it was a propane tank. Then they started saying someone set it. But you see these scorch lines up here? You see how high they start?"

"Good lord!" the attorney cries. "What is happening?"

This alarms the chairman, who has actually leaned forward across the table for a better look.

The attorney's hands are in the air next to his head. "Are we here to talk about alternative energy?"

From the back of the room a woman calls out, "Is she right?"

The attorney points an accusing finger. "A picture like this could come from anywhere! Has she even identified herself? Dan, help me out here. Do we know anything about a fire?"

A heavyset man stands up. "I know that place. Looks like the company shed to me."

"You saying this the place got hit?" says the woman in the back. "I remember that night."

"That's right," Angel says. "But then they act like it didn't happen."

The old man from the South Puna Residential Coalition shouts, "What else is new?"

One of his mobile home cronies shouts, "What's it gonna cost the common user down the line? That's my question!"

A woman from the Sacred Lands Foundation has stepped out into the aisle. "As long as we're talking about lying to the public, I'd like to mention the access road, twice as wide as we were told it would be . . . and the forest they have clear-cut to get their trucks in and out . . ."

From all corners, the voices are rising. Clemson booms above the others, a man pushed to his limit and beyond his limits. His face has lost its weary patina. It looks carved from ruddy stone.

"We have tried to be straightforward with you people! Our desire has been to work with you! We were invited here, for God's sake!" He looks at the state senator, whose face is fixed in a neutral smile. "Day after day after day, all we get is crap like this!"

There is a tense, momentary quiet, filled by the chairman, hoping to settle the air. "Then are we understand that this is not a photograph of your shed?"

Clemson turns on him, as the frustration boils over. "You're goddamn right! That shed is not my area! It doesn't belong to my company! It belongs to Energy Source! Which is a subsidiary of Western Sun! Can anybody get that straight? They hire us to come here and drill. We bring in the rig, we drill the hole, we're gone. I am real tired of explaining away their screw-ups. You think somebody has concealed something from the public, you go talk to them!"

He is heading for the double doors, shoving past the standers and the watchers, who press back to give him room.

The attorney calls out, "Hold it right there!"

Clemson doesn't stop. Over his shoulder he grumbles, "Fuck you!"

When Angel speaks again she is like the bride so choked up she can't repeat her vows, her voice catching on the words, on all that lives beneath the words, the years of her life, the years of her father's life, who left this island at twenty-nine to make it big in Honolulu, and the mother who carries her unspoken Hawaiian secrets, and the great-uncle who can read ailments in those who come to him but cannot speak all that is in his heart. It is the catch that broke the notes in Tiny Kulima's singing voice and edged the old lament that cut through the Puna forest causing guards and gate busters and 'ohi'a trees to stand still and listen.

In the months to come, as the story of this meeting spreads, joining the stories people tell one another late, at night in the lamplight, sipping the last cup of coffee or tea or one more glass of wine, it will not only be the story of what she said. It will be a story about the sound of her words, how this somehow ignited the room, one more note in the long history of sounds that have come rising. People asking her to meet with them, talk story with them, dream with them about ways the local people can hold on to what little remains for them before it is all sold away to the highest bidder—that sound is what they listen for.

"How does Western Sun get that shed," she says, "from way over there in Houston?" She throws her arm wide. "Or from way over there in Tokyo?" She throws the other arm wide. "How can they come cutting roads through our forest? And the Manu Kona Hotel, how come that belongs to Western Sun? Has anybody talked about that today? Nobody here is talking about all the other things they own—"

"I don't think that's a secret!" the attorney says, leaping to his feet like a lawyer in a courtroom. "What we do is all part of the public record!"

"But who has talked about it!" Angel says, holding the room with her voice and her eyes. "Has anybody mentioned where Pele's steam is going? Or why these people have a right to be here drilling down into her island? What right do they have to take so many things that do not belong to them? Take the land, take the road, take the trees, take the steam? How come they can take and take and take? And when will all the taking stop so this island can live and breathe and not be forever fighting for its life!"

She does not know where these words come from. She did not plan to say it this way. In awe she listens to the voices fighting to be heard, everyone standing now, voices agreeing, voices attacking, voices of strangers and of some who know her name, voices of relatives thrice removed, and high school students and land-use consultants and loan officers from banks and retired master sergeants and golden-haired hippies in tie-dye shirts and open-kneed jeans.

Dan Clemson has reached the rear double doors just as a fellow comes bounding along the outside corridor, a crewman who stayed with the pickup and the C.B. radio. He wears a bill cap, a rain-soaked T-shirt. His wet, stubbled face says the news is bad. Moments later he and Clemson vanish into the rain. From those close enough to hear, the word quickly spreads that it has something to do with the small quake they all felt while the old man was speaking. It gives them a link to whatever might have happened at the site.

In the new clamor of questions and scraping chairs the attorney tries to make an early exit. To the chairman he says, "We should have canceled. I told you this was a bad idea."

"You can't just walk out of here. We're still taking public testimony."

"This isn't a hearing, it's a crucifixion."

"We'll take a recess, then. Give us ten minutes to clear the air and find out where we stand."

The attorney looks hard at Angel, who waits at the microphone, standing very still. In his eyes she sees distance and cold pity. She knows she'll be seeing these eyes again.

Harmonic Tremors

Ten minutes later the attorney is gone. The senator is gone, on his way to the airport where a plane waits to ferry him to Kona for a fund-raising luau. Angel is gone, along with most of the crowd. With a loud snap of the latch on his attaché case the chairman announces to the half-filled room that they will have to reconvene at a later date. It is turning out, he says, to be one of those days governed by Murphy's first Law: "Everything that can go wrong will go wrong." Later on Dan Clemson will remark that this time even Murphy went too far.

The moving lava has taken a turn. It piled up beside the same low ragged ridge John Brockman imagined he would somehow detonate, a long embankment of burnt rock. The lava puddled there, hardened and puddled again, piled, climbed a bit, and hardened, until it built a ramp and breached the barrier to continue on its slow and syrupy course. The nearest edge was then a mile from the drilling site, oozing along at about two hundred feet per hour. If nothing changed, if it did not turn again or slow down or stop, the flow was still maybe thirty hours away. But the hazard had increased, according to Civil Defense monitors, because the site was now directly downslope and in the path.

About the time the old fellow from the Residential Coalition stepped up to the microphone, two roughnecks started toward the top of the derrick to begin dismantling pipe. When that long tremor passed through the region, they were lashed on with safety belts. The derrick began to sway, like a bridge tower in a high wind, causing one man to lose his footing. In the next instant the earth jumped, and the derrick jumped, as if lifted by a giant's hand. The man's leg slipped between two steel crosspieces, where it twisted, shattering his femur.

His buddy tried to pull him free, but the way the useless leg was wrapped around the crosspiece, he could not move it without screaming. The med-evac unit was summoned, and an ambulance, though the ambulance never made it through. It had to wait half a mile away. The quake had opened a broad crack in the access road. For a while no vehicles could get in or out.

No one read the crack as a message from below. They didn't have time for such a reading, nor did anyone have time to take the next call from Civil Defense, a report that would have told them the quake was followed by a sequence of harmonic tremors, which usually signal new lava rising toward the surface somewhere nearby, and rapidly. There was the injured man to be lifted out, and then bridging planks to be laid across the chasm in the road, or thick steel plates, whatever they could find. There was still the drill pipe to dismantle and equipment to evacuate, though in the end it didn't make much difference.

An hour later, as if anticipating the very hole they had planned, as if following a path upward along the course Dan Clemson had imagined would start from the top, probing downward, the fire came rising right next to the rig, the driller's will and the will of the lava drawn to the same path through the rock.

There was no moment when the side of a mountain blew out. There was a long growl of distant thunder, as the subterrenean pressures amplified, then a hissing roar of liberated steam, and the geysering started. Orange gouts came spitting upward beside the platform in a fiery wall higher than the derrick. Lava spewed and spired and seemed for a while to fall back into itself to be swallowed and used again, like waters in a public fountain. Eventually the lava began to spread across the Caterpillar-flattened clearing, which was itself an older layer that had poured outward from another fissure, lava upon lava, building, pouring, puddling around the platform, scorching paint and burning metal.

The wall of fire rose and fell and rose and fell, as a glowing mass spread toward the trees, through the grasses, making a perimeter corona of grassy fire that moved ahead of the black-orange flow, until cooling barrier edges built up to form a rough-hewn bowl. In its center the derrick tilted, charred and blackened halfway up, then white for the topmost forty feet, like one of those contradictory pieces of sculpture where half a body is perfectly made, the belly, the chest, the arms and shoulders, but the lower half is deformed, as if twisted by malnutrition and disease.

All night and into the early morning the rig leaned, melting sideways but slow to fall. As the tremendous heat softened the metal, it finally toppled into the molten pool and lay there half submerged while liquid rock continued to gush and percolate and simmer and glow.

During the next few days, lava spilling outward from the self-generating lake buried what would have been the sites for a hundred wells. On planners' maps in Honolulu and in Houston, a grid of sites had been laid out, of which this test well was to be the first, linked by roads yet to be cut through the 'ohi'a groves, linked by conduit pipe and steam converters yet to be installed, each well to be surrounded with its circular clearing among the trees, a forested city of roads and circles. Before long all these sites had been covered over by twelve feet of cooling rock.

319

Angel's Cord

For almost an hour Travis has been watching his creek of lava slither along like fiery molasses. The offshore wind is cooling down. If he stands close enough he can keep warm, but it isn't a comforting kind of warmth. As the light wanes, the earth itself has come awake. In the distance, streaks and splashes grow brighter. The time is drawing near for a decision. He has to decide what to do about Prince's body, now within range of the advancing stream, and he has to decide whether to stay close by until a plane shows or try hiking out. It's no place to spend the night.

He has tried to move him, took hold of the arm and shoulder and pulled. Prince wouldn't budge. The body has swollen until it is stuck. Even if Prince were movable, he is thinking, where would I move him to, where would I take him? Two miles out to the road? Impossible, with that much weight and smelling the way he does. But if Travis does not move him, what then? Can he stand by and watch the lava do its work?

He hears voices in the wind. He hears the mocking and incredulous voice of Lieutenant Medeiros:

And where is he now, Mr. Doyle?

Out of sight, out of mind.

How do you know that?

The hot stuff covered him.

You mean you just stood there and watched a man burn?
He was already dead. Ashes to ashes. Rock to rock.

Downwind from the crevice he squats on his haunches
and asks Prince what he would do, asks him if he minds
being left alone, if he minds being covered by this bright
rivulet that seems to have his name on it. Will this be too
horrible to imagine? Or a fitting form of burial? Will you see
it as your final punishment? Or as a reunion with the
mother from whom we all have sprung?

There is no answer. It will be up to Travis, who tries to
do what he can on Prince's behalf. He takes the spray can
Holiday left behind and sprays around the crevice a circle
of phosphorescent white, wide enough to be spotted from
above, if and when the rescue copter shows. He drags in
some large loose stones to form a barrier, thinking they
might divert a flow this size, if it doesn't stop or veer off on
its own.

As he takes a breather and regards his primitive handi-
work, he remembers the offerings. He hikes over there and
brings them back and sets them down on a flat spot between
his barricade and the sizzling edge, which is by this time
about twenty-five yards away. He sets them down with great
care, the bunch of sun-burned anthuriums and the quart of
Gilbey's inside its paper bag and the necklace of kukui nuts
and the packet of ti leaves, also showing the sun's effect,
turning brown, shredding at the edges. These are lonesome
survivors. He gives them thirty seconds of silent attention.
Does he say a prayer? Not quite. He doesn't know what to
say, but he wants this gesture and this moment to be
reverent. What the hell, he tells himself, it might help. It sure
can't hurt.

For five more minutes he watches the rivulet inching
along. Behind him lie three miles of rocks layered with
darkness. In the other direction the terrain is equally rugged,

but he knows where the road is, if he can get to it without breaking an ankle. He has a beacon light to guide him, the coastal plume, pink and orange against the twilight. He starts toward it, in his hard hat, with the canteen, and with the ready light swinging.

There is no path or pattern, just a dusky plain of broken chunks, large and small, in clumps and heaps and swales and arroyos. He is getting the hang of it, taking his time, picking his way. He is about a mile along when he leaps a rise and feels the heat of an oven door thrown open. Directly ahead a molten stripe shows through the black rock, glowing quietly. Beyond it he sees another, like a long slit eye. He is at the edge of a very recent flow, darker than the rocks behind him. Perhaps that morning, perhaps a few hours ago, in midafternoon, new lava had surfaced and rolled through. These long orange eyes are looking at him from underneath a crust three or four inches thick.

Back the way he came he sees the broad darkness punctuated by flickers here and there, like distant campfires. He remembers what Angel said when they crossed the Ka'u desert. *Ask permission. It all belongs to her.* In front of him he can see an acre or two of new crust, cracked and twisted, and striped with slits. Thinking faith and respect and reverence and concentration and luck, in equal parts, might get him across this stretch of burning earth, he sets out, talking aloud to Pele and to anyone else who might be listening in, telling her he is but a humble pilgrim trying to make his way. "Please guide my feet," he says. "Please guide my feet."

He thinks of Prince scarring his palm in a place like this. Underneath his fear of such an injury is the urge to make it happen, the hope that he too will be marked by lava, receiving the penalty he somehow deserves. They swirl together, the fear and the hope, as he steps onto the oven, where no foot has stepped before, a place so new its surface has not yet been glazed by rainfall. Each step makes a powdery crumble as he moves from block to block, testing before he puts his full weight down. Each time his foot does not push through, he feels reprieved. It is a gift. Each step a chance, each step a gift.

The heat is dry and seems to rise in undulating waves, to blur the horizon and the distant plume. Soon orange windows are everywhere around him, and respect is too mild a word for what he feels. He begins to see why old Hawaiians made all the lava places sacred, realms of wonder and glowing heat, gorgeous and fearsome. The spectacle surrounds you, and you want to give it a name, whatever comes rising from the treeless plain, and you see why the spirit that inhabits such a place has been called possessive and wild and demanding and seductive in her beauty, impulsive and changable, appearing today as a lovely, long-haired young woman and tomorrow as an aging hag. The rock you step on can be four hours old or four hundred years old, or four thousand. The ancient and the new live side by side, the black rock and the seething red, the life of the surface and the life of the underworld, the fixed look of what has been here awhile and the surging will of what is yet to become.

At the shoreline the high-rolling cloud is crimson and spreading above the cliff like a cyclorama, while beneath it a thick gusher of lava pours from the cliff in a fiery spout, arcing into the sea. Coppery nuggets turn black as they cool, heaping upon themselves, water on rock, new from old. Hawaiians call this Pele's habitat, where the unknown spouts into the known. She is a figure on the doorsill where these worlds touch, and as Travis draws nearer to the cloud of steam he thinks she might be standing there, as a person, or as an apparition. He sees an outline much like the images he has heard described, a silhouette against a scarlet backdrop.

Through the undulations he has noticed tiny shapes coming and going along the cliff. Now one of these stands motionless before a sudden fountain of sparks, a black cutout with burnished edges. As he reaches the farther side of the heated crust, it occurs to him that this figure has been stationed there to guide him in. Soon he can see, by the fullness of hair, that it's a slender woman. He is gripped by the idea that all this time he has been moving toward her.

Sulfur is in the air, and invisible steam wisps, and the wavering heat. He blinks to clear his vision, looks again, and it seems inevitable now that this would be the person he most wants to meet and the last person he wants to meet. He isn't ready for it. Not now. Not yet. He needs time to sit still somewhere and sort through this day.

In the blazing dark no one can see faces. There is a way to veer westward, past the plume, and reach the road without going near where she is standing. He has moved a few yards out along this route when his boot slides into blackness. Maybe he has stepped too soon toward what appears to be a broad flat rock. His foot finds empty air. He is falling, rolling, tucking arms and legs for what feels like a tumble into the steepest gorge. His head hits a broken edge, and he is out, his face on hot stone. He is at the rim of a swimming pool on a blazing summer day, exhausted from an afternoon of laps and diving, with his cheek against the concrete. Water bounces under murky sunlight, making flickers against the blue tile gutter, and the tiled walls around the pool. The grainy heat wakes him. He opens his eyes and sits up, nauseous from the shock. He fell about four feet.

His jacket is torn at the elbow. A surface gash runs down his arms. His jeans are torn, his knee is scraped and raw and throbbing, but he can stand on it. His head throbs too. He waits until the nausea subsides, pulls off the hard hat and sees a split down the side, a dented split. He feels in his hair for blood, feels a lump, but his fingers come away dry.

The woman is still placed between him and the billowing cloud. He assumes it is the same woman. He wouldn't swear to it. Everything he has seen out here or thinks he has seen keeps shifting. Whoever she may be, he has imagined she is waiting for him. But she is not. She has no idea he is anywhere nearby. She does not face in his direction. As he hops the final rocks and draws close enough to see her head, her stance, he sees that she is looking at the orange drama of the shoreline steam.

From behind he says, "Angel."

She doesn't move.

He steps closer, calls again. Still she doesn't move. He steps right up next to her. "Hello!"

Her head whips sideways as if slapped. "Who is it!"

"Travis."

Half her face is lit with reddish shine, the eye made large in garish light, while the other half is in shadow, darkly polished, the eye a glint in its black socket. She could be a Halloween mask. Travis is aware of being lit the same way. They are both fire creatures streaked with orange.

"How did you get here?" she asks

"I walked. I've been on the rocks all afternoon."

"You all right?"

"Yes."

"Is that blood on your jacket?"

"It's okay. I fell. How about you?"

"I don't know."

"Why? What's the matter?"

She is a long way off, as if emerging from a trance. Her hand reaches to take his, sliding from the jacket rip down along his wrist, his knuckles. It is not a sign of affection or welcome. She has to prove that someone has actually appeared next to her out of the darkness. Is she glad to see him? Annoyed to have her reverie invaded?

"I found him," Travis says. "Right where I thought he'd be."

She turns away, to face the shoreline.

"I guess he had a heart attack. He's dead. I had to leave him there."

She shakes her head, breathes a long deep breath. Her mouth moves. No words come. She is somewhere on the other side of speech and has been since the hearing broke up, as she watched the citizens in clusters amid the emptying rows. The chairman had looked up long enough to scold her with a lidded stare of familial disappointment. The Chinese Hawaiian supervisor touched her arm and murmured, "Thanks for saying what you did. It helped," while his eyes said, "Let's get together sometime and talk about this." Before she left the microphone the tan woman from the board of realtors confronted her. "You people have your heads in the sand. Nobody's taking anything. It's just the opposite. Without local control of energy, this island can't go anywhere . . ."

Angel walked away from her, out into the corridor where two more women waited, a schoolteacher who looked Korean and the Caucasian wife of an orchid grower, inviting her to a follow-up meeting on Monday night, a few dedicated neighbors who wanted to take a stronger stand, though these two would love to go somewhere right now, for a cup of coffee, to swap ideas. Angel might have gone with them, at least until the rain let up, had not Roland appeared beside her. His face was tense with all the unreturned calls and with what he'd just seen, the part of Angel that had gone public. He liked to see her sitting by his side in the pickup, not taking on the men from Honolulu. He said,

"Let's drive down to the drilling site and see what we can see," making this a little test of his charisma. She thought she wanted someone to take charge right then and decide what her next move should be. But as they reached the parking lot she said she'd take her own car and meet him there.

Outside of town she changed her route. She did not want to go back to the hearing. She did not want a cup of coffee. She did not want to ride with Roland. She wanted to see the fire and listen to its voice. She drove down to the edge of the island, where she had heard the lava was near the road or crossing the road. At the end of the asphalt she happened to recognize a ranger from the National Park stationed there to tell visitors where they could and could not walk. Most of them were stepping out of rented cars, crowding up next to the yellow-tape barrier. They all had cameras at the ready. She had hers too, in the shoulder bag. She told him she was covering it for the paper. In the dusky half-dark he let her slip past the tape.

As she left the cars and the road behind, a wind across the stone whiffled in her ears with the light whiffle of sails, while the rush of surf, invisible below the shoreline rocks, came toward her like another kind of wind. Lifted by updrafts a tropic bird rose past the cliff edge, as if released from a dark throat, from some deep place she could not see. Alive and exultant, it soared and flew a wide circle around her before it floated away across the lava plain, a pure white bird with a double tail like a feathery tuning fork that seemed to leave a very high note singing above the wind.

Near the cloud of steam she began to hear something from lower down, a hum that could have been the lower octaves of the windy whiffle and the bird-tail song, or it could have been rising from the molten underlayer, a note so low and deep and yet so close this might have been her own blood humming in her ears, or something older than blood, the call of the umbilicus that had been hidden in the high country not too far from where she stood, in a place kept secret, and now long decomposed, transmuted, absorbed into the soil beneath the 'ohi'a trees and leeched down into the stone, her *piko*, her link to the mother and the grand-mother and all the previous mothers farther back than anyone can remember or imagine it.

Against a satin sky of darkening red, the red plume had filled her eyes. All she saw was red, and not long afterward his voice, unheard, had sounded behind her, then sounded again and broke through the fiery curtain but did not break the spell. Her jacket still radiates heat, her hair, her burning eyes. She has seen the craters and the steam before and every form of hardened lava, the drips and drops and drapes and folds and stacks and sheets, but this is the first time she has seen the island-shaping fire at close range. Behind them the high glow from the inland lake makes its penumbra in the night. Below that, against the slope, a long S curve seems stamped in gold. In front of them, the dumping arc has come this far through hidden tubing, to create the steam and then light it from below. The cloud sends a pinkish glow back down onto marbled surf. At the cliff edge, between the plume and where they stand, a cinder cone is building inch by inch, built of spatter thrown upward from the shoreline surge, the sizzling union. Red-and-black gobs fly above the edge, break into fiery debris, and fall upon the cone.

They are sizzling too, burning with old fires made new. His is . . . where? In the nerve ends. Somewhere in the mind, below the brain, where the invisible voyages are fueled and launched. Angel's is ancestral, flaming in the blood. Hearing the old note, she has also felt the heat coming at her from the shoreline and from below. As if her boots are melting, as if her feet and legs are softer, she feels herself sinking into the rock. Warm and soothing, it is easy on the calves and knees and thighs. The hips are like liquid, her ribs are melting, into the soothing red . . .

Out of the night a ranger appears to tell them this piece of shore has become unstable. The cinder cone might drop away at any moment. He doesn't know who they are, can only see the half-faces. In his voice, advising them to move well back, there is an edge of wild amusement, as if he too is lit within by this fantastical show and the risky sudden-ness of where they all stand, as if running into someone in the copper-tinted night is a reason to chuckle. Others are wandering out there, in twos and threes, fire watchers and geologists and observatory staffers. But who is who? Away from the plume they are shades and shadows, geology ghosts preceded by their flickering lights.

Travis and Angel are heading for the road while rocks seem to absorb their gliding beams, sucking light down to join the day's stored heat, making the darkness that much darker. Travis feels anonymous here, unidentifiable, and he likes it this way. He has been expecting to find a police car or two, an ambulance waiting, or a fire truck, someone to report to or perhaps be accosted by, arrested by. He does not yet know about the derrick and the chaotic scene, nor does Angel know about the exodus of trucks and hastily gathered tools and pipe and Clemson's lurching house trailer, all col-liding with the in-rush of emergency crews and media people. He does not yet know a surveillance team finally made a swing over Prince's resting place, saw lava moving down below, and decided to wait for daylight. Nor does he know that Lieutenant Medeiros has come and gone. On a tran-script of Holiday's radio report, Medeiros had seen Doyle's name and Prince's together and figured Travis would sooner or later come hiking out. He was driving to the roadblock when a dispatcher called in with the news of the eruption.

As they step from the last mound of the flow and feel asphalt underfoot, the end of the road is quiet, empty. They duck under the tight-stretched tape, switch off their lights. The road's white line cuts an errie phosphorescent stripe through a night made blacker by the density of stars.

"Where's your car?"

"Not far along."

"I should get to a phone."

"Yes."

"Then back to Hilo. I'm parked at the airport."

"It's right on the way."

Inside her Honda it is darker still, thick with body scents and whatever magnetisms have once again drawn them into the globe they make and share, globe of black light that now has a crackle to it, the crackling silence of waiting expectation, neither one knowing how to manage such a sightless, lightless space, how to sit, how to touch, how not to touch. He hears the key sliding into the ignition. She doesn't turn the engine on.

"I'm not going to say anything," she says.

"About what?"

"About anything."

"It's okay."

"I don't trust myself to talk."

"Don't talk. Just drive. No law about talking."

"It's no good that way."

"What's wrong?"

"I like to talk when I drive."

"You want me to drive?"

A moment's thought, and she opens the door, steps out. He walks around and slides in and pushes the seat back and starts it up.

"You'll have to navigate," he says.

"Make a U turn and follow the line. I'll tell you which way to go. But that's it. That's all I'm going to say."

"Not talking is okay."

"I'm just going to sit here."

In the rearview he can see the plume, tiny behind them, like a feathery flame in the night.

"You should turn around," he says, "and see what I'm seeing."

She does. As she watches it recede, her tears begin to fall. In the long silence he believes he can smell them, the faintest whiff of the scent of brine. From her eyes. Or from the sea. And now they are both places at once. They are inside the car and back at the shoreline, standing in the lurid light. In front seat shadows. And in the Halloween glow. He can feel it coming off her skin. Though he cannot see her eyes, he knows the plume light still blazes there. He steals a glance at her face, faintly lit by orange-yellow panel lights, her skin glossy where the tears spread, her hair uncombed, windblown, as if a gale is blowing through the car.

"I'm going to do something," she says at last. "I don't know what."

"Where have you been?"

"You know where I've been?"

"How would I know where you've been?"

"Suppose I tried to kill you. I could, you know. Have you thought about that?"

"No, I haven't."

"I could have a knife hidden somewhere and you would not be able to see me reach for it. I could slit your throat, and no one would ever know it."

"I guess you could."

"One quick slice, it would all be over."

Next to his Adam's apple he feels the side of her out-stretched hand.

"What's stopping you?"

"Or you could kill me. You could do anything you wanted to."

"Cut it out, Angel."

"We're alone out here."

He doesn't like the sound of this. He doesn't like what he feels and sees.

"Nothing around for miles," she says.

"I said cut it out!"

He sees Crystal again, teasing, her arms thrown back as if someone has handcuffed her to the bed. It is the kind of thing Crystal would have said, giving him permission to do whatever came to mind. He can not help imagining things he might do if he chose to overpower Angel by the side of the road. Does she want that? Or does she fear it and say these words to dispel the fear?

"I'm at your mercy," she says.

"I don't like that kind of talk."

"Neither do I."

"Then let it go."

"I shouldn't be here."

"You want to go back?"

"I heard my uncle's voice today. I went to a meeting down in town. I said some things. I didn't say enough. I didn't say enough. Now you are the only one listening to what I saw. Why is it you? Why are you the only one here?"

"Who else should it be? Who else do you want to be with?"

"Maybe I don't want to be with anybody."

"That's the way it sounds."

"Does that bother you?"

"I'll tell you what I'm going to do, Angel—"

"Don't tell me. Just do it!"

"I'm going to drive straight to your place and drop you off with the car, and I'll get a cab back to the airport."

"That is so condescending."

"I'm not condescending."

"You act like I'm drunk."

"You look drunk."

"Don't take care of me!"

"Sometimes people shouldn't be driving around in cars."

"My great-grandmother used to drink like a fish. Maybe I am starting to understand why. Maybe we should stop somewhere for a drink."

"Maybe neither one of us should be driving around in cars."

"I don't want anybody taking care of me!"

"Don't get your hopes up!"

"My *hopes* up!"

"What is this, Angel?"

"That's perfect!"

"You want to yell and shout?"

"Yes!"

"Is that it?"

"Yes! Yes!"

"All right! Good!"

"Yes! Yes! Yes! Yes!"

"Start shouting! Tell me what your goddamn problem is!"

"You want to know what my goddam problem is?"

"No!"

They come pouring out then, in a word gusher, the takers and the would-be protectors who have been overrunning the islands for so many years, now crowding up her father's place in Honolulu and offering these jobs that fill her with guilt and taking her uncle by the throat, filling his world with fairways and rental cars, and right in there among the many foreign agents and entrepreneurs she lists Travis, the one who led her to the Hotel Overkill, another invader, another haole flying in from afar to feed off the body and the spirit of the island, to take up her uncle's time, squeezing to the last drop the sacred pouch where he keeps his *mana* and what remains of his power . . .

Her anger is laced with remorse and pity and self-pity,

334 and once again his heart is opened, torn open this time, while his own guilts come rising, the white man's guilt by osmosis for all the invasions large and small throughout the centuries, and below that the lover's guilt, the fear that whatever she accuses him of must surely be deserved by Travis Doyle, the Disappointer of Women. This has been going on for years, as each of the women he has chosen turns on him when he is least prepared. Listening to Angel he relives the final days with Rachel, and the final days with Marge, when he watched tolerance turn to scorn and then contempt. At the next wide place maybe he will ease the Honda to a stop and punch her in the mouth, punch her hard and watch her bleed. Or maybe he will leap out of the car and take his chances on the open road and let her drive the rest of the way alone. Yes. Yes, this has gone far enough. Up ahead he sees a turnout, a dusty crescent bordered with scrub 'ohi'a. He pulls off the asphalt, cuts the engine and the lights.

"What are you doing?"

"I'm listening."

"Don't stop here." Her voice is tight now.

"Give me a minute to think about this."

In the dark and sudden silence he is strangely calm. Tutu David is on his mind, and what Angel just said about him, which he knows is not true. David gave him a great gift, but Travis took nothing from him. David filled his chest with healing light in a way that Travis wants to trust. He trusts the eyes and the hands and the feeling that surrounded and bonded the three of them. It has given him a place within himself to sit still, to hold still, to wait Angel out, to wait for this fierce black fire in her eyes and in her body to subside, Angel, whose voice he believes, but not her words. That is, he does not take them personally. This time he does not believe what she is saying. True, of course. Up to a point. Yet not true. Or not yet true. She has been shouting in his face, her eyes blazing, and he does not take it personally. It is not about him. Or rather, it is not about them.

"Let's keep moving, Travis."

"This is bullshit."

"Yes, it is."

"All this stuff you're saying."

"I don't like it here."

"You don't believe it any more than I do."

"Don't tell me what I believe!"

"Listen to what you're saying!"

"You're such an arrogant bastard!"

"I haven't been here long enough to take anything."

"Is that so?"

"Think about it."

"What about me?"

"What about you?"

"You come in here with your round-trip ticket and get exactly what you want."

"What *I* want? What does that mean? You didn't want it too?"

"I don't remember sending out invitations."

"We both wanted it. You know that."

"How do I know that?"

Because that is the way you see things, he could have said, the way I am learning from you to see things. But he doesn't think to say it. He does not yet have the words. He looks at her, trying to find the Angel who knows everything before he speaks it. Is this his old dream girl and new teacher and wise believer in the mysterious fluid that joins each moment to every other?

"You want me to go away, I will," he says. "But that is not going to be the reason. Haole. Local. I am tired of that. It's too easy. We should be talking about Travis and Angel. Not haole and local. You want to talk about Travis and Angel?"

She sits back against the seat and stares straight ahead. He steals another glance, at a moment when her face seems to change, becomes more familiar to him.

"I haven't seen you like this," he says.

She squeezes her eyes shut, drags both hands across her face. "Nobody has. I've never seen myself like this."

He waits, then turns on the engine, the lights, swings out onto the road.

"Why is it you?" she says. "Why are you the one to see me?"

He doesn't answer. He dares not speak. The question is enough, enormous. They let it hover in the air until she says, "You hungry?"

"Yes."

He smells another kind of salt. She is opening a paper bag, releasing into the air a spicy seaweed smell.

"I have to eat something."

"I haven't eaten anything since breakfast," he says, "except the pie."

"Try these."

A little plastic tray appears close to his face, where rolls of maki sushi have been cut into bite-size rounds, rice wrapped in black seaweed, stuffed with soy-soaked carrot shreds and bits of fish. Headlights are approaching. He can't take his hands off the wheel. He feels her fingers in front of his mouth. She pops in a sushi round. It fills him with gratitude. Never has he been so hungry, nor has food tasted like this, each grain of salt, each grain of rice, the tiniest fishy morsel has its flavor and its separate life.

I have more," she says, "some of those crispy Chinese dumplings. Are they down there by your feet?"

"Here it is."

A greasy white bag is shoved back under the seat.

"Let's open that too," she says, and into his mouth she pops a ravioli-size dumpling.

He can hear her chewing. They are both chewing and crunching and swallowing. It stirs all his appetites, goes straight to his head, while his stomach is eager for more, much more. He would not call this happiness. It is a readiness large enough to include the gurgling hunger and the desire welling up and the fear of becoming lovers again, as they speed toward Hilo, their shoulders touching on the turns, her hand from time to time against his leg, as if for balance.

Angel feels that readiness too, the same hunger, the same desire, though her fear is not the same. Something is just now being revealed to her, or released in her—the old calling that may steal away from the love she will be able to give to him, or to any other man. It has nothing to do with haole or local, or who has deceived or been deceived, or who has taken what from whom. She is at the edge of knowing this. Her body knows it, already foresees the solitude this may bring into her life, and knows this could be her way, her fate. And as this knowledge, or these many knowings come upon her, she longs for all of it not to be true. Her body begins to yearn for what she already knows may never be entirely hers, which is the love that comes back to you when you can give yourself to another with complete surrender and abandon. As they draw nearer to Hilo, the fear grows within her that what once flamed between them may never flame again, or never flame in the same way.

His foot is heavy on the pedal as they race and swerve toward town. With all the windows open, humid air flows through the car, caressing the skin. At the first big intersection he has to stop. Headlights outline her brow, her nose, the upper lip that is both Polynesian and Japanese, the way its lifting edge flattens the mouth and also makes it fuller. He turns, intending to pull her close. She turns too, and in her eyes he sees a bold, reckless look. It is not the recklessness of their younger days, nor is it the thoughtful yes of their most recent days. There is no caution, no worrying about where they might end up or who might catch them in the act. It is the opposite. Her mouth curves into a bawdy smile. In her eyes he sees some edge of panic or impending doom.

He parks at the shadowy end of the lot. They straighten their clothes, to make what they think will be a quick but dignified passage through the side entrance of the Orchid Isle and up the first flight of stairs. He double-bolts the door. They kiss for five minutes standing up, mouths urgent, sliding, while they undress, unpeel each other, trying to take their slow erotic time, but this night they are driven by their hungers, grabbing, then rolling and licking as if this is an end-of-the-world farewell party, perhaps their final night on earth. Or their first night on earth, with everything new and yet to be discovered and invented. Or both. To Travis it feels both ways. The end. And the eternal beginning. He becomes a virgin, trembling with inexperience, so heated he is ready to explode, unskilled, uninitiated, unadvised except by hearsay and by whatever the body knows that the mind does not. Each time with Angel will be like this, as if the history they have is forgotten, and they are always meeting in the dark, familiar strangers desperate to remember what brings them here. His first time with her was his first time with anyone. Maybe he wants to keep it that way, the ecstatic terror of uncharted territory, appearing before her as the one who knows not what to do, how to proceed, awaiting instructions, from the bodies, from his, from hers. He is out of control, cannot contain himself. Nor can she. The first time they come, he expects to hear pounding on the walls from the next room, they are so loud, crying out with surprise, as if they have been ambushed.

While they lie there spent, wet, spread across the sheet like corpses, he fully expects to get a call from the desk clerk or the manager. As he listens for the footsteps of the messenger bearing an eviction notice, his body feels drained of all its fluids. He does not know how much time goes by, maybe half an hour, before either one moves. It is her hand, sliding across his thigh, a long moistened slide that eventually reaches in to fondle him. One hand at first. Then two. Then four. They're rolling again, and it is one of those times when they could go on all night. He keeps thinking, We can't take this any further. Yet it continues. The surfaces go numb, while desire somehow multiplies, and swells. Underlayers are awakened. They say paradise has never existed anywhere except in the mind, a dream we all have dreamed together. Certainly there is no place on the map that qualifies, no island or secret village or distant mountain hideaway has ever measured up, once you actually arrive. But there are moments that come upon you unannounced. Angel was his first lover, and his last lover, and maybe this is it, being with her. At just this moment. Not fucking. That is, not merely fucking, for its own sake. Though they are. Long and deeply. Over the years he has done a lot of forgettable fucking. This is something else. This is the entering of one by the other. And being entered. To take and be taken. "I could die right now and have no regrets," he tells her, his lips inside her ear. "Being here. With you. Like this. So close. Is more. Is so much more. Than I ever expected. Could possibly come to me. In this life."

Does Angel agree? Or not agree? Is this, for her, the long-sought-for Garden of Earthly Delights? From the way her tears begin to fall again, it might seem so. She is above him now, gazing through the black strands and ribbons of wind-blown hair hanging past her cheeks and chin, straddling, rocking, and the tears run past her nose. Some fall onto his nose and cheeks, tears of pleasure, tears of greeting, tears of union, tears for what she cannot say yet already knows, tears for what they might never be again, loving this moment and knowing how it feels for him, and knowing that her love of it and need for it is not as great as his, and yet of course it is only by arriving here, with him, the two of them, traveling together to this dark threshold in the midnight room, that she can know and understand this much, gazing down at him and through him into other places she has seen this day, this night. They are gazing through each other, and passing through. Though bound, as if their edges had been joined by the welder's torch, they are somehow passing through each other . . .

A wave begins to throb, like a sound wave, pulsing outward. That is how it seems to Travis, something he can see from somewhere behind his mind's eye and hear from somewhere behind his ears, throbbing outward in a slow crescendo that makes one long undulant roll, and he is in it, rushing, invisible, wingless, borne forth upon a broad band, a violet glow pulsing against the dark of night, the band so broad and thick it becomes a pool of violet, spreading the way they say the universe spreads, or curves. It rushes outward even though there is no border to be reached, just the borderless, infinite, endlessly surging pool. And Angel is not with him. She is here. Yet she is not. She is plunging toward some source of heat far below them, heat rising from below the bed, from below the room, below the grounds outside the room, below the island, below the sea, and

340

the dark sea floor, the deepest chambers of the island-birthing heat. Is it rising? Or is she sinking toward it? Or both at once? Rising and sinking and rising and sinking. A shadow with magnetic bulk has drawn her downward, while it rises, as if some new sea mount is emerging from the depths, like the submerged island she has heard of but never seen, somewhere offshore, to the south and east, a mile below the surface of the water, but rising from the hot spot, the next island, the newest island, pushing upward layer upon layer. Loihi, they have named it, *loihi* meaning long and tall and distant, so far down the gushering is silent, the orange gouts of wet fire burst and float and settle, as the layering lava pushes upward like a dream, like the oldest dream in the world that is new for you when it finally breaks the surface, erupting, spewing geysers in the salty air.

The Lieutenant's Tale

All night the rivers move, seen and unseen. Steam boils at the shoreline, as the bright arch pours into the surf. Around the stranded derrick, a new lake glows. Channels appear, then disappear, across the slopes of lower Puna, tongues and twisting creeks, among them the rivulet that finally rolls to a stop just short of the crevice where the corpse is pinned.

When the med-evac crew touches down the next morning, it takes three men to pull him clear so they can fit a sling under the body for the airlift. These are local county workers and much affected by the sight of offerings so close to the last lip of a flow. In the early sun the new lava lies like dark pudding across the older rock. Its forward edge has hardened into a curving fold, about ten inches from the weathered anthuriums and the ti leaf packet, which stands like a rumpled guardian.

In Honolulu the next day's *Advertiser* picks up the story and runs a page 4 headline: DID OFFERINGS PROTECT FALLEN HIKER? For the fellows on the med-evac crew, who will each describe what they have seen a dozen times this week, the answer is yes. For Tutu David the answer is yes, and for Angel, who flew down there with the first press contingent to take the picture. For Tiny Kulima too, the answer is yes. He is satisfied that the island has spoken. The body was spared, he will tell Travis, because the man went out there to make his peace, while the burial of the drilling site is a clear sign of Pele's disapproval. Tiny has a friend, a lift-truck driver, who once went into the hospital for a kidney transplant, but it didn't take. "The body didn't want it," Tiny says, his eyes filling with sad amazement. "It's like a splinter in your thumb. Your body gets rid of it, makes the white stuff that pushes out the splinter, and cleans up the infection too."

This imagery is lost on Carlo, who caught the eruption on the ten o'clock news. He saw the derrick tilting and the remains of the shed go up in flames. It had five minutes of national coverage. Now he wants to know why Travis has been so long getting back to him. Two more days have passed, he says, and time is still money.

Travis would like to take it step by step, but his boss and confidant is too impatient to sit through it all. Travis knows, as he listens to the voice across the water, that he won't be seeing Carlo again for quite a while, knows that what he's about to say will bring to a timely end his career as a claims adjuster. The report will soon be on your desk, Travis says, and it could be very short.

"What do you mean by short?"

"Maybe three or four words."

"Today is not my day for kidding around. The snake who bought this building just raised everybody's rent."

"An act of God. How does that sound?"

"We don't use that vocabulary any more. It's out of date."

"Certain people here are calling it an act of Goddess. Does that feel any better?"

At the end of a long silence Carlo says, "I'm trying to run a business, Travis. You know that. We don't have much room for theology when the time clock is ticking away."

What has happened to Travis Doyle? Does he agree with Tiny Kulima that the island, like the human body, can have a will of its own? Does he think ti leaves can actually halt the flow of lava? Leaves of tribute? Leaves of faith? Can flowers and gin and kukui nuts convey the necessary spirit of recognition and reverence?

How he deals with such questions will depend on who he's talking to. As he sees how many ways people can get the wrong idea, he will learn to be careful when the subject is gods and goddesses. Some will think he is a missionary. Or a nut. Others, like Carlo, will think he has lost his grip. Others will say, as the eyes soften, "I know exactly what you mean," and a couple of days or a couple of hours later the phone will ring and he will be invited to a meeting, "a very small gathering, all people I know you will enjoy."

Travis is not a joiner or a worshiper. He would not go out there at dawn and leave offerings at the edge of Halema'uma'u the way Angel will be doing. He would never see it as his place to do this. Pele belongs to the Hawaiians. They have kept her alive and kept alive the old, old dialogue. From them he will learn how the gods and goddesses thrive on dialogue and disappear if it dies. In volcano country, where the earth speaks all the time, the dialogue has never died. In the hearts of those who live there, something has always spoken back, and in the loaded air these voices mingle. This is what he hears in the throat-thick chants, in the cracking, bluesy note that is both lament and celebration, in the unison calls of the dancers layered with ferns and vines, as a dance is dedicated to the one who made the mountains and the canyons and the shorelines waiting to be born.

Each player, of course, reads the signs the way he has to read them. For Dan Clemson, it is all another roll of the terrestrial dice. With so much lava flowing in so many directions, the chances for synchronicities and symbolic moments gather and multiply around you. Steam is steam, lava is lava,

and humans learn by trial and error how to prevail and turn
a profit.

"I prayed, for Christ's sake! I spread leaves around the
platform like Tiny said! What the hell difference did it
make?"

Clemson is fed up. He has lost a derrick. He lost a month
of payroll. Two of his men are badly hurt. He is going back
to West Texas, where the world makes more sense. He is fed
up with Hawai'i, fed up with geothermal, fed up with
Western Sun. If there was a curse on this project, he tells
Travis, it was Ian Prince, God rest his soul, the under-
qualified and overly excitable son of the former vice president for Alternative Power Sources. "You take that fire.
Now that he's gone there's no harm telling you he shouldn't
have been anywhere near the compound that night. He was
supposed to be in town at a hotel banquet schmoozing with
the mayor."

According to Clemson the clearing had been scraped, but
the rig was still in pieces, some of it waiting to be trucked
up from the harbor, some of it en route by barge. He had to
spend a couple of days in Honolulu with the shippers, and
while he was gone Prince talked the local security guard into
taking a drive with him one afternoon in a rented heavy-
duty jeep. They started down a muddy track toward the
land he had been trying to see. The local fellow thought he
knew the way, but the track was so overgrown they lost it
and slid into a drainage ditch. They had to abandon the
vehicle and hike back up to the compound, arriving just as
night clouds rose to fill the sky with thunder. The security
man went home to check on his family, promising to return,
though he never did, and that left Prince alone in the
vibrating and enormous darkness . . .

As he talks again with the driller and with Tiny, with the
fire chief and Holiday and Connie again, and the counselor,

Travis calls it "tying up loose ends." He takes notes, as if he's still working for Carlo, but he is already self-employed, compiling for himself a version of Prince's life he will carry around and dip into from time to time, like the scrapbook of a lost relative whose face and gestures and surroundings can hold you captive.

In this biography Prince saw himself as a man of reason, and he hoped the laws of cause and effect that had worked for his father would somehow work for him. He had an MBA, two condos, a growth portfolio. He belonged to the Pacific Union Club and the Outrigger Canoe Club. He subscribed to *Forbes*, *Newsweek*, and the *Wall Street Journal*. As the days went by he could not tolerate the thought that two lightning strikes so many years apart were in any way connected. Or rather, his belief in this connection ran so deep that he had to fight it. He asked the fellows on the engine crew to keep to themselves their rainy memories. On the phone to Holiday he said it was a policy matter, the less talked about the better, and if the pilot could help the company in this small way, Western Sun could surely return the favor. Brockman's letters came along just when Prince needed them. But then the pickups stalled and Travis appeared, asking uncomfortable questions. On the morning he walked away from his French toast, Prince drove back to the office to redraft the claim. Sometime before lunch he asked Connie to put in a call to Holiday Air, to arrange the flight that would have taken him and Angel over the remote terrain he had not been able to reach on wheels. Connie was dialing when he rose from his desk and told her to hang up. His face looked flushed, she says, as if he'd been caught at something. "The next thing I knew he was out the door and heading for Maui."

To Connie, who kept the books and handled the billing, he had called the overflight a scouting trip, advance siting for the cable route. He kept to himself his long-range plan, which was to pick up this and other properties where the island-hopping towers would one day be erected. He had already formed a land company with a dummy board of directors who would eventually lease the parcels back to Western Sun. A modest scheme, by island standards, the counselor tells Travis, the kind of thing his father had done with great success. "Ian knew exactly how it worked," she says. "The problem was he never felt quite right about about doing it. Poor Ian. He always wanted to be tough and ruthless. I think he may have frightened himself to death."

On the day Travis is called in take a deposition, to explain in detail why and how he happened to come upon the body when he did, it is just a formality. Medeiros already knows what he needs to know. He has seen the rescue report and the coroner's report. Angel calls him the kind of guy who always knows where the bones are buried, a guy who listens carefully to everyone and remembers everything he hears. Angel also calls him Tommy. When Travis told her he had once been warned to keep his hands off her, she wagged her head with a tolerant smile and said, "He could hurt you, or have you hurt. But he won't. Not yet."

"What do you mean, not yet?"

"You haven't been here long enough. Like you said. And he is not that close to Roland. He asked me out himself a couple of times. More than a couple of times."

"Isn't he married?"

"Sure he's married. Let's go to another island, he says. Let's go to Lahaina. Let's go to Waikiki."

His office is located on the breezy side of the building, so his cool and unwrinkled clothes are ventilated by the trades. They talk mostly about John Brockman, who was picked up at Honolulu International trying to check a suitcase of explosives through as ordinary baggage. Later Brockman will tell Travis that he envies the precision of the rising lava and likens it to a surgical strike by a flight of fighter bombers, the kind of thing the air force will try when there is a single target, one uncooperative dictator to be excised from the political map. He only wishes he'd had another eight to ten hours to organize his attack. In the lieutenant's view, Brockman is too much trouble to be running loose. "He's an amateur," says Medeiros, who had been ready to go along with Prince's accusations. If some kind of case had been put together, where would be the harm?

"Would you have let it go to trial?"

"It would never get that far. The charge would never stick. But Brockman would still get the message."

"Which was?"

"Keep moving."

Medeiros lets this hang in the air. As a warning to Travis? It might sound that way, but it doesn't look that way. The lieutenant's eyes wait, as if ready to smile if Travis says the right thing.

"You mean because he's a haole?"

"Don't get touchy."

"I'm not touchy."

"Some of my good friends are haoles."

"As long as they don't stir up the water."

Medeiros looks out the window toward a large flame tree in the distance, rising against the shine of Hilo Bay.

"I have to get along with a lot of people here. Some of them want the geothermal coming in. They see it as good for the islands. Personally I can take it or leave it alone. A power cable from here to Oahu? I don't know. That's a lot of cable. A lot of headache. But that plan is not going away. There's too much money behind it. Washington money. Private money. Somebody has to spend it. Engineers from Houston have already been out here looking at their back-up sites. Meanwhile I have a kid in his second year at Santa Clara. Room, board, tuition, airfare three times a year. It's not easy, you know." He shrugs and muses a moment. "And our friend Brockman is nothing but bad news. So it's a relief he is out of the picture now. Haole. Local. I don't worry much about that. I just can't stand fooling around with amateurs. You never know what they're going to try next. He did a lot better dealing dope. We never could pin anything on him. As a revolutionary he doesn't think." Medeiros taps his temple with a forefinger. "Tying himself to the scaffolding over there in Kona. Bringing that stuff through baggage. That's not the way to do things. Here in the islands there is always a certain way to do things."

He is growing friendlier as he talks, as if softening Travis up for something. At last he gets around to it.

"For the record, could you find me a print of that picture you took?"

"Which picture is that?"

"The one Evangeline Sakai flashed at the hearing."

"What makes you think I took it?"

For a moment Travis feels cornered again. Has Medeiros uncovered some misstep that will give him new leverage? And is this another way to say "Keep moving?"

An odd smile has crossed the lieutenant's face. In his eyes Travis sees a look he has seen somewhere else. He is no longer a cop. And Travis is not someone with a deposition on file. They are two men regarding each other, men who take an interest in the evidence of things not seen. His cop's eyes have become like Angel's, with that same glow of receding blackness.

"It's for my personal file."

"Sure. I'll get one to you right away."

This photograph, taken in innocence, in ignorance, will continue to work for Travis, as people will hear of it and learn how he handed it over to Angel. For those who follow the underhistory of public events—and on the Big Island there are many who do—it soon will hold a small place of curious significance. The very snapping of a shutter will open doors that otherwise might have remained closed. When police lieutenant Tommy Medeiros asks for a print, it means, among other things, in the gift-giving culture of this self-contained island world, that Travis will one day be able to ask a small favor of him.

Later he will learn that Medeiros has a streak of Hawaiian in his blood, though you would never guess it from his looks. He too has his official record of this episode, and his unofficial record. He happens to belong to a partnership—the local word is *hui*, meaning alliance, union, club, team—that controls the land Prince had hoped to buy. He would never have agreed to such a sale, and he will resist any offers to secure this land for a power line or future drilling rights. Privately Medeiros believes Western Sun has already gone too far, grown too big. It pleases him to have a print of the one surviving shot of the damage that may or may not have been part of Pele's early warning system. Prince destroyed all other pictures showing any sign of lightning. Everything else—the beams, the split post, the fallen debris—has been surrounded by lava and burned. It is all gone, the access road, the trees that bordered the road, the fencing, the gate where the demonstrators made their stand and where Angel and Travis met—all buried under the wrinkled acres of new rock, with just a few charred scraps and chunks scattered around like driftwood.

Restless Sleepers

At San Francisco International he had left his car in long-term parking, thinking he'd be gone a week at most. Now six more weeks have passed, and with those weeks his long-imagined reunion time with Angel has also come and gone. And is it over now between them? Or are they waiting once again? He isn't sure. That is, he does not want to say for sure. Dreaming about her for all those years, that was one thing. Living with her was something else, living with the two-way mirror of daily life. And yet, as the plane touches down, he is already missing her, wishing he could have stayed another six weeks, or six months.

"I'll call as soon as I can."

"Yes, please," she said, "and I'll call you."

As she stood with him at the Hilo airport, outside the metal detecting gate, these were her farewell words. Her eyes were brimming with unvoiced questions. Perhaps, like him, she was remembering the first time she had seen him off, from Honolulu, with a lei of maile vines to drape around his neck, when they were both sixteen and vowing with their lips and arms and brimming eyes that they would always be together.

Taxiing in, waiting for the shuttle, he is sure his car has been vandalized or towed away after all this time and sold at auction. But no, it's right there, the aging Volvo, spotted like a leopard from the days of rain and sun and fog and sun. He pumps the pedal a few times. She coughs and snorts and finally starts. For what it's going to cost me to get out of here, he thinks, I could have had my brakes relined.

Heading toward his mother's place he follows elevated viaducts to the high road above Millbrae, which gives him a view back down upon the airport, where jumbo jets roll along beside the silky waters of the bay. Across the water he sees a white fringe of cities below the long Diablo Range, parallel to the line of ridges now carrying him south. They are twin mountain borders for the inland sea that used to cover this broad floor from edge to edge and spread on down past San Jose.

As he lets this panorama screen out the replays of their parting, he can almost take it in with new eyes, with the eyes of the newcomer or the homecomer gone long enough to be refreshed and see again, as if for the first time, these inlets and bottomlands and rumpled peaks above the bay. At the reservoir called Crystal Springs, steep trough that marks the route of the San Andreas, he turns west toward the coast, climbing a narrow, tree-lined road that has the sudden look of wilderness, a forest road among soaring grassy domes, while the sky ahead is brighter above the as-yet-unseen Pacific.

He swings south again at Halfmoon Bay, to curve along the ocean lined with swells pushing shoreward. Between the surf and the coastal bluffs there are benchlands where brussels sprouts and artichokes grow in close-packed rows. Against a sheen off the endless water, a lonesome tractor is pulling a harrow through dark soil, through fields plowed right out to the drop-off edge of the final cliff.

New Years Island is like an atoll mound inside this sheen, half a mile out and tied to shore by a narrow reef you sometimes see at the lowest tide. As the coast curves inward, below Davenport, Monterey Peninsula comes into view, like another off shore island, farther south and twenty miles across the water, promising something, always promising, promising, promising. That is how it looks to him as he hurtles homeward, the coastline vibrant, everything shimmering yet strangely still, with a polished and oppressive stillness, as if held in check for this one singular and suspended moment.

It is late afternoon when he makes the final turn, up the family driveway toward the two-story frame house his grandad bought back in the 1920s, when there was nothing else around but empty slopes and live oaks and redwoods. Now other houses show on parcels his dad sold off, but from the driveway or the yard you can't see them. Orchard still keeps the old place screened. Mixed in with the madrone and the eucalyptus and pine there are date palms for the subtropical touch. He has never thought of it before, palms growing this far north. Whose idea was that? What island did they have in mind?

He parks away from the house, at the edge of the trees, thinking he will walk across the yard, as if returning from the mailbox. Leona doesn't know he's coming, any more than she knows where he has been for the past couple of months. He is the itinerant prodigal son hoping now she has not given up on him.

He is halfway across the yard when the ground begins to tremble, as if a sea dragon has risen from below. It shakes so violently he loses his balance. He pitches sideways and lunges with one foot, bends his knees and braces like a sailor on a heaving deck, and watches the house quiver at such a high vibration he thinks it may dissolve.

His anxiety is not that it will crumble and split. He stands ready for the unknowable, and it seems to him that the frequency of this tremor has softened whatever glue holds the molecules together. The house becomes transparent, as if assuming some more primal form of energy. In another instant it could be gone. But the tremor subsides. Something in the aspect of the building offers one more tiny shiver, as if all its parts—the walls, the wraparound porches, the window casings, the eaves and pitched roof—have agreed to remain awhile longer in this particular shape, and the house settles into the position it has occupied for ninety years or so.

354

There is an instant of loaded, postquake silence, after which the nearest porch gives way. He sees one corner drop a few inches, with a clunk. Then it is silent again, and his mother steps out onto the porch. She wears jeans, a long-sleeve shirt. Her hair appears to be electrified, hanging out away from her head, gray-white, glowing like silver.

"My God!" she cries. "It's Travis!" as if the earth just announced his arrival, surprised to see him, yet not surprised. In her mind he is the child of this terrain, the son whose bones are made of tremors.

She comes running down the stairs and throws her arms around him. They hug like a mother and the long-lost son, and they hug like you do after a big shaker, grabbing the closest person, whether friend or stranger, hugging to squeeze away the helpless sense of frailty.

"You all right?" he says. "Inside, is the house all right?"

"Yes, I think so."

"Anybody else in there?"

"No, not today."

"We'd better stand away, until we're sure it's over."

"Yes, we'd better."

She takes his arm, as if for support, though she is leading, out into the middle of the yard, halfway between the porch and the trees. Looking at each other they both begin to laugh. The timing of this quake has freed them, the mother and the son, to see Leona and Travis, two humans at large on a planet that can throw you around its surface like a beachball in the wind.

They stand there talking, catching up, waiting. After ten minutes or so he goes to check the water line, the gas line, sniffing for leaks. Inside he checks the ceilings and the paneling for signs of movement. In the kitchen a shelf of dishes fell. The brick chimney may have cracked today, or it may have been cracked for years. In the hallway the photo of his father from 1945 has fallen and the glass has shattered, but the frame is okay. He hangs it up again with a new hook, the kind that slants against the wall and is said to be quakeproof, thinking he will soon replace the glass, but he never does. He likes it better without the glass. No glare from the overhead light. No reflections to distort the smile.

On his way through town he picked up a baked chicken. They move a table and two chairs out onto the grass and eat the chicken and drink a bottle of wine. It is one of the most astounding evenings of his life, sitting around with his mother. He never imagined such a thing was possible, just the two of them, drinking and talking. She tells him stories he may have heard before, during the years when he wasn't listening. She tells him the story of her father's life, and her mother's life, and things about the family he has never heard. His grandmother, for example, his father's mother, had lived through the 1906 earthquake and fire. As a young girl she ran barefoot into the early morning streets of San Francisco. Until the day she died the last thing she did each night was to place by the bed a pair of shoes she could step right into. Leona talks about the life of Montrose too, his later days and his untimely death and how fitting it would be if she and Travis could go together to visit his grave one day soon, though there is some place nearer by she wants to visit first.

While they are eating, his brother, Grover, calls to see how she is and suggests, as he has already done a couple of times, that she move into town instead of staying out in the country alone where no telling what might happen. He is wrong about that, Leona tells him, she is not alone, Travis is here, and she will have plenty of company if Grover and his family will stop by soon for a visit.

As Travis will learn in the coming weeks, she likes her solitude for half the day, and then she likes to mingle. In the

year since the funeral she has turned the house into a kind of community center, with classes meeting and weekend seminars. She is into everything from textiles to toxic wastes in the streambed you cross at the bottom of the hill. The solitude catches up with her at night, she confesses, when the slightest sound will wake her, and she will lie there for an hour listening to nothing. She will remarry before long, that is his guess. It's hard for Travis to imagine her in the company of a man other than his father. But Leona has several admirers. She's an attractive woman, with a piece of property, and she still has her health.

A fellow from Palo Alto has been offering her quite a sum to sell all the orchard they have left so he can subdivide it. He talks about "a leisure community, townhouses, tasteful, for the midrange, midlife buyer." From one point of view this would make her comfortable for the rest of her days. Yet she resists. "Where are you then?" she says to Travis. "Where do you end up? *Who* are you?" In their family they have never had much money, but they've always had some land. To Leona, living in a condo or a retirement village sounds like oblivion. She is tied to this place, and Travis wants to be true to that. It is another way of being true to the spirit of his father's life and the spirit of his grandfather's life and the call that brought him this far across the continent.

In the barn where his father used to work, Travis will soon make an office for himself. He will take over his father's desk and tool bench, along with other duties around the place. They still have acreage in Red Delicious, and this has to be attended to. The road, the yard, the house, it all needs work. The chimney will have to be rebricked and the porch jacked up while some new timbers are installed. He will discover that his lifetime of clumsiness with appliances and tools wasn't clumsiness at all. It was old-fashioned rivalry, a refusal to accomplish anything his older brother was good at.

Travis will saw boards with his father's saw, remembering skills Montrose had tried to teach him when he was ten, remembering how Grover always got it right the first time, while Travis would manage to chip a sawtooth or cut his thumb. He will remember how Grover and Montrose would argue and do battle. With eyes. With hands. Montrose never fought with Travis. There was never the showdown that is supposed to clear the air, and for a while he will wonder if this is why he joined the army. Did Travis watch his father mixing it up with Grover and come to see fighting as a form of loving? And was the army some way he thought he could earn his father's love? After he came back from overseas Travis had seen no sign of this. Eventually it will occur to him that he did not want to see such a sign. If his father had loved him, if Travis had allowed himself to see some sign of love, he would have lost an obstacle, lost the one to blame.

These things wash over him, in waves of grief and waves of affection, as he tightens tractor fittings with his father's wrenches and returns them to his wall of tools, learning ever more about him, who he was, how he stood, how he lived and used his time.

In this fashion, feeling what is here and waiting to be felt, he will stay put and, after so many years adrift, find a footing for himself, a place to stand and to return to. Before long he will be imagining that Angel might one day join him here, though who knows how or when, now that she is among those working to protect the wild soul of the island. She has told him she can't live anywhere but there. Before he left she was pulling together her best photographs, black-and-whites from Puna, Kona, and Ka'u, for an exhibit called "Who Owns Hawai'i?" The young county supervisor, Herman Yee, had appointed her to his Conservation Task Force, and they were laying out plans for a lecture tour to take from town to town, a public forum on energy efficiency, with slides and charts and blowups. Zeal was often in her eyes. Sometimes he will hear it in her long-distance voice, when they are talking late at night. Then her voice will change, soften, drop to a whisper, and he will almost see her standing in the yard between the pair of redwoods outside his window. He will try to answer, try to send a beam twenty-four hundred miles across the water. He has heard that transmission like this can be instantaneous, if you put your full attention on it. He will tell himself they are still connected by these filaments of spirit light, no matter what else has been said or done.

Now another month has passed, and Evangeline Sakai turns in her bed with a grunting snore, shrugging and stretching, half awake and alone out there in the middle of the ocean. In the humid night she sprawls and turns and sweats and listens, with a random arm flung wide, wishing for rain to come and clear this wetness from the air.

Is she thinking of Travis? Yes. And no. Travis, plus everything else. No man in her bed since Travis left, and tonight, this morning, is one of the times she wishes he were somewhere closer. She would like to be able to talk this through. Right here. Right now. On the mattress, in the dark and in the breezeless quiet. Should she call him? Yes. Early. Before eight o'clock, to get the discount.

But what will she say? How will she phrase it? And what kind of reaction can she expect? What kind does she *want*? Will this news please him? Or scare the hell out of him? Maybe words alone won't be enough. Maybe she won't call. She wants to see him when she tells him this, see his eyes, his mouth, his hands. Maybe she will fly over there. Yes, that would be better. Take him by surprise. She thinks she knows a way she could do it. The Task Force might be sending someone to meet with the Sierra Club and other Bay Area supporters. She'll talk to Herman Yee. He controls the money. He might want some kind of favor in return. But she controls the favors.

In Honolulu she could stop to see her mother. And she will have to tell Papa too. Sooner or later. If she does not lose it, the way she lost the last one. That was the one she wanted to lose, or thought she did, because it was Walter's, although now she sometimes wonders how he would have looked at age two, at age three. She knows it would have been a boy, and she knows, within a week or so, what would have been his birthdate. Sometimes she hears him scamper past, the invisible child she might have had. As for this one, yes, the timing is wrong, with her hands so full, so much to do, so much before her, and caught again, just like that little girl on Marilyn's volleyball team who has to drop out of school to waddle around the house while her body swells and blooms. The timing is wrong, and Angel has imagined flying to the clinic in Honolulu to do what Brenda has now done twice. But she won't. She already knows she wants it, and she believes Travis will want it too. This is what she has to see with her eyes and hear with her ears. For this she cannot rely on faceless telephone words.

Uncovered, with a sheet thrown back, she places hands below her belly where there is flat smooth flesh to feel and beneath the flesh a change she knows too well. No mistaking or denying it now. Did it feel this way before he left? Well, yes. And no. Almost. Not quite. Her period was late and had been late before. She wasn't ready to talk about it or dwell on it, though she knew, and she could have told him and maybe kept him on the island awhile longer—which was exactly what she did not want. Not then. It was time to fly

back home. For his own good. For *their* own good. It was too soon to set up housekeeping. They had reached an impasse. How would they live, if they stayed together? And where would they live—her island, or his? Her cottage was too small, with Marilyn always on the phone, and he was running out of money. They had tried to talk it through, of course, yet they had not talked about everything. On the way to the airport Travis knew there was something she was not telling him. He thought it was about Herman Yee. He was wrong. But he was also right. That's what made her angry.

It started with a joke, Travis joking about the way Herman always ends up sitting next to her at meetings, and a certain look he has seen in the supervisor's eyes. Jokingly Angel told him there was nothing to worry about. Herman is strong in his convictions, she said, but too methodical to fall for. "If there is going to be another man in my life, it will surely be you."

In the edgy spirit of that ride she must have figured this would pass as another form of joking. Travis didn't take it that way.

"If?" he exclaimed. "What kind of bullshit is *if*?"

The harshness in his voice rubbed her wrong. "I'm just trying to be honest about how I feel right now."

"It's this local stuff again," he said.

"That is the farthest thing from my mind."

"Maybe what you've wanted all along is a guy from here."

"I'm not looking for guys from anywhere. That's not it at all."

"Isn't Herman Yee part Hawaiian?"

"Yes he is."

"So he fits right in."

"Right in with what?"

"All this stuff you're working on."

"That is so petty, Travis."

"It's not anything I take personally."

"You sound like Walter used to sound."

"I'm just trying—"

"Don't. Please. I can't believe you're saying this."

Nor could Travis believe he was saying such things in their last thirty minutes together. In his eyes she saw a stricken look. Suddenly it was like the night they drove down from Volcano, they were strangers again, talking through fog and rainy mist. At the counter, after he checked his bags through, they hugged and both apologized. Neither of them could have said, at the time, what the apologies were for. She had brought along a double ilima lei, tightly woven necklaces of orange striped with red, and he had brought for her a last-minute gift, a pair of earrings, hammered silver from the Phillipines.

What a clumsy and painful good-bye. It filled her with such confusion and regret she started for Tutu David's place, not knowing quite why, not having words to explain her need to be with the old man. Then halfway across town she changed her route, changed her mind. She was already hearing the story she needed to hear, or needed to remember. It began to move through her head as if David were next to her in the car. Hearing it, she understood how part of her was still keeping Travis in a category. And she saw why she had done this, kept that last bit of distance, even as their lives grew daily more entangled, so that when he left again, as she feared and knew he would, she could tell herself he was, after all, a mainland haole, so what can you expect.

What did Herman have to do with this? They talked a lot, and without doubt there was an attraction. He was both fatherly and brotherly, a mentor and an ally, with Chinese hair and Hawaiian eyes. Over coffee Herman would say things that worked on her. Blood is thicker than water, he would say, seeming to speak about the work at hand and how best to get it done. Island people are the ones we can count on, he would say, echoing what her father used to tell her when she was growing up, old warnings about these fellows coming in from overseas to steal the women.

Heading home from the airport she heard Tutu's voice rising up from somewhere to tell the story of his wives. When had he first told this to her? How long ago?

"You know, my mother married two times, sister. I was married three. Once to a Japanese, Mariko. Once to a haole, Ruthmarie. Once to Nalani, a Hawaiian woman who was a fine singer, and we used to work together in the clubs over there. But I loved that haole woman too. She had a good heart, lots of aloha in Ruthmarie. That is what you look for. You trust the heart. Not the color. When you only see the skin you don't see enough, especially when you think you see the colors people are supposed to see. Haole means white, yeah? Used to mean anybody coming in here from some place else. Nowadays it means anybody white. But think about white. My shirt is white. Are white people this color? Only if they're sick. By the time they're in the islands one week they get browner than the brown people. Or they get pink. They could be red as a lobster. We still suppose to call them white. In my life I never met a Japanese who was yellow. Your grandpa, I remember him. He was kinda brown. A lot of Japanese, they are whiter than the whites.

Mariko was like that. And think about red for a minute. This hibiscus blossom, this is what I call red. Can you show me an Indian with skin like this? One time in San Francisco I knew this Cherokee fella, told these real long stories. His skin was the same as mine. You call me red? Who started this anyway, telling us what color we suppose to be?"

Alone in bed, with her arms outstretched, Angel hears the story again, almost as if she is telling it herself. The old voice fades, then returns, coming toward her, or rising through her. This time he is speaking Hawaiian words she does not understand. But she knows the sound. She knows it is a naming chant that David will say when he passes his family name to the one who grows inside her. And she knows that after the baby comes, he will take the umbilicus up into the high country, the infant's *piko*, to the same spot where her own was placed how many years ago, and she will go with him, hiking out across the windy rocks to find the narrow crack stuffed with pebbles and know that place for the first time.

Wherever it is, wherever he places and blesses the new umbilicus, half of it will come from her and half from Travis. Already she feels it, the ancient cord inside that ties her unborn babe, looping back from child to mother to mother to mother, and wound around with threads from all the fathers too, the long long braid of fathers and mothers and fathers and mothers. Already she hears the frail and slender voice of Tutu David floating over the plain. What timeless channel has been opened now, so wide the old words fill her head? She hears them swelling from within, the sound of rocks and kinship. And who knows where one ends and one begins. Is there any way to measure it? Fiery rock is the mother and the father too, whirled outward from an exploding sun, burning speckles in the fountains of suns, to cool and thicken and whirl and hum. The mind forgets, but the body can remember and hear that oldest calling. Angel hears it, cooler now in the predawn air, her limbs at ease, waking in Hilo, where a rim of pale light edges the twin humps that loom behind the town.